Advance Praise for
What Once We Loved

"Masterful storytelling continues in this real-as-rain portrayal of the Oregon-California 1850's frontier. Big-hearted heroines face past and present challenges with unswerving dreams and hardscrabble labor. Eventually, their faith and friendship triumph over daily struggles and wrongheaded past decisions... A compelling tale." —CRAIG LESLEY,
author of *The Sky Fisherman* and *Storm Riders*

"Jane Kirkpatrick's *What Once We Loved* is a mesmerizing tale of strong women in a heart-breaking time. A priceless story not to be missed!"
—ANGELA ELWELL HUNT
author of *The Note*

"Fascinating, courageous women in a beautiful, yet challenging setting come full circle in their lives and loves together, making this the crowning glory of the Kinship and Courage series." —RANDALL PLATT
author of *The Cornerstone* and *Honor Bright*

"I am proud to hand-sell this incredible series on a daily basis. *What Once We Loved* brings our eleven frontier women to their final purposes. Again Jane weaves their individual stories together with tenderness and great compassion. Following these women along their historical paths has been a powerful journey." —ROBIN POWERS
St. Helens Book Shop

"Jane's characters live on the page. *What Once We Loved* is a book that draws the reader in to lie in a cool stream on a hot day—first your toes, then your knees.... Before you know it, you are swimming and the book becomes impossible to put down." —LINDA HALL
author of *Sadie's Song*, *Katheryn's Secret*, and *Margaret's Peace*

What Once We Loved

OTHER BOOKS BY JANE KIRKPATRICK

NOVELS

KINSHIP AND COURAGE SERIES

All Together in One Place

No Eye Can See

DREAMCATCHER SERIES

Mystic Sweet Communion

A Gathering of Finches

Love to Water My Soul

A Sweetness to the Soul

(Winner of the Wrangler Award

for Outstanding Western Novel of 1995)

NONFICTION

Homestead

A Burden Shared

A SISTERHOOD *of*

FRIENDSHIP *and* FAITH

What Once We Loved

JANE KIRKPATRICK

AWARD-WINNING AUTHOR of *ALL TOGETHER in ONE PLACE*

WATERBROOK
PRESS

WHAT ONCE WE LOVED
PUBLISHED BY WATERBROOK PRESS
2375 Telstar Drive, Suite 160
Colorado Springs, Colorado 80920
A division of Random House, Inc.

Scripture quotations are taken from the *King James Version.*

The characters and events in this book are fictional, and any resemblance
to actual persons or events is coincidental.

ISBN 1-57856-234-1

Library of Congress Cataloging-in-Publication Data
Kirkpatrick, Jane, 1946–
    What once we loved / by Jane Kirkpatrick— 1st ed.
        p. cm.— (The kinship and courage historical series ; bk. no. 3)
    ISBN 1-57856-234-1
        1. Female friendship—Fiction. 2. Women pioneers—Fiction. 3. Oregon—
Fiction. I. Title.

PS3561.I712 W48 2001
813'.54—dc21

                                                                2001039016

Printed in the United States of America
2001—First Edition

10 9 8 7 6 5 4 3 2 1

*This book is dedicated to
my brother, Craig Rutschow:
a man who chooses to stay within reach
of his wife, his children, his faith, and his kin.*

CAST OF CHARACTERS

The women of *All Together in One Place*

Mazy Bacon, a dairy farmer
Suzanne Cullver, a former
    photographer
    Clayton and Sason, her boys
Tipton Kossuth, a newlywed
Sister Esther Maeves, a cleaning
    lady and attendant to
    Suzanne; former contractor
    for mail-order brides
Ruth Martin, a horsewoman and
    auntie to Jason, Ned, and
    Sarah, and mother to Jessie
Elizabeth Mueller, Mazy's
    mother and a baker
Lura Schmidtke,
    a businesswoman
    Matthew, her son
    Mariah, her daughter,
    a young horsewoman
Adora Wilson, a shopkeeper
    Charles and Tipton,
    her son and daughter
The surviving Celestials:
    Mei-Ling and her daughter
    Naomi and her daughter

Additional characters

Chita, housemaid
    to Nehemiah and Tipton
Angus Flaubert, an actor
Seth Forrester, a white-collared man
Gus Grotefend, Shasta City
    hotel owner
Nehemiah Kossuth, Crescent City
    packer, husband of Tipton
Burke Manes, a Jacksonville area
    farmer and pastor
Michael O'Malley, a former
    pit boss and miner
Joe Pepin, the Schmidtkes' teamster
Sterling Powder, tutor
    to Clayton and Sason
Zane Randolph, a.k.a. Wesley
    Marks/Beckworth,
    Ruth's husband
Matthew Schmidtke, a cattleman
David Taylor, mail carrier
    and Mazy's stepson
Grace Taylor, David's sister
Oltipa Taylor, a Wintu Indian
    woman, wife of David
    Ben, her son
Estella "Esty" Williams, a milliner

Thou maintainest my lot.
The lines are fallen unto me in pleasant places;
yea, I have a goodly heritage.

PSALM 16:5-6

Where, except in the present, can the Eternal be met?

C. S. LEWIS, *CHRISTIAN REFLECTIONS*

If you always do what you've always done,
You'll always get what you've always gotten.

CONTEXT ASSOCIATES

poverty flat

Fall 1853

Whipped-cream clouds danced across a stage of blue before an audience of oak. Shadows softened the sun's glare on the water, allowing Ruth Martin to peer beneath the river's surface. She'd seen that wily trout. Today she'd catch him without getting her feet wet.

She retied the bent sewing needle at the end of the butcher's twine. California morning sun glinted on beads of water dotting the wet string like pearls. "Just one more little nibble and I'll have you," she said. Firm yet slender as a whip handle, Ruth sat astride her horse. Old miner's pants covered her legs. Jumper, her horse, wiggled his ears, lifted a back leg to scratch at a fly, splashed when he set his hoof down. "Don't lose concentration now, Jumper," she whispered, more to herself than the horse.

Certain the needle was firmly attached, she flicked the willow fishing pole and watched as the breeze picked up the string, then set it and the makeshift hook adrift along the riffle. A reddish leaf broke loose from a willow, gentled in the stream following her line to the shaded pool. She eased the hook across the water. Waiting.

She'd have to head back soon. She still had pack boxes only half filled. Flannels needed steaming and hanging, and the wagon wasn't nearly loaded. Then there was that Joe Pepin to contend with. The wrangler'd said he'd take them north, but he'd been acting scarce of late. Still, Ruth Martin could make it happen on time. She was sure. She just wanted to bring in this last big trout before she headed back. Astride Jumper, she could do it without getting wet. She smiled.

Redwing blackbirds chirped in the tall grasses drooping with their weight. Sun warmed her face. Her eyes closed.

She felt a tug. Sitting straight, she jerked the willow and set the hook. "Gotcha," she said. Skillfully she lifted the pole up and over the horse's head, changed hands, then back again as the trout twisted and tired in the water before her. He was a big one. When it felt right, she said, "Back, Jumper." She barely touched the reins and squeezed her knees, easing the big animal back toward the riverbank. "Just a little more," she said. Then with perfect timing, she slid the trout out of the water and onto the grassy bank. "We did it!" The horse lifted its head up and down as though to agree.

With one leg raised over his mane, Ruth slid off, still holding the pole. She stunned the fish with the hard end of her whip that usually hung coiled at her hip, then slipped the fish into the canvas bag with the others. She had over a dozen. This one alone weighed as much as a pork roast. A good morning's catch. Plenty for them all at the big affair Elizabeth had planned. She tightened the strap of the bag, then draped it over the horse's neck. "You're a good fishing partner," she told Jumper, hugging him and inhaling his scent before gripping his mane in her hands and pulling herself up and astride. "The best I've ever had."

She pressed her knees and set a fast pace back to Poverty Flat. Riding always invigorated, took away any agitation or worry. It was one of the few luxuries she permitted herself, a woman with responsibilities. Today, with so much yet undone, she needed that burst of power.

A flock of geese lifted from the Sacramento as they raced by. She ducked beneath the oaks and through the pines embracing the meadow known as Poverty Flat and home—but not for much longer. She squinted.

Matthew Schmidtke and the children were pushing something on a cart. Coopered barrels. They were all laughing. Surely they hadn't already gotten all their chores completed. She didn't see any blankets on the line, and no one stood near the butter churn. What had they been doing? She squeezed her knees, and Jumper sped forward.

"Hey," Matthew said as she approached. "Brought breakfast, I see."

"Supper," she said. "Have you children finished what I asked you to do?"

"We're helping Matthew," Ruth's nephew Jason told her. His cowlick stuck straight up in the back, and he absently pressed his fingers against it as he talked.

"And it's a surprise," Jessie, her five-year-old daughter, said. "For you."

"Don't tell her," Sarah warned, acting older than her eight years.

"I won't," Jessie answered.

"I don't like surprises much," Ruth said. She removed her floppy felt hat and wiped her forehead with her forearm. Her eyes caught Jessie's troubled look, and she softened. "I'm sure this one will be fine. We just have a lot to do."

"You'll like this one." Matthew smiled at her.

"We have to be out of here this week," Ruth said, squaring her shoulders.

"Maybe some of us wish you weren't in such a hurry," he said, his blue eyes never leaving hers.

"Wait'll you see it," Ned said. Her younger nephew pulled at his stockings tucking them up to his knickers. He stood with his hands at his hips just the way Matthew did. Neither wore a hat this morning. "It's gonna be real chirk."

"Let's let her tend to her business while we take care of those fish, boys. Then we can finish up here." Matthew sniffed the air. "Is that you or the fish?" he teased. The children giggled. "Must be the fish. You'll like our surprise for sure, if it isn't."

3

Ruth grunted, never quite sure how to take his teasing. She didn't have much practice with friendships with men. Mostly they were obstacles to her finding the independence and peace of mind she sought. Matthew approached the horse, patted Jumper's neck, then lifted the canvas bag of fish. A breeze brushed at the strip of white hair that faded into black above Matthew's eye. He winked, then headed toward the porch. "Let's get these cleaned, boys," he said. "Then it's back to hard labor and Ruth's surprise."

"Surprises leave me cold," Ruth said as she reined the horse toward the barn.

"This one'll warm you to your toes," Matthew called after her. The children's laughter only added to her irritation.

Mazy Bacon drove the milk wagon from Poverty Flat into Shasta City. It was morning, and by midafternoon she'd be riding back again to milk her cows and tend to the calves she kept at Ruth's place. She felt tired. Probably from all the people out there right now. The Schmidtkes bustled about, all three of them. And of course, Ruth and her four until they headed north. Pack strings showed up and pitched tents before heading into Shasta. Even wagon trains found the wide flat inviting, giving people a place to catch their breath before dispersing to places north and south and farther west, seeking new lives, drifting like leaves to the fall winds.

Mazy had stayed at Ruth's when her cows were calving. But then Matthew Schmidtke and the wrangler Joe Pepin arrived, bringing the rest of Ruth's mares and yearlings and the Schmidtkes' Durham cows. And they brought Marvel, the Ayrshire bull that belonged to Mazy. Or did until she'd discovered that bovine was really owned by her dead husband's brother living in Sacramento. Another of her husband's betrayals uncovered. She'd have to get the bull to her brother-in-law before long.

Ruth had even asked that Mazy move the bull out now. Find a pen for him in town.

"He could injure the mares or colts," Ruth said. "I know you wouldn't want that to happen."

Marvel's long horns were worthy of respect. Mazy knew that first-hand. But Ruth would be gone in a day or two, and then the bull would have free range with Mazy's cows and the Schmidtkes', too, if they wanted. After they were bred, she'd take the cow brute south. Until then the pen of split rails seemed sturdy enough to hold him. Mazy had said as much to Ruth. Ruth had set her jaw, then stalked off.

Mazy pulled up the milk cart, tied the mule to the hitching rail, then dropped off the tins of milk at Washington's Market in Shasta City. "We'll take all you can give us," the proprietor told her. "Cheese be coming one of these days?"

"I'm just doing milk and butter for now," Mazy said. She wiped her hands on her apron, lifted another tin.

"Shasta's a growing city," Washington reminded her, taking the milk from her hands. "We need your busy cows to supplement the food shipped in from Oregon. How else we going to feed the hordes of miners spackling this country like flies on tent canvas?"

Mazy smiled. "I'm doing my best."

Mazy finished her delivery, taking some tins to the St. Charles Hotel, another to a new boardinghouse, which had sprung up almost overnight. She accepted the final payment for the day, wrote down new orders, and promised to bring more butter tomorrow. She stuffed the coins into a bag kept beneath her seat and caught a scent of her own perspiration. The work was hard but invigorating. She had a strong back and firm hands. "Formed of sturdy stock" her husband had always said. She needed to be sturdy to survive as a widow in this West. Fragrant sturdy stock, she thought, as she unhitched the mule from the rail. A bath would feel good.

Back at her mother's small room above the bakery, Mazy dabbed at her upper body with water from the flowered washbowl with a rough huck towel, her eyes glancing at the quilt pieces. Ruth had drawn the design Suzanne had described, and Mazy had promised to sew it for their blind friend. Each of the women had made a block to symbolize their experiences together coming across from the States to California last year. Mazy hadn't even decided what her own block would say, but she liked the idea of making a story out of the pieces, making it look like the pages of a book.

A dream she'd had the night before came to her mind. Usually her dreams were like hiccups, disrupting without rhythm. This one had actually been a story. It had a beginning, middle, and end. Even color. Her bath completed, she dried, then treated herself with a cup of spring water. She sat to stitch, remembering the dream's sequence.

She was in a schoolhouse, taking lessons. The teacher was her old pastor. He wore his long frock coat and on his feet the mud-stained boots of a farmer. Someone had a photo book they shared, and across the room, people carrying carpetbags on their arms bought tickets to take a stage somewhere. Mazy knew she belonged at that schoolhouse, was there to learn something. Yet she was suddenly striding out, kicking up the hem of her dress, the fringe of her shawl tickling her bare arms as she walked, her shoulders square and sure. She felt happy knowing where she was headed, the wind blowing her auburn hair. She met a wagon loaded with candle tins and wooden buckets and trunks like those the women had brought across the trail. A woman stood from the still-moving seat. She remembered her now; it was an acquaintance from back in Wisconsin, Kay Krall! Kay pulled the red-seated Studebaker wagon to a stop. She spoke to Mazy, "Are you in service?"

Mazy had answered with great joy, "Yes! I am!"

The woman had smiled and moved on, saying as she waved good-bye, "That's good. Because it's my job to make sure that everyone is in service."

Again Mazy had hurried on, sure of what she sought as she made her way through fields of buttercups and purple birdbeak blooms. At a log cabin she'd stopped, knowing this was where she was meant to be. She knocked on the door. When it opened, there stood a young man with a wife and child. "Do you need service?" Mazy'd asked. "Yes," he'd told her and invited her in. They'd walked through the house to the back, and Mazy was so happy, so pleased to be doing just what she was meant to do in life. He opened the back door, and they stepped into the blazing sunlight. Mazy looked down. They were in a hog's pen. "Can you clean up this mess?" the young man had asked, and Mazy had smiled, nodded yes, and then woke up.

She was still shaking her head when her mother walked in. "What're you smiling about, Daughter?" Elizabeth Mueller asked. The older woman puffed a bit, from the stair climb, Mazy imagined.

"Oh, one of my crazy dreams," Mazy said. "But this one told like a story."

"Something to ponder," her mother said. "What was it about?"

Mazy thought. "Travel, I guess. Securing tickets, going somewhere. Arriving. There were old photographs and some new ones in it too. And pigs." She laughed. "And a woman from Wisconsin, Kay Krall."

"Ah," her mother said.

"Ah, what?"

"You're missing Ruth, I'll ponder… Dreaming of old friends left behind and someone going on a trip. Here, I brought you a biscuit. Feed your tummy, and maybe your heart won't feel so empty."

"I don't feel empty," Mazy said. She put the quilt piece down. "I'm happy for Ruth. Glad she's doing what she always wanted to do and feeling strong enough to do it. I'm doing what I want now too. I'll be expanding the dairy. I'm a…businesswoman." She thought of her stepson recently met. "Maybe I'll even see if David Taylor has an interest in what was his father's idea."

Elizabeth's voice quieted. "You can be happy for Ruth and still feel sad she's leaving you behind."

7

"I'm looking forward to living there, closer to my cows," Mazy said. "We're both getting something we said we wanted."

"It don't hurt much to tell yourself the truth," her mother said.

"Ouch," Mazy said, realizing she'd poked herself with the needle. She sucked on the bleeding finger and said, "Now see what you've made me do?"

"Not made you do anything except notice you've started saying good-bye," her mother said. "And that can bring a body some pain."

Ruth watched the performance of the changing California sky as she shivered inside her wooden cubicle. Her husband's old pants, her shirt, and drawers hung over the rough-sawn boards. Dozens of details awaited her before she could head north to Oregon with the children, but something Elizabeth Mueller had told her clanged in her ears right then, as loudly as a cowbell. "If you always do what you've always done, you'll always get what you've always gotten. If you want something different to happen, you've got to make the change, not wait for someone else. Some folks just never get that figured out."

Ruth swallowed. What she had always done was take life seriously and assume it was best lived alone with work as its hub. What she anticipated daily was not the delight Elizabeth seemed to bathe in, but the delivery of bad news sure to come. Ruth'd decided to let today be different. Maybe she was worthy of richness. She'd had a good morning fishing, had made progress on gathering things up, and had given in to the children's lament that she close her eyes and let them lead her to these four walls that made up the shower, their surprise.

She stood in a copper tub that would collect water for later baths. It was private behind her wooden screen. Still she felt exposed. She resisted the urge to just get dressed again and get to work. Instead she pulled back her tawny hair and tied it with a section of yarn. Over the top of the boards, she gazed out at her herd of horses and the yearling foals. Her nephew and daughter now headed with a bucket of grain to feed Jumper, her "horse of high hopes." Jessie skipped, looked happy. Good. How long it might last was anyone's guess.

She took a deep breath and looked up, her hazel eyes squinting into the sunlight dappling the oak leaves. Matthew and the boys had placed a coopered barrel on a shelf they'd build up in that tree, and a hemp rope hung from a plug that had a leather latch on it. She moved her whip and boots well out of the way, then tugged on the rope. She pinched her eyes shut and waited for the shock.

She gasped. Cold water cascaded down over her face, her bare shoulders, and splashed at her feet. Goose bumps answered the water, and she laughed out loud then, sputtering as she patted, eyes closed, for the small shelf in front of her. She was like her blind friend, Suzanne, patting for things she couldn't see.

She smelled the mint, and her fingers found the partial soap cake her daughter Jessie'd made the day she'd been seized by Zane Randolph, Jessie's…father. The faint scent reminded her of Jessie's caution in things since she'd returned.

Ruth lathered her body. Jessie must have added sugar to her soap to make it suds up like it did. Ruth loosened her hair and scrubbed it as well. She wouldn't think of Jessie's pain now, nor of all she had to do yet. She wouldn't expect only the worst. A second pull on the rope and another blast of icy water. Next time she'd ask them to sun heat this spring water. She cupped her hand and pushed the soap and water down her arms, her belly, and legs. Next time, she remembered. There wouldn't be a next time. They were leaving.

That fact made the effort of this shower creation all the more frivolous; perhaps all the more precious. She patted for the huck towel that hung on a nail over the side of the boards and pressed it against her eyes. She wouldn't think sad things. She'd practice doing something different as Elizabeth advised. She'd enjoy a gift given and laugh out loud, alone.

"We're 'posed to feed Marvel, too," Jessie reminded her older cousin. "Mama said. So don't let Jumper have all the grain." The children approached the stallion grazing in the meadow.

"I know it," Ned told her. "There's plenty."

Jumper lowered his head into the bucket and pushed it to the ground. "He likes me," Jessie said, patting the place between his ears.

"Me, too," Ned said. He scratched the sorrel's neck as the big animal crunched away at his feed. "Mrs. Schmidtke says stallions aren't usually so gentle as this one is."

"I could ride him, I bet," Jessie said.

"Have you ever?"

"Not by myself, but I could." She stuck her chin out. "There are all kinds of things I can do by myself."

"Me, too," Ned said. "Here, we better pull the bucket from him, so we got some left to pitch over the fence for the bull."

"I guess," Jessie said, yanking back on the bucket. Jumper resisted, stretching his neck and pressing the side of the bucket with his nose. Jessie's apron snagged in the bucket's rope handle as the children pulled his feed away. Ned released it, and Jessie stepped backward, almost tripping over the long meadow grass, brown from the lack of rain. She caught herself and giggled. "He'll trail like a lamb," she said. "Wanna see?" She skipped away with the bucket then while the big horse whinnied, lowered his head, and raised his feet to follow.

With the soap out of her eyes, Ruth watched Jessie and Ned make their way across the meadow, Jumper following. A Quarter-Pather breed, he had Copperbottom blood in him, from her father's Virginia strain. Bred with the thoroughbred mares she had, Jumper's offspring would make good army mounts—nice, easy dispositions; sturdy animals with endurance as the military liked. She couldn't have picked a better horse on which to build her future. Strong, long-legged, yet gentle enough for Jessie to ride with her. Mariah Schmidtke had even ridden him alone. Jumper had been harder to handle with the mares back from Oregon. Even Koda, Ruth's gelding, acted proud cut, as though he had to compete with the big animal now that mares were around. She'd have to let Mariah ride Jumper a few times more before they left. The girl would miss the horses more than she'd miss Ruth and her kin, Ruth guessed.

She pulled her wet hair back and squeezed it over her shoulder, watching the water dribble in the tub now nearly full at her feet. Matthew was right; she had needed a shower, and this had been a pleasant surprise. Her task was to accept it, a joy as worthy and true as the tuned freighter bells she heard jingle just then, announcing the arrival of a pack string. She dried herself. She'd let Jessie know she had water to bathe in from the copper tub. The girl liked to bathe. Was that new, her wanting to sit in the tub and just soak?

Matthew stepped out of the cabin heading toward the new arrivals. "Need any help?" He grinned.

She wrapped the towel around her head. "Not from the likes of you," she said.

He tipped his hat at Ruth as he walked a discreet distance past her wooden cubicle, toward the meadow. Ruth blushed and dropped her head. It was good that she had plans to leave. Matthew could become a distraction from the dream she had for Oregon. She wasn't ready for that.

Dressed, she stepped out from behind the walls of the shower. She looked for a tree stump to sit on to pull on her socks and boots. This little bathhouse operation could use a good milking stool, she thought.

She heard the shout, almost a scream, and stood up. Jessie? Was that Jessie? Her hazel eyes scanned the meadow. And then as though walking in oozing mud, she turned, aware not of goose bumps refreshing her skin, but of needles of dread.

Mazy made her way to the garden. With a twig she pushed out dirt stuffed beneath her fingernails. That feeling of packed earth at her nails was always a bother. She should have borrowed a pair of Ruth's gloves for this. The lamb's ears did not like to have their roots separated, she decided. They resisted. But unless she broke them up now they wouldn't flourish, and then she and her mother would have no soft leaves next spring to use for bandages. Lamb's ears leaves were better than muslin, soaked up more, and she was sure there was some healing quality in those leaves. But come fall, the roots had to be divided and replanted and this plant, at least, didn't like it.

In her diary that morning, Mazy'd written *gardener* as she thought of a quality of God's character. It was one of the things she let herself take time for, this morning musing. Any dream she'd had would get written down there. Maybe even her mother's observation about what it meant. She found it helped to write when she wandered in her "wilderness places" as she called them, times of struggle and indecision.

She did so like the peacefulness of gardening. Gardeners changed the earth, but the soil changed them as well. Perhaps more. Take her little herb garden. After the Shasta fire scorched her plant starts last year, she'd thought she'd lost everything. But they'd come back, the lamb's ear, the lemon balm. The balm she planned to send to Mei-Ling, as she'd heard it attracted swarms if a hive was rubbed with it. It supposedly eased gout, too, and drove away depression. "Strong courage" her mother described that kind of wilderness time. She needed that right now, strong courage. She disliked change, that much of what her mother said was true. And Ruth's leaving meant change.

The clods resisted her fingers. She'd let them go too long. Some gardener she was: lazy and self-indulgent and—

No, she wouldn't say those hurtful things to herself anymore. She wouldn't talk to other people that way, so why mumble to her own mind like that? *Mind mumbling.* She'd make a note to tell herself that was what it was, mind mumbling, whenever it happened. What mattered was that she was out here, doing what must be done. She looked at her hands, then retied the kerchief beneath her chestnut hair right at the back of her neck, feeling the perspiration of the heavy braid and the afternoon sun.

At least Matthew and Lura and Mariah would still be here along with Mazy and her mother and Adora and her son, Charles—Dear Despicable Charles, as Mazy thought of him. Still, that was all that remained of their wagon group here in this place. Why did everything have to change? Why did Charles Wilson decide to stay and take advantage of his mother? He always leered at Mazy when she walked by their mercantile. Had she done something to invite his interest? Maybe the lemon balm would work for his gout, and he'd stop showing up at Poverty Flat asking for fresh manure for his foot treatment and then spending the day watching others work. Or maybe she was destined to attract men she didn't favor. *Mind mumbling,* that was what she was doing again. Useless.

She just didn't want Ruth to go, that was why she was mind mumbling. Her mother was right. Ruth'd become like a sister to Mazy. She brushed at her eyes. She took a deep breath, kept pushing at the roots of the medicinal plant.

She'd made a friend, a lifelong one forged from the difficult days along the trail and since. Friends were new for Mazy. Even Kay Krall from her dream had been someone Mazy admired more from a distance. That woman had two children, helped midwife the arrival of others. Kay always had time to listen to people, and now that Mazy remembered, she'd been a fine gardener, too. She and her husband actually held hands across their horses when they rode together, though they must have been married for several years. Mazy hadn't revealed much of herself to this woman, now that she thought of it. She wished now that she had.

Mazy had taken a risk with Ruth. They'd been through much together. But her friend was leaving. Mazy didn't know if she could make another friend like Ruth nor maintain their friendship once they were separated by a mountain range and miles. Oh, she did want Ruth to have a good life, to follow this dream she had to build up a herd and sell horses to the military, to be a good mother and auntie, a woman, standing alone. A friend supported another's dream, didn't she?

But still, Mazy felt, oh…envy maybe, that Ruth had the excitement of something new in her life. She had a daughter and kin to grow old with. Mazy would miss Ned and Jason and Sarah and Jessie, too, when they were gone. They said funny things and saw the world through spring-fed eyes. Mazy sighed. Ruth was a woman she didn't have to win-now her words with. Who would understand her as well as Ruth did? Ruth, too, had made a poor decision in choosing a mate.

Mazy pushed against the root-bound plant, spoke out loud to it. Her mother told her to talk to plants and tell them what she'd be doing to them so they'd cooperate. Not likely, Mazy thought, but she did it anyway. Maybe she'd become some old crazy lady that the children whispered about, someone who had no friends and talked to plants and scratched at herself without remembering where she was.

"Let go now," Mazy said out loud. "I'm just going to replant you. It'll feel new, but the place I picked is nice soil. Let go," she told the roots, forcing her thumb between the clods. She gave extra pressure this time and, with a crunch, the ball broke free.

"Well," Mazy said, sitting back on her knees. "Maybe you'd like to be transplanted in…Oregon, with Ruth and the children?" Now there was a worthy plan, a way for Ruth to take something with her, a reminder that strength came from clods, sometimes from being broken and planted in new soil.

Smiling, she held both clumps in her hand and was about to place one new root in the hole she'd dug, then find a container for the other to take out to Ruth, when she felt a small hand warm against her back.

"You again," Mazy said. It was one of the orphaned Indian children who'd become regular partakers of her mother's breads that they'd been leaving out. "I don't think she has any here, right now," Mazy told the child. She was never certain how much English they really understood. Most of them slipped in at nighttime, took the food, and disappeared. So it surprised Mazy to actually recognize this round face with a scar beneath her right eye and an upturned nose. And her face was puffed up as though full of air. Was she ill? The mumps? Mazy'd never seen that look on any of the children before. An epidemic would be the worst thing possible! However would they get medicine and a physician willing to treat them? Where could they house them? Her mind raced with the possibilities of all a major illness could mean before she recognized a flicker of mischief crossing the child's brown eyes.

The girl clapped her cheeks with her palms, spraying water right into Mazy's face.

"Hey!" Mazy screeched, standing.

The child crouched back.

"It's all right," Mazy said, when she saw the fear in the child's eyes. "Cooling me down, are you? It's hot enough, that's sure." Mazy smiled broadly, wiping her face of the water with her dirty hands. The child laughed then and pointed, and Mazy guessed she was streaked with earth. Mazy chuckled too and then turned. She moved toward the little pool where a spring dribbled down the side of the rockface that marked one border of her herb garden. She willed the child to stay, could feel the dark eyes on her back. Mazy lifted the heavy braid at the back of her neck, then cupped her hands. She caught the cold liquid in them, then quick as a fawn's tail twisting, she turned and threw the water at the girl. Mazy smiled as she watched the spray cascade toward the child's wide eyes.

"Ayee," the girl said, lurching out of her crouch, but she didn't run. Instead her eyes held Mazy's for just a moment before she grinned, revealing an open space where two front teeth should have been.

Must be six years old, maybe seven, Mazy thought. Jessie's age. The girl giggled and slipped past Mazy toward the spring, began splashing water at Mazy. Mazy showered her back until both she and the girl stood dripping wet.

"I'm hungry," Mazy said then. "Want a cookie that looks just like a dog?"

The girl's face became still, then she nodded just once.

Mazy reached out her hand. "Let's go inside and get one," she said.

The child pulled back, hesitated, then dropped her brown palm into Mazy's. She stood still.

"Well, come along," Mazy said. From the corner of her eye, she caught sight of another in the shadows. A woman in tattered clothes. The adults rarely came close. Her heart pounded. The child's mother? An auntie? Mazy reached her free hand out. "You come too," she said.

The girl pulled on Mazy's hand then, and the woman followed quiet as the morning dew.

Good enough, Mazy thought. That was how friendships began. One step at a time, often led by a child.

Ruth's eyes scanned for the children, the source of the screams. She heard neighing horses and a bellowing bull, then shrieks and groans. Dust filled the air near the barn. Ruth swore later she heard the ripping of flesh, but of course, she couldn't have, not from where she stood, not with the towel about her head. She could see Matthew run, his boots kicking up red dirt near the corral. His face looked strained, and her eyes searched for Jessie and Ned, Jason and Sarah.

"What is it, Auntie?" Sarah asked, stepping out from the house.

"I don't know," Ruth said, moving forward, searching.

She saw the two youngest out in the meadow now, close together. She wondered why Matthew pushed at them, moved them toward the freighters while one of the Mexican handlers turned a string of mules away from the corrals. The animals bucked and brayed in upset over what? Ruth didn't know.

Her eyes worked across the meadow. She could see Koda and the mares running into each other. Odd. Then the dusty fog near Marvel's pen cleared. Ruth watched as Matthew grabbed a goading stick to push at the big bull. He was loose? The bull was loose? The animal's nose lifted to the dusty air. She heard him bellow as though in triumph. Clods of dirt pelted the ground like rain as the brute pawed and twisted raising a red-earth cloud.

Had Matthew stumbled? She couldn't see! When it cleared, the bull lowered his head, his horns angled to attack. Her heart pounded. She heard a crack, wood against flesh, and Marvel's bellow. That high-pitched scream again. Matthew's goading stick lunged, and the animal moved back, the ground throbbing with his agitated weight. The brute was so large, and yet he twisted with the ease of a dog snapping at meat thrown in midair. Matthew shouted. The brute circled, disappeared inside the dirty cloud.

When it cleared, the bull was in the pen next to his own, and Matthew rushed forward to slide the oak latch. The animal pawed, head lowered. He bellowed but didn't lunge the gate.

Good, Ruth thought. He was back in. Everyone was all right. But what was that screaming, that— She stepped forward, barefooted, onto the warm earth and moved as though sleepwalking toward the corral, aware that her body knew something her mind would not admit.

"Ruth, stay back!" Matthew shouted to her now, his palms extended, his hat held as though to shield her eyes.

"Why? What's wrong?"

And then her eyes slid down to the lurching form just inside the log corrals, the struggling sorrel form of Jumper.

The horse lay groaning, snorting, a muffled scream now, weakened. His head lifted, then dropped. His hooves carved graves into the dust.

She let her eyes move like sunset sinking, threatening blackness. She smelled the acrid scent of blood, of seeping life, heard the bellowing of the cow brute, long horns held high as he circled the paddock, heightened too by the smells, the sounds of groans and dying.

"Ruth, please…" Matthew said as she neared him. He grasped her arms, urging her to stay back. "The bull…it's gored him in the… artery…"

"I've got to," Ruth said, her voice far away and aching like a dream lost to the morning. She shook free of Matthew's hand.

"He could be…could hurt you. Not meaning too. I'll put him down, Ruth. No need—"

But she was already beside the stud, sobbing now, a deep and awful bawling broken by gasps of choked air like a child exhaling in anguish with her loss. Then she met his eyes, her Jumper's eyes. Her grieving must have frightened the stallion as he lay in the pool of blood, red and black beneath his belly, the horn-rip of his belly, gaping like fresh meat, laid bare. A shiver of horror swelled through her in a raging wave. Eyes wild and staring, the horse tried to rise when he saw her, as if he longed for her to take the pain, to set him free.

She bent to his big head, barely touched his jaw and his ears twitched back, the pain so great. Her eyes throbbed with the knowing. She pulled the towel from her head, tried to push it against the blood flow.

"Let me," Matthew said. Ruth couldn't answer. Matthew held the towel to the horse's sheath but was unable to stop the bleeding. The big horse tried once more to rise, to lift his head with a gasping snort.

Ruth wept into Jumper's neck, a selfish moment taken before she'd free him: have to free him.

But even in his dying, the big horse gave. Jumper strained his neck, tried to lift his head as she crooned to him, "No, no, stay still, stay still," until he seemed to sigh, his legs no longer scraping, the screams of pain lessened. His breaths came shorter. His nostrils moved in and out; his heaving slowed. His eyes wide with fright, he sighed once more, then died.

Ruth stayed with him that way, wrapped around his neck until she felt only brittle cold. She stayed until the moon came up, until the stars filled the night sky like distant, dying fires. She stayed until she felt the blanket Matthew draped around her shoulders while he sat beside her in silence, while she said good-bye to a dream and what once she'd loved.

the fog of indecision

Sacramento City

"But what good will it do to teach him finger signs?" Suzanne Cullver asked. "I can't see them, or haven't you noticed, Doctor?" She spoke his title with the disrespect he deserved. She should have gone to a dentist or one of those hydropaths instead of this quack. She knew her face burned red with frustration. "I won't know what my son wants if he did use those…those things you said. And I'll have to have someone teach them to me as well, just to be able to tell him things. Which makes no sense. He can understand, he just can't say anything back. No, there has to be another way."

Her voice sounded strident, irritated. Well, she was. She'd done what she thought she was supposed to do, surrendered to uncertainty more than at any other time in her life, trusting that freedom thrived inside. No more putting her children at risk just because she wanted to do things by herself. No more singing or making music in the mining towns, no more taking risks without focus. Suzanne shook her head. *Focus.* It was still a strange word to pop into the head of a blind woman even if she had once been a photographer who knew the meaning of the word quite well. But it didn't just mean clarity; it meant hearth, that which warmed a person to the center of their being. Suzanne's focus was her children, pure and simple. That was what warmed her.

What this doctor suggested was pure foolery.

"Maybe I could teach you," her friend Esty Williams told her, taking Suzanne's hand from the place her fingers fluttered at her neck. Esty covered Suzanne's fingers with her own. "Is there a book of some kind?" Esty must have turned to face the doctor, her voice seemed directed away from Suzanne.

"The Indians use some gesticulation, of course," the doctor said, clearing his throat. "These have not been written down, but remembered. For the military. I can make a list of several if you'd like, with drawings. Nothing elaborate. The child is only three. But it could reduce his…frustration when he wishes to tell someone something but can't make himself understood. You can make up little signs, of course. Be…inventive." The doctor had leaned close enough to Suzanne that she could smell the herb santolina on his wool jacket. He must have used it to keep the moths down. Or perhaps he'd expelled so many worms from young patients with it that the scent was forever on his skin.

"But he never will talk if we give him a way to avoid it," Suzanne said. "No. I think it will divert us from finding out why he refuses to speak." She pulled her hand from Esty's, clasped her own together in a prayerlike position. Took a deep breath. "Is his mouth all right? Are his teeth formed so he can talk?"

"Everything appears to be physically as it should be," the doctor said, his words clipped like a man patting a pestering dog.

"But you're not a dentist, after all."

"The signs could perhaps help teach him to talk, in a way we just don't understand. I've seen it happen."

He'd probably taken up medicine when his interest in farming or horse racing ran out. The thought made her ask a question. "Do you think that accident with the horse last year could have caused this, when the animal kicked him in the side of the head? Or losing his father to cholera—could that have frightened him into silence?"

"It is futile to seek the cause, to lay blame," the doctor pronounced.

"You haven't anything to lose by trying this, Suzanne," Esty said softly.

"Of course you don't, my dear," the doctor said. "Nothing at all. See here. Clayton," he called the boy. "Clayton, look at me now. Would you like more water? Yes? Good boy for nodding yes. And here is how to tell me 'more.'"

Suzanne waited in the silence, her heart pounding with the reminder of what she could not do for herself. Then she heard her son giggle. "Oh, look at that," the doctor laughed now. "He's pointed to the dish of sweets and made the sign, Mrs. Cullver. He learns quickly." He paused. "He's a handsome child. Favors you with his towhead." He cleared his throat.

"Did he, Esty?" Suzanne said. "Did he use the sign?"

"He put his little hands into a ball with his fingertips pointing together, Suzanne," Esty said. "Oh, and look, Sason just did it too!"

"My baby?"

"I'll make inquiries among my colleagues to see if there are others who could assist us in further…diagnosis, Mrs. Cullver. Meanwhile, a sign for 'help' might be of use. Or one for 'eat.' I'll draw a picture for Miss Williams here—"

"We have a Wintu friend," Suzanne said. "I'm sure she can show us. We don't need anything more from here."

"Oh, well, of course," he said as Suzanne stood, "though I assure you—"

"Come, Clayton. Take Esty's hand now. And you have Sason, too?" Esty tapped her hand and placed it over Suzanne's cane as they rose to leave.

Suzanne stepped out into the Sacramento air, breathing a sigh of relief as she heard the door latch behind them. Her dog, Pig, stood up, and she reached for his stiff leather harness and followed him down the steps.

In the carriage, Suzanne listened to the clop-clop of the horses and let it soothe her. The stage trip south had been a backbreaking journey, and Suzanne had arrived tired and the children cranky and the dog barking, barking at this fabulous city still recovering from floods and fires of the year before. But she'd been determined to seek help here for her son. To accept help.

Suzanne sighed as she listened to carriage sounds, tried to identify the scents of trees, cooking fires, even the hog pens they passed. Esther had been a dear to find the doctor with whom they'd spent the morning discussing Clayton. The specialist was said to work well with children who were slow. How would she explain to Sister Esther that the man was a finger-talking quack!

"Mommy!" Clayton said. He struck his mother in the arm, forcing Suzanne to the present.

"Clayton. Stop that!" He could startle her so, coming at her that way. And he was strong for someone so small. "Mommy. Mommy," he chanted, punching her with his tiny fists. She grabbed at his hands and held them in her own. He started to wail, bounced against her and kicked.

"Clayton! Cease!" Suzanne said.

Esty must have found something to distract him for he quieted, even the bells on his shoes stopped tinkling for a moment. He still let Suzanne hold his hands. "Do you really think the signs the doctor suggested make sense?" Suzanne asked Esty as they jostled about in the buggy.

"What can it hurt? Oltipa can show us a few."

"I'm afraid…well, that people will think he isn't…all there," Suzanne said, finally naming the fear riding the doctor's suggestion. "I remember a man back in Michigan who couldn't speak or hear, and people were wretched to him. But his eyes had such light in them I always thought he could understand. Do Clayton's eyes have that light?" Suzanne asked.

"They do," her friend told her, patting her hand.

Suzanne sighed. "Sister Esther will have to know too. And anyone he's with. Oh, if we could just find out why he's this way and fix it. I just want to get things tended." Suzanne kissed the knuckles of her son's hands. "And everyone will know now that I haven't."

"They already know," Esty told her.

"That I'm a failure? Why did they tell me to stop worrying then?"

"They know that he has something wrong, not that there's anything wrong with you. They just don't know what they can do to help. At least the signs are something. And it will show us if Clayton can locate sighted people to ask for help. It takes intelligence to do that."

"Sighted people. Yes," Suzanne said. "Sighted people. Not his mother."

She turned her face away. She couldn't see through them, but her eyes could betray her with unexpected tears. She knew this had to be, this having to rely on others at so many levels of being a mother, a widow, a woman. It pained her. The boy beside her must have sensed something as he jerked his hands free, stood up, and touched her face. "Mommy," he told her, the only word she'd heard him say in months.

"Yes. Mommy." She pulled the boy to her, then kissed the top of his head. She patted his little arm. And then he did the strangest thing. First, he hit her shoulder as he had before, then he lifted her hands from the cane across her lap. He placed them like two cups, pushing the fingertips together.

"He's showing you the sign," Esty said. "For *more!*"

"Is he?"

"What had you done? Do it again," Esty said.

Suzanne thought. Stopping him from hitting her? The kiss? The hug? She reached out for him. "Let me hold you," she said, and he melted into her, then turned so his back nestled against her breast. She kissed the top of his head. "Let me hold my boy," she said. He made the sign

24

for *more* then, her arms still wrapped around him, and she felt him nod and grunt, then she kissed his head again. The dog panted and yipped.

"He's making that sign, Suzanne. And he's smiling. But no bigger than you."

Crescent City, on the California Coast

The salt spray forced Tipton Wilson Kossuth to pull the shawl tighter around her slender shoulders. Sunset usually promised a wind and a chill, but she didn't want to go inside just yet. The ball of red sinking on the horizon still felt warm against her face, and she found she could think more clearly at the shore.

Nehemiah, her husband, was a good man. Everyone said so. So she didn't know why this recent request annoyed her so. He rarely asked a thing of her that wasn't reasonable. Maybe that was it. He was always so…reasonable, telling her things "for her own good" as though his sixteen more years of living gave him some superior right to tell her what to expect, how to behave. Her mother was always telling her what to do. Her brother, Charles, gave his advice freely, when she couldn't avoid his presence. Now she had a husband who thought it his duty to educate her mind and soul…and body. She shoved that thought aside. She would be seventeen in less than a month. She guessed she knew a few things about living, about how a young wife was supposed to behave.

She bent to pick up a clear stone. An agate. She'd have one of her own to show him. He'd like that, though she supposed he knew about this beach full of them. He was always talking about the pretty rocks he picked up on his journey inland to Oregon when he brought supplies for the mining communities growing there. "An entire agate desert lies in the shadow of two strange land formations people in Jacksonville call Table Rocks."

Some days she felt as though she lived in a desert too, nothing more than a shiny object her husband polished toward perfection. At least Tipton had made her mother happy. Tipton sniffed. Her mother would say she'd made a good marriage with a man both kind and aspiring. Hadn't he recovered his assets after being wiped out by a fire? Hadn't he already arranged financing for warehouses that stocked his pack string? And he spoke more openly now about running for political office. Everyone Tipton met said he should. They needed a good representative from this northern end of Klamath County. And everyone treated the Kossuths as though they'd always belonged at this far reach of the world shadowed by transport and timber.

So what was wrong with her? She quickened her pace, her linsey-woolsey skirt whipping around her high-top boots. Tipton glanced toward the shore. No Indians. Nehemiah warned her that the Takelmas and Klamaths and other bands weren't as friendly as those who had helped them on their journey across from Wisconsin to California. Little sandpipers quickstepped against the foam that left a line as thin as lace against the sand. It was hard to keep everything straight in a new place. She didn't like the strong winds or the sudden weather changes either, changes that could take a dark, distant skyline to the heavy fog.

Sometimes the fog stayed out there, something she could see but didn't feel at all. Other times, it moved in to cover the land the way laudanum crept over her when she took it to soothe a hurt. She knew it would arrive to make the world hazy and slow, just not when or for how long.

She'd told Nehemiah about the ocean storms, especially the fog and how it chilled her, made her want to sink inside the cabin and stay a month.

"I'd have thought someone with such dramatic inclinations would enjoy the vagaries of the ocean," Nehemiah told her, "being so similar in temperament." Her husband was gentle in his saying of it, held her to him with one big arm as their boots sank in the sand. But his words still wounded. She wasn't "dramatic" as he implied and certainly not as changeable or as impulsive as his word "vagaries" suggested. She'd had to look that up in the dictionary he'd purchased. She'd been surprised he used a word meaning "odd" or "whimsical" to describe her personality. Sometimes she wondered if Nehemiah did that sort of thing on purpose, to make her feel young and inexperienced, as though she was his student and he always the teacher.

As Tipton saw it, Nehemiah was the one who demonstrated vagary ways like the weather, not her. His marriage proposal had come the same day as the fire that wiped out Shasta City, and they'd left to begin a new life the day after their wedding. The memory of her mother's betrayal that day, strong. She pushed it from her mind.

She stumbled, caught herself on the tree roots washed up onshore all stripped and bare and stacked like a witch's knotty canes against the sandbanks. Tomorrow, in a wash of storms, the beach could be swept clean as Chita's kitchen. *Chita's kitchen.* The Mexican house girl who worked for them owned that room. Tipton felt displaced even in her own house—it was as though her mother had come with her.

Her mother. The wind picked up swirling leaves and twigs. Tipton walked with her back to the wind then, letting it push her from the beach toward their cabin. Grass refused to grow beside their home, the salt and rain pelting it, leaching it of life. Maybe it was the constant shade of the tall firs that pierced the sky over their home that made her feel…closed in, somehow.

She did love the tangled foliage, the huckleberries and elderberries that tasted sweet and the flowers that bloomed soft pinks even in the fall as it was now. It was all so lush and humbling, this ocean place. She felt so small here. So very small.

That was what she'd wanted her husband of three months to understand.

She changed direction again, walking the other way now, facing the sea. The fog bank moved closer, tightened her chest. A steamer cut the horizon. Tipton wondered if it was the *Cameo* and if it would dock in Crescent City or head on north to Portland and Vancouver. She could use a new issue of *Goody's* to peruse. That brightened her spirit. And maybe there would be a letter from Mazy. She'd heard nothing from her mother, and she probably wouldn't. Her mother had Charles now. Nehemiah would get his newspaper from the ship too and disappear inside it. He kept on top of the political news in New York and Washington, sometimes reading to her of subjects like the Kansas-Nebraska Act passed earlier that summer. He got agitated by some law being repealed, something in Missouri that had happened thirty years before. And *abolitionists*. What on earth was that? It sounded like a sneeze or the stomach ague, what she was sure she'd suffered from herself this past week.

"Nothing more than eating seafood when you're not accustomed," Nehemiah told her, patting her arm in that gentle way he had.

"Chita's hot sauces more likely," she'd countered.

"Now, Tipton," he'd said. "We are the foreigners here. Remember that. We need to learn the newer ways, not them."

She didn't like that part of California at all, the foreign influences. California had dozens of them. Why, Nehemiah had informed her that five nations' flags had flown over California. "Do you know which countries they were?" he'd asked as if she were a dolt.

She guessed Spain and Mexico right off. Then thought of the United States. But she never did guess the other two. He'd been almost smug, twisting at his red beard when he said, "Russia and the Bear Republic. Yes, we were once our own little country, not unlike Texas."

She just never got used to hearing the languages spoken on the muddy streets, and unlike Mazy, Tipton didn't find them the least bit interesting to listen to. She just marched right on by if she encountered a Celestial or one of the native people with their solemn faces. Or were the Indians the natives, she wondered? That made the Mexicans, what, foreigners just as she was? It was all too confusing.

Which made Nehemiah's request all the more difficult to understand. Why did these California people use so many foreign words still? They'd been a state for nearly three years. Yet half the things Chita said ended in an *o. Pronto. Pequito. Gordo.* She'd heard that *gordo* meant *fat,* a word she'd also overheard and hoped had not been meant for her. Tipton had been diligent about what she ate. She was very careful to stop at the first sign of pressure against the whalebone busk, taking small bites of any new thing offered. She could never be sure what those people put into foods anyway.

So why did her husband want her to learn their language? That was the frustration. She didn't need to actually learn the language outright to be able to converse with their Spanish neighbors. They were all learning English. That was as it should be.

"You'll feel more at home if you know some Spanish, Mrs. Kossuth," Nehemiah insisted. He always used her full name after she'd asked him not to call her "Tip." She hadn't told him Tip was the name Tyrell had called her.

Tyrell. The man she'd come west for. The man death had cheated her of. She wondered if Tyrell would have made such a request of her. He spoke of kindness, of treating people as good neighbors, expecting the best. He seemed more concerned that she have a good heart than that she be able to talk to the maid, not that they would've had a maid if she and Tyrell had married. But she didn't think he'd have said, "Learn to talk the way the Mexicans do."

"This was Mexico once. All of it, Mrs. Kossuth," Nehemiah had said. "Just a courtesy to remember that. It's for your own good I ask it. I want you to have friends."

She couldn't imagine being friends with Chita. Besides Chita could understand her English perfectly well. That was what she'd tell Nehemiah. That she'd given it her "ocean thought," hated to disappoint him, but she was her own person as his Mrs. Kossuth. She would learn to manage the household, give orders and directions so his needs were tended, but she would do that in her own way, in English, and make her own friends. Yes, that was what she'd tell him. She inhaled deeply. The ship looked larger on the horizon. Good. It was coming onto shore. Something to look forward to. She turned her back and headed for their home.

Reality was what happened when one started to hope. Ruth had allowed herself pleasure. Morning fishing. A shower in the middle of a fall day. She had considered something besides preparing for the worst. She'd even decided to move forward, to do something different, not just wait to react to the trials she attracted like dead vermin enticing wasps. See what it got her? She'd lost a dream that would've sustained her through difficult days. She'd lost the sureness of reaching *for* something, not just batting something bad away.

It was the second day after Jumper's death. Ruth wanted to go to the barn, saddle Koda, and just ride out into the timber and never come back. But Mazy was there milking her cows, and she didn't want to talk with her or see her. Her fists clenched with the thoughts. Even if Mazy hadn't been there, Ruth wasn't sure she could give herself permission to ride Koda, for fear she would find joy in that moment.

There'd been other things to occupy her time anyway. First, there'd been the settling of Jessie and Ned, discovering what had happened, how the brute had gotten loose—not that it mattered now. The morning after, she'd tried to tell them that she was glad they were both safe and had not somehow gotten between the cow brute and the horse. Her eyes ached from crying, and her voice was as stiff as new leather.

"We was just feeding grain to Jumper, and he must have followed us when we fed Marvel," Ned had told Mazy when she'd come that night.

"But why did you grain the brute?" Mazy said. "Why were you in his pen?"

"We were just being nice," Jessie defended. "He's always been nice to us. He just watched us and chewed his mouth. He didn't mean no harm. He was all alone in there while all the rest of the cows got to be together."

Even in her grief, Ruth noticed the child kept looking at her, seeking assurance, Ruth imagined, wondering if all the goodwill they'd been storing up would now be washed away like yesterday's dirt.

"Being nice," Mazy scoffed. "You were told to never, ever go inside his pen."

"We closed the gate after we left, Aunt Mazy, we did," Ned said. "And we just poured a little bit of grain on top of his hay. That's why we had to go in the pen like that. To put the grain down. In the manger. So it wouldn't get all stomped on. I couldn't pitch it over the rail, so we went inside. I'm sorry. I am. But we slid the latch just like you always said."

"Somehow it got opened," Matthew told them, "and I don't think it was the bull or horse that did it. You kids deserve a good lick—"

"I'll handle them," Ruth had said.

It was no one's fault, not really, and they'd suffered enough. Remorse rode their little shoulders hard. Even in her own despair, Ruth could see that. And she didn't like the way everyone thought they could just discipline her children. Her children had a guardian. Maybe it was just from habit, from when she'd pulled back and let others do the raising up of them. Well, things were different now.

The horse had obviously followed the grain and, after the children left the corral wandering toward the freighter's bells, somehow the latch had worked loose—or was worked loose by Jumper's nudging at it. She'd known Koda could unlatch a gate; she didn't think Jumper could. But it might have happened that way.

Jumper had gone inside, snuffed around in the hay. The bull defended, possibly coming from behind with his horns lowered, gouging then twisting into Jumper.

The morning after, Ruth'd found herself still there, sitting beside him, talking and petting Jumper.

Mercifully Mazy had not tried to talk with her, but had stood beside her for a time, then touched her shoulder. Ruth felt cold as iron. She couldn't bring herself to nod or sink into her good friend's touch. Instead she'd continued the ritual of hand over hide, laying Jumper's hair smooth, flattening the rough spots, the tiny nicks and scars that marked a horse's life.

Matthew left briefly to get biscuits, and as the sun rose higher, he returned, squatted beside her and suggested softly that they'd need to do something about the animal. She could see herself that the flies were gathering.

"I want his tail hairs," she said then, "and mane. For a mecate."

"Joe and I'll do it," Matthew said. "It'll make a good rope. Good idea, Ruth. A way to take him with you." He'd cleared his throat. "Do you want us to bury him? The packers would help, I think—"

She shook her head. "Haul him into the woods. Cut him up." Matthew frowned. "For the dogs. The freighter's dogs."

"Ruth, I—"

"Jumper'll go on living that way. He won't have died for nothing."

"You're a remarkable woman," Matthew said then as he pushed against his knees to stand. "A remarkable woman."

"The raccoons and coyotes and bees'll clean the bones," she said knowing she sounded…callous, cold maybe, but it was her way of holding on, of keeping herself together. "Only the bones'll be left. You can bury those. After I've gone. I'll get the shears and cut the hairs myself."

"Ruth, you don't need to—"

"You can help," she said, her voice softening. "You are." Her eyes met his.

She'd let him cut the mane but had pulled on the tail hairs herself, scraping mud and manure from the long copper, black, and brown strands with her fingers. She felt the tightness in her chest and the sobs rise up from a place that felt empty already. She wondered if she'd cried this much for her brother or for her baby when they'd died. Yes, she guessed she had. The thought relieved her, somehow, reassured her.

Elizabeth arrived then, as the drover Joe Pepin and Matthew and the freighters placed ropes around the big animal and towed Jumper into the woods. Ruth couldn't watch. Someone must have told Elizabeth, or maybe she'd been headed this way on her own. No. She'd been out there the day it happened, Ruth barely remembered. There'd been no going-away gathering. Someone must have cancelled it. She had let Elizabeth put her arms around her, and she had cried, embarrassed by the flow of tears. "The children are fine. No one was hurt," Ruth told her.

"I know, Ruthie, I know."

"I can't wait for Jeremy's brother to come claim that brute," Mazy'd said. "I'm so sorry. I should have just sold him off. But no, I was wanting to build a herd, had a plan—"

"It wasn't the bull's fault," Elizabeth told her. "No one's fault. Always easier if you can lay blame but don't do you no good in the long run. Miserable results are still there, looking up at you." She patted Ruth's back. "You just got to move on."

Elizabeth's presence today would be soothing and would be a buffer between herself and Mazy. She had to refocus, as Suzanne would say. Begin the thoughts of moving on though they were confused now. What was the point of leaving without a stallion to sire a dynasty? What was the point of staying?

Mazy loaded her milk tins on her cart, carried the butter molds, and emptied them into damp linen for transport. Ruth watched her friend snap the mule's harness and drive away, relief and sadness mingling in her mind.

She stepped into the shade of the barn now, pulled halters and bridles from the tack area and placed them in a box.

"Ah, Miss Martin?" It was Joe Pepin, the wrangler with an active

Adam's apple. He fingered the brim of the hat in his hands. "I know this is a poor time, ma'am, but I'm here to tell you that I can't be taking you north today."

Ruth blinked, tried to concentrate. "I expect we'll need a few more days before we're ready," she told him. She motioned to all the tack and tools still not loaded.

He coughed. "See. I can't be taking you and the young ones at all. I'm...I got me a stake in a gold mine, and soon as the rains come, we'll be sluicing. I ain't getting any younger, and digging gold's got more promise than wrangling."

It almost didn't surprise her. "I'm sorry to hear that, Joe. But you made a deal with me."

"Yes ma'am. But as Matthew says, sometimes the wind changes. Guess people do too."

She stared at him, then waved him away. She shouldn't have counted on him in the first place, she thought. She watched with disinterest as he left and Matthew approached.

"So he told you."

"How long have you known?" she accused before turning back to lift a silver bit.

"Just since we dragged...handled Jumper," he said. He then leaned against the manger, tipped his hat up higher on his forehead, and found a strand of wild rye grass to chew. "I've been thinking since." He cleared his throat. "If you're wanting a guide to southern Oregon, I've been there too, you know. I know the way."

"Matthew, I—"

"And together, we could get twice the free land."

"Half a section will be enough for me," she said. She polished at the bit with her shirt sleeve. "And I need a guide and wrangler, not a partner."

"It's not given to single women," he said quietly.

"What?"

"Maybe...Ruth, maybe there's no reason to go at all now." He stood straight, looking tall and older than she knew he was. He was five, maybe six years younger than her. All of eighteen. Maybe nineteen. "You can't build a herd with no sire. Why not wait a year, see if one of those yearlings look promising. Put your hopes on that."

"What do you mean single women can't—?"

"Oregon doesn't give land unless you're married. Or male. I thought we'd hitch up maybe…that's why so many young girls are. Shoot, Mariah's old enough if we were to let her…which we won't. Fifteen is just too young. But I heard about a gal just eleven. Played outside with the neighbor's kids while her husband took care of the dishes and parched the coffee beans up."

Ruth's ears burned, and she wondered if her neck blotched. How could she not have known that she couldn't expect the same rights as a man? Now she'd have to use what little cash they had left to buy land. Or she'd have to sell some of the mares. Or maybe Matthew was right, just not go at all. And then what? Stay on here with Mazy and her…bull? Let Zane Randolph, Ruth's husband, just walk right up and find them all again? And just what did Matthew intend with his suggestion that they could have twice the land together?

"It's pretty country. Good soil, black not red like here. Orchard country. Good for cattle and timber. With California growing as it is, there's plenty of folks to buy all that Oregon's rich soil can grow: apples, grain, hogs, beef, even horses a man…or woman could raise up." He cleared his throat again. "Partnering isn't such a bad idea."

"I already did that once in my life. Officially, I still have a husband."

"Talking business here," Matthew said. He cleared his throat, then grinned. "'Course I'm willing to take it up a step or two if you'd like. Anything to please a little lady."

Ruth felt her face grow hot. "If your offer is to guide us, I'll consider it, Mr. Schmidtke." She emphasized his name. "But I prefer to decide my own future, not just fall into someone else's idea of what a little lady needs."

She stomped out of the barn even though that was where her work was. She heard his boots on the ground, felt him follow her out. "Ruth, I didn't mean—"

"It's Miss Martin," she said, her words gouging like a hoof pick. "I think—"

"Look. I have this habit, like my Pa, saying things in ways that come out wrong. I didn't mean nothing…anything. I wouldn't want to say or do…you've had enough bad times. I…"

She didn't hear him, had already closed her ears to whatever he might be saying. It was all a fog anyway—something said to get back in her good graces, not meant for her but for him.

She heard a wagon freighter's bells jangle as the rig turned off the red road into the meadow. He drove a two-span hitch, four mules, and sat high on top of his wagon. Maybe she should try freighting, sell all the mares and buy up mules, and just go back to farming the children out. "If you always do what you've always done…" the words echoed. No, the children had to come first. She'd already been through times when that hadn't been so. She'd missed them too much. They were a team, a family. She just had to find a way to raise them well and still not do what she'd always done that kept her distant.

The freighter driver waved to her, and she welcomed his invitation. "Got lots of baubles for the ladies in Shasta City," he told her. "Even a few feathers for hats."

"I'm sure they'll be pleased," Ruth said. "Mine doesn't appear to need any."

He laughed. "That floppy felt of yours is still becoming, Miss Martin. Say, where's that big stallion of yours? He always liked my maple candy."

Ruth winced, her eyes watered. "He…there was an accident. He—"

He swept his hat and held it at his chest. "Sure sorry, Miss Martin. Indeed I am."

She wondered how long it would take before she could talk about it without fighting the tears. At least in Oregon no one would know about Jumper. That alone was a good reason to leave. She walked around the far side of the wagon box. "Need help unharnessing?" she asked.

"Always," he said. "Leave the jack tied to the back though," he said. "'Til I can hobble him myself. He's a character." Ruth looked up at the bigheaded jack. The animal stood almost as tall as her Jumper had been, sixteen hands at least. "Old Doc picked him up. Someone coming on Noble's Trail sold him. Imagine making it all that way across and then just having to let him go."

Like Jumper, Ruth thought, having to let him go. *If you always do...* She'd have to try something new, even a new way to grieve loss. "What will you do with him?"

"Oh, break him if I can. Or breed him to some fine mares. He's good stock even if he is a little ornery. I guess they all are. The army's always looking for mules. Some of the big ranches east use 'em for haying and such, now that people are back to working instead of just crazy for gold. Yup," he patted the big black mule and raised a puff of dust. "I figured I'd find some use for him."

"Or sell him to someone who would?"

severing

French Gulch, Northern California

"Hand me Schimmelbusch's kit, the complete one. Yes, yes, hurry. With the stop-cock bottle."

"You will not use the ether?" a woman said.

"No. Chloroform. It should have been done earlier...I don't know. We'll be fortunate to save that portion of the leg now."

"He wished you to wait."

"Too risky now."

"Will he live?"

Zane Randolph heard the voices as though far away. Above him loomed a night sky of heavy black broken by the sounds of crickets. No, not the sky but dark wallpaper of reds and purples with squares like crossed prison bars marching around the perimeter. The sounds were clicks of metal against tin.

"Hold the lantern high, dear. The fumes."

"Oui," the woman said.

The lantern's light flickered against a blade. Zane smelled something. Kerosene.

As he came out of this delirium, Zane became aware of his body. It felt heavy, as though a horse had rolled onto him, pinning his limbs beneath water. His arms did not belong to him. The hand he raised to reach for the knife was pale and white, not his. He was so tired of these people always pushing at him, poking. Prison guards, holding him hostage, smelling like antiseptics. He'd ridden away from them, hadn't he? No, he'd made his way to them, and now they did this. He lunged for the blade.

"Here, here, no need for that," the man said. "I'm a doctor."

Zane heard heavy breathing and wondered if someone else hovered in the room. He tried to turn his neck to look, but a sharp pain stopped him. His head burned with fever. "Where am I?"

"In my surgery. Someone brought you in, barely alive, I might add. You've been in and out of delirium for days. Now, we must do something more. You have serious lesions and infections. I'm afraid…your leg…must come off."

Zane grabbed for the scalpel again, reached the woman's arm instead. She squealed, tried to jerk back, the lantern casting a hollow light against wood walls.

"Non!" the woman shrieked.

"It must be done," the doctor said, prying Zane's weakened fingers from the woman's arm.

"Why should I…believe you?" Zane managed.

"You have no choice."

Zane clutched the man's shirt sleeve now. "Who are you?" he whispered.

"I'm a doctor. A surgeon. You've nothing to fear. We'll get started if you just lie back down. Chloroform will put you under. You won't feel pain. Please. You're frightening my nurse."

As if frightening a woman was a foul thing.

Zane leaned on one elbow, panting. The room spun around him. He willed himself to control his mind, his thoughts. He must not let himself do something impulsive, something to later hurt his plans.

He let go of the man's shirt, lay back from the frightened eyes of the woman.

"Do you have a name?" the man asked, leaning over him, the light behind him turning the opening of his nostrils into dark caverns, dark holes in prison walls. "Do you remember your name?"

The little squares on the wallpaper moved now, circled around and around the ceiling edge. Zane heard a buzzing sound in his head, felt a linen mask drift like cobwebs onto his face. The table was a casket board, hard against his back. He could tell now that the sounds of labored breathing came from his own throat. He was alone with the doctor and nurse in this room.

"Your name. Before we cut." They were waiting for him to speak.

"Beckworth," Zane told him, pulling the name from something he'd read or heard. "Wesley Beckworth." He willed himself to remember for when he would awaken, hoping that he would, had to. "But only cut away the infection. Leave the leg. Leave it. It will heal."

"My good man—"

"Leave it!"

"Spray the chloroform on his mask, dear. Careful with the inhaler. Yes. That's right. Now then. Let's see if we can get rid of something you won't be able to live with."

Zane looked up at the woman, she was ghostly and far away. She reminded him of someone, he couldn't think whom. *Ruth,* he thought, his dear wife, Ruth. He heard sounds of metal splintering the fuzziness of his head, the knife hitting the side of a tin pan. He took in huge gulps of air. He would not be confined, not with a missing limb, not with Ruth laughing at his imperfection. Better death than that. Better death.

"No!" Zane ripped at the linen mask.

"Careful! The lantern! You'll cause a fire, man!"

"You take my leg, I'll have your life," Zane finished. He was sinking, sliding down a slope of talus, sure that at the rocky bottom his head would separate from his body.

As in a nightmare, he heard the doctor say, "When we've amputated, we must get his name from that poster we saw. I am sure it is the same man, though the name he told us is different. Send it to the Shasta post office. Whoever is seeking his whereabouts should know quickly..." And then Zane's world went black.

Mazy pushed her head into the side of Jennifer, one of her Ayrshire cows. Her fingers strong and firm, Mazy pulled at the cow's udder. The smell of the fresh milk and the hard splash sounds into the foamy pool usually soothed her. Not now. Ruth hadn't spoken a word to her directly since this dreadful thing happened. Oh, Mazy'd allowed herself time this morning—while it was still dark—to write and have her conversations with God. "Ponderin' with the Lord," her mother might say, that was what she was doing. Asking why bad things had to happen, why good people ended up hurting, bearing more than their share of suffering and separation.

She was thinking about Ruth's suffering. Ruth had been different since Jessie's return, more willing to let others...come close. Then just when she'd taken that leap, to make a difference in her life with her family intact and old lies out in the open, this happened, this tragedy stealing her hopes. It was the first thought that had filled Mazy's mind when she saw Jumper lying there. Ruth's dream, gone.

The second thought had been of her own miserable self. It was her fault that the brute had been there at all, her procrastinating about getting the bull south. She'd waited for Jeremy's brother to come and get it if he wanted it so badly. That was her right. She was within her rights to wait like that, to make him come forward. See what her stubbornness had gotten her? She was right, but being right didn't make her happy. She was also sorrier than she'd ever been in her life. At the very least, she should have found her own place to live long before now, and taken the animal there so it wouldn't have been here for Ruth's Jumper to encounter. Or she should have asked if David Taylor could take the brute to his cabin at Mad Mule Canyon.

But Mazy was building her cowherd up, she reminded herself. She'd wanted the breeding to be perfect, knew just what days to let the animals breed so she could plan when the calves would come. She had plans too. *Her* plans. See what they'd gotten her: tragedy for her friend and perhaps the severing of their relationship forever.

It was Jeremy's fault, this whole thing. For buying the brute in the first place, for selling her home, making an emigrant of her. And then he'd had the gall to die. No, she had to stop blaming. It just kept her stuck in the muck.

Mazy had stood at a distance when her mother held Ruth the morning after Jumper's death. She noticed that her friend would not look at her and turned away when Mazy started toward them. Then, still wearing a blanket Matthew had draped across her shoulders, Ruth had disappeared into the dark of the barn. Mazy followed, finding her friend bent over a pack box half filled with her bridles and spade bits and spurs.

Ruth straightened at the sound of Mazy's entrance, but she kept her back to Mazy. Mazy moved around so she could see Ruth fingering silver bells that lined the leather of a Spanish bridle. The tiny silver globes ended at the spoon spade bit.

"That looks like it would hurt a horse," Mazy said, nodding toward the steel hump of the bit meant to touch a horse's tongue. "But Seth said the vaqueros use them because a horse can go farther without water with that bit. You probably knew that. I guess it keeps their mouths moist. The Indians use little pebbles the same way. Have you heard that? Funny that something that looks to hurt could have anything good in it."

Ruth remained still, gazing down. She wore a shirt and pants meant for miners she'd probably bought at Adora and Charles Wilson's mercantile. She just kept rubbing the bridle, not saying a word.

"Of course your animals are tough anyway. They weathered the trip across in fine form," Mazy babbled. "Seth was amazed when I told him that you let Mariah ride Jump..." She cleared her throat.

Ruth just kept rubbing that bit.

"Can I help you? That's what I came to do," Mazy said. "Just tell me what you want in which pack box. I'm good at organizing things."

Ruth stayed silent.

Mazy looked out through the open barn door, her heart pounding with the disappearing of a friendship. "Koda looks good," she said. "Maybe you should go for a ride. It always made you feel better."

The little bells at the bridle in Ruth's hands shook.

Mazy just wanted to hold her, to take her in her arms and make the hurt go away. Instead she said, "You're a good horse trainer, Ruth. Those yearlings, they'll need some work, won't they? That'll keep you busy. Keeping busy is good for grieving, it is."

Ruth threw the bridle into the pack box then and pushed past Mazy into the morning sun.

Later in the day, with Ruth and Elizabeth and a few others standing about, Ruth spoke to someone else when Mazy asked a question. Ruth turned to answer Elizabeth when Mazy was talking or nodded toward Matthew to have him hand something to Mazy that was easily within Ruth's reach. Her friend didn't want to talk to her, or look at her, and surely not touch her. And Mazy couldn't bring herself to say what she feared most, that she'd somehow lost a friend in this, just as Ruth had lost her horse.

Maybe it was just as well, her not being able to bring the subject up. Ruth was leaving, and Mazy would have to live without her friend around. Maybe this was God's way of making it easier for Ruth to leave. Something good rising from the rubble. She'd keep telling herself that.

Mazy grabbed at the cow's tail just before it swatted her in the face. "Almost done here, girl," she said. The cow danced a bit, raising her back hooves up and setting them down. "Almost finished."

What good could come from this? Mazy wondered. There had to be something. Maybe she'd spend more time with her mother this way. But Mazy would have done that just with Ruth's leaving anyway. She might take Mariah under her wing. The girl was quick with her letters and such and compassionate with David Taylor and Oltipa's little Ben. And she was a good hand with stock, had always liked riding and looking after the animals. They might find something more in common now that Ruth was leaving. Mazy thought she'd put the lamb's ears cutting into Mariah's hands instead of giving it to Ruth. Ruth might not want to take anything Mazy had to offer her.

Maybe Jumper's dying was a sign that Ruth was supposed to stay! Ruth could make her way here, with help from her friends, instead of pushing herself north to a place she'd only heard of, where she said she could get a land grant of nearly a quarter-section just by showing up. Oh, she knew Ruth liked to do things on her own—what woman didn't? But Mazy could help her buy this place. They could own it together! They could buy Poverty Flat instead of Ruth's leasing it as she had for a year.

She warmed to her subject, milked faster and harder now, ignoring a small voice inside that said to slow down. To not let her hopes outrun her reason.

The cow stepped sideways, her tail flicking at Mazy's face. "Now, now, Jennifer. It's all right. Sorry. Didn't mean to pull so hard."

She was mind mumbling. Ruth would never want to go into a partnership with her now. Mazy sighed. It couldn't be fixed; they couldn't go back to what was. Ruth would leave, and Mazy'd have to take the cow brute south. Mazy might not have a pure dairy herd if she bred her cows with a Durham bull, say, or some of the Mexican stock, but she'd still have good milkers and she'd get rid of this…bad memory. For now, Mazy didn't want to miss a chance that she and Ruth could bridge this rushing river the bull had tipped them into.

Mazy pressed her fingers at the small of her back, rubbing. Bending over to milk was hard on a tall body like hers, having to squat on a stool. Probably on a short frame, too. It was worthy work though.

Milking required a commitment to routine, that was certain. And anyone who said every milking was the same—just like any journey—had never done it more than once. Something was always challenging a dairywoman: A cow with porcupine quills stuck in her nose at milking time or a calf refusing to suck required thinking. And yet Mazy always ended satisfied, as though she'd completed a chapter of a good book.

She carried the milk to the river trough she'd built for cooling. She poured the white gold into flat tins to wait until the cream rose for churning, then emptied another bucket into tins that looked like chimneys settled in the water. She had to move the cooled tins from a previous milking and place them at the end of the trough where she'd pull them out in the morning for delivery in town. She'd ask Mariah to skim, then churn the risen cream. She'd be glad when that goat and the treadmill she'd ordered arrived. The goat could do the hard work then of churning cream into butter. These were tasks with beginnings, middles, and ends that filled her like good bread. She'd begun feeling empty and alone this evening. Yet in the rhythm of pulling and squeezing and listening to cats meow and cows chewing their cuds, she'd found a respite from the ache of splintered friendships.

Mazy watched as a mallard paddled off in a pool of rushes near the trough, the sun glistening on his emerald neck. Browned grasses eased in the breeze and Mazy inhaled. A pleasant place. That was what she had always wanted. She and Ruth had that in common. Maybe that shared dream would be enough to mend them back together.

The younger children sat along the wall like lily pads around the outside edge of a swirling pond. Eyes moved back and forth between herself and Matthew, Ruth noticed, as she cut the noodles, stopped, then held a knife to punctuate her point, waiting for Matthew to counter, his own knife sending whittling chunks of alder onto the wood floor.

"You wanted my honest opinion," Matthew said. Ruth nodded.

"I think it's nuts. Crazy. Break 'em for working cattle? You got to be kidding."

"And to sell to the military. Look at the freighter market alone," Ruth said.

"You don't see any mules drawing stages though, do you?"

"But good solid, big mares, bred to a big jack would bring about a sturdy animal. It would. And it would still have the same agility because they're built differently. I just never paid that much attention before, but it's true. And with people getting back to field work, growing crops and making hay, big mules could be a premium to the Spanish ranches right here in California."

"So are you saying you'd stay here, in California?"

"Now Matthew's getting interested," Jason teased.

Ruth frowned. She lifted the strips of egg noodles and hung them over the towel holder behind the washbowl, checking their thickness. She busied herself, made a new hole in the mound of flour on the dough boy, broke an egg inside, added oil and beat them, pinched in more flour until it felt right, and she pressed the new mass flat.

"Got enough noodles there for an army," Matthew said.

"People are coming out. Mazy, too, I suppose. I wish your mother'd sharpen my knives," she growled then as the dough bunched up along the blade.

"Maybe she doesn't want any weaponry within your reach," he said.

"I know how to make noodles, and I like the idea of going north with big jacks. Maybe because that's where Jed and Betha and me hoped to go all along. Maybe because I don't really like all the memories of this place."

"New diggings don't change a person or their memories," he said. "It's how they see what they got already that does that."

"Sometimes a change of scenery can take the work out of what you have to look at though. And I don't want to see…what happened to Jessie or Jumper in every rock I stumble over."

A part of Ruth wondered why she even had this discussion with Matthew Schmidtke. He wasn't her brother, no kin at all. He had given her his honest answer, which she'd asked for though. And he did know some things about stock. He'd been clear and truthful, who could ask for more? So why was she so irritable?

"You said you thought I could go north with the children alone. Why is my wanting to take a couple of jacks along so much different?"

"Because they don't herd well. One would be bad enough, but two?"

"Jumper's foals will be good size, or should be. I'll breed them and their mothers to good jack stock."

"Too small," Matthew said. Ruth raised the blade in protest. "Well, they are. Fine looking brood mares, don't get me wrong, but they don't bulk up the way you'd want for what you're talking about."

She thought to argue, but she had to agree. She just wasn't ready to say that yet. "If I can find myself a good jack, he'll make up for their smaller size. It would work. Who knows, maybe they aren't so unruly with other jacks around the way stallions and geldings can be."

Matthew laughed. "Have you ever been around a jack? They're the most stubborn beasts known."

"And you'd know this because…"

"Shoot. Ask anyone from the South. They use them to farm down that way. You can hardly train 'em to stay inside a corral is what I always heard. That's why they run wild on the deserts."

"I didn't know you were an expert," she said as she brushed flour from her face. She pulled off the towel she'd tucked into the waistline of her pants, rolled it into a bunch. Sarah scrambled from the bed where she sat and took it from her, slipping out the back to shake it in the wind.

"You'll have your work cut out for you, with or without a jack, and besides, these mares are already bred back to Jumper. So you can't start a…dynasty until next year anyway. Why not wait to find a jack in Oregon? Herding one north will just add to your misery."

"Who's starting a dynasty?" Lura said, entering with her daughter,

Mariah, close behind. No knocking, no howdy, just walking right in. "You? Matthew Schmidtke? Well, it's about time."

"Ma, we're not talking about me," he said as he rose and gave her a peck on her forehead. Ruth remembered that Elizabeth always said a woman could tell what kind of husband a man might be by watching him with his mother. *Why had she thought of that?*

Matthew squeezed his sister close, held her for just a moment, and Ruth noticed that she let him, the bond between brother and sister a tender touch. "We're talking about Ruth here."

"What's Ruth up to?" Mariah asked.

Ruth filled her in while Lura sucked on her empty clay pipe. Matthew shook his head, frowned, and Ruth wondered how he could have been so encouraging of her going it alone yet act as though her ideas were more squirmy than worms.

Mariah, familiar in Ruth's kitchen, popped the raised noodles into a boiling pot of water, then sent Jessie and Sarah out to collect tomatoes from the garden and the last of the lettuce, too.

"Is that it then?" Lura asked when the girls had left. Ruth nodded. Lura tapped her pipe on her palm while she sat, kicking her foot draped across her knee. Her white-and-blue striped skirt bobbed up and down as though she were dancing. She was always in motion. "Let me think how that would work," Lura said. "Exactly."

"She's talking new uses for stock, now, Ma," Matthew said a bit condescendingly. Ruth caught her breath. "It's a little complicated."

"I know all about stock," Lura snapped. Both Matthew and Ruth turned to look at her. "People been talking about such things at the store and before that while I banked at the casinos. Lots of talk about seeing in new ways. What you're suggesting is mixing up 'livestock.'" She laid the pipe in her lap. "And you can count me in."

"Count you in on what, Ma?"

"Look," Lura told her son, standing then, quick as a hungry fox. "Best thing for us to do is to sell those Durham cows of ours to Mazy Bacon."

"Sell them?"

"She's got herself a herd then, dairy or beef, and she can dump that Marvel cow brute with an easy heart. She'll get herself some good help. Maybe David Taylor, her stepson of sorts. We can take some shares in her dairy instead of cash, if need be. Then we bag that money, and we buy ourselves some stocky mares, some from that Primrose blood out of Virginia, bred back or not. Maybe a couple of heavy Quarter-Pathers, too. Then the next few days, we roam these hacienda hills for the biggest, the strongest, and the prettiest jacks anybody ever saw—maybe two or three days. We buy them up. We breed them to any open mares we have. Next year they meet up with Ruth's mares, or by then you may be ready to sell them, too, Ruthie, and get yourself some of our stocky brood. It won't matter whether you like the breeding part or the training. We'll have plenty to do in this…dynasty you're proposing. We'll need to break them, and we'll need people to sell them to the army, the farmers, and cattlemen. Maybe some good buggy mules'll sell too. They'll all need tending, that many animals."

"Ma," Matthew said. "I think maybe—"

"'Course we got to find land enough to house us all and the mules, too. It'll be worth investing all we got. This could become the biggest moneymaker from a common thing since…brass tacks. You're a whiz, Ruthie, a true whiz. I had no idea you carried around such innovating thoughts in that pretty head of yours."

"Me neither," Ruth said. She felt spun around like a bottle at a party. She sneezed from the flour that dusted her face. "I only wish I'd thought of it myself," Ruth said as she sank onto the stool.

"This came in for Miss Martin," the editor at the Shasta *Courier* told Elizabeth. "You're heading out that way?"

"Indeed. Tonight's the big shindig. We hope to have a few fiddlers and plenty of food. You could join us."

Sam Dosh adjusted his printer's cap and shook his head. "Got to get the paper out. I'm going to miss her. She was a fine lithographer."

"She's a fine artist," Elizabeth said.

"It's not polite to read another's mail…" Sam said. "But hard not to when the writing's on the outside."

"Well, thank you, Sam," she said as she pulled the letter from his hands. "I'll see that Ruth gets it."

It was all happening too fast with too many things to sort through. Ruth listened and watched and wondered how her life had suddenly become someone else's. She looked around, wanted to concentrate on what was simple and sure.

Elizabeth whipped the cream. Mariah scraped on a chunk of ice Mazy brought out from the butcher's cave in Shasta. The little scoop below the blade filled up like pieces of crushed glass. She dumped the half-moon-shaped shavings on a pewter plate. Lura poured berry juice over the top. Only the whipped cream remained for the oohs and aahs to commence. "Ned, you going to sing for us tonight? Maybe 'O Susannah.' I always liked that one," Elizabeth said. "Helps me not miss Suzanne and Clayton and that Sason quite so much."

"Joe Pepin taught me one called 'Dinah Had a Wooden Leg.'"

"I bet that's a real foot stomper," Elizabeth said.

"Supposed to make cows get sleepy, that song, what Joe said," Ned continued.

They'd eaten the noodles with venison stew poured over them, finished off the lettuce, and sliced the last of the tomatoes that hadn't been dried by Sarah and Mazy. Fresh basil and oil covered the last slice, and Mazy ran her finger around the plate, lifting it to her mouth and sucking on the oil and herbs. Mazy'd been quiet all evening. Now she spoke.

"So you're going to sell your cows," she said to the Schmidtkes. "And you think I should buy them?"

"Expand your herd fast," Lura said. "Be dairying just like you wanted in no time. Your new kin there, David Taylor, he could stay home nights, not be driving a stage away. Protect his Indian wife better. It'd work out perfect."

"Maybe he likes traveling," Mazy said. "Some people do." She looked over at Ruth. "What about your work at Adora and Charles's store? Don't they need you there?"

"They'll get by. I've got new things going," Lura said.

She certainly did, Ruth thought. What had been her own journey to Oregon had suddenly become a crowd. Ruth knew she should speak up. She didn't know why she couldn't, wouldn't. She and the children would be joined now by a man she had some confusion about, a girl who adored her, and their…mother. That was the only word she could think of to describe Lura right then that wasn't unkind. "Don't know of another good jack in these parts, do you?" Lura asked. "Ruthie picked up one named Ewald. Black as the night."

"My Hans always used to say of someone pigheaded that they was 'stubborn as a German jack,'" Elizabeth said. "He saved it for the most bullheaded, stiff-necked patients he had. Ones who refused to listen to what he told them to do, even if it killed them. Which it sometimes did."

"I once heard Pa say you were as stubborn as 'a bobtailed mule,' Ma," Mariah said cautiously. "Remember that?"

"I don't."

"Jacks are that stubborn—not like you, Lura—but like a bobtailed mule that can't switch at flies. Here, scratch some brown sugar into this cream, girls, and we'll plop it on those piles of berries and ice. I got a pie I brought out too," Elizabeth said. She cut the slices, and each took a piece on a tin plate, putting the crushed ice on top.

"Have you ever seen anything prettier?" Elizabeth said. "I like that new ice shaver you bought up, Ruthie. Always something new to marvel over."

"A frivolous luxury," Ruth said. "One I don't deserve. You can have it, Elizabeth. My going-away gift."

"Oh, Ruthie, I wasn't—"

"I know," Ruth said. "I…" Ruth took her pie outside and sat down. Stars popped out. She really just wanted to be alone, to think.

"All right if I sit beside you?" Mazy asked.

Ruth moved over stiffly, and Mazy sat down on the shallow stoop, her knees in front of her. She fumbled balancing her plate, then moved behind Ruth, giving her back a solid rest. Ruth supposed that leaning over cows to milk two times a day must put some strain on a woman so tall.

"I always like seeing the stars come out," Mazy said. "Remember that night Mother took off and we didn't know where she was? I felt like we became friends that night. You even washed my hair. Remember?"

Ruth nodded.

"After that was when all the deaths came. That was the last night Jeremy put a quilt around my shoulders. But he didn't stay awake with me. You did. And I'm grateful, in case I never told you."

Ruth heard her set the tin down on the stoop and decided her own back could use a rest. She pressed crumbs on her finger, licked them clean, then sidled her way beside Mazy, setting her tin on top of hers. Crickets filled the night air.

"I miss fireflies. Something they don't have here in the West," Ruth said. She sighed. "I wish this hadn't come between us, but it has," Ruth said. "I know Jumper's death wasn't your fault."

"Oh, Ruth. Thank you. For understanding. I am sorry beyond description." Mazy touched Ruth's hand, felt the woman stiffen and pull back. Mazy brushed at her apron, picked at imaginary lint. She cleared her throat. "Funny thing is though," Mazy continued, "I think I know now what Jeremy might have been feeling, watching people ready to head out into something new, something they thought would be better. There's something…seductive in anticipation, looking forward. Scary, yes. But a little like that crushed ice, all fresh and new looking scraped away from something old and familiar." She picked up a pebble and threw it.

"You're putting off the inevitable," Ruth said finally. "Not wanting to accept what is."

She heard Mazy swallow, her voice develop a quiver. "Some of 'what is' I can accept. Everything bad that happens isn't my husband's fault. It's not always my fault either." Ruth looked at Mazy and saw moonlight glistening on the wetness of her cheeks. "But I don't want to accept that our friendship has a strain on it that can't be buttressed. I mean, what kind of friendship can't endure a stone or two thrown against it. Won't it make it stronger in the end, like stitching up a tear in a quilt? It just gives it another...story."

Ruth grunted.

"I can't accept that people come into our lives and then leave," Mazy said. "I just can't."

"You may have to," Ruth said.

"Just say it's not forever. Tell me that you'll forgive me for having a mad bull around, for imposing myself on your place all this time, for not moving along the trail a little faster. I am so sorry," she whispered then. "You know I am."

Ruth wished she could take them back to before it all happened, bring Jumper back, return to the safety of a relationship with Mazy. Maybe this was why she didn't have many friends. Keeping them rubbed her raw, took her inside places she didn't want to visit.

"Can't we just pretend we're still good friends?" Mazy persisted.

"I'm not sure what that would look like," Ruth said. She picked up another pebble and threw it into the darkness, listened for its plop.

"Just acting like you believe it's so, I guess," Mazy said. "Maybe agree to answer my letters when I write—you wouldn't have to tell me all that's happening inside you, but around you. The daily things. Maybe let me tell you what's inside me. Let it be all right for me to hold you in my prayers."

"So you can convince yourself everything is all fixed?"

"No. Because it's what friends do. Even over years and miles. Families, too. I guess it's what loving requires. Finding ways to close the spans that open when we least expect them."

The two women sat without speaking, a mooing cow, a coyote's howl, and the chatter of people in the cabin behind them filling the silence. The evening turned cooler, and Ruth heard Elizabeth saying that she needed to be leaving, then looking for something, wondering where she'd left it.

"It'll be all right. It will, Ruth," Mazy said.

"Maybe. In time."

"We don't have time, do we?" Mazy said. Ruth heard a catch in her voice. "You're leaving, and we may never even see each other again, not ever. I don't know if I could live with it like this, you gone and our… not…settled."

Ruth shrugged. "You'll have to."

"Can you ever forgive me?" Mazy whispered. "I guess that's what I want."

"You've come to the wrong place for that," Ruth said. "Forgiveness isn't something we humans grant anyway, isn't that right?"

"We have a part in it," Mazy said.

"Not me," Ruth said. "I live alone." Ruth's tone sounded stiff as a wagon tongue, even to herself. "We're on opposite sides of a cliff, and if either of us move, we'll disappear inside darkness," Ruth said.

"We're friends," Mazy whispered. "Surely friends—"

"People come into our lives for a reason, and then they go away. Maybe we came together to help each other on the trail, and now it's time to move beyond that. Maybe it'll make my leaving easier, this way," Ruth said.

"You've withstood so much, Ruth. I admire you so. You've found a way to live with loads I don't think I could have carried."

"Maybe now I'll find out who I really am," Ruth said.

"You don't have to leave now," Mazy said, almost pleading. "I mean, without Jumper, you might take the season here and find another stallion. Maybe at the hacienda you visited last week. Maybe yours was supposed to be a California-bred herd. And surely one of your mares will foal a stud colt in the spring. There are even some nice-looking yearlings you could hold back, see if one of those would turn into another stallion of high hopes."

"Don't…don't say it that way."

"Why risk leaving when you have everything you need right here?"

"You're taking over this place," Ruth said.

"We could all stay. There's room. I was thinking." Mazy turned to face her directly. "We could build the house I told you about. Lumber's coming down in price. Share the lease, maybe buy the old man out. I'll get Marvel south. I will. I'm going to ask David and Oltipa and Ben to come live here. Mother, too. We could be all together, just like we were. Once. You could spend time with Mariah. She so adores you. And we'd have time to mend this. Why go now? The maple tree we brought from Wisconsin is here. We've celebrated here, Jessie's return, all kinds of good things."

"I can't get past it."

"Mother always says *can't* means 'won't.' It's a way of avoiding choosing," Mazy said.

Ruth felt herself stiffen. "Your mother was speaking to you, Mazy, not to everyone in the universe. Not to me anyway. I…can't get past the image of your bull, nose high in the air while my Jumper…" Ruth shuddered. "Look. Things change. We change. And I'm not going back on what I said I'd do. It was a good decision, my choosing to go north. I think it's best we just learn to say good-bye."

"Oh, Ruth," Mazy said.

Ruth stood and walked toward the corral. She knew Mazy couldn't come after her, wouldn't.

a jack-of-all-trades

Poverty Flat, near Shasta City

Elizabeth Mueller's hip ached, her brain felt fuzzy, and she found herself more than a little irritable. She knew she shouldn't eavesdrop, but she'd heard their conversation, then watched as Mazy stepped inside, her cheeks streaked with tears.

Well, she couldn't fix it. She could only offer solace. Every wound healed at a different rate, despite the salve placed on it. Why, her own palms that burned when Shasta did were still tender, so she could just imagine what Mazy struggled with, her heart being scorched so and nothing but time to cool it.

This commotion at Ruth's had tired her, she realized. Maybe she was just getting old and couldn't take all the hubbub of children anymore. *That'd be sad,* she thought. She was still wondering what she'd be when she grew up, and now here she was thinking she was older than dirt.

Elizabeth looked around for her small bag, found it and the letter, and walked to the corrals to find Ruth.

"Here's the post I was bringing you, Ruthie."

Ruth read quickly, the color draining from her face.

"You seen a ghost?"

Ruth showed her the poster—a drawing she had made herself of her husband when he'd kidnapped Jessie. "Zane's in French Gulch. Some doctor's treating him. I'm not running," she told Elizabeth.

"I know that. Still it's wise you leave. No one needs to know just where, exact, unless you let us. That way, he can't find you."

"I'll have to risk his knowing where I am anyway, so I can have divorce papers filed. I just want to be a distance north before it's done."

"I could take them for you. What could he do to a tough old woman?" Elizabeth grinned.

"He could do more than I'm willing to risk." Ruth shook her head. "No. I'll let my lawyer do it."

"You might ask David Taylor. He has some unfinished business with that man."

"I imagine he does." Ruth stood quietly.

"And as for my daughter…" Elizabeth nodded toward Mazy. "She's a good woman."

"I know," Ruth said. "I just…"

"You need some time." Elizabeth patted Ruth's arm.

"Tell her that for me, will you?" Ruth said.

The commotion, sounds of harness and hames, cows bellowing and wagon wheels crunching, took Elizabeth by surprise. "Who do you suppose that is, so late?"

Then the sounds of wagons and dogs barking and a big "howdy" coming out of the night brought people out of the cabin, scooped Elizabeth up into the middle of children and oxen, soft laughter and stars.

"Another wagon train on Nobles Emigrant Trail, I'll ponder," Elizabeth said.

"That you, Elizabeth?" a familiar voice called out.

"Who is it?" Mazy asked.

> "Mazy, Mazy
> She's not lazy.
> Got herself a dairy.
> That's what she'll marry."

"Seth Forrester!"

"Hey, Seth's here!" shouted Ned. Elizabeth stepped aside to avoid the stampede of children heading for Seth Forrester, wagon master, gambler, friend.

Elizabeth watched her daughter cross her arms, then drop them and stride out to meet the rider stepping off his horse. She put her arms around the tall man in a giant embrace.

"Or maybe I should have rhymed the last word with 'lazy' and said something like, 'Some say she's crazy.'"

"You don't think that now, do you?" Mazy asked.

The big man bent and swept Sarah up into one arm and Jessie into the other. "You two pistols are packing extra lead," he said, laughing.

"Can't be from Ruth's cooking," Lura told him, fast-walking right up to him, wiping her hands on her apron.

"We do have extra venison and noodles. Though with that endorsement, you may want to pass," Ruth offered.

"You didn't answer my question," Mazy challenged. Elizabeth could hear lightness in her daughter's stuffy-nosed words.

"I've had jerky enough, but I suspect some of the folks in this wagon train would find a meal prepared by others' hands welcome indeed." He set the little girls down. "And no, Mazy Bacon, I'm not one to call a woman following her heart crazy."

Were they sparring friends or *spooning* as they used to call it in her days? Elizabeth wondered. These young people. Who could make sense of them? Well, old-fashioned hospitality was still available, and Elizabeth walked out toward the wagons with kerosene lamps casting yellow shadows on the faces of men, women, and children. "Welcome to California," she said, speaking to the first woman she reached.

"You just survived the worst months of your lives, I'll bet," Lura said, close behind Elizabeth.

"That's a certainty," someone said. Tired and drawn faces nodded to Elizabeth as they busily unyoked oxen, keeping them inside the circle of wagons Seth Forrester had guided them into.

"You're among friends now. May still be foreigners in a foreign land, but you got yourself some guides, folks who have made it. A year ago now, but we did it. Like you. Where you all from?" Elizabeth said.

"The States," a man answered.

"The states of confusion and exhaustion, if you ask my wife," added another.

"You'll be right at home here in Shasta City," Lura told them. "You've joined a select group of folks, bewildered and weary."

"We're from Missouri," a woman told her, saying it with that soft "ah" sound at the end. "Most of us. A few from Ohio. Some from Kentucky."

Elizabeth noticed the faint smell of licorice on the woman's breath and wondered if she imbibed in Sweet Cicely wine or had used the plant for a snake or spider bite. "You bring healing herbs with you?" she decided to ask. "My daughter Mazy's growing such a garden, and any starts you got to share I know she'd appreciate. She'll share too, I'll ponder."

"Traded some Cicely with Indians a ways back," the woman told her. "They ate the seeds and said they'd use the roots to catch wild horses with."

"That a fact. Wonder how that works?"

The woman shrugged. "Me, I chew the leaves. Keeps my stomach from churning up. It's been doing that plenty."

"Does it? I like my spearmint for that," Elizabeth said.

"Maybe we can make an exchange," the woman offered.

"Love to. Be a big help." Elizabeth noticed the woman's eyes lit up a bit. There was something refreshing about giving to another, however small the gift.

"Speaking of churning," her eyes sought Mazy as she called out, "do you have some more cream, skimmed and cooled, Daughter? I'd be up to whipping up another batch. You folks think the taste of fresh cream after so many months without would take the grit from your teeth?" The murmur of agreement was all she needed. "I'll get right on it,"

Elizabeth said. As she walked she noticed that her step had a spring to it, and she was no longer tired.

Ruth's head still spun with the rapid changes. She couldn't escape change, had to embrace it, grab it like the Giant Stride ring swinging her around a pole in the schoolyard, taking her ever wider and farther until her feet were nearly straight out with only the air and the grip of her hands keeping her lifted. The more children who grabbed adjoining rings, the faster they all went, wind pushing their laughter down their throats as smiles froze on their faces. She and her friends played at the Giant Stride so often their running feet had dug a pit into the ground around the pole. She had loved it. Once she decided to jump on.

Then there was the problem of getting off. Two choices. Each child could will themselves into the center, pull in tight as they held on and wait until the others slowed around. Many was the time she'd been hit by a ring let loose by another while she stood with one hand over her head at the center, her heart pounding, waiting.

Or the better second choice was to swing as far and fast as she could for as long as she could and then…to simply let go, to give herself fully to the wind's embrace. She'd fly through the air then, skirts and crinolines billowing out, barely softening the drop as she landed in a heap on the grass, far beyond the chaos of the Giant Stride pole. Relief and loss always greeted her there, watching the others still spinning. Once she'd broken her arm, and her father had chastised her for choosing a boy's game, one demanding both skill and strength. And risk, she told herself. It took some risk to go on the Giant Stride. But the pain was worth it.

She hadn't thought of the Giant Stride in years. Funny name for it, though today she felt as though she took a giant stride toward something new, something risky.

They'd ridden to a hacienda, she and Matthew, who had initially been dead set against taking two jacks north—until his mother stepped into it. Then he was all in favor of it. They hadn't even asked Ruth if their presence in her plan appealed to her or not. The next thing she knew, everyone made decisions around her. Mazy bought up the Schmidtke cows—all but one—borrowing money from Seth Forrester to do it. Lura let the Wilsons know she was heading north and wouldn't be working at their store next week. Everything was settled almost before Elizabeth served the second batch of whipped cream to the new travelers.

Truth was, she needed help to go north. Suzanne's adventure in the mining towns told her what could happen if she didn't accept her limitations. Suzanne had put her children at risk performing songs and declamations before rowdy miners, rejecting marriage proposals from men she'd just met. Clayton had even cut his hand on one of Lura's sharpened knives. Ruth would have preferred just Matthew heading north with her and the children, not his whole family. Well, that wasn't true either. She enjoyed Mariah. It was Lura who troubled her.

She knew she'd have to talk with Lura about just exactly what part in this stock adventure she thought she had. The Schmidtkes were purchasing a jack, she knew that. But whether the Schmidtkes were buying mares, hers or someone else's, she didn't know. And she didn't know at all how she felt about Matthew. How on earth would she discuss so many tender topics with him? How could she afford not to?

His company wasn't all that unpleasant—without his mother to contend with. Except for that boisterous exchange they'd had before Lura arrived, he'd treated Ruth with nothing but dignity and respect. The shower he'd created for her had been as fine a gift as any of the jewels Zane Randolph had ever given her. She just didn't know what it meant. She didn't know what price she'd have to pay for accepting his kindness. But there was always a price, always some payback for experiencing joy.

Koda shied away from a cluster of dried leaves along the trail, and

Ruth returned her attention to the matter at hand. They rode beneath the wooden gateposts of the small ranch her Mexican friend had recommended. The jack they looked at was the color of the red dirt road and bore the name of Carmine.

"His name, it means vivid red," the jack stock handler told them. "He leads like my mama's little dog." The animal stood fifteen hands tall. He had one eye that wandered while the other one stayed straight. Ruth commented on that. The handler shrugged his shoulders. "*Sí.* Each one is very special," he said, emphasizing the word *very.* The handler led the jack around the paddock, and Carmine did trot easily to the rope. He performed the same when Ruth led him while she rode Koda.

"He's broke to ride?" Ruth asked.

"*Sí.*"

"Must be an easy rider," Ruth told Matthew as she walked around the animal and patted his back."

"Why's that?"

"No little tufts of gray from saddle sores where the hair's grown back in after being rubbed raw. It's what I always look for."

"Not a good clue," Matthew told her. "If you rub bacon grease on a saddle sore, the hair comes back in the same color." She stared at him. "Just something I've always known," he said. "We always kept bacon grease out in the barn, though Mariah's kittens got the most of it."

"He has a white tuft on his left forelock," Ruth noted. "You suppose they didn't put bacon grease there?"

"We'll take him," Matthew said. "Ma always liked red. He'll look good with your mares." Ruth glanced at him from the corner of her eye. So, were they partners or not?

"I will keep him for you until you're ready to go," the handler said. "You can trail him right from here. I will feed him a day or two more at my expense. Then I'll take your gold eagles when you pick him up."

"Done," Matthew said before Ruth could protest.

Ruth thought the time leading Carmine back to their own corral would have been well spent, them getting used to him and he the same with them. So much for that. Well, she had her Ewald, black as a cave hole.

"Means someone who is always powerful, Ewald does," the freighter she bought him off of had told her. He smiled sheepishly after he said it, wiped at his mouth with the back of his hand. "It's my brother-in-law's name, Ewald. He is stubborn. So it was fitting. They're all stubborn," he hastened to say.

"This jack going to give me trouble?" Ruth asked.

"No, no. He likes human company." The jack lifted his head at that, and the man scratched between his ears.

"I'm company," Ruth had said, settling the deal and beginning her grand adventure.

Ruth said little as she and Matthew rode back to Poverty Flat.

"Where's the second jack?" Lura asked as they unsaddled near Ewald's corral.

"We'll pick him up on our way out," Matthew shouted back to his mother. "Saves us the feed for a day or two until we leave. I don't care how much that jack is supposed to like people," Matthew told Ruth. Puffs of dust rose as he patted Ewald's rump. The children stood at his head. "Odds are good he can only tolerate so many at a time."

"That appears to be the perfect opening for me," Ruth said, clearing her throat.

Matthew turned to look at her.

"You kids run along now. We need to have a few words."

"Had all day to talk," Jason said.

"You listen to your auntie now," Matthew said.

"I don't need your help to manage my children," she said. Ruth nodded at Jason.

He pushed his brother and yelled to Mariah, "Let's play anteover one last time at the privy." They took off, running behind the cabin.

Jason looked back over his shoulder, and Ruth urged him on with her eyes.

Matthew stared at her, and for a brief second, she wished the children hadn't gone. She heard her heart pound and wondered if Matthew could hear it too. Why was speaking up for herself so difficult?

"I wasn't intending to intrude," he said. He put his foot up on the bottom rail beside Ewald and tipped his hat back so his face was fully exposed. Then he turned to face her, staring into her eyes as though no one else in the world existed. She felt weak to her toes.

He does that on purpose, controlling with his blue eyes.

"Sometimes boys'll listen to another man better than a woman," he said.

"They need to learn to listen to me," she said.

"True enough. That what you wanted to talk at me about?"

Ruth cleared her throat. "I wasn't wanting to talk *at* you at all."

"Poor choice of words. One of my many failings," he said.

"Nor to speak of your failings, as you put it."

"I best be still," he said with a smile. "I'm just digging myself deeper."

Ruth took a breath.

"I didn't plan for your whole family to be going north with me," she said. "It was my wish to manage for myself, my way of tending to the children. Then Jumper…and then I thought to give my heart to this new thing, a new way of making our way, with the jacks and all. And suddenly your mother and you and…everything's mixed up. I like things neat and tidy," Ruth said. "So I need to know, about the jacks. Are we partners? Are you planning to buy some of my mares? What? And I need to know your intention about staying on. I mean, are you taking a claim or wanting to work for me?" She swallowed as his jaw dropped while she talked, hurried on. "Will you be buying an interest in my mares or buying some of your own? I can use the help in trailing them north, but after that I just need to know what your intentions are.

About the stock, I mean." There. She'd said it. She turned away and brushed at dust on her pants.

"About going north," Matthew said, "I had hoped to go back some-day myself. So I'm not doing you a favor. And you had a good idea about the jacks, I figure. But sure, you can own one."

"How generous of you, Matthew Schmidtke," Ruth said.

"Ma'am?"

"Don't tell me what I can or cannot own. I'll decide that for myself."

"Didn't mean to undercut you. You bought Ewald. That's fine. Or you could take Carmine. Whichever."

He adjusted his hat, pulling it up and then down. He'd taken his foot off the rail and then put it back. Well, good, he was nervous too. She wasn't the only one struggling with strong feelings.

"That's straight then. I like…Carmine, even though I found Ewald first."

"The wild-eyed one? Oh, Ruth, I'm not—"

"And your jack, Ewald, you'll breed to…?"

"We'll buy half your mares. If you'll sell. Or we'll get others. Keep everything businesslike."

"Your mother will approve?"

"I'll talk to her," he said.

"So we may not end up exactly in the same area," she said. "Once we're in Oregon, I mean. If I'm buying land and you're getting yours free. Because you're a man."

"Looks like it."

"Good. Then we have an agreement for traveling north together only. After that, we'll part company. Go our own way."

"Looks like it."

"While we're settling things, I also want to say that I'll be directing the children as I see fit. And I'd appreciate it if you'd refrain from telling them things. Seems to me you have your hands full with your sister and your ma. Your mother," she corrected herself. "I wouldn't want you to become…overburdened raising me and mine." She swallowed. "Do we have an understanding?" There. She'd clarified this relationship once and for all.

Matthew stopped adjusting his hat and stared. For some reason her heart rate increased, and his blue eyes moved like a lightning strike right through her.

"Do we have an understanding?" she said again, blinking.

"Looks like it, Miss Martin," he said, sweeping his hat from his head. He held it at his chest, gave her one last look, then turned on his heel and walked away.

She'd said all she wanted to, up front and clear as a freighter's bell. She'd taken a giant stride forward. So why did she feel as though she stood with her hands pressed over her head instead of flying free with the wind in her face?

Matthew Schmidtke hefted sacks of grain onto the back of the wagon with a little more force than needed. Who was he to think he understood them anyway, any woman? Not his sister, not his mother, and certainly not Ruth Martin. He wished for the hundredth, no, the thousandth time, that his pa was alive to ask. But based on the changes he'd seen in his mother in the year since his father's death, he guessed the man might be scratching his head just as Matthew was, if he'd been alive to witness Lura's transformation. She'd once been a mouse of a woman who'd do whatever his pa had asked.

"Fix us some sassafras tea, Woman," he'd say, or, "Get me my tobacco and pipe, quick like now. I don't have all day." It never seemed unkind. Just his pa's way. And his ma just moved like a…rabbit to comply. Most times.

Now that he remembered, she did have another way about her.

Sometimes she moved slower than a terrapin. "You in a hurry?" she'd say, handing his pa a pipe they all knew he didn't like, that clay one she'd taken to chewing on since his pa had died. She'd give it to him and he'd say, "Now, Woman, you know this one don't draw good. Should throw the thing out."

"It was my pa's."

"He could have afforded a better one." He'd motion her to go back and get another, and this time she'd bring it...but not the tobacco. "Lura," his pa would say. *Lura* instead of *Woman*. That was a sign he was getting upset. "Your pa was a seven by nine if I ever knew one." His mother would scowl and quick-walk away. She returned with the tobacco—but without a flint—and they'd start arguing about his grandfather, a man Matthew truly loved. "Just a seven by nine, that's all that man ever was. Not a dream in his head. Not a vision. Raised himself a daughter the same as him."

"He made his way with his head held high," his mother would defend.

"Because he jutted his chin out telling people his opinions," his pa would respond. "But not keeping his thinking sharp." Sometimes Matthew wondered how his parents had ever found each other, let alone decided to marry and stay that way for twenty years.

"He told my mother every day that he loved her," his ma would say. "Put his arm around her. Every day."

"That's because your mother would forget from one day to the next, he *had* to tell her every day." His mother's eyes would pool. "Oh, don't go pumping on that handle now. I told you I loved you when I married you. That hasn't changed. Don't need to keep repeating a thing. Only seven by nines need things repeated."

Matthew'd wondered about that phrase his pa used. He'd even asked him once, within his mother's hearing, what it meant.

"Huh?" his pa said. "How would I know?"

"Your pa don't worry over origins of things. Nor what their impact might be," Lura told him and then answered the question her husband couldn't. "Used to be the size of common windows, a seven by nine, and people who're common—"

"Don't you be filling your head with words and such," his pa had countered, pointing with that pipe. "There are no solutions in reading. Experience, that's what you got to learn from. It don't matter what that term meant once. Enough said."

"She was just saying, Pa."

His father had sat right up in the chair. "Don't you go back-talking to your pa now, Son. Don't worry over women none either. They'll come along when they're told. It's the way it was meant to be. It's the way it is." His pa had sat back in the leather chair. "You put your concentration on cattle and land, Son. That's how you'll take care of your ma. And how you'll find yourself a woman. You don't worry about this 'touching 'em' every day with sweet words and all. You give her land, and she'll come to you like a bear to honey."

His mother had snorted. "Ask your pa if that's how I came to him." His father had lifted an eyebrow. "I'll answer that one, too. Your pa came to me, my being an only child. And my father having land with a house on it with windows larger than seven by nine. Now who's talking honeyed words," she'd said and slammed the long-handled spider to the stove.

Funny he should think of that day while he was dealing with Ruth. He guessed he wanted to say and do what would be a comfort to her— he didn't want to agitate her. He wanted to be more like his grandfather, using loving words every day, even if his pa thought it wasted effort.

His ma seemed to be enjoying the readying. He was glad she'd be with him and Mariah instead of sharpening knives for butchers and whatnot, taking that little cart around with things from the Wilson's Mercantile to sell to folks up in the ravines. He didn't think that was safe, a woman going alone like that. "Pa said I was to look after you," he'd told her when he arrived in Shasta City.

"He couldn't look after himself," she said and sniffed.

"Ma!"

"It's true. Oh, he loved me. I know he did, in his way. But I cooked and cleaned and mended and ran for him, and he mostly told me I was nothing but shucks. Well, I'm more than that. And so is Mariah, and so are you. I'm proud you took the cattle on ahead. Proud you tended Ruth Martin's horses all that time. But while you were growing up, we were doing things to tend to others and ourselves, too, back there on the trail. We were growing up too."

"Mariah looks a little worse for wear," he said under his breath.

"Mariah does? She's doing fine. She's a big help to me."

"She ought to be in school, Ma. You don't want her ending up as some...seven by nine."

His mother hadn't responded, but she'd thumbed her eyes, quick like. He figured he'd hit a nerve.

His little sister, Mariah, had changed. Taller, prettier, a good rider. He guessed it was all that time with Ruth's horses. But she wore a sadder face somehow. Joe Pepin, the wrangler who had come all the way from New York with them, had commented on that too, how Matt's little pipsqueak sister had "grown the eyes of a lonesome dog." It wasn't exactly how Matthew would describe it, but he knew just what Joe meant.

Maybe his ma hadn't been available to her like she should have been this past year after his pa's death. Maybe his ma's push for business was her way of numbing the pain of it, and Mariah had paid the price. He had to step over the fact that his mother had worked in a saloon and been part of a traveling musical troupe to mining camps with slobbering men hanging around. She'd done what she had to do. Couldn't fault her for that.

At least he'd had Joe Pepin to help guide him this past year. Not so much about the ways of women; Joe had little experience with that. But about cattle and horses and keeping his head even when he was grieving the loss of a loved one. That was what he'd needed. He'd almost lost more than his head in the tangle of Oregon country. They'd given up some horses to Takelma Indians wearing paint, the braves pointing those bows laid flat out from their chests, the way he'd seen pictures of Englishmen holding crossbows. A good trade, three horses for their lives. He'd made sure they were the Schmidtkes' horses and not Ruth Martin's. And they'd learned later that the braves always wore paint; it was when they put on white dye that they meant to use those bows against the whites.

He and Joe had lost two cows to broken necks from falls off ridges they shouldn't have been on. Eventually they'd found a route he later learned was part of the Applegate Brothers' Trail. They'd pushed the stock into a valley in the shadow of two flat-topped hills sticking up like tables just before the first snowfall. A river that folks sometimes called Gold and sometimes the Rogue flowed beneath the table rocks, and Matthew said that was where they'd stay, take the animals on to The Dalles in the spring where he'd agreed to meet up with his ma and Ruth Martin.

It was the wasted time that had distressed him, the sense that he'd somehow lost his way and not kept his word to meet up along the Columbia River when he'd said he would. Ruth would be waiting for them there, he was pretty sure, and she'd think he'd taken off with her treasures if he didn't arrive. Treasures! After this past winter, he knew that just living was the treasure. He wouldn't mention that to Ruth just now, that the snows in Southern Oregon had been so bad the horses had eaten moss from the trees to stay alive. He'd save that and some of his other tales for telling over the campfires on the trail, if she was interested. Right now, he was just grateful she'd agreed to their partnering up, however stiff the terms.

"Well, ponder that," Ruth heard Elizabeth say. Seth stepped away from in front of the oak tree near the cabin on Poverty Flat. Behind him, a ladder rose up through the leaves.

"For you and David and Oltipa's boy, Ben, when you come visit," he said. "We boys here built it ourselves."

"Well, ponder that," Elizabeth said again, her handkerchief moving the warm air before her.

Adora Wilson and her son, Charles, had come out too, it being a Sunday, their mercantile closed. Who had invited them? Ruth wondered. Couldn't there be an event without everyone being included? Was there some written rule that whenever those who traveled on the widows' wagon gathered in a group, that all of them within trotting distance had to show up, even one who had created more problems for them in the first place? Charles Wilson with his jagged ear was slime on a rock, as far as she was concerned, slick and full of trips and falls if one stood too close.

Besides, they were just putting off the inevitable. No one wanted to say good-bye, but that was what was needed next. Then came this tree house unveiling. Now all the children would have to climb up into it, and there'd be cake eating up there and drinking eggnog while retelling the stories about building it and whatnot.

"When'd you find time to do that?" Mazy asked.

"While Ruth and Matthew here were off gathering jacks and you and Lura were negotiating Durham cows," Seth told her. "Me and the boys, we just pitched in and got 'er done."

"I helped," Jessie said.

"You did. And Sarah, too. And Pipsqueak there. She holds a hammer right well. You'll be glad to have her in Oregon." Mariah blushed. Ruth supposed it was Seth's use of the nickname said most often by her brother.

Oltipa, David Taylor's wife, held her baby on her hip. She dressed not in traditional Indian clothes, but in a dress David gave her, purchased from Adora's mercantile.

Ruth was just anxious to be gone. Just making a mile or more the first day gave impetus to a journey, moved their eyes forward instead of hanging back, which was where she'd been for the last five years, always looking over her shoulder. Outdistancing her husband's betrayal. She was past that now and liking the lightness of that burden. Moving on, that was what she wanted. Nothing to hold her back, everything to drive her forward.

"Let's us check the wagon one last time," she told Jason loud enough for all to hear. "Poor old oxen have been yoked since noon, and they're ready to go. Can't say as I blame them."

"Why don't you just plan to leave first thing in the morning?" Mazy asked.

"That's a good idea," Elizabeth said. "Give you time to come on up here." She called down from the tree house. The children had helped push her up, laughing all the way.

"Now that's just what I thought someone would offer," Ruth said, answering Elizabeth. "But no, we've got a three-week journey, and we'd best be off. Nights are getting cool, and we could have an early winter. Wouldn't want to get stuck in the snow of the Siskiyous just because we wanted an extra piece of cake from on top a tree."

"You're right. It won't get no easier," Elizabeth sighed. "We'll get the rest of you up here later. We'll play plenty then." She made her way down.

Mazy blinked back tears, and Ruth felt her eyes pool too, a sensation she tried to ignore.

"I picked up a little something for you, Ruth, and the rest of you travelers, too," Mazy said. "Little packages you can open on the trail. Or when you arrive. Just something to remember where you came from, here. In Shasta." Seth stood beside Mazy and put his arm around her like a big brother, pulling her into his side.

"You didn't have to do that, Mazy," Lura told her. "But I love a good surprise."

"I just wanted to." Mazy shrugged off Seth's arm and walked fast to a box where she pulled out packages wrapped in paper and string. It looked like lamb's ears had been set in an old boot filled with dirt. Butcher paper was stuffed around it. "You can use the paper for writing a little letter now and then," she said, looking sideways at Ruth.

"Truth be known, she bought them at our store, she did," Adora cooed.

"The wrappings, yes," Mazy corrected. She carried the packages and placed them in the back of the wagon through the puckers and stood there a bit as though collecting herself before she turned to say her final good-byes.

Ruth didn't know why, but the presents annoyed her. Maybe because she hadn't thought of giving something herself to commemorate all they'd been to each other, all that had happened here at this place. Or maybe because it was one more way Mazy hung on or smoothed over a relationship too wrinkled for ironing.

Ruth did have a package of her own that had taken her a fair amount of time to gather. But it belonged to someone…deserving of its special sting, to be given when the time was just right. When they were far away. David Taylor was going to see to that.

"You'll survive, Mazy," Seth said. "Come spring you'll have calves aplenty, and their antics'll keep us laughing." To Ruth he said, "You just head off. You got your work cut out for you trailing jacks." He nodded toward Ewald. "You picking up the other on the way?"

"Carmine. Yes."

"More power to you," Seth said. "I hope that jack's disposition is better than the family reputation."

"Whose family?"

"Don't get defensive. I was talking about jacks and mules in general," Seth said.

"He's a good-looking animal," Ruth defended.

"Not saying he's not," Seth said, pushing his hand against the air as though to calm her. "Just what I always heard was that two of them was worse than tying cougars together at the tail."

"They act fine to me," Ruth said. "And I have full plans to keep them separated on the trail. Once we're north, we won't be sharing pasture. Not that it's any of your account."

Seth raised an eyebrow but didn't speak. Ruth wondered if she sounded spiteful. Men often raised an eyebrow when she spoke more forceful than she meant to. She was just sharing information, that was all, telling things to people's eyes. Men did that all the time and expected people to just accept it. When a woman spoke her mind, they acted as if she was some kind of…wild one. People took her wrongly, but she couldn't account for how other people listened. She had things on her mind, and they'd just have to accept that.

She motioned for Jason to join her. The boy came, along with Jessie. They stuck their heads in the back of the wagon and with Ruth scanned the trunks and boxes there, a wooden rake, pack boxes with tack. Her eye lit on the one she knew held a few bones and the tail hairs of Jumper. *Taking you with us.* She was glad again for her decision. Everything they needed was loaded, including Lura's knife sharpener and flour and salt to last them a couple of months.

Koda stood saddled and tied to the wagon along with two other green-broke mares that Mariah and the boys would ride. Jessie had chosen the wagon seat where Lura and Sarah would sit, a move that surprised Ruth. She'd always been so willing and wanting to ride. Now it appeared she preferred sidling up next to Lura.

"Let's head out," Matthew said then, and Ruth shot him a grateful glance.

Matthew moved toward his mother who was hugging Adora and patting little Ben on the head and making the rounds to Elizabeth and the rest. He touched her elbow, and the woman nodded. Sarah approached and Matthew lifted her like a paper fan, her little pinafore billowed out as she stepped down into the box. Then he unhitched his big gray gelding named Sailor and said, "Step along, boys. Ma. Come on now."

"I don't believe I'm ready to leave just yet," Lura said. She lifted a mug of cider she'd placed in the box and drank from it. Lura's cheeks were pink. Perhaps from her singing "Pop Goes the Weasel" with the children not long before. "Got my pipe to chew on. I'm ready. Feels like I been living out of a wagon for over a year now."

"Let's be mounting up, children," Ruth said.

A kind of frenzy began then, with David helping Seth check the harnessing of the oxen, Elizabeth carrying last-minute food bags from the cabin. Mazy, too, busied herself, scraping butter from the mold and wrapping it in wet cheesecloth and placing it in the wagon.

Matthew sat with his hands crossed over the saddle pommel.

"I thank you," Elizabeth said. "For the laughter and the special thoughts and all the rest you gave us to ponder by your presence. And we ask for traveling mercies for you all."

"We'll think of you every time we make angel pie," Sarah said, waving down at Elizabeth. "Won't we, Jessie?"

Ruth thought the girl would be crying any second, and she cleared her throat, hoping she wouldn't do the same. She brushed up against Mazy setting the butter into a camp box. Ruth heard her sniff.

"Let's just get these hugs and holds and good-byes said fast as we can," Mazy said then, stepping away from the wagon, nearly stumbling over Jessie who'd slipped out and come to wrap her arms around Mazy's apron. The woman knelt down so she could pull the child to her, kissed her head. Ned came next to brush against her, stick his hand to Seth's to shake.

"We'll float that wagon away if we're not careful," Mazy said, dabbing at her eyes with her apron. "You won't be able to drive it off."

"Thought that might be what you had in mind," Mazy's mother said.

"I can accept the inevitable," Mazy said, pushing against her knees to stand. Her eyes glistened. "But I don't have to like it."

Mazy stepped over to Ruth then, fingered the rawhide hanging from the front rigging ring of the saddle. "You take care of yourself now," she whispered, looking up at her. "You write. When you're ready."

Ruth felt a tearing at the fabric of her heart. These were people she'd come to love, she realized. They were as much a part of her family as her brother and his wife had been, stitched to her through service, caring, and time. Ruth wanted to say something, to make this easier for Mazy—she had always been kind to her—but Ruth wasn't confident of speech. She swallowed, touched Mazy's cheek with her palm.

The familiar faces looking up to her sitting atop Koda blurred. She had to leave. She reined the horse north.

strands of hope

"And before that?" Suzanne asked. "Where were you employed?"

"That were my first job, Missis Cullver. Before that, my pappy paid me good to look after his kin."

"They weren't…your kin?"

"Well, with his second wife, yes'um. But his third, well, them were her children he paid me to tend. He didn't have no young uns with her. Now his fourth wife, she were younger than me, but they had one. So I got baby time, too. That's how I got such good ideas for herding little tykes, like what I told ya."

"Indeed. You did." Suzanne took a deep breath. The woman before her was barely grown herself, judging from the pitch of her voice. She smelled of lavender, fresh and tidy, and probably worked hard to look proper for her interview. But she wasn't right for what Suzanne needed, what her boys needed.

These interviews were just going nowhere. Surely there were educated women in Sacramento who, like herself, had come west with their husbands hoping for wealth and who woke up only to discover they'd not find it in the rushing streams of this state. Surely they'd be seeking something more to feed their children.

That was the other problem she'd discovered in the interviewing: People wished to bring their own children with them. Suzanne wasn't prepared for the taking on of an entire household. Esther had said the

fire last winter had wiped out a goodly number of business establish-
ments, and they hadn't all come back full force. So there had to be
people interested in work, especially work that kept them indoors, warm
through the winter, and well fed. Suzanne was offering a profession
here, of tutoring and training. It required respectable women.

Even Esty had come up empty. She hadn't found a single reference
from the women whose hats she created at her little shop, not one
woman she could send to Suzanne with at least some kind of letter of
introduction. All the young girls Suzanne had interviewed had arrived
in response to the ad Esther placed. Esther said the Sacramento *Daily
Californian* ran her advertisement right next to notices written by husbands back in the States offering rewards for their "runaway wives."
Maybe they thought her job announcement a trick of some kind, so
only women of insufficient skill applied. She hadn't thought of that.

"Missis? You all right?"

"I'm fine. I'm sorry. I got distracted. Just one last question. If I asked
your...pappy to describe you to me, not how you look, but your
virtues, what's inside you that drives you toward your wishes, what three
adjectives might he use?"

Pig snored at Suzanne's feet, the only break in the silence. *At least
she must be a kind girl, or Pig would not be sleeping.*

"I'm guessing I don't know for sure what that word *ad-chu-tives*
means, ma'am," she said at last. "But I'm pretty sure I don't got any of
them ver-chews. I never did take up chewing or smoking tobaccy, either,
and I been real healthy. I wouldn't bring no nits or worms into your
house. No need to keep valerean around neither. I don't have no hyste-
ria or nervous disorders needing such kind of herbs. I'm sound as a trail-
savvy ox. See, got all my teeth yet. Oh, you can't see. Want to feel
them?"

"Thank you, Miss Edina. I'm sure you are...quite capable. Just tell
me what your pappy might say about you, if he wished to compliment
you, say something nice."

"He wouldn't cotton to such talk, Missis. It be prideful to speak kindly of kin."

Suzanne remembered to make herself smile. "I'd say you're honest and sincere. And since I'm not kin, I can tell you that and hope you hear it."

"My hearing's real good, Missis. Was you wondering over that?"

"I think that's all for now, Miss Edina. Can you find your way out? I'll be in contact if I need to speak to you further."

"Yes'um. Thank you, ma'am. And tell your boy it were real nice to shake his little hand."

Suzanne heard the swish of Miss Edina's skirts and the heavy thump of the girl's feet as she left. A large girl, most likely. Able to lift Clayton or Sason if need be. But certainly she'd be unable to teach them a thing about good grammar. Suzanne had thought to tell her to stay, that she'd find some work for her, even if it weren't teaching her children.

No, she had to find the right person, not jump in too soon, not get frustrated and slip off a rock in her haste to make it across this stream. At least Miss Edina was the last interview for the day. Suzanne had forgotten how much energy it took to listen to everything a new person said, to hear the lilt in their voice, the length of a pause, the boldness of a question. What did the shuffle of their feet mean? If Pig barked but thumped his tail on the floor, was that different than if he stood and slobbered at the person's skirts? If they paused, were they thinking, or scheming, about how to answer? Did they sneak little candies from the bowl right in front of her, or did they sit and look at her as though she could see even though she couldn't? She hadn't realized the comfort that came in familiarity, in not having to wonder about every detail of a relationship. She removed her dark glasses and rubbed at her eyes. How could they tire when they did nothing all day?

She stood, said, "Pig, go," and waited for the dog to stand, heard him stretch and yawn, then press beside her with the harness she held to let him lead her. She felt for the leather, then started toward the door.

"There is one more," Esther told her, startling her.

Suzanne put her hand to her throat. She'd forgotten Esther was in the room. For some reason, Suzanne resisted simply hiring Esther as the boys' tutor. Perhaps it was Esther's chuckle when Esty told her of the finger talking. As if it was a joke. Esther was set in her ways and came quickly—too quickly—to conclusions. But Suzanne had promised her she would officially consider her for the position. She didn't want to hurt Esther's feelings, though she knew by delaying she was.

"Would you mind terribly waiting until tomorrow, Esther?" Suzanne told her. "I'm very tired. This is more work than I'd thought it might be."

"I wasn't thinking of my own interview." Suzanne heard frostiness in Esther's voice. "However, there is still another. A gentleman, who has been waiting quite patiently."

"You didn't tell me there was a male applicant. I don't think that would work at all."

"I told him as much. He said he was hoping to 'press his case,' as he put it. Seems he had a brother once who was a mute."

"Clayton is not a mute! He has words! You didn't say anything like that in the ad, did you?"

"Certainly not. But I brought Clayton past him each time you had the applicants talk with the boy. And he asked me, having heard nothing come from the child's mouth. People must know something's amiss, or you wouldn't be seeking a 'compassionate, patient, skilled tutor of young children and reliant mother.'"

"Maybe the word *reliant* threw him off," Suzanne said.

"You didn't want 'needy,' you said. And you aren't. You simply have specific needs. That's different."

Perhaps she should just give in and let Esther be the one to tend her children, herd them—and her—around. It would be easier than explaining to people about her son. Yet she didn't receive a sense of peace when she thought of Esther being in her employ. That in itself would change their relationship. There'd be the effort of maintaining her fondness for the woman with the worry of offending Esther if she had to correct her actions as her employer. Her boys were counting on her to do what was best. She'd never forgive herself if she said yes to Esther because she didn't work hard enough to find the perfect person. "I'd best interview the man," she told Esther, hoping her prayers for guidance and vision would be clearly answered.

"Hey! Is anyone there?" Zane Randolph listened but heard no sounds in the room beyond his own breathing and raspy voice. "You! Surgeon! You going to cut me free? Let me starve to death? What kind of doctor are you?"

He thought he might've heard the scurry of a rat, twisted his head to see. Beady eyes stared at him from beneath a dresser. He hissed, and the animal darted behind a cabinet that stood with glass doors open like a dead man's mouth, nothing inside. He looked around, saw the room reflected in a mirror near to him. His own image stared back, a wasted man with broad but bony shoulders. A full beard covered his face, and his throat itched of it. He squinted. White hair? Could that be possible? His hair had turned in a fortnight? A month? How long had it been? He'd heard of that happening, to fearful people.

His eyes lifted, scanned what he could from his position on the cot. The room was eerily empty. The cabinets no longer held chloroform, bandages, or scissors. A cuplike structure of leather attached to a wooden peg leaned against the bed he lay on, his arms still attached by bandages to the bedside. A spider ran up the wall. But for it and the rat, he was alone. His heart pounded, he felt hot, his chest tight.

He needed to relieve himself.

He listened for street sounds and heard none. It was morning, judging by the light streaming through the lace curtains, early morning, so few would be about in French Gulch. Surely the doctor and his wife had not just gone off and left him, not still tied as he was! "Hello! Is anyone there?"

Silence.

Yes, he'd made demands on the man, but no more than anyone would, confined as they had him. What could he actually do to hurt them? He couldn't stand alone, couldn't get away without help. So what did they have to fear? Even when he'd gotten that last drink of water they hadn't trusted him, so what was he to do now, after they'd doused him with laudanum "to keep him calm," they said while he raged against his bonds. How long ago had that been?

He heard his raspy breathing, the sign he was starting to panic. How dare they just leave? How dare they take his leg and then leave him to starve to death, alone. *Dr. Hollis.* He'd find the man, he would. And when he did…

His body betrayed him.

He felt the warmth, smelled it, before he saw the stain against the sheet that covered him.

Suddenly he was small and young and frightened. He was at a horse race, his father too busy to hear his pleas. Blue linen shorts he wore now stained. He heard the laughter as his father doused him in the horse trough. He swallowed water and fear as he fought against the pressure of the man's arms holding him down. He struggled for breath, his father's face distorted in rage through the ripple of water. Muffled sounds of someone—not his father—shouting, "No, no, Randolph, you'll drown the boy—" pulling him up. He gasped for air, gasped for life, scum from the trough clinging to his face. All the way home he sat beside his father in the cab. He shivered in his blue suit, dreading the sting of his father's whip he knew would finish his night.

Calm, calm. He steadied his breathing.

Dr. Hollis would pay for this, he would. No one who harmed him escaped. Not this doctor. And not Ruth.

Ruth. She put him here. She sent him to prison, kept his child from him, and ran west to escape him. She caused him to take their child, to pursue the blind Suzanne, to take the Wintu woman, too. She made his foot infected, and even now she was why he lay here humiliated in his own stench, bound to a bed, mutilated and aged, waiting. *How dare these people abuse him! How dare they simply leave him here to rot in his own stench?*

He heard a door open then, the sound of feet coming through the house.

Zane swallowed. "Hello!"

"Ah, so you're awake," a man with an Irish brogue said as he came to the side of the bed. "Let's be a good one then, Beckworth, and I'll cut you free. Doc said you could flail a bit in your delirium and to advise you what I was about afore doing it. Are you ready to be moving then? Getting something to eat?"

"Who are you?" He made each word a sentence.

"Michael O'Malley, former pit boss and miner. Can't say which wore me out more." He laughed as though he often made the joke. He looked at Zane's soiled sheet. "Ah, and I was getting here too late for you to relieve yourself like a man. Sorry then. But we'll have you cleaned up in no time. Me uncle had a wooden leg. Got around right smart with it. Took it off and threatened the wee ones with it when he wanted a rest. Never hurt 'em, mind you. Just waved it about to get him some peace. Let's cut you free now. I got me knife here."

"Dr.…Hollis…"

"Headed out as planned. Never meant to be remaining this late. Surely he would have been in New Orleans and married by now but for your needs. And then on to Oregon, so he says. Near death, you were, as I hear tell. He paid himself from your funds and my wages, too, for a time. Thought you wouldn't mind paying for your care." He cut the bonds. "There. That's better."

Zane lunged for the man, his breathing raspy and raw.

O'Malley coughed, pushed his hands up under Zane's, and pushed himself away.

"Here, here. No reason for that now. I've been left to help you. You won't be making it without me."

Zane flopped back onto the narrow cot, his heart pounding. He was weak as a kitten. He rubbed his wrists. "Cut my leg free," he ordered. He scratched at his face, the beard, winced at the pain in his leg when the bonds on his good foot were set free. "Help me up."

"Going to sting a bit, you not having weight on it for so long. Your good leg'll feel worse than the bad, but it'll come along."

The Irishman was a big man, and he lifted Zane's arm over his shoulder, then swung his leg over the side of the bed.

The weight of his leg and both thighs dropped down, sending shards of pain so great Zane wanted to cry out. But he imagined Ruth instead. Focused his venom on her. He gasped with the effort. The Irishman twisted him back up onto the cot.

"Fortunate you still got the knee," he said. "When you're ready, we'll attach the harness and peg. You'll be hopping about like a young lamb in no time. You rest a bit. We'll try again. I've a crutch made for you."

"Why would you do this?" Zane asked.

"You're paying me, sir. Good wages. A gold eagle a day from your gold pouch. No need to be thinking you're taking charity. You're paying. I hope we made the peg the proper length. We'll be bringing you food and tending. You'll be taking baby steps. It'll take time, mind you. You've got to strengthen your good leg, get your muscle back. You'll be walking alone someday. There now. Steady. I'm sure a lad like you has places to be going."

Oh, yes. He had places to be going.

Chinatown, outside Sacramento

Sometimes, the Celestial known as Naomi dreamed she was Chou-Jou, became that woman who had once been her friend. Naomi remembered the dead girl's pocked face, her wide, flat nose; a Celestial who longed to be accepted as she was but who succumbed finally to living in another world where she was not herself at all. Chou-Jou's world turned wild and full of angry outbursts just before she died on that wagon train of women. But before that she had been quiet and sweet. Thick cords and bonds of silk must have kept her tied inside her heart where no one could see but Chou-Jou.

In her dreams Naomi felt the warmth of the Seth man's hand as he helped Chou-Jou from a wagon, the smile of Ruth who wore a whip at her hip. A breeze brought the softness of the woman named Elizabeth who held people in their hurts. Perhaps they saw Chou-Jou as she was. No, no one could do that, except perhaps The Heart One Sister Esther often talked of. She could not recall the name inside her dream, only remembered him as The Heart One, who could see through everyone and loved them just the same.

Sometimes in her dreams as Chou-Jou, Naomi felt seen through, the way the sunlight flashed through a butterfly's wings. Known inside and out and yet loved fully. She would rest when that happened, feel light and purposeful and safe. Then she'd stop the dreaming and fall instead into a deep, deep sleep.

After those sleeps, Naomi would wake, no longer Chou-Jou on her way to dying but as Naomi, wife of a disappointed Chinese miner, living inside a hovel not fit for his goats, let alone his wife. Naomi would wake as a Chinese woman longing to die, but for the mewing sound coming from the corner. A mewing sound that was her child. A girl child considered useless by her husband. She was her mother, a failure, not having given him a son; the husband seeing through her to who she really was.

She had hidden the fact of the coming infant from him. He had work for her to do—washing laundry in steaming tubs, scraping dung and blood and mud from the clothes the white miners brought her. She made her husband more money than his other slaves, her countrymen whom he forced to sift gold from the once-deserted mines until they paid off the cost of their passage.

Once she had asked to spend a small amount of his gold dust to visit Sister Esther and her friend Mei-Ling. He had struck her face and hissed like a snake over her cowering on the floor.

The pains had begun after that. Naomi dreamed that the child floated in the water of her womb despite its pressing early to come into life. Aching, she kept her legs crossed, inhaled long and deep though the infant pushed, demanded to breathe the California air. And then Naomi could hold back no longer, and the wetness and the scent of life had filled the room. With the sight of the girl child, Naomi knew their lives would be no better, no better.

"You stupid girl!" Dow Yuk had charged when he saw the infant, tiny, suckling as she could at Naomi's breast. Naomi raised her arms across the baby's head to protect it from the blow she knew would come. He struck Naomi's cheek. "Get rid of it," Dow Yuk demanded while her face still stung.

The welt he left joined many scars, the puffiness of her eyes a common sight.

"Best put some raw beefsteak on that blow," a miner bringing his laundry told her. Squinting, he said, "Whooee. That's a bad one."

She'd taken the blows to her head and her face as though she deserved them. Hadn't she given him a useless girl child? Hadn't she come to him not the beauty he believed from the photograph of her cousin but a common girl, trained in fieldwork and simple house chores, not the refined woman he imagined he would bed? Hadn't she arrived with feet larger than some men, a sign her family did not care enough for her to bind her and then tend her, as she'd need in order to survive? Yes, the welts and hits she deserved. She was not a woman complete unto herself despite what Mazy Bacon said each woman could become if The Heart One loved her and they returned that devotion.

She defied Dow Yuk's order about the infant, hiding her daughter, placing her palm over the tiny mouth when she cried. As long as Passion lived, she'd stay.

She'd named her Passion. A time on the trail, Sister Esther said the word meant "deep feeling." Naomi had such deep feeling for her baby. She willed her child would have it too, so she would live.

So tiny, Passion slept inside a box that once held rolled tobacco. On cool mornings, Naomi placed the child at the warming oven of the stove, watching her, picking her up at the first sounds of discomfort. Naomi vowed that she would not dream to be like Chou-Jou as long as Passion looked into her eyes each morning. Instead she would remain the quiet mother, worker, protector.

When the infant was strong enough to hold her head and then sit and watch the world of her father wearing wide sleeves as he exchanged coins and gold dust with men of pale skin, Naomi would place the child on her back to keep her safe. When no one was looking, she would brush the miners' clothes with more speed, while quickly filling a tiny buck-skin bag she kept tied around the baby's waist, filling it with gold dust, readying their escape.

Once when she had delivered washing to a new district, the clothes piled high on top of her head, the baby on her back, she thought she had seen the blind woman led by the dog. The dog barked at her, and the woman calmed him. She recognized the voice. "Who goes there?" Missy Suzie asked.

Naomi had almost spoken when Missy Esther came out of a shop. She looked straight at Naomi and gasped, her fingers pressed against her mouth.

"What is it, Esther?" Missy Suzie asked.

"I think it's…"

Naomi had disappeared between the buildings, cobwebs brushing her face as she ran.

"Have you learned a few Spanish words?" Nehemiah asked.

"One or two," Tipton told him.

"Splendid! And as your reward, I have a gift for you." He handed her a stone.

"Oh. An agate."

"They bore you," he said.

"They're lovely. I just don't know what to do with them," she said to him.

"Eventually I'll put them into settings," he said. He drew a design with a pencil on a piece of paper before him at the table. "This would make a lovely brooch. And this one, for a silver letter opener."

"You have so little time when you're here for dabbling in such things," she told him.

"Designing soothes me. Perhaps you should draw more."

"I'm occupied with…study," she said.

"I think of you always while I'm gone," his words softened. "Soon I'll be campaigning." He cleared his throat. "Unless we were to begin our family."

Tipton stood, dropping the agates onto the carpeted floor. "I'll put these in a jar and cover them with water," she said. "They look like rainbows then." She hurried into the kitchen, catching her breath. She had no intention of discussing such intimacies with her husband. She was quite sure her parents never had talked of those "private things," and she certainly wasn't going to. She hadn't even allowed him to see her unclothed, and she wasn't sure she ever would.

"I am sorry, Mrs. Kossuth," Nehemiah said, following her into the kitchen. "I…fumble at these things." He reached for her hand, held it. She knew that she shook. "It's just that I am not getting any younger and—"

"*Progresso,*" she said, spinning away from him. She slid the curtain back from the little cupboard, moved things around. "I'm sure that was one of the words Chita told me about. It means making progress," she said, holding up a wide-mouthed jar.

"Something we apparently aren't," her husband said.

That first afternoon out had gone well. They'd agreed to tie Carmine to the wagon and keep Ewald moving in the rear. Then the next day, they exchanged it, tying the black jack to the wagon. They hobbled both animals that night, letting Carmine loose in the morning. There were no mares open, Jumper having bred Ruth's animals; and the stocky mares Matthew had bought up were said to promise foals come spring. At least Ruth hoped she had no open mares. From the size of the jacks, she could tell there'd need to be some accommodations made to get her mares bred when the time came. She didn't want it to be happening on the trail north, didn't want foals born next year just before winter.

She eyed the dusty trail ahead as it meandered around clusters of oak or an occasional pine that acted as prelude to the dark timber covering the hillsides farther ahead. It wasn't a well-traveled trail though it was well marked. Matthew said folks talked about a stage run that would head this way someday, north through Yreka and into Oregon. Ruth didn't see how. There were sections that required bringing the mares single file, with the wagon wheels barely narrow enough to keep to the road. The children walked then, and Ruth drove the wagon. Not that Lura couldn't, but the older woman appeared to dislike looking down onto the manzanita and oak trees that dribbled off below her into steep ravines.

Ruth kept thinking about Jumper, couldn't seem to stop it. His presence would have made this new journey so much richer. Even Koda acted strange, as though he knew that something was wrong, that one who'd once traveled with him no longer shared his trail. Ruth was silly, she supposed, imagining that horses missed each other. Just struggling with her own missings—of her brother, her boy, her horse, and even Mazy, she decided.

Koda did not like the black jack. He snorted and shook his head as Ruth stood off to the side of the trail allowing the wagon to pass with

Ewald tied behind. Ruth couldn't ride Koda anywhere near the animal, not that she wanted to, his being Matthew and Lura's now. But once or twice the day before, when she rode back to tell Matthew something, the black jack brayed out of nowhere, its trot-trot gait full speed toward them, nearly skidding to a stop in the dust just before he would have crashed into Koda's side.

"I believe that jack knows exactly what he's doing," Ruth said. "Running up, all threatening. Maybe we should hobble him." She backed up a nervous Koda who raised and lowered his head in irritation, his bit and bridle jangling in the autumn air.

"Got his own personality, that's for sure," Matthew told her. "He'll be all right."

"I just wondered how far you thought we should go tonight before making camp?" Ruth asked.

"Whatever's your pleasure."

"You've been this way, so I'm deferring to you." She didn't know why she needed to explain to him her request for information. Maybe she was still feeling a little embarrassment about their conversation, his assumption that she'd "partner" more than just for jacks or to get cheap land. "And you've done a good job choosing," she said, offering the compliment both as something genuine and as an olive branch against their sparring.

Matthew nodded. "Would have gone over the Trinity Mountains through French Gulch if you hadn't gotten Elizabeth's letter when you did," he said. "He will have received it by now. What you sent on."

"And be roaring mad if I know Zane. And I do."

"Nothing wrong with being angry. It's what a man does with it that counts him," Matthew said. He cleared his throat. "We should make it to a place across from a ridge that looks just like a backbone," he said. "Rest there for the night."

Ruth felt an edge of disappointment that he'd changed the subject from her future to resting places. But it was no one's business but her own, she guessed, though Elizabeth's last-minute announcement had made it pretty public.

David Taylor had agreed to deliver the divorce papers she'd had drawn up. There was little left to do but wait until Zane responded through her solicitor. There would be a messy court event, but with her and Jessie in another state and his own body ravaged by the amputation, perhaps he'd realize the futility of resisting. That was probably wishful thinking, and she'd promised to tell herself the truth.

"You rub that whip handle," Matthew nodded his hat toward her right hand. "Tells me you're hungering for something. I figure if you're ever going to use it on me, watching your hand'll be fair warning."

They rode side by side for a ways, the white-topped mountain Matthew said was called Shasta shimmered in the distance.

"I was thinking of my future," she said. "Well, maybe hanging on a bit to what I left behind, too. And about what I hope to find in Oregon."

"Shasta's a lot hotter than Jacksonville. Fewer folks there too. Table Rocks are interesting. I want to climb them sometime. Supposed to have unusual flowers up there in the spring."

Ruth nodded. He was so much more talkative about weather and land and…things.

"Carmine's a good-looking jack," Matthew said as they prepared to camp for the night. "I'll catch him up now, if that's all right with you. At least he doesn't race toward a body the way Ewald does."

"So far he's demonstrated better manners," Ruth said. It was the last bit of gentle conversation she had with Matthew for the next few hours as they attempted to round up her jack.

Ears perked forward, the big red animal let her and Koda approach. He lowered his head like a tame goat, then thrust his head up, bolted, and ran, kicking up his heels so close to her horse, he nearly got Koda in the neck. Ruth jerked the reins back, while the gelding sidestepped. But the jack took this as a challenge, and he turned. This time with ears back and mouth open, he lunged for the gelding.

"You're not hurting this horse," Ruth shouted.

She spun Koda away from the jack who quick-trotted up the side of the trail then down into the mares, pushing them aside, biting a neck, kicking at a hindquarter as he moved against the tide. Just as Ruth would get close to him again, the animal would forge up the trail, pass the wagon on the ravine side, and end up in front of it as though to harass the oxen who were lumbering along and braying as though he did it for sport.

The sounds and quick movements and kicking and nipping got the mares all skittery and startled. Then Ewald, still tied to the wagon, brayed and pulled back when all day he'd been happily plodding along with the herd.

Ruth realized it was the first time they'd tried to catch Carmine up. He'd been corralled at the ranchero, tied up for them when they rode out the day before, and kept that way until today.

"Maybe he can be roped," Jason shouted from his smallish mare who sidestepped and snorted as the red jack approached.

"Give it a try," Ruth shouted. She watched the boy swing his rope, surprised at his skill for someone just ten. A few missed loops, and then it was Matthew who swirled his lariat closest. While he tossed the rope to Carmine's head, the jack lowered his ears, bucked and pulled and got himself so woven within the trail herd that Matthew's rope slipped off.

"Let's wait until we're into a more open area where we can round up the mares in a rope ramuda," he suggested, wiping beads of sweat from his forehead with his arm. He replaced his hat and stared at Ruth who nodded agreement.

Once over a ridge, they located a spot wide enough. "String that rope from that oak there, to that big pine," Ruth shouted. "Mariah, you tie off the other end. Soon as the mares are driven into the center we'll try for the jack." While they did that, Ruth noticed the whitish row of hide at Carmine's left fetlock, and something rang a bell inside her head.

She dismounted carrying her whip at her side. Carmine trotted back and forth beyond the rope corral, acting as though he wanted in but was not likely to stay settled even if they let him. Ruth walked slowly, staring at those dark eyes, one wandering to the side, and when he saw she had no rope, he slowed his trot but still moved back and forth before the mares and lone milk cow.

"Easy does it, Carmine. Easy now," she cooed, swirling the whip at the ground. He stopped once or twice and stomped with both front feet toward her, but she stayed steady, didn't back away. "Like fishing for trout," she whispered to herself. And the next time he ran back and forth in front of her, she acted: She cracked the whip, winding it around his left front foot just about where that white hair ran its ring. He stopped as though struck with a club. Carmine never moved a muscle. It was as though the rawhide around his foot was a cage of steel, a bear caught in a trap.

Ruth walked toward him, keeping the whip taut around his fore-lock. The animal breathed hard from his running, hung his head low, but made no action to bite at her or lunge or pull away. "I wondered if your feet didn't do your thinking for you," she said. Ruth smiled. Elizabeth always said that the scars of a person's past gave clues to what would hold them hostage. "Bring the hobbles, Jason, and a little grain," she said. "We've got this one figured."

"It's only for a short time, David," Mazy said. "I want to take the bull south, to meet your uncle and give him his due. Unless you'd rather," she said.

David Taylor shook his head. "I've applied for the mail run," he said. "Between French Gulch and Weaverville, here and south. I'll be home most nights that way. Keep Oltipa and Ben safe."

"If you could, if you would, handle the cows for me—"

"I've never milked a cow," he said. He sounded annoyed. It reminded Mazy of David's father.

"It's easy enough. Reliability is what matters. Having someone I can count on being there to do the work two times a day and make the deliveries, too."

"What about Charles Wilson?" David said.

Mazy scoffed. "He's reliably unavailable for any real work," she said.

David rubbed his chin with his hands. Mazy didn't want to push him, but she wasn't sure who else she could ask. Seth had agreed to go south with her, and they needed to head out before it got cold if they were to make it back before the snowy season. "I need some time to think about it," he finished.

"I understand," Mazy said. She stayed to take a bowl of Oltipa's acorn soup, asked her how she made it. It smelled heavenly and tasted the same. She'd come up with something else, maybe hire a packer to drive the bull south.

"I'll let you know in a few days," David said. "And I'll think about it, I will."

Back above her mother's bakery, Mazy broke a tendril of thyme and rubbed the stem on her forehead. Her mother said it was good for head-aches and fainting and sleeplessness, too. That, she could use. Something to help her sleep. She just missed Ruth, she guessed. Ruth and the chil-dren and what was familiar.

No time to sleep now, she thought. She hadn't seen her mother all day, a fact that surprised her since her baking was usually finished by late morning. They often took lunch together. She drove back out to Poverty Flat to begin the evening milking.

She had more cows now, with the Durhams. But she decided she'd wean only a few of the calves so she would have less to milk until later. She might sell some stock for beef this winter. She would be able to get a good price, she was sure. The miners had scared wild game so far into the hills even venison was becoming a delicacy.

She finished with milking, grained the bull in his pen, and stood watching the sunset. She'd have to move her things from town soon, take over the cabin. She didn't have the heart to try to build another place even though the man she leased from had said she was welcome to do it. The Sacramento River looked gold in the twilight, shimmering, promising ore but delivering something quite different: steamers bringing passengers; ferries bearing wagons of people from miles away, all stepping into new places. She wasn't alone, and she was better off than most. She knew Poverty Flat. Ruth would have to learn a whole new place. Tipton had already, discovering Crescent City's coastal ways. And she still had her mother as a friend; neither Ruth nor Tipton had that. She should remember to be grateful. It was so easy to think complaining thoughts when all around her was abundance. She took a deep breath. She had to trust that she had stepped out onto a cloud of faith believing she would not fall through. So far, despite the loss of an unborn child and a husband who both betrayed her and left her widowed, she'd found faith enough to take the next step. Why should she think she deserved more?

She placed the wooden bucket back in the barn and noticed a pale light coming from the cabin. Who could that be? Maybe David had decided they would come after all? She picked up her skirts to move more quickly toward the cabin, more curious than concerned.

6

a woman she wasn't

Crescent City

"Chita, what ever did you put in those beans?" Tipton said. "My stomach is a tumble."

"Just what is always in them," the Mexican girl said. "As Señor Kossuth say to fix them. A little vinegar, to take the wind away."

"Please. Don't even say that word." Tipton held her side, and then put a hand over her mouth before retching into the pan Chita held for her just beneath her chin.

"I've never been so sick in my life," Tipton said, wiping her mouth. Her knees buckled when she stood, and Chita steadied her. "I must look a fright," Tipton said.

She wobbled toward the mirror and peered at herself.

"You are lovely, señora," Chita told her.

Tipton pulled at the skin beneath her eyes, revealing dark pockets like heel prints in the beach sand. Her usually creamy complexion looked pasty as a wet sand dollar.

"Maybe it is *la niña?*" Chita told her.

"Niña? What baby?" Tipton said. She lifted her chin to stare at the round face beside her in the mirror. The girl had eyes so brown they looked sable, hair so black and shiny it was the night sea. Beautiful, that was what she was. Maybe that was why Nehemiah kept her around.

Tipton pinched some color back into her own pale cheeks. "What baby?" she repeated. "Did you let someone bring a child into our kitchen? You know how dangerous that can be."

"No, no." Chita pointed and smiled, those dark eyebrows opening up her whole face when she did. "The baby inside señora."

"What?" Tipton turned to stare, too quickly, and the room started to spin. The kerosene lamp smell made her sick, and she pushed her hand over her mouth again, her eyes searching for the retching pan. Chita found it. Tipton filled it. Then with a clay cup Chita handed her, she rinsed her mouth of the foul taste.

The stale beer did little to improve her disposition or her breath, but their water supply was dismal. Everyone had taken to drinking wine and beer brought in by ship. At least until the rains filled the streams and reservoirs.

"Your peppers, that's what it was," Tipton insisted. "Women… indisposed…get morning sickness, not evening sickness, Chita, not that I should even be discussing something so intimate with you. No, this is from your cooking. Don't you pawn that off on some nonexistent condition."

"You lay down now," Chita said. "I will get a cool cloth for you, yes? Mr. Kossuth, he comes home. We will clean your face and put fresh linens on you. He will be so happy to know he is a father, pronto."

"Oh, just stop that. I guess a woman knows if she's…or not. Well she does. There is no way I *can* be, Chita. I know that much."

Chita grinned at her. "How do you think this happens?"

"I know," she said though she wasn't totally certain. "That's why I'm sure it could not be happening to me. Not that it is any of your business." Tipton took the cool cloth Chita offered her and settled it on the back of her neck. "I have never once, not ever, sat on my husband's lap. That's how I know." She closed her eyes. "Which is exactly what my mother warned me against doing to avoid an…unplanned event of that nature."

Chita laughed out loud.

"What?" Tipton pulled the cloth from her neck.

"Is all right, all right," Chita said, her palms defending. "You have other story maybe to tell why you have no flow for two months."

"Chita!" Tipton stood now, started to pace.

"I wash clothes. I know this. Two months. You tell Señor Kossuth you have bad beans. Give you time, but Chita knows." She touched her finger to her temple. "How you will explain why your *estómago* grows, that will be different." Chita laughed again as she left to empty the bowl.

Insolent girl, Tipton thought as she gathered her skirts up around herself and curled onto the divan. Had it been two months? Her face *was* a little fuller and her corset actually hurt a bit, pushing up against her breasts. But even on the trip across, her flow had changed, stopped for a time. Elizabeth said it was because of how she ate. So, there. That was the explanation again. Beans, nothing more.

Tipton lay listening to the wind sighing in the huge redwoods standing as a sentry around the cabin, allowing her mind to drift. *A baby.* How that would change her life! And not for the good. She turned over, not wanting to think of such a thing. Too intimate. Back home, she had had to hang her father and brother's unmentionables and her own underdrawers up at night, and her mother would rip them from the line before first light. "No one should see such things," Adora would say. Maybe that was why her mother resisted Tipton's doing laundry for the miners last winter in Shasta, even if it did allow them to survive. Tipton sat up. Maybe that was why her mother was so anxious to marry her off. Not for Tipton's happiness but to avoid the embarrassment of her daughter tending strange men's unmentionables.

She moaned and lay back down. She couldn't be with child. She just couldn't be. A baby meant hours of paying attention, something she wasn't up to, not right now. She rubbed her arm in that achy place that meant she wanted to escape. That was what Elizabeth told her.

A baby. There'd been those times, in the quiet of the night, when she'd felt loved and tended as Nehemiah lay beside her, his hand stroking her hair, his kisses soft and lulling. She'd fallen asleep, hadn't she? No. Gone away, more likely. She'd had frantic dreams after, she remembered now, full of wildness and unfamiliar scents. She sat up straight in her chair. *Perhaps it had happened then?* There had been that one night...

How could she be sure? She couldn't ask Chita. She couldn't discuss it with her husband. She'd never even undressed in his presence, had always insisted the lamps be put out before she stepped out of her underdrawers and donned the white muslin she slept in, covered from head to foot.

A baby? No, it had to be something she'd eaten. She was hungry now, her stomach fluttering with the foreign thoughts. Roasted apples, that was what she wanted, or something fresh to bite into. She rose, made her way to the back porch, and reached into the barrel. She lifted a smallish Maidenblush apple that Nehemiah said came by ship all the way from New Jersey. Well, originally from that far but now there were trees bearing the waxy yellow-skin fruit in Oregon. She found the corer and stripped the apple of its seeds, then took a bite. Her stomach felt better already. The queasiness came from how she'd been eating.

She wished she could ask her mother. She snorted to herself. What would Adora care? She could ask Elizabeth. She'd write to the older woman, find a way to get the information without telling her what she needed it for. Just curious, she'd tell her. She'd describe the beans and the effects. That woman knew everything about food.

She took another bite of the round fruit. It would make a good cider, she thought. Something better to put into her stomach instead of that stale beer. She picked up two more apples and began slicing them. *A baby?* She couldn't be expecting Nehemiah's child. She still wasn't sure how she felt about him.

"Honest. Creative. Warm-hearted. My three adjectives," the man told Suzanne with no hesitation. She wondered if Sterling Powder had overheard her question to each of the candidates or if he was just inventive. He said he was creative, after all. Suzanne would have added *charming*. She hadn't even wanted to interview him, but she felt sorry for his waiting all day and then having Esther ask him to return. She'd told him as much, and his interest must have been great since he had come back.

"I understand fully your reluctance. The propriety of a manservant for a gentlewoman would certainly be questioned, Mrs. Cullver. However, I would not be your servant in the usual sense."

"No. A tutor is what I'm hiring. But I did hope to have a second value met in that person becoming a part of my...family."

"The word *family* in Latin comes from *famalus,* a word meaning servant, this is true."

"You knew that? I'm...impressed." Details and facts were important for a teacher to retain.

"Still, you yourself will have need of a personal caretaker, if I may be so bold to suggest. Someone to assist with your morning toilets." Suzanne had nodded. "And perhaps keeping the...functions separate, a man to tutor your boys, a woman to assist you, would ultimately help you *focus*." His use of *that* word surprised her too. It was almost as though he'd been eavesdropping on her life. "And any tutor you employ must have a way with children. Quiet children, as it appears your son is."

"Quiet." She liked that characterization. Not mute.

Pig had been whining at Suzanne's feet, and she thought once she heard what might be the dog sniffing and then the shuffle of a smooth boot where Mr. Powder sat.

"Is the dog a bother for you?" she asked.

"Not at all. I'm sure we'll become good friends. He seems well trained."

"Thank you." Suzanne reached to pat Pig's wide head. "He saved my life once. Before I knew I wanted that." Her fingers brushed at her throat. "I've thought of perhaps training other dogs. Be a teacher myself, of sorts. We've done well together, haven't we, Pig?" The dog made slobbery sounds into the silence.

"I see you like lavender. I can smell the scent," Mr. Powder said.

"And you, rue," she said, becoming more formal. "Have you been in court lately then?"

"Aha," Sterling Powder told her.

"My sense of smell is quite acute."

Sterling said, "No, no time in court. I do not hold as some do that the rue herb wards off the plague or evil spirits. The plant does, however, bear full foliage and looks ominous on a judge's desk. Touching it, as you may well know, leaves a red lesion on the skin, it's said. So perhaps it does ward off defendants who might otherwise get too close to a judge's throat. I would never have such a plant where children are about. For that reason."

"Your use of it?"

"Aha. Boiling rue with gun flints improves accuracy, you may have heard."

"You're a marksman then?" Suzanne asked. It would be good to have someone about who might be able to protect the boys if need be.

"I'm more taken with the manufacture and design of firearms than the function," he told her. "I find them lovely works of art, even those without elaborate carvings. The designs, history, engineering, the selection of wood, all intrigue me."

"I see."

"But nothing intrigues so much as seeing children, young boys, become competent young men. That is truly important. Your boys will have need of a man in their lives, Mrs. Cullver. A good man. To show them how to be respectful of a mother, how to use their minds and skills to become good citizens, to someday care for a family of their own. To demonstrate strength. These are important values built into my lessons." His use of the word "important" sounded like "im-pour-dent" the way people from North Carolina would say it. It soothed her some-how, reminding her of an aunt of long ago, and comfort arrived on the lilt of his words.

She wished she could have talked with his former employers, but they were back in the States. She had to trust that the letters he read to her were accurate portrayals of his skills. And he confirmed what she'd been struggling with: how to meet both her own needs and Clayton's. Hiring a tutor and a personal assistant would define and separate those two roles, would help give Clayton all he needed without sacrificing her own care. Perhaps he'd hit upon the way she could avoid disappointing Esther, after all.

"If my friend Sister Esther finds you suitable and my son begins to develop some words after a trial period, we can then discuss a perma-nent position for you. And of course, we'll discover if you are truly cre-ative, honest, and warm-hearted."

"What about the dog?" he said.

"The dog is a part of this family," she said, alert to something besides his gentle voice. "I thought you found no objection?"

Sterling laughed. "Not at all. Though my cats might."

"Cats? Neither he nor I fancy cats much. Cats? Plural?"

"Cats. Three."

Mazy moved to Poverty Flat.

After months of hovering like a dragonfly over the pond of her life, always trying to get back to what had been, Mazy decided. While she packed her few belongings into trunks, finished digging up herbs for transplanting, brushed the linsey-woolsey dresses and folded the new underdrawers her mother had made her, she assessed this new step in her life. She was no longer Jeremy Bacon's wife. She was a milkmaid, a businesswoman, someone indebted to another, a woman hoping to serve. She had made some good decisions and some poor ones. It was part of living. She was a widow, yes, and a stepmother and a young woman. Perhaps she wasn't totally dependent on herself, but neither was she dependent on a husband, father, brother, or son. She was her own person for the first time in her life, and at this moment she was strong and firm and stepping forward with a plan not to avoid or intrude but to advance. At last, it felt right.

After delivering the morning's milk, Mazy loaded the milk wagon with furniture in Shasta City including the trundle bed and the linens and her settings of herb plants and the backing for the quilt squares, her Bible and tools for writing. She drove Ink, their family mule, out to Poverty Flat.

"I can help you move your things in," Seth had told her the day before, his hat pushed back on his forehead. She'd declined.

"The only heavy thing is the bed," she'd said. "And even that can be moved in pieces, so I'll be fine. I'm looking forward to just taking my time. If you come help, I'll need to be fixing up a meal afterward and deciding right off where to set things. I suspect I'll be cleaning awhile before I even move the canvas from the wagon."

"You got frame houses nearly built, I hear."

She nodded. "Yes. It surprised me how far that lumber I'd bought for my house could go."

"I imagine those Indians are pretty pleased to get the shelter. How many do you have out there now anyway?"

"Maybe twenty," she said.

"That many?"

"Mostly children. They're safe there. I didn't know about all the… bounty for scalps or that the Shasta longhouse had been burned." She shook her head. "They're good help, they and their mothers and kin. At least they all seem to get along like kin. Even a little scolding at each other. And it isn't just their long-tailed dogs." Seth grinned. "They won't milk though. The cows scare them."

"It's a good thing you're doing anyway, Mazy."

She shrugged. "I'm not doing it to be good. It's almost like I'm doing it because I'm not good. It's my own self-interest that keeps them there, so I can sleep nights without worrying over them. Sula started it. Her name means "trout." Did I tell you? She's the little feisty one. But they all have more light in their eyes now. Does that make me…condescending, that I enjoy seeing the light in their eyes and feel as though I have some part in it, however small?"

"You're asking me?" Seth said.

"Is anyone else here?"

Seth laughed. "I'd never describe what you're doing as condescending. Caring would be a word I'd use. Taking action. Making love a verb." Mazy looked at him, and he turned away.

"That's the poet in you," she said. "I hadn't thought about love being an action. I saw it as just a feeling, a passion. But it is something we do, now that you mention it. What good is the passion if we don't act in some way."

"Can you feed them through the winter?"

"If I don't panic and think everything is up to me! People at the church have been helping. Several women have agreed to come out to finish the women's quilt. I always thought of them as kind of snooty," Mazy said. "And not all that anxious to help last year. But now, without my even asking, they've offered. Some of them are…well, a few work at the saloons. One was a friend of Esty's."

"So you're opening some other doors."

She nodded. "I guess."

"They'll help you unload if you need it," he said.

"I'm looking forward just to doing this all on my own."

Truthfully she wasn't sure how she'd handle this being alone, not waiting for her mother to share tea, not "doing" every spare moment. Maybe it was just as well David and Oltipa hadn't taken her up on moving in with her. She could use their help with the milking, but with the women and boys doing so many other chores, she found the milking itself not as tiring. She was already up to ten cows now, morning and night.

"It'll give you time to find pleasure in your own company" was how her mother put her moving, adding that people who could do that were their own best friends.

"Kinships take a little tending," her mother told her. "Got to stake 'em up before the winds buffet. Goes for taking care of you, too, Daughter. This'll be good, this time with your own place without others sharing your roof."

"You just want to take your baths without feeling rushed by my waiting for the water," Mazy'd laughed.

"That, too," Elizabeth told her, as she brushed a tendril of Mazy's hair back behind her daughter's ear.

"You need to take time to find the miracles in the pages along the way and not just go rushing through your book to find the ending," her mother said.

Hadn't that been the most important lesson Mazy'd realized after nearly a year of avoiding the journey south to see the solicitor about her husband's wayward ways? She'd kept herself from pleasures that lived right down the road from her, if she had only known, if she had only risked letting go of the past so she could grab on to the ring marked "future." She might have avoided still having the bull, would have avoided Ruth's terrible loss. She shook her head. *Mind mumbling again.* She would not think of that now. She would save bad thoughts for a certain time of day and give herself over fully to them then.

The cabin at Poverty Flat still held a scent of Ruth and her brood, something of lemon and leather. Well, the leather scents might have come with the Wintus and Yuroks now bedded down in the frame houses. She scanned the two little rooms of Ruth's cabin wondering how Ruth ever housed four children, plus Mariah, herself, and then the whole brood out here after the fire. And other guests from time to time, like the night Seth brought the new wagon train in. Today that quiet room breathed…spacious with just her few things there.

It took her very little time to drag in the trunk that would serve as a table until she could build one. She pounded a board into the log wall and stacked on it Johnson's *Dictionary of the English Language, Uncle Tom's Cabin, The Scarlet Letter* and several little books she said were "written by men in a hurry" that she bought at Roman's Books. The words weren't well phrased, but the stories romped, and Mazy could lose herself inside them on a rainy night. She found an old sock slobbered by Pig, and she smiled, stuffing it into her high-button shoe to keep the leather at the ankle from sinking in and cracking. In no time at all, it seemed, she was finished, and she turned slowly around in the room. *Her room.*

She felt more than heard the stillness: her quiet breathing, the rustle of her hands fidgeting with her apron, even the pound of her heart. A cow bellowed in the distance. Lemon scents drifted to her. The silence comforted like a quilt.

She should go out and see how the children were doing, check on those cows, the weanling calves. Or transplant the herbs into the window box, or perhaps now was the time to read that chapter of Acts suggesting she go out to serve without worry of where food or shelter would arrive from. She could write down the thoughts that scripture brought to mind. Her eyes scanned the room. She'd placed the Bible beside her bed lantern.

Perhaps she could make notes about that dream, about what people were carrying in their carpetbags that would allow them to arrive prepared once they reached their journey's end. It reminded her of Ruth, and she wondered if her friend had reached her destination. She should write a letter to Ruth, offering one more time to bridge the darkness but telling her she was strong enough now to live knowing she'd once had a friend like her and that doing the work to make another was a worthy effort.

No. She was doing it again, running off to fill the silence, using study or service or other distractions to keep her mind busy so she couldn't be touched.

Couldn't be touched by what? she wondered. *The silence?* She made herself sit down on a maple chair she'd purchased from a newcomer arrived on Noble's Trail. She put nothing into her hands. She took in deep breaths, the way she did as a schoolgirl before having to stand and recite in front of the class. It was not laziness to be staring out at the world from a comfortable place, she reminded herself. After all, she wasn't going to sit forever in that chair. She was just stopping for a moment, to savor the quiet. There must be a reason she was here alone. Now. There were things she was meant to learn by experiencing what she could smell and see, what sounds she heard or didn't, how her body fit into her clothes, what space she filled up with her being. Hadn't she read in the dictionary that experience meant "to be present"?

Her mother's comment about kinship came to mind, about tending it for friendships. Perhaps that was why she'd developed closer ties on the wagon train than at any other time in her life. The women saw each other every day. They survived difficult times together. They adjusted what they ate, when they slept, how they tempered their tongues, and they laughed together. Yes, those friendships had taken a toll. She'd found qualities inside some of the women that she would never have given a second thought if she hadn't been forced to see them the next day. Qualities she guessed that she needed to pay atten-tion to in her own life. She'd have shared a meal with Tipton or sewn something for Suzanne, but she never really would have known them. Nor let them get to know her. She swallowed, fidgeted again with the thought.

She'd let few people really know her. She'd come closest with Ruth. A thrust of pain pierced her heart. With Ruth gone, Mazy had no one to be herself with. Her mother, yes, but time with Ruth had been dif-ferent. Heaviness weighed against her chest. She didn't want to cry, not here, all alone. It did no good! She breathed a prayer of safety for her friend, of healing with no permanent scarring for their friendship.

But this wasn't about Ruth, not really. It was about…kinships and the meaning that hovered inside them.

She started to get up but didn't, her legs weak and achy, her heart heavy yet empty. She took a deep breath suddenly tired beyond belief. Maybe she was just lazy. Maybe she wasn't formed of "fine pine," as her husband had once said, wasn't sturdy stock after all but merely timber that looked tall and straight on the outside but was eaten by worms from within. Jeremy. The last time she had been by herself for a night with no other human around had been the two weeks before Jeremy brought the bull back from Milwaukee. That was the last night she'd spent in her own home. Alone. Until now.

Afternoon light poured in through the imperfect window glass, and a spider made its way to the upper corner. A crow called out in the distance, a cow bellowed again with insistence. She felt pasted to the chair, her body big and bulky, taking up the space. She sat alone, totally alone, more frightened than she'd ever been in her life.

"The Lord knows my lot," she said out loud. She spoke the phrase as a reminder of his promise and as comfort to herself. "He makes my fences fall on pleasant places. Pleasant places. Fenced-in places, but not necessarily confining ones." She had to remember that.

An old proverb Esther had quoted came to mind. "Silence is the fence around wisdom." To learn the lessons and find the wisdom in her days, she must learn to savor silence. It was a way to tend relationships. She breathed deeply inside her fence, entered the gate called prayer.

"So tell us another Oregon story," Jason urged Matthew. Firelight flickered against the boy's face. After only a few days on the trail, they'd fallen into a routine with Matthew telling tales at night.

"Well, let's see. Leave the red leaves alone on the trail. I learned that one the hard way. Those madrone trees, the ones with bark about the color of…a red sunset."

"Or Mazy's hair," Mariah said.

"Or Mrs. Bacon's hair. Right. Hers is a bit darker though. Well, those red bark sheddings, they mix in with…poison oak leaves." He leaned way into the fire when he said "poison oak" as though he was some kind of monster from the Brothers Grimm stories.

"Do you have to eat the leaf for it to hurt you?" Sarah asked.

"Just touching them can make a body sicker than you'd know. And itchy! But the real reason to pay attention to those leaves and never touch them…is that that's where rattlesnakes hide and they'll leap out at you!" The children all leaned back as one with stiff necks and wide eyes when Matthew shot up from his seat at the word "leap."

"Snakes don't jump that far," Jessie said.

"Some do," Ned told her.

"And then there's the Table Rocks," Matthew said with a shaky tone to his voice, rubbing his hands into an imaginary ball.

"I thought you said they were beautiful," Ruth said. "That wild-flowers grew there and all."

"Taller than Independence Rock back on the trail and flatter, that's true. The Rogue River runs right below 'em. Two flat rocks. Side by side."

"What's scary about them?" Ned asked.

"Beings from the sky, from faraway stars, sing songs that sound like babies crying, and they come swooping down to settle there in the night. And they look out across the land, eyeing…little children to snatch up for supper." He lifted his arms like wings. "Late at night," he whispered. "And when they can't find them, they lay eggs all over the ground at the base of the rocks. Those eggs will hatch in the heat and—"

"Which is why some children grow up to have heads as hard as rocks," Ruth said, looking directly at Matthew. She stood at the wagon back, wiping the tin plates. "And that baby-crying sound is a mountain lion for sure, nothing from the night sky. And those pretty stones I'd guess are agates, not eggs. Come on. Time to bed down." A chorus of groans followed, but the children moved forward and were soon settled in bedrolls near the fire. Mariah and her mother took a lantern into the pines for their necessary time, and Ruth chose the opportunity to talk.

"You shouldn't scare them so," Ruth said as she hung the towel on the backboard. She'd agreed to help with cleanup while Lura assumed all the cooking. It had worked well. The children assisted too, along with tending the stock. The rope ramuda allowed them to post minimal guard on the horses, and hobbling both jacks had proved wise too.

Matthew whittled a piece of burled wood he'd picked up along the trail. "They love it," he said. "Just stretches their minds."

"I'm not sure Jessie does. Her eyes were big as boulders when you talked about things coming out of the sky to get them and take them away."

"She knows it's a story," he said. "She's a smart kid."

"Maybe. But she's different since she got back from…well, you know. She cut her finger on a rock this morning, and you would have thought she'd broken her leg again." Ruth sat beside him on the log and looked at the bark. "This isn't poison oak, is it?"

He laughed, shook his head. "Seems to me your Jessie was always a tiger," Matthew said.

"You remember her from the wagon train?"

"A little. I was keeping an eye on Mariah and comparing her some with the other girls, even though she was lots older. Jessie always walked like her chin knew just where she was headed and she was just along for the ride."

Ruth wondered if for some strange reason he remembered her, too. She'd only thought of him as that young wrangler with the white streak of hair against coal black. Now he seemed much older, wise beyond his years. And those blue eyes of his had a way of seeing into her soul. She stopped herself. She couldn't afford to see him as anything beyond a wrangler helping her move a herd north. She had to stay a loner, just be there for the children. That was the path she walked on just now.

"Jessie is different," Ruth insisted. "It's not like she's wanting attention, but that she's really frightened about something. Lura clanged the Dutch oven against the wagon wheel before supper, and Jessie got that same big-eyed look and started breathing real fast. I asked her what was wrong, and she didn't even seem to hear me. And I touched her, and I could actually feel her heart pounding through her pinafore. She was scared. Over nothing. Kept it up until I got her a drink of water, and then she didn't seem to know what I was talking about."

He sat without speaking. "I'll try to be more careful," he said. "Maybe it's just all the changes she's had. Knowing you're her mama for certain, being stolen and coming back and now, on the trail. Maybe it brings back old thinking, like when her auntie died. You said they were pretty close."

"Betha was her only mother," Ruth agreed. "I hadn't thought of that. Thanks," she added after a time of quiet.

"For what?"

"For taking me seriously, about Jessie and telling tall tales. I…it's hard for me to ask things," she said.

"I consider myself honored then, and I'll try to be worthy of it. Guess I best check on our jacks." He stood.

"Don't let anything come swooping down out there and whisk you away," she said.

He cocked his head to the side. "I'm honored again," he said. "That you might grieve my going."

"I feel badly whenever I know you're doing my laundry," Suzanne said. Esther scrubbed at a board, and Suzanne could hear the rub of the cloth and occasionally the throb of knuckles against the rough tin. "And I can't do a thing to help."

"You just keep playing your harp there. That's your job. Gives me pleasure while I work. The steam doesn't hurt the wood in your harp? I just now thought of that."

"I don't think so. But Esty said there are dozens of Chinese willing and needing to do laundry in Chinatown. It's how they earn their wages to send back to China. Why don't we employ one of them?"

"I can do the work as well," Esther said stiffly. "And that's not the only kind of work those poor people are asked to do for a mere pittance."

"What? What else?" Suzanne asked.

"Just…things. Cooking and such," she said.

"Do I not pay you enough for our personal care? I could offer more—"

"Nonsense. I'm doing fine. You need your money to pay for the children's teaching. And for this house. I'm grateful we worked out what we did," Esther said.

"Maybe I'm just feeling useless," Suzanne said. "I can't even clean the lamp chimneys without someone having to redo them. I know you do that, Esther. No need to protest. I'm as useless as a wax dropping on a gentleman's napped hat."

"You're your children's mother, first. That's your task, and you're tending it well. Just play," she directed.

Suzanne strummed her troubadour harp. She stopped. "I could give children music lessons."

"Not many children around here free for lessons, Suzanne. This is a hard place, this mining country. Not kind to men nor to women and certainly not to children. Most of them are working, helping at boarding-houses, with gardens, ironing, all kinds of things to make ends meet. You're lucky in some ways, not to have to see it. Not so hard here as Shasta City, but still not much time for frivolity."

"I did all right entertaining in the mines," she said. "People need music and plays when they're feeling destitute and empty. It lets them forget."

"You got yourself some gold, certainly, but you paid a price."

"I know," Suzanne said, chastened.

"Besides, I'm not sure forgetting is what'll help people who are look-ing for a way through a life they don't feel is worth living," Esther told her. "Doing what you did—getting clear and getting courage—that's what helped you, and that's what'll help them."

Suzanne sighed. "All the more reason why you should stop cleaning that theater. Get you away from all that."

Esther didn't speak, just kept up her scrubbing. Perhaps Suzanne had gone too far. Esther had cleaned at the Sacramento Theater for the past year, late at night, and she had not once complained, as far as Suzanne could remember, not in her letters, not in her speech since Suzanne and the boys had arrived. Esther was paying off the contracts from the failed marriage arrangements of the Celestials she'd brought west. But she suspected Esther got something more out of that theater attachment than simply paying her bills. What, she wasn't sure.

"I'm sorry. I have no right to tell you what to do or not," Suzanne said. "I guess I'm just feeling…restless, wanting some excitement, some-thing to anticipate. Mr. Powder has the boys in hand. You have me in hand, and I have…hands with nothing to do." She lifted her palms.

"Idle hands are the devil's workshop," Esther said. "So you best strum that harp."

tell it to my eyes

She was more like an older sister than a stepmother, David Taylor imagined, not that he'd known either before he met his father's widow, Mazy Bacon. In one year, he'd gained an Ayrshire cow, a Wintu wife and her child, a stepmother, and even a grandmother. And he had a deeper knowledge of the life his father'd lived after he left the gold fields of California. Still, David wondered why his father never wrote, never let him know he was alive back there in Wisconsin.

"Maybe he hoped to see you, to tell his story to your eyes," Oltipa told him when he thought out loud about it all.

"Tell it to my eyes." David nodded agreement. He stacked the armful of split wood in the wood box of their cabin, preparing for another frosty night. "A story like that would tell better face on, wouldn't it? Hard for a man to pen that he had two families. A double mind of sorts."

"Your father believes his brother would be with you soon. If he writes to you, then his brother knows of his strange dealings far away in Oui-scon-sin." David liked the way she said the name of that state, as though it had a French twist to it. "Your father chooses his own time to tell him. Waits to say words to his eyes. But he joins the Up-in-Being first."

David nodded. What she said made sense, and he guessed it did little good to swirl the murky past into the present. Like dirt in a bucket of water, if left alone, it would settle soon enough, and then he could see clear again.

David scanned the room. This cabin was finally getting to be the home he'd always imagined, and he wasn't sure he wanted to leave it all to take up farming with Mazy Bacon. Her "plan," as she called it, arrived too soon.

There'd be some complications with Mazy Bacon, he knew. He didn't want to talk about them with Oltipa, but Mazy Bacon saw him as a cowhand, he was pretty sure of that. Hadn't she given him an Ayrshire, him a stranger to her even if they were somewhat kin? Milking cows wasn't something he ever imagined he'd be doing. He tried to see himself burying his face in a cow's udder on a frosty morning. He shook his head. He'd thought to keep one cow, maybe, for milk and butter and such, for his own. One, a woman could milk. He wasn't interested in a dozen that needed milking morning and night. That was what Mazy Bacon had in mind to manage. She had a big plan, all right.

He walked back outside, lifted his ax and chopped thin slivers from the edge of the log, for the kindling stack.

He hadn't liked discussing it with Mazy Bacon either. She had kind eyes, a warm smile, and was generous to a fault, but there was something about the way she got things happening that made him wonder how well she might actually listen to a fellow who saw things different than she did. He didn't know if moving to Shasta was something Oltipa wanted either. She'd stayed alone in this cabin during the past winter and did well, until that Zane Randolph came around. And now they all knew: That crazy man wasn't all that far away. Still dangerous, even with a cut-off leg.

It might be safer at Mazy Bacon's. He'd have to find out how Oltipa felt. Maybe she'd feel buffaloed by this well-intentioned woman too. He'd have to ask, talk to them both, he guessed. He swallowed. He didn't like talking about what he felt. He had trouble finding the words. He preferred speaking with hostlers and horses to women any day.

Things just got complicated with kin around. He'd forgotten that in the years since his father left and he had had no one to be accountable to, no one to please or disappoint. But he was learning again right fast.

David watched Oltipa fixing her acorn soup. He'd acquired a taste for that golden meal. He wondered if his father had ever eaten it. His father had been a dairyman in Fort Vancouver and now, he learned, Wisconsin, too, before he died. It might just be that dairying was inside David's blood. At least that was how Mazy Bacon put it to him when they met to say good-bye to Ruth Martin. Oltipa had a special place in her heart for Ruth's girl, Jessie. Otherwise, they would never have joined in.

"I spent my life driving the big Concords," he told Mazy. "Meeting people from here and there wearing tall hats and speaking with accents. I like that. I'm not so sure about cows. They seem to be pretty much everyday creatures without much changing."

"Meet up with some unsavory folks driving a stage, too," she said.

His face felt hot as she talked, reminding him that he'd never really confronted Zane Randolph the way he'd hoped, that he'd failed to protect this woman he'd grown to love and married.

"I take people places," he told Mazy. "It's honorable work."

"I'm not saying it isn't. But so is dairying, and it has the advantage of predictability," she'd insisted.

He had predictability traveling the same route daily. But it also kept his mind alert, his body engaged in handling ribbons of reins and thousands of pounds of horse flesh. In rain or snow or hot sun and dust, he watched the world spin by from the height of a tall stagecoach. It gave him perspective that he didn't believe he'd find seeing the world through the underbelly of a cow.

"I'll be needing thinking time for that," he told her, and to her credit, she'd accepted it, at least for a time.

He'd felt...maneuvered by her. The way he would sometimes get a horse to harness, feeding it a handful of grain and talking nice while all the time knowing that his little treat would be short-lived and soon the horse would be hauling instead of standing and eating.

Or maybe she was just being direct, asking for what she needed. He didn't know much about the ways of women. Women looked at things differently, now there was the truth. He'd barely begun to understand how Oltipa thought things through and now was adding the rise and swoop and dip of another woman's thoughts, winging through the air like a hungry hawk. He wasn't sure he was up to it, he just wasn't.

The smells of the soup were so rich his stomach growled before he could even say thanks to Oltipa who set a bowl of it down in front of him. She lifted her boy and held him on her lap. Then she snuggled the child to her breast, and he began suckling. David reached for Oltipa's hand and bowed his head, saying a table grace he'd learned as a child, adding a prayer for guidance at the end.

Oltipa stroked the boy's thick black hair as she stared at David slurping soup from the side of the wooden spoon. With the fork, he poked for a hunk of cheese Oltipa had laid out too. "You talk like you talk to friend," she told him.

"To you, you mean?" David reached for Elizabeth's baked bread, tore it off and dipped it into his soup where the cheese melted slowly.

"When talk to Up-in-Being," she corrected, the fingers of her small hand pointing gracefully to the sky.

"Speaking to God like a friend. I guess I do. My mama always said to give him thanks but to be sure to talk things over with him too. He wants to be that involved in our lives," he told Oltipa. "Even about little things."

David savored the soup, then looked up at his family. Oltipa's dark hair, wrapped with twists of calico cloth, hung over the boy's hands. Ben touched one lightly in his fingers. She hummed a song to the child. They both looked like children, so young. He wondered how old she really was, how many summers she'd seen before becoming a young widow, a mother, and now his wife. She looked up at David then with such devotion in her eyes, such a look of peace upon her round face that his stomach tightened. She brushed at the boy's cheek, and he noticed still the scars on her wrists from where the ropes had burned into them, from the time when Zane Randolph had held her. His eyes filled up then, an overflow from his heart.

He set his bread down and leaned back in the chair, relishing this moment at his banquet table, mixing family and faith.

Ben finished nursing and sat up, pushing against his mother to be let down. She set him on the floor, and he pulled into a crawl. He rocked on his baby knees, squealing.

"You heading my way, partner?" David asked. Ben laughed, rocked again, his arms like a young colt's legs just learning to stand. His little elbows locked stiff while his knees flattened under him. He pushed up again, looked down at his palms flat to the floor then scooted with his bottom. He took a sprawling squat forward, landing on his nose.

Oltipa swooped, leaning toward him.

The boy didn't cry at first, instead offered up a look of surprise.

David held his hand up, and Oltipa stopped. "Let him be," David said, smiling encouragement at him. He held his arms out. "He's working his way through this. Just needs some confidence from us." Ben kept his eyes glued to David's, he pushed back up, moved one hand out and then the other, just far enough to inch forward, stay balanced, and still make progress. Ben looked up at his mother and grinned. He grew bolder then, pulled himself up on David's pant leg, took a step, wobbly, still clinging to David's leg. "See," David said. "What'd I tell you? A fellow's got to take a few falls in new territory before he makes any real progress."

Oltipa smiled. Maybe that was a good reminder for himself, too. Mazy Bacon's plan did offer him a way for more of this. He could have time closer to Oltipa and his son, watch over them, keep them safe from those who saw Shastas and Wintus and the other tribes as property to be used up, sold, or discarded. The land at Poverty Flat did offer safekeeping, at least more there than at this isolated cabin. He doubted Mazy would let someone come bullying in to claim Oltipa as a vagrant even if David was away. And if they lived there with Mazy Bacon, Oltipa would have woman company. She might like that. It could all work out well…except for him, feeling stuck with cows every day.

He watched the boy plop down on his bottom, then stand up and move, hanging on to the table until he reached his mother's skirt.

"That boy keeps on trying," he said. "Pretty soon he'll be doing what he wants no matter where he starts from." David's face broke into a grin.

Ruth smelled smoke as they rode. Matthew said it came from Indians burning underbrush to clear out meadows for hunting deer. They rode side by side, Matthew occasionally moving off the trail to keep the mares gathered; Ruth often trotting ahead to check on the boys, talk with Mariah, then back to see how Lura was faring driving the wagon.

"You never told me," Ruth said, "how it was you came to be in Southern Oregon when you were headed for The Dalles."

"You didn't want to hear any more scary stories," he said. She laughed. "And I never heard how it was you came to end up in Shasta instead of heading north."

"So we both have a story or two."

Matthew rode quietly, the jangle of the bridles and bits broken by the sound of leather creaking as their bodies shifted on their saddles. "Couldn't have done it without Joe," he said finally. "He just kept us looking one day ahead and not worrying over what we couldn't fix. Guess, like you, we thought the way we went would be a shortcut but it wasn't. I wrote to tell you and Ma, of course. But I wrote to The Dalles 'cause that's where I thought you and Ma and Mariah would be. And then we found out you were that close to us that whole long winter." He shook his head.

"Just as well you weren't in Shasta. It snowed and snowed," Ruth said.

Matthew nodded. "They said it was an unusual year. I was feeling pretty glum to have carried snowshoes all the way from Laramie to never use 'em until January came. The people we bunked with, the MacDonalds and their five kids that took us in, well, we couldn't see out their window on account of the snow. That's when the animals started bawling. Mares looked thin as hatpins. I knew some would abort come spring. And they did. But that little buckskin filly," he pointed into the herd, "she's a feisty one. And she pushed herself through some snow I wouldn't have thought she could have and got snarled up with a fir tree. Branches poked out and threatened to rip her tender hide. But when I got closer, I saw the strangest thing. She wasn't fighting the branches, she was eating them!"

"Isn't that a marvel?"

"With those snowshoes, we could make our way to trees, saw down branches and get into places where the snow wasn't crusted enough to hold the horses. We dragged the ones with the moss on them back to MacDonalds' for the rest of the herd. Fed all that moss to the cows and horses," he said. "Must have something in it good because the animals lived off it. All started with Puff, that little filly." He sat thoughtful. "My grandpa used to tell me when I wanted something that I thought I needed real bad, to 'be patient and have a little faith.' He told me once there would always be a way if a man kept his head and if what he was doing was part of God's plan. I never forgot that. When I saw that horse eating the moss I almost blubbered like a baby. 'Til then, I thought if we lived I'd be telling you about your losses. Then the snow melted."

"And the floods came. It's always something."

"They said that was unusual too." He laughed. "I think that's the word for southern Oregon, *unusual*. That Rogue boiled out of its banks, ran like the Columbia does year-round, a river everyone should see once in their lives, by the way."

"How'd you happen to see it?" Ruth asked.

"Oh, I made a side trip of a couple hundred miles." He grinned. "Not a shortcut either. Joe and me decided one of us should go there and find you or a letter or something to know where you and Ma were. I got picked. Pretty country. Mountains and ridges with grass so high, Sailor here didn't need to lower his head to eat his fill."

"Will Jacksonville have grazing like that?"

"No ma'am. It's got more settlement and a little more rain from what I figure, with timbered ridges that slope to meadows and creeks. And like I said, good, rich soil. Once we're over these Siskiyou Mountains, we'll be in Oregon, Ruth." He pointed ahead. "North of Mount Shasta, I think you'll find just what you've been seeking."

"I'm sorry, Mrs. Kossuth, I truly am," Nehemiah told his wife. "But I brought you something special, truly special this time. Cashmere. Pink. It's difficult to get and so soft. Feel it."

She brushed it aside. "You promised. You said we could take the ship to San Francisco, and now you say we can't. It'll be too late to buy up things for Christmas and send them if we don't go soon. And why do you get to buy things but I can't?"

"The backers came here," he said. "So there's no need to go south right now. They'll leave tomorrow, and instead of our going on the ship, I can take another shipment into gold country. It's very profitable, Mrs. Kossuth. And we need to concentrate on profit...and making sure people have what they need before winter sets in."

"Your backers. Let them back you up when you come home to a cold fire," she said.

"Tipton."

"Mrs. Kossuth to you," she snapped.

She could see the hurt in his eyes beneath those bushy red eyebrows, and still she couldn't stop herself. She felt as though angry cats had taken refuge in her head, and she couldn't get them out no matter how much Nehemiah tried to calm with his words.

"My head hurts." She rubbed at her temples.

"Shall I fetch the doctor? Here, take the cashmere. It's warm. So soft. Please."

"I just need to rest. To go to bed." She shrugged the cashmere from her shoulders.

"I'll fix you tea," he said. "I'm sorry."

"No!" She hated it when he was nice to her when she was being wretched to him. Worse, when he apologized and didn't know why he apologized. He didn't intend to never do this again; he just wanted her to not be angry. And he'd say anything to make that happen. She hated that about him…about men. Tyrell used to do that too, at times. Just try to find a way to appease her without ever really knowing why she was upset. What was worse, she often didn't know why she was upset either. Like now.

A pale light broke through the shutters. Tipton turned over. Her husband was already up and gone. But she knew he'd come back for a final good-bye before he left for his pack trip. She hated it when he left her all alone. Well, fine. She would go out too. For a long ocean walk. If she made it back before he left, so be it. If not, he would know how it felt to be counting on something and then find himself disappointed.

She grabbed the cashmere shawl he'd given her, ran it across her face, then threw it on the bed. She didn't feel any better. Those cats were still in there, having their way.

Even though the sun had barely risen, she could see well enough to stride out fast along the rocky beach. And the long walk with the wind at her face did soothe. Maybe she was just being petulant. Nehemiah did have his work to consume him. She supposed that was part of what troubled her; she had nothing that engaging. Even her painting had never sparked her interests the way Nehemiah was fired by finance and shipping and supply routes and even the detail of which mules worked best with which handler.

And then he had his plans to run for the county commissioner from the region. He could be famous someday, a man with a head for business who was also compassionate and kind. He said she could help him, knowing Spanish or Mexican enough to converse. It seemed to her there were lots more Chinese and Indians around than Mexicans. But they couldn't vote, she guessed. The others could.

"You can be my eyes and ears when I'm not here," Nehemiah had told her once. "It will legitimize gossip for you," he'd said, smiling.

She'd looked that word up—*legitimize*—and been surprised that he thought there was anything that would warrant telling secrets about others. It must not have been what he meant.

She had told him about talk at the mercantile of men who called themselves the Crescent City Militia. They'd said the men had ambushed a group of Tolowa Indians and made wild threats about bounties for their scalps and burning their babies. She'd shivered. Nehemiah had said it was probably just out-of-work miners bragging themselves up, then told her not to walk the beach when he wasn't with her.

She tugged on her old shawl, wishing she'd brought the new cashmere one with her. Once when she'd been outraged over something as insignificant as dandelion fluff on a Newfoundland dog, Nehemiah had actually walked across the room, put his arms around her even though she batted her hands at him, and he held her. She had been screaming and crying and shouting all at once, and he had just wrapped her into him, let her sob and sink into his arms. He hadn't told her it would be all right, hadn't said he was sorry. He had just held her, made sure she knew she wasn't alone. She had never felt more loved. Even by Tyrell.

She inhaled a deep breath. Marriage must demand that kind of love. She didn't know if she was capable of that, reaching out to wrap her arms around someone pushing her away. But he'd seen through her, that was it. Seen what she needed even when she didn't know it. She wasn't that kind of a wife, would probably never be.

A sea gull chattered on the shore before her. She stepped to avoid stringers of kelp curled on the sand. Nehemiah was a good man, a husband she didn't deserve. Truth be known, he didn't deserve the likes of her either. Truth be known, she thought. She was sounding just like her mother.

Zane hated the look of it, the thin thigh. A narrow knee. Half a leg ending at a rounded nub like a knurled tree root cut off. It throbbed less now, and he could actually bear weight with the odd contraption of leather and wood that attached around his waist with a strap, gave his leg length. He couldn't wear it for long though. The stump ached, burned almost, whenever the contraption was strapped on, and he would have to take it off again.

Sometimes he could actually feel his lower leg and foot even though he knew it wasn't there. He wondered if that could be possible or if he was…no. He was of sound mind, he was sure of that. He wanted to scratch there though, or rub where it ached, where the child had jammed his foot with the stone, where the horse had stepped on it and scraped him in the creek. But it wasn't there! His leg was gone.

It could have healed. A decent doctor could have healed it—unless he needed practice amputating legs. If Zane could feel the hurt, that Hollis should never have severed the limb. The man had experimented on his leg! Zane snorted. It was a poor physician who would amputate a limb with blood still flowing to it, blood and feeling that stayed, even after the limb was severed.

And then the snake of a medicine man had run out on him, had left an ignorant immigrant to tend him.

Maybe it wasn't healing right. Maybe Zane had gone overboard when he lost control and grabbed at them. Sent the man away with his mousy nurse when he still needed a doctor's care. He must not lose control. People refused to listen to him; that was all it was. And they underestimated him. Ruth, too.

At least the crutch helped. Zane hated leaning on the man. The big Irishman had some ulterior motive, he must have. Tired of mining in the narrow gulch. Too stupid to make it on his own so he hired out, providing a way for the doctor's escape.

He had asked that a carriage be brought around. "A man does not need both legs to drive a wagon or a buggy," Zane told the Irishman.

"A driver would be the better way."

"I do not need a driver," Zane growled, though he had the resources to pay.

That, too, was an oddity. A stranger had found him beside the stream, his foot festering, his mind drifting with fury and pain. If Zane had encountered such a person, he'd have ridden a wide berth around them. But this stranger had brought him here. Hadn't even taken his purse! The fool. He could have been rich beyond measure, but apparently he had emptied Zane's bag only enough to replace what he'd purchased in food for him. Hollis, the doctor, had taken little more, leaving Zane's fortune intact. Admirable, these people. And stupid; O'Malley among them.

If only they had listened to his cries to simply leave him be, leave him whole. He wasn't sure he could live as just half.

But, for now, he had a plan. He'd told the Irishman what he wanted, and the following day O'Malley had brought the two-wheeled open carriage with a folding hood to the front of the house. It was painted as purple as a week-old bruise. It was perfect.

What he wanted next was to take a trip out to Ruth's. She lived just down the way in Shasta. Where she'd been, taunting him out in the open, acting as though she didn't care whether he found her or not.

That would change. He'd been foolish to become distracted by the Wintu woman, even his own child that day he took them. He'd lost his way, his focus, as dear Suzanne would put it. Ruth was at the center of all his trials, all his pain. She needed to atone for her sins. Yes. Knowing Ruth would suffer must remain his reason for living.

He thump-hopped to the door with the crutch, catching a glimpse of himself in the mirror as he did. He cringed. He ambled like an ape. He'd seen a big ape caged at a circus back in Missouri. The primate lunged at him, and Zane had laughed, sneered at the lack of control the ape had over his own movements, junk that looked like tears stuck in the beast's eyes. Tears. Now here he was, almost as caged, almost as pathetic.

But not quite. He had no tears.

Zane squinted into the sunlight, feeling lightheaded and weak with the effort. He needed to build up his strength. He'd start today, by driving the shay to Ruth's. The horse stomped impatiently at the hitching rail as Zane gasped for breath in the doorway.

"Knew you'd be needing a tad of help then," O'Malley told him, stepping out from beyond the shay. "Later on, you can be doing it on your own, but for now, best you be accepting."

Zane seethed at his need. The image of that blind Suzanne and her pathetic hunger for assistance flashed before his eyes. His leg throbbed. Tiny flickers of light made him blink. He let go of the crutch without meaning to, felt himself sink.

"Let me be getting that for you." The man began lifting him.

"Not back inside! Take me out to the shay."

Zane lunged forward, pushed against the Irishman in an effort to do it alone. Took one step and his good leg collapsed. He hit the ground, the pain searing up toward his head. He gasped, cursing Ruth, just before he passed out.

David hadn't slept well again. He wasn't sure if it was Ben's knees pressed into his back or David's own worrying over whether he'd roll over onto the child. David sat up. He guessed it was anticipating meeting Zane Randolph by the time this day had ended that really disturbed his sleep. He decided to get up though the sun wouldn't be up for a time yet. He listened to the breathing, heard the more rapid hushed breath of Ben mixed with the steady sounds of sleep coming from his wife. *His wife.* He loved the sounds of those words.

Their marriage had changed things, mostly in good ways, but this sleeping with a baby had hit him broadside.

"I just figured we'd have our own...bed," David told Oltipa that first night. Elizabeth had offered to keep Ben to give them time alone, and David had thanked her and accepted. Then he noticed Oltipa's face darken, that shadow cross her eyes like a hawk's wings over a rabbit.

"Something's wrong," he said.

"Baby will miss his place of belonging," she told him. "Will wonder what he has done to be left behind."

David's face turned a little hot as he realized he had put his own needs before the child's. Of course Ben was still reeling from his mother's being gone. David should have considered that fact before he accepted. So he'd thanked Elizabeth for her kindness, then politely declined her offer.

Oltipa had smiled gratefully and lowered her eyelids in that shy look of hers. It hadn't really been a problem that first night at all. The boy fell asleep sitting up in his basket-board, and David and Oltipa had found pleasure in newness of sharing their bodies in marriage. Their union had been everything David had hoped for, his inexperience a catalyst for discovery and not a cause for embarrassment. He must have told her one hundred times how much he cared for her, how grateful he was she'd consented to be his wife.

He didn't know when Oltipa had brought Ben to bed with them later that first night, but when he awoke and rolled over to place his arms protectively around his wife, he'd felt the child's head and chubby neck nestled at Oltipa's breast though both still slept. The scene had warmed him, made him send his "arrow prayer," as his mother had called those instant conversations sent heavenward in gratitude. He hadn't thought he could be this happy.

But just now, the boy's knees had poked straight into David's back. He was sure he had little red marks turning to bruises beneath his shoulder blades. He yawned. His head felt fuzzy.

It was probably not the boy at all but his own difficulty in talking with Oltipa about the sleeping arrangements that bothered him most. He hadn't come right out and said he wanted Ben to have his own little mat. Every time he cleared his throat and said something he thought would fall easily on her ears, like "I didn't know that boy could roll so much in his sleep," she'd do some sweet thing like bend to kiss his nose or run the tips of her fingers across his lip. Or she'd offer him a taste of plumped-up huckleberries or whatever else it was she was fixing.

David wondered if his own mother had been like that, cutting his father's words off with her acts of distraction? The thought hadn't occurred to him before—just how it was that a man and woman worked out these…details. He guessed usually they had time to grow together before they added that third person. This was different, all right.

Only once had she sounded as though she knew he wanted to talk of something he found hard to say. But when he'd barely gotten the words out, she'd stopped him with, "It is the way my people sleep with their children. To keep them safe."

So it wouldn't be an easily changed arrangement. He wouldn't be able to just offer a solution like "I'll frame up another bed for the boy." First they'd have to agree there was a need for change. And then find a way to reassure her that the boy was safe sleeping just a few feet from them. From the sound of it, negotiating that meant bringing his ancestors and hers back to life, a few more people than he cared to have discussing his bed habits. And it might mean bringing up what had happened to her when she'd been left unprotected by Ben's father and then later, by him. He feared she could never forgive him for allowing the likes of Zane Randolph to torture his family. He'd failed her, them. Oltipa had rescued herself and Ruth's girl. All David had done was pray and keep looking. Who would want to trust a man who'd let that happen?

David got up, stepped outside to relieve himself, then returned to pull on his shirt and pants. He yanked at his boots, never feeling fully dressed until they were on. He didn't guess Ben would share their bed until he moved on to his own marriage bed, so there must have been a time when even Oltipa's people pushed the little ones out like a mother bird freeing her babies. David could only hope that day wasn't years away.

And while he was thinking about kin, he realized he ought to reach out to his sister, Grace. Now that he was a married man, his uncle might let her live with him. He'd gotten a letter from her. She was with their aunt and uncle in Sacramento. He could have seen them when he took Suzanne Cullver south, if he had taken the time. But he had been anxious to get back to Oltipa and Ben, to get married and keep them safe.

Grace would have to wait. He poked at the fire, hung the black pot filled with water on the andiron. Waited for it to heat while he found the tin of barley coffee.

Today, he would meet Zane Randolph face to face. He would just have to do that on his less-than-rested best.

Legally the man had done nothing wrong—that was the sick of it. Claim an Indian and take her, leave a baby to die, flee with your own child you haven't seen for five years—none of that would even be challenged in a court of law. David felt his face grow hot with the outrage of it. The situation begged for justice, yes. So today, he would hand out more than Ruth's packet of her divorce intention: He'd hand down justice of his own.

the signs of hunger

They were not even a day's ride out from Jacksonville when Carmine took off again.

"You should have hobbled him," Matthew shouted as they watched the animal quick-race south of the trail through an opening in the pines.

"I can get him," Ruth yelled back. She pressed the reins against Koda's neck and headed after him, ducking as they rode beneath the huge pines. A hobbled animal looked so pathetic, hopping as though it had two legs instead of four. Besides, she could catch him now, with her whip or a rope. She just had to get him into the open where she could swing out and snag that left front leg.

A shout behind her, a crash of branches to her side, caused her to turn. Carmine had doubled back. She saw the rascal pitch and turn again, this time circling the mares then biting at their hindquarters. To the bellowing of Ewald who was tied to Lura's wagon, Carmine pushed the mares back through the stand of pines.

Matthew would not be happy. Neither was Ruth. She turned Koda back into the trees, riding a parallel course, keeping one eye on the mares and the other on the low hanging branches. So she didn't notice until they reached the other side just what lay ahead.

"Matthew," she shouted. "Jessie! Boys! Come on through!" She waited until she heard them behind her, then kneed Koda, and they stepped out into open sunlight.

A timbered ridge broke into a low wrist of land that flared out like webbed fingers of trees and shrubs separated by the meadow below. Nestled in one section of wood was a cabin. Mounds of grass hay were stacked lopsided not far from the house. No smoke rose up. A half-finished split-rail fence lined a portion of the perimeter. It was as peaceful as a painting.

The mares had already started down the side ridge and spread like a swarm of bees over the meadow. A still-warm afternoon sun spilled over the sorrel and black and bay backs. Like a twist of moss-dyed yarn, a stream still licked at green despite the late season. Ruth could see tiny dots of black on the water. Geese or ducks. Further from the banks, and working up the side hills, grass waved brown beneath oaks and scattered pines, and a herd of deer ripped at the blades as though alone in the world. It reminded her of a Saint Louis city park.

Ruth became aware of Matthew beside her.

"Pretty, ain't it," Lura said then, not asking a question. The woman puffed, pushing her way through to stand between Ruth and Matthew's horses.

"Indians have cleared it with their fire," Matthew said.

"It reminds me of your prayer, Sarah," Ruth said. "About the valley of love and delight."

The girl wrinkled her eyes in her small, heart-shaped face. "Mariah's the one who told that, Auntie," she said.

"What prayer's that?" Jessie asked. The girl wiped at her eyes, and Ruth wondered if she might be getting a cold or if it was smoke in the air that irritated.

"'When we come down to where we ought to be,' that's the line I member," Ruth said. "This place feels like where I ought to be."

Water, grass, timber. Off the trail but close to it. It had a southern exposure for a garden and home, yet it was snug, tucked up beneath the trees. She scanned the horizon.

"Looks like old Rumpelstiltskin spun his gold here," Jessie said.

Ruth smiled. The children's story had been one of her favorites, too, of a little man spinning straw into gold and the queen who outwitted him to avoid giving up her firstborn. "It does have that look," she said.

"So we're home?" Jessie asked.

The question jarred her. *Home?*

"Someone else probably owns this already," Matthew told her. "And it's nowhere near those Table Rocks I told you about." He turned in his saddle. "I'm not sure exactly where we are. We might still be in California."

"Is it as good as the place you wintered in?" Mariah asked her brother as she made her way to stand beside him. She patted his horse's neck.

"We were holed up north of Jacksonville." He looked toward the mountain range to the east, getting his bearings. "The MacDonalds lived north, the folks that took in me and Joe. If they're still here."

"So we are in Oregon then," Ruth said.

"There was talk this summer of making part of this territory and some of northern California into a separate section to apply for statehood. Might have happened by now."

Why was he talking about things like that now? Ruth wondered. It was almost as if he didn't want their traveling to end.

"Well I like it, wherever it is. Sometimes a place just talks to you. This one is saying my name," Ruth said. The land rolled easily toward the stream, an apron of gold edged in green. Ruth could almost see the girls running down the gradual slope with their pinafores blowing in the wind. The boys would be whooping and hollering as they rode. She thought of young colts wobbling their first steps across the grass. Just then a red-tailed hawk swooped over to cheer them on, confirming Even Carmine fit right in, his reddish hide looking copper as he kicked and squealed. Water. Grass. Shade. Family. Privacy. Peace. It fed her, this land did. This could be the place where the pebbles of her life tossed across a continent could now settle, find their angle of repose. "The landmarks should make it easy to describe, to find out who owns it," Ruth said.

"We're too far away from civilization to be settling in here," Lura said. "'Cept for tonight, maybe. Got to be closer to town. I want to get me some chickens and a goat or two. Can't sell goat's milk if we're living too far from thirsty miners."

"Thirsty miners'll travel," Matthew told her.

"Yeah, but not for goat's milk."

"I rather like it," Ruth said. She could see that the valley might be a bit narrower than she'd want in the long run. Trees could be cleared out and burned to make pasture. And who knew how the land claim was divided up—she might end up with the side hills rather than the valley, then she'd have to buy hay and haul it from a long distance. Maybe even haul water, though from the look of the lush pasture, if she set barrels out as cisterns, they'd have water enough. The horses could drink from the stream.

They rode closer, and she could see that the cabin was really just a shack. It might not be practical to stay the winter there unless they could shore it up. Yet something about Lura's suggesting they *should* move on pushed Ruth toward staying.

"What do you think, boys?" Ruth asked. "Jessie says we should make this our home."

"Build a corral at that narrow place," Jason said, pointing, "maybe catch up Carmine without having to rope him."

"I like it, Auntie," Ned added. "But I'm tired of riding too."

"Sore bottoms do make for hasty decisions," Lura said.

"Best we see what's available for land claims," Matthew cautioned. "There might not be an adjoining one to this." He looked at Ruth. "And this one might not have a title a man could sell even if he wanted. Don't go getting your hopes up, Ruth."

"The only thing I'm inclined to do right now is to get Carmine roped so he doesn't lead his harem off somewhere," Ruth said. "And find a place to get the wagon through the trees. The children and I will stay here for the night. See what the morning brings."

"We could still make the Table Rock site," Lura said. "Do a comparison."

"Ruth's made up her mind, Ma," Matthew said, and he reined his horse away.

Nehemiah Kossuth lost control, just that one time.

His young wife permitted herself to be seen by him standing before the lamp in her night linen, for a moment, a breath-holding moment. Then she blew out the lamp.

It was what he thought of now watching the campfire dwindle into ash. He listened to the stomp of mules and the night sounds of crickets and packers turning in their sleep. The coast range mountains gave off cold. The moon cast barely a shadow from its pale opaque.

He turned on his bedroll, unable to move his beautiful wife from his mind. Tipton was a woman-child whom he'd never seen completely, not as a husband should see a wife. He'd thought to be patient, to stay forever close to her, giving her the time she needed. Then he'd done a thing he had told himself he would not do. She hadn't pushed him away, but she hadn't been welcoming either. It was as if she'd gone away for a while, and then returned when it was all over. Hurt pooled in her eyes.

That was when he'd chosen this occupation of packing supplies into Jacksonville.

He could have found a way to take her to San Francisco. This separation had been as much a way to avoid looking at the accusation in her eyes as getting needed materials into the mining camp before the snows came.

He lingered with the packing. It would be nearly two weeks before he returned, and something in her look bothered him. He thought he saw puffiness in her perfect oval face. And a sadness. She seemed so irritable of late. He knew it was his fault. His weakness that had caused it.

He imagined her in the firelight as he had that night some months back, an image of white like porcelain, of beauty and perfection. Pearl. Ivory. Opal.

He'd seen a blue opal once, traded to him by a Warm Springs Indian in exchange for dried meat and fruits along the trail. Nehemiah had accepted a dark rock that the Indian said inside contained "a moon river stone." He'd cracked it open and found an opal as near to perfect as anything he'd ever seen. A blue opal. He'd hoped to work it into a setting of silver. But he'd gotten involved in other things—a mule giving him trouble; digging out a mud slide, a slipped pack. There was always something to contend with on the trail.

When he returned to the opal a week or so later, the blue had disappeared and a dark crack like a lightning bolt fissured through the stone. Exposure to the elements, disregard, neglect, had all destroyed it. Who would have thought that the ugly-looking facade could hide such exquisiteness? Or that stones untended could deteriorate so quickly? Tipton was like that opal.

He worried over his marriage that he'd thought solid as rock. He had enough love for both of them, he'd always thought. Tipton just needed time, tending.

And then he'd lost control.

He wanted her to come to him, to assume her place as his wife as one willing, not just in name, not just because she'd married him. He'd committed to wait, wanted to do whatever it took to give this woman he'd discovered on a cold December day a lifelong place of security and love. People didn't take risks unless they felt safe, unless they felt respected and confident. This he understood. It was why he'd offered to bring her mother with them to their new home. But Adora Wilson had chosen otherwise. Had chosen her son over her daughter. They'd never even discussed his mother-in-law's unexpected decision except for an occasional mention on his part that perhaps there'd be a way to mend the break someday.

He'd edged around that topic like a wary man encountering a cougar.

Tipton hadn't permitted discussion. She started rubbing her arm and then just went away in her mind if he came too close to some subject she wanted dismissed. He barely mentioned his meetings with the new political party, fearful that his talk of readying himself to run first for the county office, then on to the state house might send her to that distant place far away and alone.

He tried to involve her in his life, suggested she be his eyes and ears. But even that might not have been wise. Her story of the Crescent City folks talking Indian troubles wasn't something a young woman needed to be exposed to, especially when he was away from home so much.

He tossed on his bedroll again, the roots of the redwood lumped up into his blanket. He got up and poked the fire. He didn't talk easily about the things that mattered. Never had. Especially about intimate things. It was easier to remain formal, to speak to people...as a teacher might.

Teaching, that was familiar. He'd had to instruct young recruits in the Mexican War seven years previous. And he had inspired confidence in them despite many being close to his own age. Drawing from his vast knowledge gave others security; they liked knowing about plants they might eat, how to respond when mules balked, ways to repair firearms and analyze battle plans. He'd read the classics, too, on warfare, philosophy, and such. It was gratifying knowing that the books he read or the lessons learned from the times he'd lived in the timber could serve a useful purpose. He made a point of listening in such a way that the boys spoke of their needs too, when the occasion demanded it, for those facing battles come morning. A few of them even called him Reverend, though he was far from that. Telling others what he'd learned was a natural way to gain respect.

Perhaps that had been his error all along with Tipton, taking on the role as "teacher" with his young wife. Maybe her youngish attitudes and actions made him treat her as a child.

Oh, he wasn't blind to her flightiness, but he could see through it to a fragile soul that did not believe she had much worth. It was his hope to give her worth by sharing time and knowledge. He blinked at the night sky, breathing a prayer of confession for being too impatient, for the sin of taking advantage. Not that saying he was sorry meant he'd never do it again; though he'd try not to, he would. But the fessing up brought him closer to the relationship that could heal his hurtful act, fill his emptiness, maybe even help him understand why he presented what wasn't his to offer. After all, a person was created with worth. Tipton had to decide to believe that on her own.

Knowledge, not that he could give, but knowledge in the biblical sense, between a man and woman, was something else again. He was a student just as she was in that regard, and he found it impossible to talk of it. Yet didn't he know that talking of a thing made it less fearful? Didn't he say out loud to his troops that they might die come morning? It had opened the door to spiritual talk beneath stars that some saw for the last time.

Instead of talking of what he wanted most for her, for them as husband and wife, he'd lost his breath when he watched Tipton walk toward the lamplight that night, blue ribbons fluttering at her neck, her hair like twisted strands of gold cascading down her back.

"Leave the light on," he'd said, the croak of his voice startling him as much as her.

"Never," she said and blew it out.

"Tipton," he'd said then, his voice a wail.

He'd feared she might not slip beneath the coverlet to share his bed. When she did, he felt so grateful he hadn't frightened her away that he'd lost control. Instead of merely holding her, stroking her hair as he had for weeks since their marriage, gentled her head into his chest until she fell asleep, he found himself drowning in the fragrance of her, in the smoothness of the linen formed over her gentle curves. He'd become not Nehemiah Kossuth, former hotel owner, teacher of recruits and one young girl, packer of supplies and family provider, but Nehemiah Kossuth, husband.

She had never spoken of that night and he found he couldn't either.

A coyote howled as Nehemiah squatted at the flames. Sparks flew high into the Oregon sky. He told himself it was his right as husband, that he'd been patient, surely that was true. And yet he'd wanted it to be a mutual giving. Perhaps the fifteen years between their ages was too much for her. Perhaps she had married him not because she felt a single spark of love, some level of devotion that might grow, but out of duty, to tend her mother. Surely that spark would disappear into the dark night just as the ones he watched here on the trail. He should have thought of that before. He stood, restless, amazed at the depth of his denseness. Did she even realize what had happened? He rubbed the back of his neck, scratched at his muttonchops. *Poor child.* Listen to him. That was how he thought of her, just a child.

He heard a horse nicker and stomp. A night owl hooted and swooped.

"You up for a reason, Boss?"

"Just restless," Nehemiah told the Mexican man.

"Sun comes up. We make an early start. Be back home soon. You greet your wife then. Tell her all you see along this trail. Teach her much."

"Yes," Nehemiah said. "That's exactly what I'll have to do." Only it wasn't just her who needed to be taught.

"But surely we could remain here at the boardinghouse until you're certain this...arrangement will work," Sister Esther told Suzanne.

"It is working, Esther. We just need to modify some. Accommodate, remember? Wasn't that you who recommended accommodation?"

"It's the cats, isn't it? They're troublesome, that's certain."

Suzanne sighed. Every step of this move had been a trial. Not as difficult as coming across the prairies, but difficult nonetheless. She had tried to keep her vision forward, tried to stay focused. Practice surrender, she told herself. Try new and different paths. But she'd encountered little stones along the way, little pebbles unexpected that she'd stubbed her toes on. Esther's reactions, for one. It was as though she held a secret of some sort that she wouldn't share.

"I need a good yard for the boys, fenced in. I need rooms that I can keep the same way. So I can learn my way around. And private rooms for the boys' lessons. For you. And for Sterling Powder."

"And his cats."

"And his cats." Suzanne continued, "He's done well with Clayton. The boy doesn't cry out or throw fits as he used to, which is pleasing. And he seems more gentle, not surprising me with his fists as he did."

"The man has him working the soil." Suzanne couldn't tell if Esther approved or found that worrisome. "He encourages the boy to dig in the dirt he warms by the fire, until his face is a mess. Then allows him to splash in the copper tub."

"He told me as much," said Suzanne. "Something about wanting the child to 'feel' things, take them inside himself to really learn them, Mr. Powder says."

"All the handwriting was different, at least, in his letters of introduction," Esther clarified. "I noticed when I read them to you."

"What are you suggesting?" Suzanne turned to face her.

"He was certainly patient waiting through all those interviews."

Esther must have busied herself with something because Suzanne could hear scissors snipping again. It would be easier to let this conversation die right where it was, but Suzanne was finding that not talking about a thing didn't necessarily make it go away, didn't keep it from exploding later into conflict.

"Esther, I want this to work for me, my boys. And for you, too. I don't want you to be upset or offended. When you find fault with things, I feel…guilty and angry and sad because you're my family. What I think we all need is a place for privacy." She hoped the words had the effect she intended.

"Privacy. Yes," Esther said. "You're right." Suzanne heard more snipping. "I should have thought of that." Esther said it as though she already had.

Could the woman have been this inscrutable on the trail? She'd seemed so predictable then, so sure of herself, marching toward California with her promised-brides, figuring out how to resolve the broken contracts. She was different back then.

But so was Suzanne. She wondered when she would stop comparing everything to that trail time, as though it was the standard for when life began and how much she or others changed.

"Maybe we should visit Mei-Ling," Esther suggested then.

"I'd like that. The children would too. After we find a new place. We could invite them to visit us then, something hard to do at this house, you must agree."

"She has done well, though I fear for her. They will move the Chinese out before long."

"Out of Chinatown?"

"Out of all California. She and A-He will have to leave then."

"I haven't heard of this," Suzanne said.

Esther sighed. "Sometimes, I wonder what kind of place I brought her to. I thought I was doing what was right. But now I see so many Chinese are…badly treated, Suzanne. The women especially. Most are mere girls," Esther said. Her voice rose in pitch. "Young girls, but they are…employed by Tong leaders, men who treat them like pots and pans to be used up, tossed about as though life was a dirty kitchen. And Naomi—"

"Perhaps we could go see Naomi," Suzanne suggested, her voice kept light to contrast Esther's intensity. Esther could talk at length about the Chinese, Suzanne found, and without seeing her face, Suzanne couldn't decide when to interrupt, know when Esther might be finished or if she ever would be. "We could all go for a little visit."

Esther paused. "In this rainy weather?"

"Yes. We could see Mei-Ling and take her with us to visit Naomi. With the children and Sterling Powder. A man's presence might soothe the matter, and we could see for ourselves if Naomi's all right. We could bring a gift for her baby."

"Suzanne," Esther said. "There is something—"

Suzanne turned to the sound of a bell.

"It is I, Mrs. Cullver," Sterling Powder answered. He had a formal way of speaking, Suzanne noticed, not unlike Esther. "I have taken the liberty of removing the bell from your son's shoe, which I hold now in my hand. I thought it an important first step."

Suzanne frowned. "It's how I know if Clayton is about," Suzanne told him. "Where is he?"

"We have gathered flour and water for paste, and he creates colored treasures for you with pieces of melted wax and cloth. But we do have a decision to make. The boy uses the sound to tease you. He has found clever ways to remove the bell when it suits him. He even allows the cats to play with them thus confusing you more as to his whereabouts."

"He has? I didn't recall being confused."

"You will not have noticed. But, yes. He has. Just this morning he was in the room with you while you played your harp, with Pig lying at your feet asleep. You were unaware, as the boy had slipped his shoes off. The bells included."

"But why? Why would he bother with such deception? He's only three years old."

"Perhaps he wished not to disturb his mother," Esther said.

"Why indeed. That is our challenge, gentlewomen. Children only manipulate when their needs go unmet. So we must discover what wish he has that tricking you achieves so we can create opportunities for him to learn other, more acceptable ways."

Esther snorted. "He can't talk with her, that's plain enough. He can't tell her what he wants. That's what his need is. When you teach him to speak, that will be placed in the past."

"So he follows her about. Until what? She notices him or stumbles over him because he's removed his bell and she is not expecting him? Is that what you think, Mrs. Maeves?"

Suzanne heard bluntness, not just honesty, in the man's words and annoyance and impatience inside Esther's. Her fingers fluttered at her neck as they spoke about her.

"Please put the bells back onto my son's shoes until such time as we've discussed this further, Mr. Powder. Meanwhile, Esther, if you would be so kind as to ask that a carriage be brought around, I wish to make a trip to a land agent. We're going to be moving to a new home, Mr. Powder."

"This fits precisely into another issue I must raise. I have taken the liberty of preparing a calendar," Mr. Powder continued. "There is entirely too much disorder."

"I keep our rooms well," Esther defended. "You—"

"In routine, not physical space, Mrs. Maeves. It intrudes with Clayton's learning. He needs routine."

"Mr. Powder, the children like to go visiting and surprises. So do I. Rainy weather mustn't keep us housebound—"

"Whose wishes are being addressed here is the question to be asked. There will not be room on the calendar for our locating a new home, as you put it, until…perhaps Thursday, next."

It was time, Suzanne decided. Time to stand firm with their need to find a larger place. And time to set the limits for Sterling Powder. Maybe Esther, too. Suzanne smoothed her skirts. "Very well. Let us plan our trip for next Thursday, you said, Mr. Powder? Meanwhile, please put the bells back on Clayton's shoes, and I'll think further of why he might be taking his shoes off. Unless it has become a part of his routine."

David rehearsed just what he wanted to say. He wouldn't push him too far. He just wanted to face Zane, to tell him that his attempt to harm others, his intent for evil would be used by God for good. Oltipa had come into his life as his wife now, not a purchased slave of Zane Randolph. She was safe and couldn't be touched by the likes of him. He would inform Zane that his hope to harm Ruth hadn't met its mark.

Ruth had begun a new life. He'd say that. Not where she was, but that she was heading on with her life and he best do the same. Then he'd hand Zane the divorce packet and be on his way. David stood tall. He was ready.

David decided that if the man looked pathetic, he'd temper what he had to say. It wouldn't be easy. The memory of Zane's having nearly choked David to death last year caused him to straighten his neckerchief, rub at his throat. Still, there was nothing courageous about taking advantage of an invalid, David thought. He just wanted the deed done, so he could redeem himself. So he could get some sleep having faced the man who had brought such misery to the ones he loved.

David watched as a couple of flakes of snow melted as they touched the ground. Another early winter? He hoped not. David's heart beat as much from frustration as anticipation as he made his way to the house at the end of the French Gulch street. Outside, a purple shay waited and a horse stood head low, one leg bent in respite. *Must be the doctor's rig,* David thought. He swallowed hard. At last, his time had come.

He knocked on the door, rustling the lace curtain sheltering the hand-blown window glass. He carried the white packet wrapped with a black ribbon in his hand. It reminded him of funeral missals, the black marking a death. He guessed Ruth's package did mark a death—of a marriage gone wrong. He knocked again and finally watched the pale outline of a man shimmer behind the curtained glass. Even hunched over, he looked to be the same height as Zane but his hair was white, all white. *Must be an elderly gent, this doctor.* David removed his hat.

Then he noticed or rather heard the shuffle-thump, shuffle-thump sound as the man walked, then stopped, fumbled at the latch. David heard something scrape against the wall as the door opened, saw the crutch fall and the man curse as he bent, one leg in a bracelike contraption.

David replaced his hat and quickly bent to retrieve it. The body that stood before him looked ravaged by coyotes, worn and torn. *White hair? Zane hadn't had white hair. The man had aged a decade. Pathetic.*

"Here," David said. "Let me help you." He reached for the man's elbow.

Zane Randolph raised his head slowly, and the eyes that met David's were cold and empty, eyes he'd first faced at a flesh auction a year or more ago. When they recognized David, they hardened even more.

"Here to steal more of my property, are you?" Zane said. He wrenched away from David's touch as he handed him the crutch.

"Me stealing from you?" David said. He sounded defensive. Zane had drawn first blood. "I helped a woman get free from your clutches, that's all I did."

"Defend your own thievery by blaming others—such gall! How'd you find me? Come on. Speak up, boy!"

"I...we got a poster. The doctor..." He had to get a handle on this. David looked beyond Zane to see if anyone else was there.

"What poster? You've been hunting me, have you? You and your warped virtues, rescuing savages." Zane scoffed.

"No. Miss Martin—"

"You know my Ruth?"

"I...she's—"

"Now you found me. Now what?" Zane laughed.

"I ain't been hunting you. I just came to give you something." He was under control now. Had a purpose. "From Ruth Martin. The woman who bested you," David said. He could tell from the flinch in Zane's eyes that he, too, had struck blood. "She sent you this," David said, thrusting the packet at the man. "You'll be divorced come spring." Zane jerked back as though receiving a blow and lost his balance.

"Take advantage while a man's down," Zane said, scrambling and reaching for his cane.

David wasn't certain what to do. His inclination was to help, but when he extended his hand, the man growled. "Ruth. Always Ruth," he said. "She sends a boy to tower over me."

"I'm not towering over you!" David said. "Here. I'll help you up."

"She thought sending you would keep me from going there to get her?" He laughed. It was a laugh that made David wish again he'd never met this man. He was glad Ruth Martin was on her way. "Nothing will stop me from getting my Ruth."

"She has someone to defend her, to help her out. She doesn't need to worry over the likes of you anymore," David said. He should just go, not worry if the man couldn't get up. It was pointless to try to defend Ruth or himself to such a person.

"Out there, brazen, in the open meadow." The man talked even while he groveled for the crutch, lifted his pegged leg, pulled himself up against the door, struck at David's legs with his one good one. David stepped backward. "She's just teasing me as if I was a lame cat and her a succulent mouse," Zane said. "Well I know where she is—"

"She's safe, I tell you. Safe. Away from you."

Zane glared at David, his eyes in a hollow shell that made David think of a dead coyote's stare. David felt his skin grow cold. He could almost smell the rot of the man. David felt the blood rush to his neck, his face. The man might appear weak, but his spine was made of the devil's fork, just as straight and piercing. David's fingers ached to reach out and press his hands at the man's throat, push against the soft flesh until he felt the spine, shut the eyes that mocked him as he stood.

"And my little Ruthie, ran off, did she? Still fearful?"

"Not of the likes of you. She headed straight to what she always wanted."

"She went north. Didn't she?" he seethed. Zane's words cut like rawhide against uncallused skin, going deep. David willed his eyes not to flicker. "Her brother put Oregon in her head. That's where she's put her tail between her legs and skulked off to, isn't it? Answer me, boy!"

"I—"

Zane laughed then, ending with a raspy breath. "Your eyes answer," Zane said. "You cannot tell a lie even when a life's at stake." Spittle formed at the side of Zane's mouth. "Not a solicitor in the state who won't tell me what I need to know. I've been served papers." He nodded with his chin toward the black-ribboned packet that had fallen to the floor and slid beneath a cabinet. "She may have thought filing for divorce would be the end of us. But Ruth was never one to think things out. You tell her if you see her again before I do. You tell her this from me—if I can't have her, no one else ever will."

With that, he poked at David with his crutch, pushed him out, then slammed the door.

the fence around wisdom

They found a place to bring the wagon through into Ruth's meadow. She already thought of it that way. Her meadow. She dismissed a sudden ache of missing Jumper and took a deep breath from her belly. She'd make this a worthy place to start over if it was the last thing she ever did.

In the morning Matthew and Ruth saddled up to ride into Jacksonville. Matthew must have had words with his mother about it because Lura scowled and slammed the spider in the fire when she cooked up flapjacks for them all. She rattled around in the camp box in the back of the wagon, grabbed a tin of syrup and said, "Waste of time to just ride in there without taking the wagon and getting us vitals, you ask me."

"Time enough for that, Ma," Matthew told her.

Lura wore a hat with a flounce rather than a bonnet, and Matthew touched the ruffle as he spoke, a gesture of affection, as Ruth saw it. But Lura jerked her head away from his hand.

"Time enough for shenanigans, you ask me," she said.

"I haven't," Matthew said, straightening his hat, pushing it forward and back on his head.

"This is no time for courting," Lura said. Ruth felt her face blush.

"We're getting business done here, Lura," Ruth said.

"Business would be buying up supplies, settling on a land claim—"

"Ma, one thing at a time," Matthew said. "We'll be back before sunset."

They rode in silence, Ruth wanting to thank Matthew for his clarifying with Lura, but she found herself shy. Besides, she wanted to savor having found such a fine spot on her own. Well, with Carmine's help. But it was good to have a place to choose, not one chosen for her or requiring Matthew's intervention.

Ruth watched Matthew check his father's pocket watch. "Time's more important than miles in this country," Matthew said by way of explanation. He put the watch back. "On a map it looks like so many miles from here to there, but the underbrush in places or the winding trails makes it a longer journey than you'd think."

"How far north will you look for a place?" she asked.

"Oh, it'll be within a day's ride of wherever you light," he said.

Now she'd find out if he really understood the limits she'd set on their "partnering" in coming north. The land would change their relationship. They were in the mordant stage, the land like the alum and tin that prepared wool yarn to accept dye. She hadn't thought of gathering wool or spinning for a long, long time. Not since Betha, her sister-in-law, had taken the time to show her how. They'd laughed together as Ruth's hands, that were capable of carving fine lithograph designs, fumbled with the alum. Betha had explained each step, then told her, "When the wool is ready, free of lanolin and soap, then it will accept the new color, each strand though different now, ready to become one color, Ruthie. It's not unlike a marriage. The strands are still themselves, but they've blended into one."

"How do you know if you'll get the color you want?"

"Oh, Ruthie, that's the loveliest part. You can't go back. You can't ever get it to be what it once was. You know that going in. So you do what you can to prepare the wool. You choose what color you think you want. Imagine it in your mind, hold that image, that dream to guide you forward. Then I say a little good-bye to the fibers I hold in my hands, knowing they'll never be the same. But the new things I get will have grown out of what I had before. Then I just give my heart to it, to accepting that whatever arrives was just what was meant to be."

"What're you grinning about?" Matthew said, breaking into her memory.

"All the different strands of color there are," she said and kicked Koda to a trot.

They splashed through a wide creek to enter Jacksonville. It proved to be a much smaller version of Shasta City though it bustled with miners and packers. The tip of a Chinese laborer's hat could be seen in the distance. And here, an Indian or two stood tall, prouder than those she saw scurrying in Shasta. Not just a woman or child either, but braves.

As the Chinese man drew closer, Ruth made out a yoke across the man's back with two laundry baskets hanging from either end. A wide-faced man with a heavy body turned to stare, and as they passed him Matthew leaned to her and said, "Kanaka."

"Is that a tribe?"

He shook his head. "Not Indians from here. They were brought here from the Sandwich Islands by Hudson's Bay people. Been here since '51, working the gold mines. Most of them stay at One Horse Town just west of Jacksonville. Along with the Chinese, Negroes, and a few whites. Sometimes you can hear their conch shells blow. I even saw one stout fellow play a flute with his nose."

"His nose?"

Matthew nodded. "All that good breathing learned from diving for pearls in their homeland, they say." Men turned to stare, and Ruth wasn't sure if it was because she wore pants, rode astride, or the mere fact she was a woman. She looked around. Flowers had been planted in a window box or two, so she knew she wasn't the only female in the place.

They soon learned that the section of land Ruth admired could be bought, or at least a land patent applied for. Talk of the stage route coming north added to people's reluctance to set a price for property until they knew for sure if the value would go up or down. But all that mattered to Ruth was that the current titleholder might be willing to sell.

"Section next to it ain't available," the land agent told them. "No good for farming anyway less you want to scratch a field in between the pines." He had a thick neck with layers of fat so that his chin seemed to just sit on his chest. "You can graze the timber. You got goats? Might need them for the brush. Didn't I see you earlier this spring with horses?" He squinted at Matthew. "Out near the MacDonalds' place, wasn't it?" Matthew nodded. "Yup, yup. I remember now. Why don't you set claim on that section then? MacDonalds and their kids moved on. There's more room there. Got the river and all and the view of those flat rocks."

"I like what I picked," Ruth said.

"Got a town and trees between those two sections," he noted on the map. "Be hard to run both places."

Ruth bristled. "I'll run my own place. Mr. Schmidtke here is merely helping me…settle, bring my things north."

"Is he now," the fat-necked man said. The wink he gave Matthew sent a flash of fire to Ruth's face.

"I'll take the current owner's name, if you please," Ruth said, grabbing and releasing her whip handle at her hip.

The agent wrote the name on paper, dropping sand across the ink to dry it quickly. "Yes ma'am. Or is it miss?" he said, hanging on to the edge of the paper longer than needed as he handed it to Ruth.

"It's Missis," she told him, surprising even herself that she would seek safety in that fragile status.

Tipton felt her stomach, stood sideways in the oval mirror. The letter she'd just read from Elizabeth lay folded beside the rose-flowered wash-bowl. There was no doubt about it. She was putting on weight. Chita was right, though she just could not believe yet in Chita's explanation. Still, last night, lying alone in her bed, she'd felt a movement inside of her, a strange fluttering as though a dragonfly had gotten captured inside. She'd sat right up in bed and called out Nehemiah's name before she remembered he wasn't there. He hadn't been there for several nights. Even when he wasn't out on the trail, he'd taken to sitting up in the big chair reading or "keeping the books," he called it. When he came to bed—if he came to bed—she was already asleep. And he was up before she awakened in the morning.

"Taking care of business," he told her. Oddly, his eyes looked sad.

At least she'd gotten Chita to agree to keep their secret. She'd threatened her with the loss of her employment if she breathed a word to Mr. Kossuth, not that she would have. The help didn't speak of such things. Or did they? Chita must have been teasing when she said she'd tell him. Tipton couldn't figure when people teased or not. Tyrellie had said that of her, that she took everything as though meant to damage her rather than the dance of give and take that happened between friends.

But she and Chita were not friends. An employer could not become friends with her employee. It wasn't acceptable, not even here in California where anything seemed proper. Well, she'd been taught how things worked in her father's store back in Wisconsin. And her parents would never have had a conversation with a clerk about his health and certainly not about something so intimate as the state of his gastric juices.

But this small bulge below her waist was more than gastric juice, and the noises it made were far from a sign of her hunger. She wished she could talk with Nehemiah about it.

She imagined him riding through those tall redwoods, he called them, huge trees that towered and made her feel smaller than an ant when she'd seen them the first time. Some of the mules were actually stashed in a barn formed out of a redwood hollow. How could a person feed themselves to fullness in a place where the land dominated, where the winds howled and massive trees disappeared into dark points at the face of the sky? This was a shadowed place—except when she walked on the shoreline.

She looked for her wool shawl, found the plaid bonnet Nehemiah had given her shortly before he left, all the while trying to understand how this…thing could have happened.

Her letter written to Elizabeth must have been so vague that the woman didn't have a whit of insight to give her when she wrote back. She just talked about the tree house and such and just before her closing said that *marshmallow root boiled in butter might relieve gastric ulcers,* if that's what she was having. *Fennel works as a mild laxative, if you've need of that.* She could just see Elizabeth grinning when she wrote that. Then she advised her to try rosemary and quoted the old saying that *where rosemary flourishes, the woman dominates. Not that that's ever been a flaw of yours, now, Tipton, lacking in domination. So I suspect your rosemary plant is large and fragrant. Chew on some and it might help.* Then she'd advised her to get out and take the sea air, that she'd heard it was good for a person, no matter what ailed them. *Dominate your life, Tipton,* Elizabeth had finished.

Tipton didn't dominate a thing in her life. Her husband was off on a long trip taking supplies into mountain towns; her employee acted as familiar as a friend. And now her body was doing things that totally confused her. Gastric ulcers? Indigestion? Hunger? Her arm ached, and she was breathing fast. She placed her tongue on the roof of her mouth to calm herself. Was she hungry? She checked. She had no hunger in her mouth, no hunger in her stomach. But in her heart, she starved.

There was no denying it. A baby. She was pregnant, and she wasn't ready. She tried to let the idea settle in. It could fill her up. More likely, it would empty her and there'd be nothing left. Going away in her mind had not protected her from this. Had probably caused this.

The wind howled against the house. Sand pitted against the boards, sounding like rain. Then it was calm, and she opened the shutter to the shoreline, the ships, and beyond. Funny how the weather could change so abruptly. The vagaries.

Maybe it wasn't too late to change that baby's mind. Maybe if she took enough fennel or if she boiled enough marshmallow root she could cleanse herself of what she wasn't ready for. First a marriage she had just let happen and now this. Dominate your life, Elizabeth had said. Well, she would just do that, starting with finding a way to make this "baby thing" go away.

Ruth wasn't sure what Matthew decided about the north piece he'd eyed. She'd taken the paper from the fat-necked agent and stomped out onto the boardwalk, seeking fresh air, leaving the two men inside. She wondered again how Suzanne had managed to find a good place in Shasta, wandering with her children and Pig as she had. Angels must have been watching over her that day, Ruth decided. She stood in front of Koda at the hitching rail and scratched at the horse's nose, keeping the paper from him, then took in a deep breath.

The climate was hot but dry, not heavy with wet as in Missouri. Matthew's gray horse nickered, and Ruth turned to see Matthew standing behind her. He nodded with his hat across the dirt street. The sign read "Robinson Hotel." Banjo music floated over them. "'Little's Trading Post,'" Matthew read the signs aloud. "'Westgate and Little's Saloon and Bowling Alley.' Maybe we could get a *little* direction, since it seems Mr. Little knows which way the wind's blowing."

Ruth frowned. She wanted to do this alone, but the trip in had taken an hour, and who knew where the owner of her place just might be found?

She started across the street aware that her arm touched Matthew's, his wide hand for just a moment at her elbow. She let it rest there, warmed by his presence, then she pulled away. A woman would be safer in a mining town if she was married. Well, she already was. Best she leave things at that. She stepped away from Matthew's hand. They dodged horse droppings on the dusty street.

After asking a few customers, a man named Smith, whom they

discovered was the owner of her parcel, left the saloon to come outside to talk with Ruth. He eyed her miner's pants and for just a moment, Ruth wondered if her wearing them might prove an obstacle for Smith.

He wasn't really interested in selling, he told her, and kept glancing at Matthew as though wondering why he would "allow" this woman to do the talking and Smith was being asked to indulge her. He frowned at Ruth, kept looking at her. He probably thought her a little daft, wearing the pants; and Matthew her keeper, standing silent beside her. Well, so be it.

Ruth negotiated well, she thought, countering Smith's reluctance to sell at all, and then appealing to his good nature by mentioning that she was raising her brother's children. She didn't fill in all the blanks, of course. He finally relented, having upped the price Ruth had offered by an uncomfortable amount.

Ruth chastised herself when he did, remembering Lura telling her to "never tell your price until you get the seller to name his. You might get it for less than half of what you were willing to pay."

Finally, they came to an agreement and, after he handed the paper to Matthew, Smith said, "Sign right here, sir."

"It's my land to acquire," she said.

"What?" Smith turned on Matthew. "You wasn't just letting her negotiate for practice? Well now. Well now," he said as though for the first time aware of Ruth in her own right. He rubbed at his stubble beard. "How can I be sure you'll make the payment then? I've got to have some guarantee. I'm letting you have use of my place, my land I've cleared, my investment, and what're you offering me? A little cash? I don't even know you, anything about you. A woman alone, right?" He eyed Matthew who nodded.

"With kids? What can I expect from such as you?"

"My word," Ruth said. "I've made it this far, all the way from Ohio. I keep my commitments. I'll sign a contract." She still had some of her brother's estate money, but little after buying Carmine, tending to the children. The divorce filing had taken some. And if she used all the rest to increase the down payment, they'd have nothing to tide them over until she sold the yearlings come spring. "I could make semiannual payments instead of once a year."

"I don't know." Smith pawed the side of his cheek.

"I can make a higher down payment. Maybe a bred mare—Copperbottom strain." She felt her hands grow wet, wondering if it all would just slip away.

"We can find another spot for you, Ruth," Matthew said. "There's no need to—"

"How many?" Smith said, light gleaming in his whiskey-bathed eyes.

"I don't know. Maybe…how many would you want?"

He scratched his chin. "Three mares with foals. But I want standing foals and the mares bred back. And you feed 'em through the winter. No sense my keeping 'em alive."

"Two," she said. "And no cash down then." Ruth swallowed.

"And your fellow cosigns for you."

"No! He's not my fellow. You have my word, my signature, too, if you'll hand me the agreement to sign. And three mares, then, with babies at their side. What more could you possibly want?"

Smith sucked his lip. "I'm thinking this ain't such a good plan." He scratched his reddish nose that led Ruth to think that he'd probably spend any cash he got at Little's Saloon until he only had a little left. "Naw, I think we should just count this up as an afternoon of jawing and let it go at that."

Ruth risked it all: "And a payoff in the spring. In full. Or I forfeit—"

"Ruth! There ain't no need—"

"In full?" Smith was suddenly acting as clever as a hungry coyote.

"Or I forfeit it all." Her heart pounded, her mind raced. She could sell the stud colts as geldings next spring, get them green-broke this winter. She could rent Carmine out to other farmers in the area for a fee.

One or two might want to raise their own farm mule. Maybe she'd have to sell Carmine and wait to see if she had a good colt to raise up as a sire. Or she could take a job doing…laundry as Tipton once had. The yearling fillies could be sold to make the payment, all of them. She'd still have the mares to breed and her jack. It would set her back a full year, but she'd have the land. She'd have to count on last winter being "unusual" in truth and hope they had hay enough without needing tree moss. She couldn't afford to lose any mares or yearlings. It would take all her energy and the children's, too.

She ought to talk with the boys and Sarah and Jessie. See if they were ready to take this on as a family venture. They'd understand, surely they would. Hadn't they found nurture in their land? Their land! It was already hers. She just had to take the risk. She just had to believe she could do this.

"Every penny of the down and the three mares and any improvements made will be yours. I'll move on if I fail to pay you in full."

Smith dropped his hand from his face and grinned. "Oh, I'm a reasonable man. Tell you what. The cash down. Two mares with foals standing in May and you pay me in full then."

One didn't get what one wanted without a little struggle. Betha told her to imagine the color she wanted and then just believe. And Elizabeth said that *believing* in German meant "to belove." Enough belief birthed love which birthed miracles. She'd count on that.

Mazy loaded her milk tins and a ten-pound lard bucket now filled with milk onto the back of her cart. A Yurok Indian woman, a Shasta, and a Wintu worked beside her, helping her lift. It was a strange alliance, begun that night she'd seen the cabin light. They had been outside, leaning like weathered sheaves of wheat against the logs.

The child answered, "They sell hair and head," she lifted her own braid to emphasize, "in Shasta City. They give money to men who carry hair. Make marks and get coins." She held up her fingers, counting to fifteen.

Their faces looked thin as brown paper, eyes distant and lost. "I can't stop the…hunting. I'm only one person," Mazy had said.

"You give bread in Shasta. You. The baker woman. We follow you. Maybe you have milk and place to sleep. Safe."

"Mothers have no milk," the Yurok woman said. She was big-boned, but her cheeks sank in like an old empty squash.

"Milk. Yes. I can get you some that's cooled. And you can stay the night here," she said. "I…I'll have to think of something. Tomorrow."

That had been weeks ago. She'd gotten them some milk. They chewed on wind-dried meat, and then she'd ridden back to town, letting the mule Ink make his way to her mother's. Her mother would have some advice.

Her dream drifted back, the part with the carpetbags and people buying tickets for a journey. She'd been on a trip too and realized then that she still was, would always be. And the pastor at the schoolhouse looking formal yet wearing earth-laden boots meant this, she was sure: that she had lessons to learn on her journey. Sometimes they were shared in sermons on a Sunday when expected. Sometimes they surprised, arriving on familiar soil seen in some new way. She got the lessons if she remained in service. "Are you in service?" her friend had said. These Indian women had offered her a way.

Carrying the lantern beneath a harvest moon, she stabled the mule. "You're late, Daughter," her mother said.

"I had company. At Ruth's." She told Elizabeth of the evening's happening.

"You take out some bread in the morning," Elizabeth said. "I can bake extra."

She'd been afraid they might just stay and told her mother as much. Elizabeth smiled. "Being a servant feels a little different when it's

157

closer to home, don't it? Can't put the need out of your mind so easy." Mazy nodded, dropped her eyes from her mother's. "No need to feel guilty. Even the Lord wanted time to himself. But he always returned to meeting needs where they arrived. That's what you've been given, Daughter. And isn't it time you stopped calling it 'Ruth's place' and made it your own?"

Mazy'd ridden back out in the morning. She brought in Jennifer and Mavis, her Ayrshires, and then herded in three of the Durhams. She separated the calves into one pen and their mothers into another, trying to ignore their bawling. She knew the babies would eventually accept that they could no longer suck. Her Ayrshire calves had already been weaned. After she skimmed the cream from the flat tins that cooled the previous night's milk, she fed some to the calves. She made sure they had rye hay, then poured the cream into the churn and brought the rest of the pale milk to the women.

Then, thinking, she began loading the tins of whole milk from the cooling place at the creek. She couldn't just keep giving the Indians milk. She'd need some for the calves and had planned to use the rest of the skimmings for the pigs she hoped to purchase. And she still wondered if just giving them food for a while would make any real difference in their lives.

She'd leaned over into the water to pull at the handle and lift up the heavy tin, then felt a hand take some of the weight from her.

"Thank you," she said, surprised to look into the eyes of the auntie who had accepted bread and cookies from her that one day in town. Two older girls fiddled with the butter churn, and Mazy signaled them to wait, that she'd show them in a minute while one of the women picked up the scythe near the barn and walked out into the tall grass and began cutting.

"That'll be wasted effort," Mazy said more to herself than anyone else. "The Durhams will stomp it down before it can be sheaved."

"We will take the cows to the trees," one of the older boys said, having obviously overheard her. She nodded agreement. With a stick they began moving the large cows with still-sucking calves slowly away from where the Yurok woman worked. The way Ruth's boys used to, Mazy thought.

She heard a baby cry and told Sula to give it some of the skimmed milk. She watched the mother soak a cloth in it and dribble it into the baby's mouth. Such a simple thing; so essential, her husband might have said. They had found a way to meet essentials through mutual service.

In town, Mazy carried in the milk from the cart while that lazy Charles Wilson watched. He was hatless, so the gouge out of his ear seemed accentuated. She always wondered how that really happened, but no one ever said.

"You're just the kind of man I'd go fishing with," Mazy told him, grunting with the effort to lift the milk tin by herself.

"Why is that, my dear woman?" Charles said. He pushed his fingers into his vest, kept his bad foot raised onto a stool.

"Because I'd know anywhere you'd choose for fishing would be a place of easy catching. A man like you wouldn't want to do any hard labor. Even fishing."

"I've gout," he whined. "Got to take care of myself. Don't want to be stepping into that cold spring out back, just to set in tins of milk. My mother wouldn't want me pushing myself," Charles said. His mouth smiled, but his eyes stayed cold as a widow's hands in winter.

"And you sure wouldn't want to distress your mama, now would you?" Mazy said.

Adora stepped out of the doorway. "He does not distress me in the least, truth be known." She patted his head, and he jerked away. She laughed, an awkward sound. "Charles's health puts pressure on him; still, he stays, so helpful. Such a sacrifice for him. Wouldn't have wanted to be tied down to a mercantile, now would you?" She smiled. "But who knows, maybe Nehemiah will take over this store when I pass. He's a good man."

Sacrifice? That word wasn't in Charles's vocabulary. Mazy wondered if Nehemiah knew of Adora's hopes for him and Tipton returning someday. She hadn't heard that before.

"We get so many requests for your butter, Mazy, especially from new arrivals. I hope this isn't just a one-time thing. We'd like to have you regular, wouldn't we, Charles?" Adora said.

"Regular," Charles said.

"Lura always said buying from you made the most sense," Adora told her.

"I usually sell all my extra to Gus at the St. Charles," Mazy told her. "And Washington's Market has been a steady contract. Just happens I promised Lura I'd bring you some before they left. Just today though. Don't count on it."

"But now with your added herd, you'll surely have enough," Charles said. "That's a long journey back and forth to town each day." His large head of tight little curls always made Mazy think of a drawing of Julius Caesar she'd once seen. Charles had a noble look if not a noble heart. "But that's right. You've taken the lease Miss Martin had and are staying on there. Finally separating from your mama. What I hear, your mama has interests of her own. So you'll be alone out there now with your dairying."

She usually didn't pay much attention to anything Charles Wilson said. But she wasn't sure what he was getting at about her mother; and she didn't like the prickles rising at her neck as she thought of Charles being the one to comment on her being out at Poverty Flat alone. Well, with the Indians there, she wasn't.

"But why won't they milk them?" Mazy asked the Yurok woman with the black hair so thick it must have weighed as much as five pounds of coal.

"They kick," the woman said.

"They kick. Well, yes the cows do sometimes, but you can tell when they're about to. If your arm is where it needs to be, by their back legs, you can avoid their kick, keep them from getting the bucket or you."

"I cut grass and bring in grain. I feed calves. We take cows to hills. Help with tins. Girls make butter."

Mazy had already offered to pay them a wage for their work. She didn't know if she had built enough housing for them. It would be cold soon, even in the daytime. Some of the children had slept up in the tree house.

The women's help with the heavy work was welcomed. But it was help with the milking that would relieve her most and allow her to take the bull south and to meet the new demands she had. She guessed she could do without pigs for a while.

But the women were afraid. Maybe she could get the children interested. After all, they'd climbed to that tree house without a hesitation. Her mother always said that fear was a way to remind herself to just take the next step. "Most everything new is a little frightening the first time," her mother said. "That's how courage is built. Don't see no babies giving up trying to walk just because they stub their nose a time or two."

And hadn't she stubbed her nose a time or two, Mazy thought. But there had always been a way to get back up, someone to help her do it. Just like now. These people arriving when they did had to be for a reason. She just didn't believe in coincidence anymore. It was all divine intervention.

"Chopped-ear man riding in," Sula told her, running out of breath. Mazy looked at the trail coming from Shasta. "Charles Wilson? Is it?"

The child nodded, still catching her breath. "I tell him you are not here."

"No," Mazy said, hesitating. "But tell him I'm busy cleaning out the privy. Can you do that?" The girl nodded. "And come get me just as soon as he's gone."

Sula signaled and the others disappeared into the trees, the boys taking the cows with them, the women moving into the cabin. Mazy went to put lime down the outhouse hole so the girl wouldn't be telling a lie. She didn't expect to hide out there long. She doubted he'd hang around with that kind of work waiting to be done. She imagined Charles riding up, staying mounted when he approached the child, dust spilling over onto the girl's bare feet.

She couldn't do it. What if he decided Sula was a vagrant, a fish to be whisked away? She turned, felt her own heart start to pound faster, and marveled at the child's willingness to stand so small beside the man's horse, to not turn and run.

In that moment, she knew she had been running long enough on this journey: from the past, from facing strong feelings, from her own fears.

She was a strong woman, a capable woman, even if she did make mistakes, even if she did sometimes cause others pain, even if she did feel fearful at times. Just because she sometimes did less than she was capable of doing didn't make her a bad person. It just meant she was human, not someone unworthy or lower than dirt. Maybe she couldn't help *all* these Indian people. Maybe she couldn't mend her relationship with Ruth. Maybe she couldn't rewrite the past. But she could certainly learn something from the effort.

And she could certainly stop the Charles Wilsons of the world from intimidating her into being a woman she wasn't. She went back to stand beside the child.

in pursuit

"I want you staying in close, Mrs. Kossuth," Nehemiah told Tipton. "No more walking on the beach for a time without me please."

"Why?" Her eyes were innocent, but her heart pounded. Had he discovered that she'd been asking around at the Chinese doctor's for ways to "cleanse herself?" She hoped not. She hadn't had any luck anyway. Those foreigners pretty much kept to themselves. It had occurred to her to approach one of the women who worked at the saloons, most seemed an unsavory sort who would know what she needed. But Lura said some of them were just banking in there, not doing the things people thought they were. Esty acted…chaste enough, the friend of Suzanne's who had opened her own millinery. She did have a flair for style, though nothing Tipton would have chosen to wear. So how would she find someone?

Tipton swallowed. What would Elizabeth say if she knew…

"Mrs. Kossuth? Tipton?"

"I'm sorry. I was lost in thought," she said. "Tell me again."

"Apparently the rumors you heard were not random," Nehemiah said. Tipton tried to remember what rumors she had told him. "Much as I hate the rain, I'll be pleased come spring to have it return. Settle these miners by sending them back to work. Too much idle time." He poked at the center of the newspaper, folded it. "And I can't understand what's holding up the forming of reservations. They were authorized to provide protection for the Indians, but nothing's happening. So these people," he poked again at the paper, "are being left for slaughter."

"What people?" she asked.

"All of them. Tolowas, Wintus, Shastas, Hoopas, Karuks, all of the northern tribes that are left. So you just be staying close at home, all right, Mrs. Kossuth? At least until this latest upset subsides."

He obviously didn't want to tell her any details of "the latest," which was probably just as well. But what would she do cooped up here?

When he left to go to the warehouse, Tipton read the *Herald.* It was not a good decision. Someone had chosen to recount atrocities done by Indians to the white settlers in years past. Pack strings had been regularly attacked, mining camps ambushed and shot up. Unprovoked attacks by Indians on simple miners just seeking gold, not hurting anyone. She hadn't thought of Nehemiah being in danger from the Indians when he took supplies in, only that the weather had been a trial! Tipton wondered why Nehemiah never told her of his business trials. Maybe he was trying to protect her? That thought hadn't occurred to her; she had always attributed his warnings to her as his way of making her behave.

It was the last thing Mazy Bacon needed that morning, Charles Wilson at her door. Just yesterday, she'd received a letter from the Sacramento lawyer saying Jeremy's brother expected her to bring Marvel, the cow brute, south. Now. Before spring. Before any more time lapsed.

David had come back from his encounter with Zane Randolph more rattled than rested, telling her he thought he might have given Zane some direction for pursuing Ruth. She'd assured him Ruth wou'' understand. "Her solicitor will most likely have to say something about where she is anyway. Maybe not detailed."

But David had not been easily calmed. Zane Randolph incited the worst in otherwise sound people.

David didn't bring up the milking, and she didn't either, deciding to let the subject just drift.

And now this. *Charles Wilson showing up.* As if she didn't have enough trouble already. He stepped off his horse and winced. The last time, she'd managed to send him off by suggesting that she did have that privy to clean.

"Mrs. Bacon," he began. "What a lovely morning, isn't it? Brisk day." He used the horse to steady himself, brushed at the heavy rubber rain gear, flashed the cape open to reveal his vest, green-striped as a melon, then rubbed his hands of the morning cool.

The weather was so wretched, she'd have to invite him in to get warm.

Maybe he really did have trouble with gout, Mazy thought, though she doubted it. His malady always appeared to serve him just when someone needed his brawn at his mother's store. Mazy looked at his wide face framed by tight blond curls. He stood just shorter than her, but had broad shoulders, a perfect physique but for the notch in his ear that now drew her attention.

"Ah, Mrs. Bacon," he said. His hand flicked at his ear. "You've made a fine place for yourself. All your little helpers nicely organized, I see." Charles nodded toward the plank huts marked by wisps of chimney smoke disappearing through the trees.

Mazy had used some of the money Seth had loaned her to buy the Durhams and pay for the lumber and their wages. She supposed they were spending it in town so people did know they were out there. Thank goodness she wasn't alone with the likes of Charles Wilson coming to call.

"Whyever would my status interest you?" Mazy asked.

"Will you never forgive my lapse in brotherly...well, filial love? I was in my own state of grief, uprooted from my home, my future, my father lost and all. Grief does unusual things to a soul. Changes a personality. You should know that."

Mazy felt her face turn hot. "When we needed you most, you took yourself far away. Leaving your mother and sister and the rest of us on that trail."

"My dear sister. Still, see how you've weathered. You're the stronger for it." He swept his arms in a wide arc. "Got some little orphans to help with your cows and their mamas to do your cooking."

"I pay them," she defended.

"Oh, to be sure. You do good things, Mrs. Bacon. To be sure." He turned back to her, lowered his voice. "You're more alluring now than ever. Nothing entices a man like the scent of a successful, generous woman."

Mazy's skin prickled as though spiders spread their legs over her arms and the back of her neck. She remembered when Charles Wilson stood too close beside her at his family's mercantile back in Cassville. She'd shivered back then, too.

"Is there something I can do for you, Mr. Wilson? As you noted, I have much work to do. You're welcome to warm yourself at the barn before you head back."

"My mother suggested I ride out to engage you in negotiations about milk and butter on a more permanent basis. Seems the demand for such in Shasta City grows along with your herd. What with your Wintus churning up a storm, in the most positive ways, certainly, we thought we might get you to settle on a contracted amount instead of this somewhat inconsistent overflow. Difficult to do business without predictable products," he said.

"I'd forgotten," she said. "You're not one of the remittance men, are you?"

This time his sculpted features hardened. "I am not a remittance man, as you well know. Those are 'kept men.' No one back in the States is paying me to keep away. My family took everything I might need back home and sold it." His bitterness surprised her. She hadn't thought he cared much for his father's business, and Adora's comments earlier had seemed to confirm it.

"You could always go back. Start again if you have a mind to."

"Ah, such passion, Mrs. Bacon, to have me out of your way. So enticing."

"Men can be thick as tree trunks," she said, shaking her head.

"Let us discuss our dairy needs then, shall we?"

She hated doing business with Charles. But it was apparently going to be one of the compromises she'd have to make in this new venture she'd undertaken. Expanding her herd meant more milk, which required wider distribution. Gus Grotefend had rebuilt the Shasta Hotel and ordered up all his dairy supplies from her now. He urged her to consider cheesemaking, too. He'd been spending time at her mother's bakery… Was Gus courting her mother? Surely not.

Back to business. She had an order in for more chickens and planned to get a goat or two in the spring to walk the butter churn treadmill, saving the children from that onerous task. They hadn't shown any interest in learning to milk yet, so she was totally on her own with that. And twenty cows two times a day took its toll in time.

She did indeed have milk and dairy to sell. She just didn't like the idea of having to deal weekly with Charles Wilson.

"I'll tell you what," he said, moving in closer to her so that she could smell the tobacco on his breath. "Let's not talk about it as a cash commodity. Let's consider what you might take in trade." He grinned at her, and she felt the spiders crawl again.

"Books of cloth," she said and stepped backward, pacing and counting on her fingers as though making up a list. She needed to do something to keep him from traveling farther along the deranged trail his voice suggested. "And leather shoes. Several pairs of different sizes. Wool blankets. And fruit. Lemons, oranges, or citric acid if you can't get those fresh. The children need them to prevent scurvy."

"Well, well. And I'd be happy to deliver them for you here," Charles told her. "And pick up the milk and butter each day. That would save you time and labor, now wouldn't it, Mazy?" He had a gravelly voice that might have been intriguing in another man, but with Charles it just grated further on her nerves.

"Mrs. Bacon to you," she corrected.

Marvel bellowed from his pen, and a new idea shot through her. "I could use your help. With a delivery."

"Anything to be of assistance to you, *Mrs. Bacon*," he said. "Anything at all."

She might pay a price for this later, but for now, she could rid herself of two difficult males with one remittance.

Zane Randolph felt strong enough to try the shay. If O'Malley had done what he was told to, the side boards would be cut down so Zane could lift himself into it more easily. If he didn't try soon to head over the mountains, it would be spring before he could. He wanted Ruth to know that he had plans for their divorce, plans to intervene. He smiled. It would all work out so well. A divorce in California was a treasure, pure and simple. Especially with an industrious mate. Ruth surely was that.

The jehu becoming frazzled told him he could take on whomever he must, despite The Stub, as he'd taken to calling his leg. Zane grinned. And see how getting rattled spoiled a thing? Ruth's solicitor would have to tell him where she was. Zane could make him. More importantly, Zane could see how easily he, too, could allow emotion to overcome him. That was what had happened before, when he'd threatened the doctor; when he'd taken Jessie while wanting to see Ruth's face in agony. He must calm himself, not allow the moment to unsettle him.

He looked out the window. O'Malley should be back. It was December, and still they'd had no snow to speak of, just some drizzles— enough to replenish a few of the smaller streams. If he were lucky, he'd head on into Oregon Territory by Christmas. What a lovely gift to give himself.

Zane reread the letter. It shouldn't have surprised him, not after all that time, and yet he'd felt a fury burst like a lantern lobbed against a wall. How dare she be the one to claim the need to be set free. He was the one held hostage—by her betrayals, her escaping west, his now mangled body. Yet she wanted out, wrote despicable things about him. The marriage, dissolving away like whiskey into sand.

He'd tossed the papers into the dirt, stomped on them with the crutch, and then the wooden peg of his leg until the stump ached from the pain of it.

That wretched O'Malley arrived to lift him up, and Zane saw the pity in the man's eyes. The same look that David Taylor gave him when he'd first seen him, before Zane had managed to rattle that kid's thinking.

"Sure now and you've gotten yourself into a state," O'Malley said, hauling him to his feet.

"Just leave me," Zane told him.

"Would these be yours then?" the man continued, picking up the papers, pocked now with the peg's impressions, brushing off the dirt.

Zane ripped the papers from the man's hands. "Help me outside," he'd hissed, his breath coming in raspy beats. "I'm heading north."

"I doubt that," O'Malley told him, and Zane had struck out at him with his crutch, flailing about. O'Malley had lifted him and carried him to the cot like a child.

The humiliation still burned at Zane's face. He must not lose control. He must stick with a plan; adjust it slowly, only as needed.

Today the plan was to see if he could indeed get himself into the shay and then attempt to drive it. Up and down the street for now. He looked out the window. Good, O'Malley had hitched the horse.

He strapped the contraption onto The Stub. It still hurt, more than he thought it should. The crutch beneath his armpit rubbed too. O'Malley had suggested Zane wait until he was stronger with his chest and arms. "Your legs'll be working, but it's your arms that'll be lifting you. And you're weakened by the healing."

Zane scoffed. Today he would hoist himself into the shay and drive it.

He made his way to the door, the crutch helping him balance. He thump-walked to the side of the shay.

The horse turned and wiggled its ears back and forward, snorted. She didn't like what she saw. Even Zane could tell that.

"Put your crutch inside then," O'Malley told him, coming up from behind him.

"I need no help from you," Zane said.

Zane stood in front of the opening to the carriage, leaned the crutch against the side, turned around. He would sit in the box at the cutaway, push back, then pull himself up to the seat, reach over the side for the crutch, lift the reins, and be off. That was his plan.

But when he turned and pushed against the shay, he knocked the crutch. It slid away, the sound causing the startled horse to lurch forward, rolling the buggy. The movement pitched Zane onto his knee and jammed the pegged one.

"Hey, hey! Hold that blasted animal!" Zane shouted.

But it did no good. The horse remained tied to the post, and Zane slid as though in slow motion to the ground beside it.

"Here then—"

"Get away from me! Away!" Zane gulped huge mouthfuls of air.

"Let me be helping you up then—"

"Leave me!"

And there he sat, struggling and pulling, grabbing the crutch, trying to get his good leg out from under him while the pegged one pointed in accusation. By the time he'd pulled himself up, hanging on to the footstep of the shay, twisting himself to grab the crutch, he was exhausted. Sweating. His leg throbbed as though his heart beat within it.

"Enough for today," Zane said. He'd begin working on his arm and chest strength in the morning.

"He's gone!" Sterling Powder shouted.

"Who's gone? The boys?" Suzanne asked, standing quickly.

"No, no. The dog. Your Pig. He's simply taken off." Suzanne thought he sounded genuinely sorry.

"Was there a cat about?" Esther asked. "He never liked cats. He chased them back in Shasta."

"We were simply out for a walk. My cats are caged, Mrs. Maeves, and I did not see any on the streets. He just bolted and ran. I'm so sorry." He spoke rapidly, upset.

"Did you call for him?"

"Oh, yes. Even your Clayton did."

"Clayton called the dog?"

"He repeated me. I was quite impressed."

Suzanne felt as though she'd stepped into a puddle of disappointment surrounded by a pool of joy. "Clayton talked. Did you hear that, Esther? What did he say? Exactly?"

"He said, 'Come back you...dog.' Of course I repeated his name and called to him despite the wary looks of others wondering why I should be calling a pig, but nothing. He leaped over a picket fence, ran through a yard, and was gone."

"The leash. Did he have it on? Will it tangle him?"

"He had only his collar. I am sorry, Mrs. Cullver. Perhaps it was all the commotion, all the changes brought on by your...activities."

"Yes, perhaps," she said. "Well, Clayton, Son, come here. You, too, Sason. So you can talk! That's wonderful." She felt for her son's head, patted his eyes and face, then brought her hand around his small shoulders. She felt something strange just at the back of his head.

"He has a nick here. A little scab?" she asked.

"While I was cutting his hair. He wiggled a bit."

"I don't remember asking you to cut his hair," she said.

"It is part of a...tutor's duty. I just assumed. I took the liberty of cutting Sason's hair as well."

"Sason's little curls? You cut his curls off? I loved wrapping them in my fingers."

"He was mistaken for a girl, Mrs. Cullver. More than once when we walked about."

"Perhaps they need less walking about," Suzanne said. She heard a quiver in her voice, swallowed. "Without their mother and now without Pig." She must think clearly about just what influence Sterling Powder had in her life, her boys' lives. Was it all good?

Ruth had agreed to let Matthew and Lura and Mariah stay. Lura had been happy enough to keep going, to find "their place." And Ruth would have been happy with them all moving off, with her and her family at last alone, making or breaking by what they could do together as one.

"You've committed yourself to making a rope with a whole bunch of strands," Matthew told her. "It's foolish to tell anyone who could help to just walk on."

"But don't you want to get your land grant?"

"I will. We will. But that doesn't mean we can't stay on here and help you through the winter before we do."

"I don't need help. I told you that before we left. Escorting me up here was fine. But now—"

"I know, I know. All right then. You'd be helping me and mine. That's the truth of it. I wouldn't be worrying over what was happening to you and the kids here, that's true enough. But there's talk of the Takelmas and Rogues acting warlike, and we'd be safer in a cluster here than all spread out. If they're peaceful, we can get work done to your place. And Mariah would have playmates and Ma a woman friend. It's selfish, I know. I'm making the offer from pure self-interest."

She glared at him. "Pure self-interest."

"Yes ma'am. You already got a roof. Needs some work, but it's shelter. Won't be any way we can build us one other than a lean-to in the woods before snow flies full. Be doing us a neighborly favor to let us stay and help get things buttonhooked before winter. You've got a pistol or two if we have to defend ourselves. There's strength in numbers. Come spring, we'll be on our way."

" 'Give Mariah a playmate and your ma a woman friend,' " Lura said while Ruth eavesdropped later outside the wagon. "Since when have I needed you to find me friends? And your sister's way past playmate time. Have you looked at her lately? She's a young woman."

"She's only thirteen, Ma."

"That's the sorriest suitor argument I ever heard," Lura said. "You've got some other motive under your hat, is my guess. The way you've been lookin' at Ruth." She wasn't sure how she wanted him to answer, smiled at his sputtering.

"I'm not her suitor, Ma. I'm her friend. That's all. Nothing more."

"Her friend." Lura scoffed. "What do you take me for? A seven by nine?"

And so they'd set to work. They assessed the cabin first. While Matthew checked the chimney that failed to draw, Jason shimmied up a tree and dropped onto the roof at the chimney, broke free a bird's nest settled there. Moss grew on the shake shingles, and he called down to Matthew with estimates of how many they'd need to replace to keep the snow and rain out.

Mariah and Lura and Sarah took the ox wagon into town with a list of the staples they needed to survive the winter. Additional flour, salt, lard, chickens if they could be had, alum, saleratus for raising dough and onions, lemons, oranges, apples, raisins, figs, or any other fruits or vegetables—dried or otherwise—they could muster in town or anywhere in between. "Pick up some cough syrup and whiskey, too," Matthew said. "For medicinal purposes."

They were also to bring back sacks of grain for the horses, nails and hammers, shakes already made, if available. Poverty Flat had provided much while they lived there and had come already furnished. Now they were starting from scratch. "I'll start us an account at the mercantile," Lura said, and Matthew nodded yes before Ruth could protest.

"You can keep track," he told her. "I know you want to do it all on your own."

"Don't you want to go along, Jessie?" Ruth asked. "Sarah and Mariah are going. Lots of interesting things to see. Might be awhile before we get back into Jacksonville again."

The girl shook her head. "I want to stay with you," she said.

"I'll be working. Got lots to do. Boys'll be splitting rails yet this afternoon. We'll need to be sweeping out the cobwebs and piling in all the bedding we took out of the wagon. Are you up to that? "

"I know it," she said, that little chin jutting out.

"You can help then," Ruth said, and they waved Lura and the girls off.

"What about the Indians, Mommy?" Jessie asked when they carried in the blankets and a stack of flannel sheets.

Ruth turned to see if they had visitors, then remembered. "Were you listening to Matthew talk about that?" she said. Jessie nodded. "Well, don't you worry. He wouldn't have let his mama and sister go off with your sister, Sarah, if there was any real danger. Besides, that Lura, she's a good shot. She could protect herself."

"But what about us?"

"Us? We're fine," she said. "Come here." Ruth pulled her daughter to her, felt again that rapid heart rate. "We're fine. We're just fine. We're home. See? This is our place. You don't have to be afraid here." She had to remember to tell Matthew not to bring up frightening things in front of this fractured child. "Your mama's got her whip, and your brothers can shoot a rifle. And Matthew, I'm sure he knows how to take care of people."

"But what can I do if something happens? What will I do?" She started to cry.

"You're safe here, Jessie. We'll keep you safe. Don't you think we can?"

"But what will I do?" She almost screamed it now, her breathing coming fast. She was going into one of those fits.

"You'll be fine. You're with me. I'll keep you safe." It was more than a promise—it was her prayer.

Tipton did slip out, just to stand in front of the cabin, her pink cashmere wrapped around her. It was getting dark, and Nehemiah hadn't yet come back. In the distance, she heard drums and high-pitched singing. How close were those Indians? She looked south, toward the bay. Sometimes sound carried farther than she would have imagined, but she thought she might even see firelight flickering at the shore. She looked up behind the house. Timbered trees and vines clung there, tree stumps twice as tall as she. She thought if she stood up on one, she might be able to see farther. But there wasn't any way to climb them. And besides, it was probably nothing. There was some dance this time of year when the Indians were said to gather. A Nay-dosh, they called it. Funny how it came almost at the same time as their Advent season, getting ready for Christmas. That was probably all it was.

She walked back in and lit the candles in all the windows. It was a still night. Nehemiah would like coming home to the light shining.

She'd fallen asleep when he arrived, rolling a barrel.

"Where have you been?" she said. "I was…worried."

"Worried? I'm sorry, Tip—Mrs. Kossuth. I went to the warehouse, and the *Columbia* came in. There was a barrel for you from Shasta City. I thought you'd want it, so I stayed late to check everything in yet tonight. You were worried?" he repeated.

"I read the *Herald*," she said. "And I heard the drumming."

"Now, nothing for you to worry your pretty head about. I think it's just that winter dancing gathering. A celebration. You were worried," he

175

said again, as though she'd just told him he was the handsomest man on earth.

They opened the barrel, unleashing the scent of mint and wood smoke. "It's the quilt," she said. "I won the first year. I can't believe Mazy got it finished. She must have had help. Lots of it!" She spread the quilt over her lap and ran her small hand over the stitching, liking the contrast of a new satiny piece next to the roughness of a worn piece of wool. She read Mazy's letter and got the news. And when her husband's eyelids dropped, she pulled her cashmere shawl around his shoulders and let him sleep.

She carried the quilt into the bedroom and looked at each block, each story blending the past with the present. They were like photographs almost, catching each event of the past, yet somehow changed when seen in this present, each observer creating something new from it.

She found Mazy's block: a log house with a black dog before it. Of course. Then her eye caught Ruth's quilt block about "telling the truth." Had she been telling herself the truth? About this…baby? Something in the stories gave her courage to look into her past and remind herself. Since Tyrell's death, the time when she'd felt the strongest was when she'd thought she was the weakest. She'd washed clothes and boiled shirts. There'd been dignity in those tasks, that was a truth. She'd tended to her mother, met all their needs, and hadn't sold herself in the process as some women like Esty Williams had. Had Adora appreciated her determination? No. That was true too. Yet she'd felt a little righteous about being the one to do it, rather than her brother, Charles. Dear Charles.

And if she was totally truthful, she'd accepted Nehemiah's marriage offer as a way to set her and her mother on a safe and steady course for their lives. She'd done all that for nothing. Simply to please a woman who couldn't be pleased. She'd come to Nehemiah falsely, and he was a good man.

Maybe God was punishing her now for her less-than-humble

thoughts. Maybe that was why God had given her a gentle man who went away often and allowed her to become with child before she'd grown up herself.

That was another truth. She was with child. No amount of walking or cleansing could wash away her tender breasts, her burgeoning waist-line, and the ache in the back of her legs. Now the question was whether to tell Nehemiah the truth.

Surely he'd be happy. But it would also set their lives on a course that Tipton had come to falsely. She'd married him for the wrong reasons. And they were both suffering. Into that, she'd add a third being who would grow up as the offspring of confusion. How could any good come of that—this mess she'd created? She needed to go away, that was what she needed.

No wind rattled the shutters. The storms that had shut down all the coast's mining activities leaving the miners in town, spending freely in Crescent City, had ceased for the night. But she could still hear the drums. She pictured the faces of the angry men she'd seen in town.

The paper had called the men "exterminators." They would rid the country of Indians. "There've been some uprisings of late, but mostly Indians defending themselves," Nehemiah had told her when he came back. "That fellow named Tipsey keeps his people riled up and yet in hand. Just get through the winter now and we'll be all right, I think. They're just celebrating. No reason for the exterminators to interfere."

She picked up the pistol he'd given her for when he was away. She'd expected the stock to feel like a snake, be cold and slimy, but the wood felt warm in her hands, firm. And when she'd later commented about it, Nehemiah said, "Snakes are warm-blooded, too. They're quite fascinat-ing. They molt, you know. Give up their entire skin every year. Most vulnerable then, to predators, though they have few. I have a book on them here somewhere, if you'd like to read more. Can never know too much." Always teaching. That was their marriage: Him always teaching, her a student who didn't like paying attention.

stimulating change

Oltipa Taylor laid her hand on her husband's damp head. She'd just washed his face with a brew of laurel leaves, hoping it would soothe away the headache he complained of. David's head nestled into her lap as she sat. Oltipa drifted the backs of her fingers across his forehead like a dragonfly skirting the water. She loved this David Taylor. It was not the love she'd shared with the father of her son. That love had been fiery, made full following the union of their Wintu families. But this love had been plucked from the strands of a broken dream, formed anew through one stranger's helping of another. This love had been sewn into the fabric of a friendship until finally, now, it was a filling-up love of a husband to a wife.

Still, she could not seem to comfort him after his time with the Randolph man. She grimaced with even the thought of that one. She shook her head. David sighed. "You feel better now, na?" she asked.

"A little," he said. He opened his eyes to stare at her. "Doesn't pound quite so much."

"You think of the Randolph man?"

He nodded. "And…the restlessness of people like the exterminators, people like that." He pinched his eyes closed. "Worried more about them right now. You won't be safe here. I don't know how to make that different."

He lay silent a long time, and she wondered if he would talk further.

She liked this talking thing he did, this speaking of his heart. The father of her son had never done this thing. Perhaps he had thought it made him weak. She did not find it weak to make such talk. A heart that could be shared must be strong to risk such wrenching and giving away and yet remain whole.

"I felt so stupid," David Taylor said. "He made me ornery. I lost my temper." He ran his hands through his hair. "Didn't avenge you or Ben or Ruth neither. Made things worse. The man looked even more mean-spirited, if that's possible. Arrogant and pitiful all at once."

"I do not know this word, *arrow-gant*."

"Scrappy and acting bigger than he really is. Like he doesn't have a bone of regret over what he did to you and Jessie and Ben."

"Nothing whips him still?"

David snorted. "Nothing whips him. That's right. I wouldn't put it past him to just show up here. Try to right what he thinks went wrong." He pressed her hand against his eyes, held it there. She could feel the throbbing at the side of his head.

"It is no good to poke at a fire gone out," she said.

He lay thinking, she decided. He thought of things often, turning them around and around the way the dog turned before it plopped down to sleep. It had been weeks since he'd gone, and still he let this Randolph man sting at their family like a hungry wasp. She wished she could take away his worry, take away his head pain, give him new things to think of. "You make yourself weary," she said. "Old wounds need wrapping, tied tight in rawhide so they do not get out to spoil what lies around them. They heal then. Leave no scar."

He opened one eye and cocked his head a bit to look at her. "Well, aren't you the wise one," he said. His face held a smile.

"I only want what is good for you, David Taylor."

He reached up and pulled her head, rubbed her nose with his. "And that's just one reason why I love you," he whispered. "Only one of many." He kissed her then, held the back of her head with his hand.

Oltipa heard the dog squeal. "Put the *sookoo* down," she told Ben, breaking the kiss with David. "Come. Sit beside me now, na?" She patted beside her as she moved out from under David's head still in her lap. She laid his head gently on the furred hide, and the dog hopped up onto the bed. Ben whimpered, but Oltipa gave him her silencing look.

"Ben's feeling left out," David said. "Takes it out on the dog."

Oltipa nodded, not liking the biting tone in his voice. She wished the tension between him and her son could be lessened. Perhaps if he could have more time with Ben, more time to play as he once talked of. He worked always, keeping them safe. She worried that he worked too much; worried that the boy could be taken. He needed her, needed her. Now, even more.

David Taylor had learned of the massacre near Crescent City. Another on the Smith River. Exterminators, they said. White men seeking revenge and bounty.

People…her people, others from the coast and lands in the shadow of Shasta Mountain, had traveled for the dancing, a time of joy and celebration. Instead they had been slaughtered while the pileated woodpecker feathers from their headdresses bobbed in the breeze. Killed while they danced. Men, women, children, even babies asleep in their boards were taken, babies asleep between their parents in their lodges, their heads set onto sticks like salmon roasted at fires.

She shivered, gazed at her husband's face, made herself see only his eyes of kindness and not the faces of so many of his race that hunted, wounded while they laughed. David Taylor was not like this.

She knew he wanted safety for her and that he could not take them with him to ensure it. She did not wish to live in Shasta City where she would be alone while he was gone. And she knew he wished to drive the stagecoach, the tall Concord, as he had before so he could be with them every two or three moonlit nights.

Mazy Bacon had once asked them to live with her, to milk the cows, but David had resisted. Who was she, a mere Wintu woman, to suggest that this was a way to keep them safe where he could still travel? Who was she to contradict what had been his answer once? "I'm no cow-hand," he'd told Oltipa.

"Maybe we go visit Elizabeth Mueller soon," she offered. "Maybe she will find pleasure in Ben and offer something for your headaches."

David nodded.

"We could take Ben and visit Mazy Bacon, too." There, she'd risked it.

David grunted.

"There are Wintus there."

"So I've heard." He paused. "Say, do you know some of those women?"

"It is likely. We all know someone who knows another until we find out who is family, who is friend. It is good to know this so a young man does not choose to love someone who turns out to be his cousin. This was not our concern, you and me," she teased.

"No. It's pretty certain I ain't your cousin." He grinned. "Families sure are made up of strange batches. I wrote my sister, and it's as though I didn't exist. She doesn't write back or come to visit."

"Maybe she does not get the letter."

"I didn't think of that," he said. His face brightened. "You're good for me, Oltipa. Keep me from always just seeing the worst. My mother used to do that. Always had a verse or two to help me through the hard places. Seems to me my father tended to the miserable at times too. I don't remember that he was, but I mostly remember him working and working, until that day he left."

Ben shouted from across the room. He was crawling near the bas-kets where Oltipa kept her dried fish and ground acorn flour. He pounded his flat fist on the basket, turned to see if he had her attention. Oltipa scowled at him, telling him to wait with her eyes. "I need to be up and doing," David said.

Oltipa was sorry they'd moved from the place in their conversation where they spoke of heart things. It had happened before. And now that she thought of it, it usually followed something Ben did.

"We go to visit?" she said. "To Mazy Bacon's?"

"You really want to go there? Well, sure. We could go see some of your friends. Probably glad they're safe there, after what happened."

"They are safe there," she said. "As we are safe with you."

"I hope so."

He worried over them, she knew. A good wife would help ease his burden.

Rain fell on the newly shaked roof, patting against it as persistently as an orange Flicker tapping out his territory. Suzanne found the sound soothing, a new noise helping her know a different place. The even rhythm blocked out the scruff and scrape of Esther's efforts to put the room in order. Suzanne supposed that if she could see things she'd feel differently. She imagined trunks and toys in various stages of finding their places. She indulged in that picture for only a moment, returning instead to the comfort of the rain while it lasted, a momentary reprieve from a gnawing emptiness.

Esther had been the one to locate the house, just beyond the burned area that had taken Sacramento the year before, a ravaging fire that threw flames into the sky so high people said it could be seen for a hundred miles. Their new house had been scorched from the heat, but its owners had dumped buckets of dirt on the shakes and had spent the night on top of their house, flapping at sparks with their blankets and shirts. Suzanne imagined them standing triumphant with soot-blackened faces in the morning, joyous for having saved their home.

"Is the house next door made of clapboard or brick?" Suzanne thought to ask as Esther worked.

"Brick. The new ones are all of brick," she said. "Came in by ship, I hear. Ballast, then sold to the highest bidder."

"So Californian," Suzanne said. "Making something go twice as far."

"For twice the cost," Esther said. "It's a tragedy that they put so much work into saving their home only to leave it a year later." Esther clucked her tongue in that way she'd begun, and Suzanne imagined her shaking her head. "Gold just keeps drawing people from one thing to another."

"I've often thought of it as their Devil's Mill, the thing that lures them in, looking like a treasure but turning quickly to ruin. I know a song about that Devil's Mill."

"When will it all stop?"

"Does change ever?" Suzanne offered. She noticed again something more in Esther's words, some underlying meaning she hadn't translated in her mind. "It can be good for a person, change can."

"I certainly hope this one satisfies you. At least for a while," Esther said. She continued quickly, "It tires you to have to learn new routines and where things go and memorize the room with your hands. It will certainly be simpler if we can get settled now and stay." Suzanne smelled the scent of lavender probably once folded into a linen. A snap of cloth and a fragrant breeze moved the air. Esther must have been making up the bed.

Suzanne had surprised herself by defending change. She'd actually convinced them all they needed to move so she could have things set forever in certain places. That was what she told them. And yet she'd found that she liked anticipating the disruption: The new sounds and smells and wash of breeze across her face felt...invigorating. She liked having to sort and decide.

"Didn't you tell me once, Esther..." Suzanne reminded her as she patted for the bedpost, feeling the smooth walnut, "Didn't you say that I had to learn to accommodate if I was to survive?"

"I can't imagine being so blunt," Esther said.

Suzanne laughed. "Moving reminds me to adjust. I haven't thought of it before, but I actually find all the chaos rather...stimulating. Ouch!" she added, having just walked into the side of a dresser. At least she assumed it was that with the sharpness of the edge and the smooth marble top she ran her fingers across. She rubbed at her hip, imagined it would turn black and blue soon. Just something else ugly she wouldn't have to see. She giggled to herself. Amazed that she recognized advantages to her blindness.

"That bureau was change reaching out to grab you," Esther told her. Then with words more quiet than scolding she added, "If only that black dog were here. He kept you from such edges."

"Well, he's not," Suzanne said. Had it begun with Pig's leaving? No, she'd been restless before then. She sighed, listened to Esther tug on the teardrop drawer pulls followed by a silence while she must have gathered items from a trunk. In many ways, these times of disruption in Suzanne's physical space made her feel…useless, too. She really couldn't do much to help, couldn't say, "Put the dresser here or there or hang that picture next to the doorway." No one asked for her opinion until after things were settled and she received "the tour" as she called it now, from Esther. So why did she persist in creating disruption in her life? In their lives?

Maybe she'd go find the boys who were being kept safely out of the way, tended by their tutor. Sason had taken to the man, that was true. The child giggled and wiggled on her lap whenever Suzanne heard him enter the room. Often Suzanne felt Sason's arms lift up and away from her as if the boy couldn't wait to go play, couldn't wait to be out of her presence. She missed his little curls.

But Sterling was a good teacher, and that was the priority now. Every high-flying kite had an occasional dip in the wind, so who was she to demand perfection from that man in all areas of his life? He was diligent in his teaching. And he did take direction, though sometimes she would have liked him to seek consultation first before he simply acted on his intentions, good as they might be.

It was for Clayton that she swallowed some of the things she might otherwise have said. The child not only showed her hands how to form the words he wanted to say, but just that morning he had actually used

two new words, putting them together, not repeating something someone else had said. A special marker on this journey.

They had been said with a kind of breathy rasp, low but still dis-
tinct. "Good. Food." The child sounded like a baritone inside a tenor's
body. He'd said it just as Suzanne's tongue tasted the eggs and melted
cheese seasoned with hot spices Esther had prepared.

She'd nearly dropped her fork.

"Was that Clayton?"

"Indeed," Esther said.

"Good food! Yes, Son," Suzanne said setting the fork down. She
reached to pat Clayton's head then quickly made the sign for *wonderful*
or *good* or something of merit. She said the word too, making herself
smile wide as she did. The boy laughed and repeated the words "good
food, good food," so deep he sounded like a little man. "Good food.
Good food," he repeated over and over as she laughed. She noticed tears
wetting her cheeks and had been surprised that she hadn't felt the wetness first in her eyes.

Her child had spoken. On his own. At last. She knew that for the
rest of her life she'd think of this moment whenever she tasted hot peppers and eggs.

Perhaps it was all the newness that stimulated his learning too. If she
told herself the truth, disruptions in routine gave her things to think of,
kept her mind from simply dwelling on what she "couldn't do." It forced
creativity, the way learning to play a harp had. Maybe that had happened for Clayton, too.

She'd always created challenges for herself. That was why she'd
learned about photography when Bryce suggested it. Why she'd chosen
the house away from the other women when they first moved to Shasta
City. Perhaps a reason she'd let that Zane Randolph become a part of
her life. Maybe the rush out of routine was even why she'd joined up
with Lura to take her music to the mines. Suzanne liked the tingly
feelings of pushing herself. She always had, and becoming blind hadn't

changed that basic part of her, she decided. She just had to be sure she didn't push herself or her children toward unmerited risk.

Maybe it was even why she liked training Pig to do new things. It required all her thought when she'd worked with the dog, kept her always from feeling sorry for herself. She'd grown quite fond of the animal that had once belonged to Mazy. He'd actually chosen her, way back on the trail, even when she'd resisted him. Such devotion, staying and caring even when she said he should go. He'd never left her back then. So she just couldn't understand why Pig had taken off now.

As she padded her way down the hall railing to the stairs, she lifted her skirts to ascend. She retraced the incident in her mind, to see if there was anything at all that might have been a lapse of some kind on her part, on anyone's part, that would account for the dog's running away.

Pig always slept inside the house, never had to be out in the cold or the rain. He'd made a sleeping place beside her bed. She could always hear him breathing in comfort, ready to stand up when she dropped her toes against the fur of his back. Why had he taken off when Mr. Powder had walked him that day?

The tutor had been genuinely grieved, even more so when she'd brought it up later, wanting clarity. He'd had an agitation in his voice, annoyed almost that she persisted. She could tell he was alarmed and distressed by what had happened.

"He simply tore from my hand, Mrs. Cullver. You can see the burn marks in my palm. Oh. I'm so sorry. You can't, but they're there just the same. Here."

He'd reached for her wrist and pressed her hand onto his open palm. She felt the raised skin of a wound, and she pulled back. Had he resisted freeing her hand?

"Was one of your cats around?" Esther had asked accusingly. Suzanne hadn't realized she was in the room with them and she felt... grateful for Esther's watchful eyes.

"The cats are caged when I walk the dog and the boys," Powder told her. "But perhaps it was all the newness..."

"I hear that dogs sniff their way around their world. They use their noses the way we use our eyes," Esther said. "Yes, those cats—"

Suzanne said. "You're probably right. All the disruptions I've caused. Pig got tired of mining camps, Sacramento, boardinghouses." Her guilt wore emptiness as disguise.

"Now don't blame yourself," Esther said. "Some changes are important."

"Perhaps Pig felt displaced."

"But why hasn't he come back?" Suzanne insisted. "Surely he felt our love for him. Wouldn't that be strong enough reason to return?"

No one responded to her that day, and now as the rain pelted the roof, and she made her way to the nursery, Suzanne thought again. She'd been talking of the dog, but perhaps the words applied to something more: to her husband's leaving her as well.

Bryce had died, succumbed to cholera. He couldn't return, of course, and yet in her grieving, perhaps she'd asked that of him, maybe even felt angry at the man for dying in the first place, at herself for not feeling that she'd loved him enough to keep him from leaving. Could that have been the case? Could she be still blaming Bryce for leaving? Blaming herself for not loving him enough to keep him here? Keeping things swirling so she'd not feel the pain?

"Is that what I'm doing, Bryce?" she said out loud. She only halfway believed he wouldn't answer.

She shook her head. Living with the loss of what we loved forced the strangest ways of thinking. New boundaries, she decided. She smelled a fire in the fireplace of Esther's bedroom when she passed, heard the crackle of the logs. Esther always read to her in the evening at the fire. Could it be evening? Already? She found it difficult to tell the time of day without the warmth of sunlight. Sometimes she relied on her stomach to tell her she was hungry, but if she napped as she had earlier, she was often confused when she awoke about just what time of day it was. Esther said Suzanne was more short-tempered at times, and she wondered if the missing light had something to do with her emotions.

Esther had been reading from the book of Acts, the second chapter, a section about the disciples being all together in one place after their good friend Jesus died and rose again. Waiting, waiting. She supposed it was sacrilegious almost to compare herself to such men of God, and yet she wondered if she didn't have things in common with them. They'd had to put behind them all the old hurts and disappointments of what they'd done that failed the one they loved, that didn't keep him from dying. She felt that way about Bryce. They'd agreed to go somewhere new by faith, go somewhere he had told them to go, to take up new risks and wrap them into old routines. Here she was, where Bryce had said they should go. The disciples traveled to a new city to celebrate First Fruits, an old tradition, Esther told her, of giving of their bounty. Suzanne wondered if her not giving anything back was what kept her feeling empty, kept her from feeling settled.

But perhaps the disciples too wondered why the one they loved had to leave them and why their love had been insufficient to bring him back.

Theirs was the much greater loss, of course. Yet she felt a kinship with them, with their willingness to risk and wait in a difficult time. A kinship of wondering why she could not keep the people she loved. Not just people, but now Pig, too. Gone. She took her glasses off, rubbed her eyes. She had to keep her boys safe. She worked so hard to make that happen.

"Are you getting chilled?" Esther asked her. The woman placed her warm hand on the back of Suzanne's, surprising her with her presence.

"I didn't hear you," Suzanne said. She shook her head. "Just missing things. People. Pig." She smiled. "Thinking theological thoughts."

"Shall I get the boys for you?"

Suzanne nodded. "If Mr. Powder is finished with them for a time." Esther's skirts swished by her in the upstairs hall. The woman smelled of fennel. *Her bowels must be bothering her again,* Suzanne thought. She was always chewing on the herb. Suzanne listened to the rain and the occasional clop-clop of a buggy or shay splashing by. She heard a cow bellow in the distance. What she wanted to hear was a scratch at the door.

But this was a new home for Pig, and even if he wanted to return, Suzanne wasn't sure he could find his way back. She'd ask Sterling Powder to please go by their old boardinghouse again, to be sure that if Pig came back there, the residents knew how to find them. He'd said he'd done it. Why did she doubt?

"There's a window in here, isn't there? In that direction?" Suzanne said when she heard Esther and the boys approach.

"How did you know that?" Esther said.

How did she know? "Just something about the difference in the quality of the darkness, I guess," Suzanne said.

"Well, I'll—"

A knock at the door at the bottom of the steps startled them both, the pounding loud enough to climb the stairs.

"We'll see what it's about," Esther said. "Come along, boys," she said while Suzanne shuffled with her hand and cane to follow the sounds of Esther's footsteps.

The pounding continued, and she heard the creak of the door opening and Esther gasp. Both boys squealed.

"Who is it?" Suzanne called from the top of the stairs.

"It's a sight for sore eyes," Esther said. Suzanne hoped that next she'd hear the sounds of a barking dog.

They had found a way to work side by side. The cabin, simple as it was, now had two rooms in addition to a loft with a floor patched up with tin flattened from lard buckets and old coffee cans mined from a dump Ned had found. The pitch of the ceiling made it impossible to stand up in the loft, but the children could sleep there, and it was the warmest spot in the house. The added room served as a bedroom for Lura, Mariah, Ruth, and Jessie, who resisted the ladder climb to the loft.

Behind the cabin, the former owner had dug a spring and lined it with rocks so buckets could be easily filled and set on the porch. A dipper hung on a nail above the rail. Any unsipped water got splashed over Lura's herb starts, sent along by Mazy as gifts. Mariah said maybe they should try some way to get the water to the house on its own, and Lura had laughed at her, but Ruth "pondered" that, as Elizabeth would say. And in the morning, she set Jessie and Sarah to gouging out a narrow fence rail into what resembled a dugout canoe. A flue, she told them it was called, and when it was finished, they set it at the opening of the spring. The water ran to a barrel set beside the house and filled it, spilling over and running back into the pool.

"Hey, that's chirk," Jason said coming back from setting fence rails with Matthew and Ned.

"We women can solve some problems, can't we, girls?" Ruth said.

Lura came out wiping her hands on her apron. "Good. Now we don't have to go so far to heat up the water for washing, which we best be at," she said.

The girls groaned. The boys, too, for washing meant all hands had a task.

Each had their other chores too. Gathering eggs was Jessie's; milking Martha the cow was Mariah's; Sarah helped with ironing. Ned and Jason worked the scythe when Ruth wasn't or when they weren't working on the three-sided shelter for the animals. Ruth hoped it would help during foaling come spring. Ruth spent as much time as she could gentling the yearlings, getting them ready to break.

The usual doctoring of children and animals took time too. Then ridding themselves of the ground squirrels who kept trying to invade the pantry moved up on the list.

"I bet that's why you got this place so cheap," Lura said.

"I wouldn't say it was cheap," Ruth told her. She heated a curling iron in the lamp chimney, took it out to crimp curls into Sarah's hair.

WHAT ONCE WE LOVED

"Well, somebody was here, dug out a spring, built a house, and then they left. Now why would that be? I say it was the squirrels. Little beggars got into the flour again and the corn seed I bought. We need to dig ourselves a root cellar and line it with rock, too. Break their little teeth when they start to chew then. Can't afford the ammunition to do 'em in."

"I'll get us some poison next time we're in town, Ma," Matthew said.

"We better make that sooner than later," Lura told him.

"Won't be long and it'll be Christmas," Mariah said. "Can we cut a tree? We never did that last year."

"Got a few treasures to buy up," Matthew said. He looked over at Ruth.

"Don't you children get your hopes up," Ruth said. "It'll be a lean year for us."

"All in how you think about it," Matthew said. "Buying gifts isn't the only way to celebrate. Tree's a good idea, Pipsqueak. If the weather holds, we might even make the Table Rock Baptist Church I heard was meeting in someone's house in town."

"You go to church?" Ruth asked. "I didn't know."

"Lots about me you don't know."

"That's only half of that story," she said. "The other half is I don't necessarily want to know more."

"Ah, you're missing a whole mine full of intelligence," he teased.

"I've had enough of mines in California," Ruth said. "That's one reason I came north."

He laughed.

"Speaking of intelligence," Lura said. "When you go into Jacksonville the next time, best you find out about their school term. Getting Mariah started again was part of our reason for coming to Oregon, if I remember."

"Can we all go?" Jason asked.

Ruth frowned. "Not this term. We've got so much to do before spring. So many animals to keep healthy—"

"We can check it out," Matthew interrupted.

Ruth noticed Jason's smile. It wasn't enough to overlook Matthew's habit of intrusion.

Matthew and Ruth saddled up, rode to town, made their purchases, some with a secretive flair. When they'd left Jacksonville, Ruth allowed herself to feel restful. That was what she called it. She had a safe place for her children; she'd made progress on her property. So far all the mares looked good, and the yearlings she worked with were gentling well to a halter and lead rope. She'd left some cash at Little's Mercantile, set aside supplies they'd come by with the wagon to pick up later. She'd even located a goat as a gift for Lura. Ruth had a vision; a plan. She smiled to herself. Those were Mazy words, planning and moving toward something. Her friend had often inspired that in Ruth, encouraged it. "A clear goal helps you keep going on the days you feel discouraged," Mazy'd said. Ruth grunted. She missed her.

Just then a band of seven Indians on horseback came out of the myrtle and oaks, interrupting her thoughts. The braves surrounded them not a few hundred yards from Ruth's ranch and her family.

"What do they want?" Ruth said, turning in her saddle as the men kicked their ponies in a circle around them, close enough that she could smell their sweat, see the pocks of their skin beneath the white streaks of paint.

Matthew signed something with his hands, and they stopped, one man lifting his chin and saying something back. "They're Rogue River Indians. Takelmas, I think. Maybe Klamaths. Seems we're approaching land that belongs to them. They pointed toward your meadow, Ruth."

"Tell them we've bought it from Smith," Ruth said.

Matthew smiled and nodded his head but said, "Keep your voice even. I don't think your purchase agreement matters much to them. Nice and easy, Ruth. It's a war party of some kind. Don't look alarmed."

The one with eyes that reminded her of Zane as a young man said something more, motioned with his hands again. "Seems they've always come through here."

Ruth heard her heart pound louder in her ears. They had black streaks of paint beneath their eyes, too; and red on their cheeks. They kept their ponies moving back and forth, circling them, kicking up dust. She could smell a strange scent. Grease maybe, on their slick hair. A leather parfleche held their arrows. She put her hand on her whip handle. "What's he saying now?"

"Winters his horses here, he says. Wonders what you'll trade to use his grass and…camas, bulbs they eat, come spring."

"Tell him we don't want the roots. He can have them," she said. "But I don't understand this about the grass. Didn't I just buy this land from Smith?"

Matthew nodded his head, still maintaining the smile. "Yes, yes, but Smith probably never talked to these folks. People are unsettled right now. That Crescent City outbreak. Deaths in the Illinois Valley, according to the talk in town. We're probably lucky we still have our heads for talking. Don't want to start a war here."

"What could they want? The horses?"

"Offer cash," Matthew said. "They're going into the winter same as us and could buy grub and such with it. Ammunition. Miners are using up the streams, and I haven't seen all that much game around either. Offer cash. Maybe the cow. But cash first."

"I don't have much cash left," she said quietly. She felt herself begin to sink back into that place where she stashed hope. She couldn't let it fade.

"I've got cash," he said. "I'll hand it to you, slow like, or you let me give it to them. Don't let this offend you, Ruth. There's a time to take help."

"Your mother'll think we're daft, paying twice for the same thing."

"It's possible," Matthew said. "But if she could see the look in their eyes and the quiver full of arrows there, and the rifles they could just as easily point at us as shake in the air"—he nodded with his chin—"she'd think different. Just go slow, and we'll show them what you've got."

There wasn't much choice, Ruth thought.

"I won't charge much interest," Matthew told her.

He handed them a roll of bills. One of the braves grabbed for it. Then the steel-eyed one took it easily from the first.

"What's he saying now?"

"He wants to graze his horses there tonight."

"Didn't I just pay to have them move on?"

"They'll move on."

"It'll terrify the children," she said. One of the braves leaned over to finger the whip at her hip. Hoping he couldn't smell her fear, she smiled as though she were at a tea party with kin.

"I'll tell them to bed down near the barn. I think it's wise, Ruth. I do."

She could just see the children's eyes when they rode in followed by seven braves in full paint. "All right," she said.

Matthew talked more with his hands, and then they turned into the trees toward the sloping ridge and the valley below.

"Could be we were just held up," Ruth said.

"Oregon style," Matthew answered.

"How much did you give them?"

"Not all that much," Matthew told her. "Bought us some neighborliness, maybe. And you're now beholding to me for life. You'll have to give up your firstborn."

"I've already done that," she said quietly, her son's tiny face flashing through her mind.

"My mistake," he said, chastened. "I was trying to ease things up. Let's just say I gave them enough so you and I will have another subject to talk over during the long winter nights."

Ruth swallowed. His words touched a place in her she'd forgotten existed.

The stillness of the forest floor softened with fir needles, and fallen leaves moist from recent snows made their horses' hooves thud as they rode. Ruth shook her head. She was down to her last gold eagle, had just paid ransom for her land.

They rode into the pine patch, down the slope to the house. This was her place of belonging. She'd found it. Not something she'd stumbled into and just stayed at as she had at Poverty Flat. But a place of her choosing when she was living free, aboveboard, no longer held hostage by Zane Randolph. She felt held hostage now.

She'd signaled quickly with her eyes when the boys came outside. They reined their horses to the house, and Matthew said, "Just keep it easy, boys. They're spending the night at the barn."

"They'll steal the horses," Jason said.

"No. They won't. We'll stay up watching. Take turns. But so far, they're doing just what they said." The boys slipped back toward the door. Ruth got off her horse, pulled off the cinch saddle and blanket, and set them upright under the porch eave.

"Keeping these close," she said. "Jason, water the horses. No quick moves. We'll stake them out in back. Let them eat at the grass there."

"Should we offer them some biscuits?" Sarah asked.

"Horses don't eat bread," Ned told her.

"Not the horses. Them?" Sarah said, nodding to the braves. "It's almost Christmas."

"We're just gonna let them be," Lura said. She gathered them like chicks to get them back inside.

"None of us will be the worse for wear if we just keep our heads," Matthew said.

No worse for wear. Ruth almost believed that.

And then she saw the look in Jessie's eyes.

intrigue

Suzanne had almost forgotten about joy. How strange that was when she had a son named Sason whose very name meant joy. Even when she'd thought about the first-century Jews as Sister Esther read to her in the book of Acts, she'd forgotten about their joy. The joy of being with friends. The delight of eating together, of supporting each other while they waited. And then the Holy Spirit had touched them, and others who saw them accused them of being drunk! At nine-thirty in the morning! Why, they were just happy, ravenous with delight at the power they'd been given, the power of friendship and compassion and hope.

Then, it had come back to her, God's gift of joy, a thing she'd never conceived she could have again as a woman blind, a widow in mourning.

Oh, she certainly didn't speak in any unknown language as those disciples had. Unless words of endearment coupled with dreams about one's future lifting like bubbles from a bottle of champagne counted as strange language. But she felt the fullness of the joy just the same, feasting with friends and food and being loved beyond measure. She believed again that all could be accomplished with faith and power and a worthy focus. *Focus. Hearth. That which warms us, the center of our being.* And she'd felt that in a way she had never imagined she ever would again. She'd given her heart to it. She'd believed.

True joy had arrived before Christmas. It came in the form of a bawling bull attached to a very wet-smelling man and the embrace of a fond friend.

"Just give me a bed. To lay my head," he'd rhymed.

"Seth Forrester?"

"None other." Suzanne heard him stomp his feet. "And Mazy Bacon, too."

"Mazy! So good to see you! However did you get away from all those cows?"

"May I help you?" Sterling Powder said. She hadn't heard him enter the hallway at all, but he was standing at Suzanne's left.

"These are our dear friends," Suzanne told him, turning. "Sterling Powder, please meet Seth Forrester and Mrs. Bacon. Dear old friends."

"Not so old," Seth said. "Though I like the 'dear' part." She heard Seth groan, "You've grown a foot, Clayton."

"Mr. Powder's been tutoring the boys," she said. "And they're doing so well. Aren't you, Clayton?"

Mazy laughed. "Clayton just looked to see if he had more than two legs."

"Did a bit of tutoring myself," Seth said.

"Did you now?" Sterling Powder answered. Suzanne heard something unpleasant in his voice.

"Yes sir. With little Chinese girls."

"I'm sure," Sterling said.

"He did. They learned very well," Suzanne defended. "Maybe we can see them while you're here. You know where Mei-Ling lives. We haven't found Naomi—"

"Let me take your wet cloaks," Esther offered.

Suzanne heard shuffling. "Clayton's voice is very deep, but he puts a few words together now. Can you get Clayton to say something, Mr. Powder?"

"He is not a circus dog, madam," Sterling said.

"Of course not. I only meant… Well, I—"

"Perhaps I should retire now, leave you with your…friends," Sterling said.

"As you wish," Suzanne said.

"This one will soon be too heavy to carry around," Mazy said. "You'll have to ride that old Pig, won't you, Sason?"

"Dog gone," Sason said.

"He is?"

"I meant to write to you, Mazy. I…we're so sorry…it's so confusing. Pig just…ran off."

"After Mr. Powder started here with his cats," Esther said.

"Shall I take the boys back to the nursery?" Sterling offered.

"Yes…no, they've missed their friends…I'll tend to them later," Suzanne said.

"It is their bedtime. They do need routine."

"This once…" her voice faltered. "Well, yes, of course. They need their routine."

"Come along, boys," she heard Sterling say along with Mazy's smacking kisses on them. His footsteps echoed in the hallway, leaving behind that scent of rosewater he usually wore.

"I thought you were Pig, returned," Suzanne said, reaching to put her arm around Mazy. "I've missed him so. I'm so sorry, Mazy."

"Me, too," Mazy said. "I hoped to see my old friend." She sighed. "But animals can be…unpredictable."

"I should have had Esther walk him. Or taken him out myself. I've thought of a hundred things I wished I'd done—"

"You're looking mighty chipper, Missy Esther," Seth said. "They say it's the lengthening of the days that brings on the bloom in a garden. You're blooming well."

"Weeds bloom too," she said. He laughed. "But you always did know how to turn a girl's head," Esther said. Suzanne could imagine her straightening the little cap that tied beneath her neck that everyone said she always wore. "Let me take your cloaks. Such a night it is."

"I've got to put the bull up," Mazy said. "Can I tie him in the back-yard until morning?"

"Of course. Yes," Suzanne said. "Your bull, Mazy? Your husband's brother never came and got it?"

"One and the same. Seth helped bring him south, and if nothing else, I'm to meet at last this elusive relative and maybe get some answers about who my husband really was. I almost got Charles to deliver him, but Seth offered to bring me south. So I took him up on it. He was pretty insistent. You must like Sacramento," she said. "Unlike Pig, I guess."

"I am so sorry," Suzanne said. "I, we can't explain. I have posters out. But people…many are hungry…coyotes…"

"Maybe someone found him and gave him a good barn to sleep in," Seth said, "As likely as the other."

"Pig never did like cats," Mazy said.

"I'll get us some hot tea," Esther said.

"Let me help as soon as I take care of Marvel," Mazy told her.

"I'll do it, Mazy," Seth said. "You go get dried off."

Mazy thanked him, and Suzanne could hear her friend and Esther move down the hall.

And then Seth turned to her, to Suzanne. "I'm reaching for your lovely hand, Mrs. Cullver."

"Suzanne," she said. She smelled wet wool as he lifted her fingers and kissed the back of it, held it for just a moment longer than he should have, long enough for Suzanne to feel her heartbeat quicken.

"Hands still as soft as rose petals," he said.

"That's because Esther takes such good care of me."

"An enviable task," he said.

The bull bellowed again, but Suzanne was sure Seth stared at her, could feel it almost, the warmth of his breath brushing her face. "You were the prettiest of the lot even then," Seth said. "Way back on that trail. Here is my truth—you're a beauty, forsooth."

"That is the most dreadfully beautiful poem I have ever heard," Suzanne said.

"I'm out of practice," he said. "No inspiration. But I have a feeling that's about to change."

❧

Ruth thought Jessie's condition would be temporary, just one of those childhood things. She stayed hopeful while life moved on around her. At times, it reminded Ruth of waiting for Jessie's return when Zane abducted the child, except here her daughter lay before her, dark shadows beneath her eyes. Still distant, almost gone.

The arrival of the braves had set it off, even though they'd settled themselves near the barn just as they'd said they would. They'd been peaceable. Jason and Ruth and Matthew and Mariah had taken turns watching the small fire flicker through the night in the center of the Takelmas' cluster. Then, in the morning, against Matthew's wishes, Lura marched out with a basket of baking powder biscuits.

"Men got to eat," she said. "Harder to kill someone who's fed you or treated you human."

Jessie watched, her eyes a glaze of terror. "It's all right," Ruth said. "See, Lura's coming back." She urged the girl to look out the window, then wished she hadn't. Jessie's breath came fast as a hard-run horse.

Ruth steered her from the curtain to the bed where Jessie shivered as though cold. Her face felt hot, and Ruth wondered if maybe the child had developed a fever.

By the time the braves mounted up and rode out, howling wildly as they passed the house, Ruth exhaled along with the others, as though they hadn't taken a breath all night. Ruth went outside and counted her horses. They were all there. Martha, the milk cow, too. Even the oxen. And in Lura's breadbasket, they'd left dried salmon and a handful of dark round roots that Ned said tasted sweet.

"Try one, Jess," Ned told her, but the girl just grabbed Ruth's arms and held tight.

"Maybe she's gotten the ague," Lura said later when Ruth swept the dirt floor of supper crumbs.

"That's a summer ailment," Ruth said.

"Haven't really had a hard, hard freeze. It could be the air still holds it."

Jessie lay pale as an onion skin. "I can't move my legs, Mama," she said.

"What?" Ruth dropped the broom, touched Jessie's damp forehead. "You're so weak," she continued. "You need to eat, and we need to get this fever down."

"I'll go for the doctor," Matthew said. "After we give our visitors a little time to head out."

Matthew rode out, bringing McCully, the doctor, back. "Looks like the ague," he said. "Just late." He offered no real explanation of the ailment and prescribed some concoctions that Lura complained would be no more effective than mud on a washcloth. Ruth insisted they be administered.

And Jessie did seem to perk up after the second week; then the days waned into more with little change. The goat and her kid arrived, a gift delivered. Jessie appeared to tolerate the goat's milk. At least she drank the mugs, a sip at a time, while Ruth held her head.

While the child slept, Ruth pushed herself to work the yearlings, her mind kept tightly focused on the animals at the end of the rope, the needs of the horse protecting her from worrying over Jessie, from wondering why bad things just kept happening.

"She's worse when you leave," Lura told her once when Ruth came back into the house.

"So are you saying I shouldn't? That I should just let the horses run wild?"

"Hey, hey," Matthew said. "No one's saying—"

"Mama! Mama! I hurt," Jessie wailed.

"Where? Tell me where?"

"Don't go. Don't go outside. I need a drink." Her arms arched at Ruth's neck. She frenzied herself, became another person, almost. She had the eyes of a horse caught unexpectedly on ice.

Ruth decided to stay close. She worked on the rope she was weaving from Jumper's mane and tail hairs, getting Mariah to bring in other strands after she brushed the snags and snarls from Koda's tail and some of the mares. Ruth heard the jacks yelled at by different voices—the boys when one jack got out, Matthew when he tried to rope that left front leg to get Carmine caught.

Few people trekked along the trail from Yreka toward Jacksonville now, snow falling in the Siskiyou Mountains keeping Californians on their side of the range. At least Ruth needn't worry over Zane for the next few months. How could he cross the mountains?

Ewald pawed the bottom rail of the corral and skinned up his leg enough that Lura had a new patient to hover over. Matthew killed a deer, and they quartered it on the plank table he'd built and hung it in the smokehouse finished just before Thanksgiving. The scent of alder swirled the air that hovered as an overcast sky threatened rain and sometimes delivered. Once the crack of thunder startled Jessie into a scream. And even Matthew's telling her that the lightning was angels playing billiards with fireballs of sagebrush across the open range did not calm her. Once a fire shot up on the ridge beyond the meadow. A squall drenched it, but not before Jessie saw it, beginning another of her long, sleepless nights.

The horses fared well. They easily pawed through skiffs of light snow that fell. Some made their way up the slopes where the wind blew the snow away for them. The little creek froze over, but the boys kept a hole open for watering stock, bringing the cows and horses down to the flat most evenings to drink.

"I heard a group of braves, seven or so, attacked a farm not far from Jacksonville," Matthew whispered to Ruth one day when he came back from buying more medicine for Jessie. "Totally surprised 'em. A survivor said one lay on his back and shot his bow using his feet. Said he grinned the whole time he did it."

"Are people forming up?" she asked.

He nodded. "They're seeking a posse."

"You aren't—"

"I won't," he said. "We'll post ourselves as guards. Ned, Sarah, Ma, Mariah, too."

Ruth's shoulders sagged with relief.

"We were fortunate," Ruth said.

"We had someone watching over us," he answered.

Matthew shared reports of skirmishes but always out of Jessie's hearing. Still the child continued to wane. Just before Christmas, Lura surprised everyone by having a cookstove delivered. Fingers of fog flittered at the valley's neck as the freighter helped Matthew unload it.

"May be the last trip over the mountains bringing supplies," Lura said. "And I figured to have it in our own house." She looked pointedly at Matthew. "But seeing as how we're here, I decided no need to deprive myself of what would make life easier while I'm waiting for something different. We'll have raisin pie for supper," she added. "That'll perk you up, won't it, Miss Jessie?"

The girl had only smiled. Ruth dabbed the wetness from the corners of the child's eyes and considered: She wasn't getting better. Surely Jessie wasn't so strong-willed she could "make" herself this sick. No child would deprive herself of being able to run and play and laugh and dance in some willful state, would she? It must have been caused by something in this southern Oregon air, something that weakened her, something unusual in this unusual place.

Jessie's dark eyes followed Ruth as she moved about the room, a small smile hovering just above a pooched-out lower lip when Ruth administered the strong-smelling medicines. The little packages Mazy had sent along with them contained dried herbs. Jessie's was full of spearmint that she took easily as a tea.

"Isn't that something?" Lura noted. "The very thing for pneumonia, and that's what that girl gets sent to her. That Mazy. She's got some way of knowing things."

Ruth hadn't thought of Jessie's condition as pneumonia-like. Her daughters' breathing was shallow but generally steady and not raspy.

Ruth wondered if Mazy might have noticed something about Jessie that Ruth had missed. They'd spent a lot of time together, making soap, she remembered. Had the child had something like this before? She wondered if Mariah or Lura ever wrote to Elizabeth or Mazy. She should write, ask her what she might know about Jessie, ask her to hold them in her prayers. Still, it didn't seem right to ask for prayers only when things were dismal and then to never show up when things were grand.

Christmas came quietly. Ruth had given Matthew a final list of items he might find in Jacksonville including special hair ribbons for Jessie, Sarah, and Mariah, a Jacob's Ladder for Ned, and two kinds of spinning tops for Jason. They all went out to cut a tree, all but Ruth and Jessie. They trimmed it with paper rings and popped corn. And Matthew insisted they had to hang a pickle.

"A pickle. I'd forgotten. Your pa's pa used to do that, didn't he?" Lura said.

Matthew nodded. "First child to find the pickle on Christmas morning gets a special present."

The children rose early, squealing and giggling, the scent of their clean hair, Castile-soaped nightshirts, and Lura's cooking mingled in the air. No one could find the green pickle, it blended in so perfectly with the fir's tight branches. Finally, Jessie said, "There it is!" She pointed from the cot she lay on.

"Good for you, honey," Ruth told her.

"You get the pickle gift. And the pickle, too, if you want it," Matthew said.

"Neither one," she said, causing the room to grow silent.

"I'll take it," Ned said. He crunched into it and wrinkled his nose. "Umm. Good," he said, the bite releasing the scent of vinegar.

"And we can split up the present," Matthew said, pulling a fresh orange from a stocking he'd hung by the stove. "Seeing as how Jessie is so generous giving things away." Jessie gave a weak smile.

The sounds of the other children happily slurping couldn't remove Ruth's growing dread.

Over sage grouse that Lura cooked—that Jason had shot for their dinner—Matthew said he'd heard in town that a woman named Emma Royal wanted to start a school and she had collected money from the miners for it. "You should send the boys," Matthew told Ruth.

"Should send our Mariah and your Sarah, too, if the weather holds," Lura said.

"Would you like to go, Jessie? If you were well enough, you could."

"I'd like to go, Mama," Jessie said.

"Good!"

A cheer went up from Jason and Mariah, too.

"That's the best Christmas present ever," Ruth said. She cast a hopeful glance toward Matthew just as Jessie added, "But I can't go to school. Who would take care of you?"

The child's words set like an anvil on Ruth's chest.

"Sinclair Taylor." The tall man standing eye to eye to Mazy introduced himself, as Mazy stood once again in the posh offices of Josh Mc-Cracken, solicitor. Just a few months earlier Mazy had discovered she had a stepson at this solicitor's desk. Now the view of family would be expanded. "Please. Be seated."

Mazy didn't like being directed by Sinclair Taylor any more than she'd liked bringing the bull to him. She'd accommodated just about as much as she could. She'd met him at a freighter station as he'd asked, so the bull could be loaded onto the wagon. Seth and the freight driver and she had done most of the work, Mr. Taylor barely prodding with his fine cane. Mr. Taylor apparently either paid or cajoled others to do work he didn't like.

Finished, the bull standing with his horns like twin arrows toward the sky, Mr. Taylor tipped his hat and said, "I see you have transport." He nodded at her horse. "I believe we meet next at Mr. McCracken's then," and he'd stepped inside his carriage not even offering her passage.

No matter. Seth would have trailed her horse back to Suzanne's, but this way she wasn't beholden to Sinclair Taylor for a thing.

She'd put up with it for one reason only: She wanted all the knowledge she could acquire about the Jeremy Bacon she'd been married to. And this man was the only road to it.

Mr. McCracken had made himself scarce, leaving his office to them. "May I present my niece, Grace," Sinclair Taylor said then, nodding to a child maybe fourteen who curtsied and then sat, keeping her head shadowed in the stiff-brimmed bonnet she wore. Mazy folded her own hands, chapped from milking cows in the cold air, and glanced at the girl. Grace resembled her brother, hair the color of Wisconsin soil, eyes winter sky blue. Her caped arms disappeared inside a fur muff. She looked well tended and content.

"It is my understanding that one of your conditions for bringing the bull south was to meet me, to ask some questions. Grace consented to come along. Curiosity, I suspect."

Mazy nodded. He was a broader man than Jeremy had been, easing toward portly. And graying, so he must have been the elder of the two. He had that same air of certainty about him, a kind of cool disinterest that Mazy decided just might be a family trait. Then he surprised her.

"I am sorry about the...disruptions my brother placed in your life," he said. "I...we were unaware of his reason to remain in Wisconsin until your arrival here in response to my letter. I understand you intercepted it on the trail west." Mazy nodded. "We knew only that he had remained in Wisconsin and that at last, after much correspondence, he was to head west, to California, to keep his agreements."

"He never told you he was married?"

"We knew he was married to—"

"My mother," Grace said.

"Yes," Mazy said. "Your brother talked of her to me. She must have been a fine woman."

"Indeed," Sinclair Taylor said.

"She has no need of compliments from you," Grace said.

"Grace," Mr. Taylor scolded.

Mazy raised her hand as though to say it was all right. She thought of what it must be like for Grace, a mere child, uncovering betrayals within her own father's life. Not that anyone could ever know what their parents thought or did, even if they had the interest or courage to ask while their parents were alive. Grace had lost her mother and her father. She was an orphan as certain as Sula was. And here Mazy was, someone threatening to disrupt memories perfectly intact.

For the first time, Mazy asked herself just what she was doing here. Just what did she think she needed to know?

"You immigrated?" Mazy asked.

"Before Jeremy. He is, was, my younger brother. There were only the two of us. We both married in England, and Jeremy had this idea to go to the provinces. Canada. And make our way to Fort Vancouver. He was always the one with ideas," Sinclair smiled for the first time. "He could always talk me into doing them first, so I arrived in Vancouver before them. We became enamored of the idea of having our own dairying, here in California. The purebred bull you delivered will complete that phase of what he wished for, what we wished for. And I am grateful."

"You won't have a purebred herd," Grace reminded him, "without the cows."

"No," he said. "But a good sire and sturdy cows will nevertheless add to the herd we already have. And your father's widow needs some just compensation. Adjustments are always called for, Grace. It's not a sign of weakness."

The girl blushed. "Yes, Uncle," she said.

"And the rest you know, I presume. He was a good son to our father. A good brother though more prone to impulse than me. He treated his wife and children well from all I know, and he left fully intending to come back, fully planning to keep his commitments. I trust that. There was an injury, an illness, I believe, that may have affected his timing."

"My father and mother and I nursed him back to health. He told me he had arrived by ship, just that year."

"Then he was less than candid with you or confused by his trauma."

Mazy nodded. This talk was revealing nothing, nothing she didn't already know, nothing that would fill the empty places.

"His son, David," Sinclair continued. "I bear responsibility for not contacting him. I hoped to know what had happened to his father first. My own…difficulties after arriving here made finding David an impossibility. I have still not found a way to answer his letter."

"Did he write?" Grace asked, casting a surprised glance at her uncle.

"Just recently," Sinclair answered. "But that is not your affair, Missis…Bacon, I believe you go by?"

"That's my name," she said.

"Is there anything more then, Mrs. Bacon?"

She tried to think. Was there something she should ask, some piece of forgotten information, some tidbit of her husband's past that in knowing would somehow make her life complete? She could think of nothing. She rose.

"I do thank you for delivering the bull. I know it was an inconvenience," he said. "I, too, am widowed." He coughed. "I've had no way to travel and still provide for Grace."

"I'm sorry, " Mazy said. "I didn't know."

"No reason you should."

"Can I take a message back for you to David?" Mazy turned to look at Grace as well. "He and his wife are helping my mother on my farm while I'm here. I'll see him when I return."

"Tell him I'll write," Grace said. "And that I'm helping Uncle Sinclair."

Mazy nodded. "I guess it's good-bye then," she said.

"We seem to have covered all that's essential," Sinclair said, his use of the word *essential* springing tears to Mazy's eyes. It had been Jeremy's word.

She rode sidesaddle, taking her time, to Suzanne's. Had she gotten what she hoped for? She wasn't sure. It was clear though, any sense of family could not be forced. There was no family here, just people who had crossed her path, intersected her life and moved away. No amount of her persisting would make that different; if anything, it could drive a possible friend away.

What she had with Jeremy was real, had been real, even with its tainted edges. To make it something more, to insist that Grace or Sinclair or even David Taylor fit some fabric she called family did them a disservice. They were simply good people going about their way. Insisting on more meant sending out an invitation for disappointment. She couldn't fix the mess. She couldn't make the past go away by trying to reshape it. It was what it was. Nothing more, but nothing less.

Jeremy had loved her. He had known what might hurt her and had not used it to harm her. He had lived with the knowledge of his deception. To his death he had refused to send her into a fault that could not be altered. Wasn't that an act of love?

"How did you find us?" Suzanne asked Esty.

"Esther sent word of your new location."

Esther had sent word? How strange. Esther had practically snubbed Esty when she'd first arrived with Suzanne, insisted that there was no room at the boardinghouse for her. Maybe Esther felt guilty about judging the woman harshly instead of seeing that she merely wanted to start a new life, move out of the casinos and saloons and into the millinery business.

"I'm pleased she did."

"Is she here?" Esty asked. Into the silence she added, "I have a hat to talk with her about."

"Esther is going to buy a hat?" Suzanne couldn't imagine Esther without the little cap everyone said she always wore. Perhaps she did wear hats, and Suzanne simply hadn't known.

"No. Yes. She's looking at some feathers," Esty said. Something in her words sounded so…lame. "There you are!" she said, and Suzanne heard Esty stand, the rustle of her crinolines telling Suzanne she was walking away.

"I…let's go to my room," Esther said. "You can find the…color that will match the feather I need. Will you excuse us, Suzanne?" The two women were gone before Suzanne could say anything.

How odd, she thought. She stood, thinking to pour some tea. She counted her steps to the sideboard, patted for the tea cozy. The doorknocker caused her to turn, and she shouted to no one who cared apparently, "I'll get it," and headed down the hall to let in Seth. She felt herself blush.

The evening before, the others had finally gone on to bed leaving her and Seth in the parlor alone. They talked the night away, at least Suzanne believed it was late though she lost track of time. Seth was an easy listener, and she found herself telling him confidences she hadn't known she was thinking.

"He worries me, yes," she said of Sterling Powder. "But I think it's just my wish to control things. I do that, you know, try to make things happen. But I'm certain his being here is important. For Clayton. And I'm committed to my boys."

"He seems a little stiff," Seth said.

"I know. But the boys come first. I'm firm about that. And he tolerated my moving us, my need to have things in a swirl." She laughed. "I used to like to dance."

"The belle of the ball, no doubt," Seth said. "You still can."

"Oh, I don't think so. My balance. I can't imagine being dragged around the floor by some poor soul having to dance for the both of us."

"Might be a poor soul out there willing."

"You think so?" She patted the bun at the back of her neck. "Maybe someday. When the boys are grown."

"You won't do them favors by putting your whole life on hold, Suzanne. You can't put them first if you don't tend to yourself. You'll be all drained out with nothing to give them."

She hadn't thought quite that way before. "Do you think that's why I keep looking for things to occupy my time? I thought about training dogs. See how that's turned out." She scolded herself. "And music lessons, singing or the harp. I'd love that, but Esther doesn't think there are many students about."

"Might only need one or two to make you feel like you were being worthy."

"Being worthy," she sighed. "That is what I long for. To feel as though I can do something well, something that might matter. I'd like to add a little light to another's life."

"I know what you're saying," he said. They'd talked about small things then, and large. She would have kept talking except for the yawn she heard him suppress, reminding her of just how late it must have been.

"I'm so sorry. Tomorrow. We can talk more tomorrow. You've had a very long day. I shouldn't have kept you."

"It was my pleasure, Suzanne," Seth said. "My pleasure indeed."

So when she found herself alone with him again, it was almost as though they had never stopped talking.

"And then there's this new vision that came to me," she said after he'd been seated and she'd poured him tea, placing her finger to the inside of his cup just as she did for her own so she wouldn't overfill it. "I've been dying to tell someone. You're the perfect person."

"Talk on," he said.

"It…it has to be kept secret. And if you think I'm…well, that I'm addle minded, you must tell me."

"You already have my undivided attention, Suzanne."

She blushed. "I want to start a theater company. Art soothes human wounds, and this California lures people with open wounds, or splits them open when they least expect it. Theater, stories, can help with that, can wrap arms around a person. The stories help us remember what we were, who we are, and where we're going." She thought she might be babbling. "I'll seek investors. We'll build a building. Or perhaps see if the Rays are interested in selling that Sacramento Theater they own."

"And you'd perform?"

"Maybe. I want to choose the plays and hire the actors and oversee things. Isn't that a funny word for me to use, *oversee*. But that's it exactly. Sister Esther could work for me then while I'm gone, and maybe not have to spend her nights cleaning. I'd hire someone else to clean my theater."

"Esther might like to keep working."

"Perhaps—"

"Keep me working where?" Esther asked, returning to the room. Suzanne could sense that Esty stood there too, smelled her delicate perfume.

"I want to buy the Sacramento Theater," Suzanne said. "To use the money I made singing in the gold mines to give something back to the citizens here. You all have your interests, and you know how consuming they are, how gratifying. I want that too."

"But you have your boys."

"I'll still have my boys. I'll still have Mr. Powder, I hope. But I want something that will, well, help stir me up and be consequential, beyond my little family."

"And you believe plays and things will do that?" Esther said.

"Shakespeare matters," Suzanne defended. "He alone touches more lives than… His stories reach to the heart of people," she finished, her enthusiasm suddenly spent. "Never mind," she said. "It was only an idea. Not well thought out."

A silence Suzanne guessed was being filled with knowing looks permeated the room. "What?" she said. "What is it?"

"Suzanne, Seth." Esther cleared her throat. "Esty and I have something…of consequence to share."

Suzanne heard the swirl of intrigue in Esther's voice, savored the taste of anticipation.

the truth shall make you free

Elizabeth appeared to be having a fine time. Carl "Gus" Grotefend, the little German, squired her to church now and frolicked before her at the Twelfth Night Dance. They'd insisted Mazy come along, and they'd even come out early to help her finish up her milking chores though that had proved unnecessary. She already had good help.

Oltipa had taken to the handling of the Ayrshires and the Durhams like feathers to a felt hat. And with her willingness to bend beneath the cows' bellies, the other Wintu women seemed to ease into the role, leaving their framed plank houses and learning the squeeze-pull rhythm of milking too.

They had discussed how to keep the women and children safe while David carried the mail and Mazy was gone for a few days. Mazy's mother and Gus had said they'd alert the sheriff to keep an open eye. "The authorities call them 'Mrs. Bacon's Indians,'" Elizabeth told her. "They said they didn't know a soul who wanted to take you on. I think they'll be safe while you're gone."

And they had been. Even David commented about the little bed Mazy made up for Ben on a mat next to his parents'. "Now you're close enough to climb up anytime you want; but safe from me rolling over you and squishing you like a bug," David said. He decided they could stay for a time longer, "What with the uprisings and retaliation and all."

They became a daily part of her life, just as she'd hoped. Strange how when she stopped "planning," things fell into place.

A goat now walked the treadmill, so the butter churned itself. Mazy could concentrate on the business side of things: breeding, calving, forming two-pound frames of butter in the hinged molds she built herself, and working out ways to get the white-gold "crop" delivered while the taste stayed sweet and cool. That was probably another reason Mazy found the winters less troublesome than some—the winters made milk cooling easier. It was only keeping the roads passable for deliveries that could throw her schedules and plans off.

She loved farming, the constant creativity of finding some new way to relate to the land—*humus*. It was a word that meant the earth and had something to do with humans, too. And humility. Surrender. She'd come some distance in her thinking, allowing the land to help shape her. She'd keep giving herself that quiet time each day to remember to be humble and grateful, too. She was hatching wisdom there, that was what she was doing.

She'd taken care of Charles Wilson with her request he take the bull south. He hadn't, of course. But at least for a few days, he'd stopped coming out, as she knew he would. Lazy men never stayed around long if a woman had a list of "dos" for them. But he'd shown up again to invite her to the Twelfth Night Dance held for the last time at the Shasta Hotel. Next year Norton and Tucker's new brick building would serve that purpose. She'd refused, of course, and instead come along with her mother and Gus to this gathering. "You're always huddled out there working your fingers to the bone," Elizabeth had said.

"You said I should settle in, and I finally have," Mazy told her.

"Digging in is different than settling, I'll ponder," Elizabeth said. "Even dirt needs to lie fallow some to grow richer crops. Time you had a little fallowing. You come with us." And so Mazy had.

Elizabeth stood nearly a foot taller than Gus, but it didn't seem to hamper their enthusiasm for the music. Mazy couldn't remember when her mother's eyes had sparkled so, couldn't imagine that she'd ever seen that round face framed by curls damp from the combination of both levity and love. *Love? Was her mother in love?* Mazy pushed that thought from her mind.

Had her parents ever gone dancing? Mazy didn't think so. It was something new her mother discovered in this western landscape.

Mazy declined the dance requests she received. Instead, she placed herself behind the table, serving lemonade from one glass bowl, hot cider from another, and helping two single women at an adjoining table with their eggnog supply. It gave her an opportunity to be a part of things, but still under her control. She smiled at that admission. That was her, all right. Always wanting control.

Well, at least she was participating, wasn't hiding herself away. And she did enjoy seeing people spirited and happy, getting acquainted with new families arriving daily, talking books and business with the owner of yet another bookstore—number five for Shasta City. Thomas Maupin stood off to the side. He owned a big farm in Bald Hills, and word had it he wanted to bring in hundreds of hogs. That made her think of her dog, Pig. Whatever could have happened to him? Sometimes not knowing was worse than a bad answer.

She watched the dancers, her eyes catching the children at the edges giggling and imitating their elders. Her foot tapped to the fiddle and the accordion. She nodded when addressed, chatted easily with a stranger or two as she handed them a cup to sip. She wouldn't have done this back in Wisconsin, not made herself be a part of what she didn't always find comfortable. She would have judged herself too unkindly, said she "didn't do well with new people" or "took up too much space" with her "ampleness." But it was good to stretch herself a bit, to make herself do things that didn't harm, but challenged. She thought of her dream of her friend in Wisconsin asking her if she was in service. Being here, handing out eggnog—was that service?

"You're looking quite thoughtful this evening, Mrs. Bacon." Mazy turned to face Charles Wilson. "You're so obviously occupied with doing good works here," Charles said, "that I hate to intrude. But what would a Twelfth Night Dance be without a turn with the most beautiful woman present?"

"And your gout…?"

He lifted his boot slightly, the new leather sole barely scuffed. "Healing nicely. Your concern is well taken."

He was a handsome man in an odd sort of way, that ear chunk and all. But like discovering a spider, his appearance made her wary. Mazy turned to stare out at the dance floor. The fiddler had taken a break, and she welcomed the flock of hot dancers seeking respite with eggnog. "Oh, looks like I'm back to work," she told him. "Perhaps another time."

"Let me help you," he said. "Lovely ladies, please forgive my intrusion." The two women at the eggnog table, sisters, Mazy thought they might be, stepped out of his way, grinning behind their fingers and flashing knowing looks at Mazy.

That was all she needed, some wretched rumor that Charles Wilson was sweet on her. It was bad enough he came out to check on "milk production." *Milk production.* The only production he had in mind had nothing to do with cow's milk but milking someone else for all they might be worth.

She scanned the crowd for her mother, glad for once that her height helped her see across heads to find the gray curls and pink cheeks. Mazy raised her chin, trying to catch her mother's eye, but she couldn't. Elizabeth was having maybe just a little too much fun, Mazy thought. After all, she was a woman nearly fifty. What did she think, laughing and clasping arms with that man anyway? Elizabeth fanned herself with her handkerchief as the little German leaned his head in as if to tell her a confidence. Her mother threw her head back and laughed. Why, Elizabeth might have a heart attack or something, with her age and her weight.

Mazy squinted. Had her mother been losing weight? Perhaps she was ill. She needed to take care of herself a little better.

Mazy spilled lemonade on her hand, apologized to the person she was handing the cup to, felt Charles Wilson press against her arm as he reached to serve someone else. She heard a woman say, "Isn't it lovely to see a man so helpful?" Mazy nodded, looked up in time to see Gus's hand on her mother's elbow as he wove her not toward her table but toward the outside door.

"It seems your mother's found a way to enjoy the evening," Charles said. "Like mother, like daughter?" he said, raising one eyebrow.

"Yes," Mazy said, placing a cup of eggnog firmly in his hands. "I could certainly use some fresh air."

Esther and Esty's unveiling stunned Suzanne into silence. "You must say nothing," Esther said.

"How many?" Seth asked finally.

"So far, six of them," Esty said.

"We might have helped more, but each time…each time there was a change, a move from the boardinghouse, Mr. Powder…it set us back," Esther said. "We had to find new routes, new places to get them to safety. Only short interruptions," Esther soothed.

Suzanne pressed her fingers to her lips. "But how did you…what got you started?"

"When I saw what I had brought the Celestials into," Esther said. "There were so many here, young girls, all being…used. I was sure God had not allowed me to be a part of something so vile. And then I felt he answered by showing what I could do that would make a difference. Be his hands in this place. If I had not come…" She cleared her throat. "Mei-Ling helps us, but she and A-He are fearful now too. Most girls are sickly, and then they're tossed aside like garbage, ravaged by dogs or tossed to the rivers. If we find them quickly, we get them well."

"That's how I became involved," Esty said.

"You don't make hats?"

"Oh. Yes. I do. We all work. But Esther thought she saw your friend Naomi. It was in an area not far from my shop, so Esther and I began working together. I have kept my eyes open for her. Today…I thought I might have seen Naomi again. I have a back room where Esther brings medicine at night. When she works at the theater."

"Sometimes, at the old boardinghouse, we had the stable to hide them. Esty took one girl by steamer to San Francisco, telling the captain that she was her servant, but it was to get her out, into Portland, Seattle, where she would have a better chance than with the Chinese leaders here. And there have been others. We give them money and hope."

"So it is both costly and dangerous," Suzanne said. "And my moving about. Moving us about. It disrupted—"

"You didn't know," Esther said. "There is no end to the suffering. No end. But nothing is impossible with God."

Suzanne couldn't seem to concentrate. She wanted to be a part of what Esther was about, wasn't sure how she could be. And then she found herself thinking only of Seth. He'd been so silent throughout this revelation.

Seth left then, to attend to his affairs, he said. Suzanne hadn't been brave enough to ask which ones. She hoped he had business details to wrap up before he committed to what Esther proposed. She pushed aside the thoughts that his gambling that everyone whispered about was still a part of his life. It was none of her business, she'd decided. He'd been sworn to secrecy whether he participated or not. She was sure he'd honor that.

Seth told her some days later that mistletoe still hung in the hallway. She fluttered her hands at her throat, must have blushed. "I hung it there myself," he said.

"Where exactly?" she said. "So I can avoid it."

"Hmmm," he said. "That's one request I'll only partially comply with. It's right here," he said and moved her shoulders so she stood in an airy place she knew to be the archway between the parlor and the hall. And then he'd kissed her.

She knew he would. And yet the startle of it, the sweetness of his lips on hers sent tingles to her toes. His mustache pricked against her upper lip. The kiss was so different from Zane Randolph's kiss to her. She shivered with the thought. It was more as Bryce's had been, and she felt herself sink in.

"I could not resist, dear lady," Seth whispered. "Forgive me."

"You'll think me a brazen woman if I don't." She stepped back, straightened the cane at her wrist.

"Think of you as brazen? Never. Oops!" Seth said, stepping away. "Blasted cats. Where did that one come from?" Suzanne giggled. Seth cleared his throat. "Did you know that mistletoe grows wild in the oaks in Oregon? It's true," he said when she shook her head no. "It's true." His voice changed, the words coming deeper and more slowly. "I thank the good Lord for giving us mistletoe, or I might never have found the courage to kiss you, Suzanne Cullver."

"You, lacking courage?" she said. She made herself seek his eyes, could feel the softness of his breath as he moved closer again. She felt herself aching to stay in the comfort of his chest, his arms—

"There's certainly no courage in taking advantage of a blind woman," Sterling Powder said from the hall.

Suzanne felt Seth move back from her as her hands fluttered at the lace ruffle at her hips and smoothed the silk at her throat.

"Holiday celebration," Seth said.

"Indeed," Sterling Powder said. Then to Suzanne Sterling said, "I believe the time has come for me to submit my notice of intent to leave. I realize this is not the best of times, during a *celebration*. However, I've found it difficult to speak with you of late, you being so occupied."

"Leave? But why?" Suzanne asked. "Haven't you enjoyed your work? The boys? Please don't go." She reached out for his arm, waved in the air before her. "Clayton's made such progress. Shall I pay you more? Is that it then?"

"The money is sufficient," he'd snapped. Then more calmly added, "I simply find my teaching approach challenged by the many intrusions and distractions the boys must endure. Clayton needs consistency. A regimen that must be honored daily."

"You're referring to me," Seth asked.

"No, no," Suzanne said. "It's the move and all. We're just getting settled in, Mr. Powder. And the holidays have distracted. Things will be more orderly now," Suzanne said. "I promise."

"I fear you will always seek distractions," Sterling Powder said. "There was no need for this new home. No need for disorder to present itself. People with…impairments need everyday patterns and habits. That concept appears to challenge you, Mrs. Cullver."

"Maybe it's all those cats around that distract," Seth said.

"The boys like them. Master Clayton calms when he pets the calico, and his words come more easily then, not that a man of your experience would understand. He'll miss them, I'm sure, now that the dog has abandoned you. Regretful, that. His leaving and now mine are just trials you'll have to bear," Sterling said. "But fortunately, you have good help, and you do seem to appreciate the challenge of change."

Suzanne felt herself blush with the truth of his words. He just couldn't leave, not now, not when the boy was at the threshold. She had to do something to change his mind. Suzanne felt the old irritation, anxiety, and frustration that once drove people from her just when she wanted their help. Had she somehow done that now? She'd have to concentrate.

"We can work something out," Seth said.

"What?" she said. "I'm sorry. I wasn't paying attention."

"And therein lies the problem," Sterling Powder said, sounding as firm as a final curtain.

"What is the problem?" Suzanne said. "Tell me and I'll fix it."

"You're not the problem, is all I'm saying," Seth said.

"And you would know, sir, about the training and teaching of young men without speech?" Sterling Powder challenged. "I think not."

"I know a rude speaker when I meet one," Seth said.

"Stop it!" Suzanne said, her hands to her ears. "Just stop it. Please."

"If my being here is a problem, Suzanne, I'll just be heading out. Never intended any disruption in routine," Seth said. With a sinking feeling, she heard him usher himself out.

Tipton shivered, wiped her face of the spew she'd just deposited in the brass spittoon in front of her. She couldn't remember ever feeling so miserable. She leaned back against the wainscoting, pushed a mildewed pillow beneath her back, then pulled her legs up under her on the narrow cot. She sipped a canteen of water, hoping it would stay down.

She could do laundry. She'd have competition from the Chinese, that was sure. But she'd had that back in Shasta City, too. Some miners wanted only white women to do their wash. How odd that was, when she thought of it. What possible difference could one's skin color have on the cleanliness of a shirt?

She leaned forward, upchucked again.

Still, lifting the hot water, hauling the heavy loads of boiled shirts back to their owners, all would take a toll on her small frame. But as she huddled in the small cabin of the steamer making its way from Crescent City to San Francisco, it was the only thing she could think of doing. She would have to do the only thing she knew how. She had all she needed. Wasn't that what Tyrellie told her? He'd added something about God giving her resources enough to serve others, but surely God would want her to take care of herself first.

She'd been ill through most of the voyage, the seas being heavy with the storm. Or had it been sickness that came to those carrying an infant? There was the real truth she had to face, the real reason she couldn't wash clothes for long.

She tried to calculate how much time she had. Chita said it took nine months, and she'd suspected a pregnancy for at least two, and it had been two more since Chita had been sworn to secrecy. That meant—she counted on her fingers—May. She could perhaps do laundry through March. After that she would have to find other work and a place to birth her baby. She'd have to worry about getting food enough, a doctor or midwife who could help... Tipton heard her breathing change, the rapid intake of breath. Her fingers started to tingle. *No!* She had to stay here, not go away. That was how she'd gotten in this condition, pretending not to know or feel, not wanting to upset Nehemiah, and so she'd allowed herself to drift away inside his passion for her, disappeared inside compliance.

She couldn't afford that now, couldn't risk going away or using precious strength worrying over her hand growing numb. Elizabeth had said she'd stop doing that to herself when she understood what disappearing took from her, when she found a better way to get what she wanted.

What did she want? She'd left a safe, warm hearth to huddle in a damp ship's cabin, and she'd be deposited in the morning on the wharf in a January chill. All she had to do to be warm was get back on and go home. Maybe Nehemiah would follow her. Was that what this was about? To be pursued, wanted? To have the happy reunion she could never have with her mother? With the fiancé who had died? She heard a rat scurry in the corner. No. She didn't want Nehemiah to follow or find her. She wanted to do this on her own.

This baby was really Tyrellie's and hers, the baby they would have had. She still had his memory, his tender advice ringing in her ears to help her raise it. She didn't need anyone else. Not her mother's love, not her brother's wretched approval, not her husband's fatherly protection.

She needed none of it. And if she was truthful—and she was learning to be—her baby would provide her with all she needed: love enough, approval enough, and even protection enough. After all, who would harm a woman bearing a child? Who would harm a mother with an infant at her breast?

Tipton smiled and rubbed her stomach. This wasn't so bad. A baby was such a little thing to give so much, but that was what a baby did: mind its mother's mind, keep its mother happy so its mother would be sure its little frame would grow and learn and change. This baby was totally dependent on her. Just her. She sipped some water. It stayed down. They'd dock before long. She wouldn't be seasick again. She'd be fine. She was having a baby. She didn't need anything more.

"Your rotten jack," Matthew said, jabbing his finger toward Ruth, "almost lost us the whole herd."

"What are you talking about?" Ruth sat up, wiped at her eyes. She must have fallen asleep beside Jessie. She turned out of habit to see if the small chest still raised and lowered itself. It did. Then she gave her attention to the madman pacing the room before her.

"That cussed Carmine just kicked off the corral panels, that's what he did. Crazy floating eye should have told us to let that…that…tarnal jack stay where he was." Matthew kicked at the ash tin set beside the hearth. A dusting of snow drifted up.

Ruth had never seen him like this. She felt her stomach tense, her shoulders stiffen. She looked at Lura, busy darning a sock. Neither she nor his sister seemed to notice.

"He ran around, stomping at the poles that held the mares," Matthew said. "Tarnal thing!"

Ruth watched Matthew tug at his gloves, hunch his shoulders up, yank at one that resisted his hands. That irritated him more. He gritted his teeth, jerked, then threw the snow-wet glove across the room.

He was having a tantrum, for heaven's sake. She'd never seen him like this, a huge bear marauding around the room, stomping and snarling. Why, he'd scare Jessie if she woke. Sarah huddled off to the side casting furtive glances at Ruth. Mariah yawned.

"Got them all riled. Storm wasn't enough to agitate them. No, your jack had to add his two eagles to the fray." He stopped, looked at Ruth as though she'd just shown up from nowhere. His shoulders dropped. "How is she?" He nodded toward Jessie.

"She's...the same."

"Maybe better give her some of that rum and add honey and the glycerin Doc McCully gave me. Ma, you got honey, don't you?"

"Traded some with a pair of Rogues," Lura said. "They use fire to burn out the bee trees, did I tell you that? I've got a mind to be trying that myself, come summer."

They mixed the ingredients, and Ruth gave her child small sips. Jessie coughed from the smoky room and begged to be held, which Ruth did. She patted the girl's hands in her own, saying words to both soothe her daughter's soul and bring some settling to her own.

"Just give the child the broth, some stew broth," Lura said. "Not the meat or nothing."

"I know," Ruth answered. Even then she wondered why she couldn't just accept what someone told her, without assuming they were making a correction.

Lura made up a new batch of onion juice, heated it, and insisted it would make the child sweat. "That's what'll break this new fever, you ask me," she said.

Ruth had nothing to lose. She dribbled the strong-smelling liquid into Jessie's mouth. The child did not resist. Her eyes fluttered some as she opened them. She even attempted a smile when Ruth brushed the damp hair behind her ears. "You'll be all right," she told her daughter, whispering it as a prayer. "You'll be all right."

"Where is Carmine now?" Ruth asked, hoping enough time had elapsed for Matthew to talk rationally about the jack.

"Dead, I hope."

"Well, of course he's red," his mother chastised. "She didn't ask you what color he was but where he was."

Matthew swatted at his felt hat, brushed off the snow melting from it as he stood before the hearth. "Ma. I said I hoped he was dead, not red. Your hearing's getting worse every day." He slowed his pace, spoke louder.

"You mumble," Lura said, laying the socks down and picking up a venison ham bone. She started to slice.

"Why didn't you get the boys to help catch him?" Ruth asked.

"Oh, they did." He brushed the water from his coat, hung it on a wall peg near the stove. The smell of wet wool filled the room. His shoulders sagged, and he took a deep breath. Tension eased out as he exhaled. "They did the best they could with that…beast."

He had immense patience, Ruth had always thought. At least with people. But animals and objects, he apparently got upset with them. Or maybe it was just this being cooped up, not being able to make any real progress through these winter months. It was too bad the school term got cancelled because a Negro child had enrolled. Except for this current storm, it would have been the perfect January for the children to go to school.

"The boys got the mares back in," Matthew continued. "But that Carmine would have nothing to do with the corral. He just ran back and forth, seducing them, I swear. Talking to 'em like he had things worth saying. Ewald's all riled up too. Don't know what's gotten into them."

"Maybe it's the weather," Ruth said. She rubbed at her arms to warm them. Rain pelted the shake roof, but it sounded like ice when it struck. "I'll go out in a bit to see if I can lure him in."

"Probably freeze good tonight, from the feel of it. Bucket handle is already iced up. Rope is fat as a well-fed snake. Which is why I don't want those mares out there. Be safer for them closer to the lean-to where we can at least keep the feed dry," Matthew told her.

"You did well to get it built when you did," Ruth said. Matthew nodded.

"Hopefully the sun'll come out in the morning and melt this all away, and your crazy mule will settle down."

"Have some coffee," Mariah told him, handing her brother a mug.

"Thanks, Pipsqueak. Best offer I've had today."

Ruth stood and peered out through the door. Next to it a scraped hide that served as a windowpane let in light. Glass would be nice, she thought, so she could see out and not just have the light. She shivered both from the cold that chilled her bones and from Matthew's earlier intensity. She liked that he could be as absorbed as a sponge in what he did—building, tending the horses' hooves, looking after all of them—but she hadn't expected his anger to carry the same kind of weight. Such stomping and shouting belonged to drunken men, not to upstanding though frustrated souls.

Zane had certainly never lost his temper like that, direct yet over with quick. No, his outrage seethed and consumed.

She closed the door, watched Matthew set his boots down, pick up his gloves to dry them by the fire. All calm. Oddly calm.

It was dusk, but from the four-paned window over the dry sink, Ruth could see Carmine in his quick-quick steps racing back and forth. "Did you try roping his left leg?" Ruth asked.

"I tried everything. He doesn't want to be caught. He didn't get caught."

"That's odd," Ruth said.

"What? Did the danged thing just wander into the corral like he was waiting to be asked?"

"Not exactly," Ruth said.

Matthew stood and followed Ruth to the window. Then they opened the door to the porch. He eased beside her. The jack paced, kicked once more at Ewald's corral despite the boys' efforts to throw a rope at Carmine's leg, and then he headed off, up through the pine outcropping and out of sight.

"What? He took off?" Matthew said.

"Just watch," Ruth told him. "He comes back."

Within a minute, the red-dirt-colored jack did just that. He trotted out of the darker timber, back toward the corral, pacing again, kicking at the poles, and eluding the boys and their ropes. "He'll do it again. Just a few seconds and then he's gone. You can almost count it. One, two…"

"Like a danged dog wanting you to chase him," Matthew said. "Some sort of crazy game he's playing."

"Ten, eleven. All right, he'll be back any second." They waited and Carmine arrived, kicked a few times, paraded before the mares whose backs steamed from the ice hitting their thick winter coats. Carmine squealed and bawled, then left, repeating the sequence.

"That jack is absolutely crazy. Needs one good sockdolager between the ears. That would fix his flint."

"Nobody's going to hurt him, are they, Ruth?" Mariah asked, shivering beside her brother, her arms wrapped around herself.

Ruth shook her head. "Get back inside. Your brother's just upset that he can't think like a jack." Ruth called to the boys, encouraging their efforts.

"Don't know as I'd breed anything to him," Matthew said. "You'll probably end up with a…mad dog rather than a mule."

"Well, if it's a game, he'll tire of it."

"I don't know. I once saw a mule slide down a hill covered with snow. Kind of on his back, his feet up high. He'd get stopped by a tree, pick himself up, shake off, and run back up and do it again. They play, those mules do. Must get that from some part of their breeding."

"I just hope the boys outlast him, keeping Ewald's corral and the mares' poles up until he does."

Carmine finally disappeared in the timber. This time he didn't come back.

"When he's hungry he'll show," Jason said as the boys came stomping in, warming their hands at the stove.

"There's lots of grass yet," Ned reminded him.

"Yeah, but he's got to travel some to find it not under the ice. Our stack's easier pickings."

"Besides, he likes his girlfriends," Ned said.

Sarah giggled.

"Well, he does," Jason said. "He treats those mares like they was his own little playmates."

"Were," Ruth corrected.

"Huh?" Jason said.

"Like they were his playmates. Your grammar. If you're not going to go to school, you'll have to accept my instruction here," Ruth told him. "McGuffey Reader awaits."

"Yes, Auntie," he submitted. "Anyway, he sure is attached."

"I'd always heard mules were herd bound," Ruth said. "More so than horses. Guess they get it from the jack side of the family."

"Funny, isn't it?" Lura said. "We always think of the females being the ones attached to kin. Truth be told, I think men are more family oriented. I remember your father being the one who always wanted to go maple syrup gathering. All his brothers and their families headed upstate, and they did more jabbering than gathering. Your pa always liked that time. And his home just so. Said it was a place of refuge."

"I remember, Ma," Matthew said. "Missing him, are you?"

"Oh, every January I expect he'll come to mind. Along with every other month of the year."

"We should do something like that," Mariah said. "Have some special event each year we look forward to."

"There's the women's quilt. We'll get that eventually, won't we, Auntie?" Sarah asked.

Ruth nodded.

"Maybe we could go back to Shasta. Have a reunion," Ned said. "We could see Suzanne again. I miss her. We used to sing real good together to those mining camps. Remember, Mariah?"

"I'll bet you do miss her," Ruth said.

"Or start our own tradition. Right here," Matthew said.

"Chasing jacks?" Lura said. She finished slicing the meat and put it into the pot to boil. Ruth was growing accustomed to stew. Still, she wasn't going to complain. Anyone who did that soon got assigned to kitchen duty.

"The Table Rocks," Mariah said. "We could hike to them come spring. You said you could see all kinds of different plants and things in the pools up there, right, Matthew?"

"Wasn't that where the treaty was signed last year? At the base of it?" Ruth said.

"For all the good that did," Lura said.

"Never been there myself," Matthew told her, nodding agreement. "But I heard you can see the whole valley from that point."

"Might be we'll be needing that view to find your red mule," Lura said.

"A red one or a dead one," Matthew said.

"I've need for a live, red jack," Ruth said, "who will spend this night separated and cold for going out beyond his limits."

They listened to the pelting ice, stoked up the stove, and Matthew directed the boys to bring in more wood to keep it dry inside.

Ruth thought about the limits of things. She was certainly beyond her limit here. She'd gone to the place her father had said each "man" must go: to the limits of her longing.

"You've got to go out so far you can't come back," he told her brother, Jed, as Ruth eavesdropped. She was just a child, but she never forgot. "That's how you find out who you really are. Can't just put your hand into a thing, Jed. You've got to put your whole body into it."

Sometimes Ruth wondered if that challenge didn't also drive her brother's love for whiskey, sinking him into the amber liquid when being out beyond his recall got to be too much. She knew her brother's taking on her case against Zane Randolph had taxed him heavily. And their flight west on her behalf had used up his life and Betha's, too, dropping their children as orphans in Ruth's care.

Still, her brother had put the whiskey bottles down when they headed west. Perhaps he'd left the States not just *for* her but because he wanted to stretch his own limits of longing, follow the passion of his *own* heart, too. Maybe that was in her blood, that needing to seek, to push, to find how much she could really achieve.

How odd that she wasn't doing it alone.

"I hope he's all right," Jessie said, breaking Ruth's thought.

"Who? Carmine?"

"No, Matthew. He sounded so...mad," she said.

"He did, didn't he? Being mad isn't bad, Jessie. It's what we do with it that counts."

"He throws gloves and stomps."

"I think he was just frustrated. All the waiting and watching. We'll find Carmine in the morning. It'll be all right." She hoped she wasn't telling her child or herself a lie.

silver storm

They settled into their beds listening to the sleet strike the wooden shakes, a sound that soothed through the night. Ruth rose early. It had become her habit to bring in wood and stoke the morning fire. Sometimes she worked on the rope she was twisting out of Jumper's tail hairs. It was almost finished. She didn't sleep well lying next to Jessie, so it was natural for her to take on some morning task. She worried she might roll onto her daughter and halt her shallow breathing. Sometimes the child complained of pain in her legs, and Ruth gave her a dose of Perry Davis's Pain Killer that the locals said treated ague. That was the general diagnosis from those who heard the symptoms. "Usually happens in the summer and leaves come cold weather," Dr. McCully told her.

But the weather had turned cold, and Jessie didn't seem much better. And the symptoms floated, Ruth thought, drifting from one part of her body to another. Lately, Jessie hadn't been strong enough to even walk without help.

Ruth was coming to accept something she hadn't earlier seen, like stars arriving at dusk. Jessie just might not get much better than she was. If that became true, Ruth would have to find a way to manage the stock, handle the spring foals and the breeding that had to begin soon after, while still tending the child. She needed to break ground to plant grain, buy cattle, and smoke the beef. Live. Provide. She just didn't know how she'd do it.

She padded in her bare feet to the door, stepping over Matthew's bedroll, hearing the boys toss and turn up in the loft. She stood for a moment watching Matthew breathe. He'd turn nineteen later this year. He seemed years older. She shook her head of the thoughts.

She opened the door and gasped. The world was awash with silver. An icy, drifting crystal mist. Ruth had never seen anything like it. It was etched out like the finest lithograph ever created.

Tree branches thick with sterling dotted the perimeter of the ranch. The corral poles lay frosted white. The pines wore sugared icing. Every blade of grass bent with a sea of hoary frost. Even the rock outcroppings had a glaze like sugared water over their edges. Small yellow flowers stood stiffly frozen, the color made more vibrant by the etching. And over everything hovered a pewter fog. No sound sifted through it.

Ruth's eyes rested then on a small canvas tent near the haystack. It, too, was covered with ice.

She looked beyond for Carmine, didn't see him. She'd check the tent to see who was there as soon as she stoked the fire. She reached out as though to touch the silver air, it filled her senses so. Then in one giant swoop her feet went out from under her, and she landed with a smack, her head cracking against the stoop. She moaned. Even the wood decking was frozen slick as a dog-licked plate.

Almost instantly Matthew was standing behind her to help her up, wearing his unmentionables. "Kind of squirrelly out here," he said, reaching beneath her arms.

"Whoa!" he said as he fell too.

Ruth grunted as his hip hit hers, but it was so slick she slid out from under him, her arms tangling with his, her head still throbbing. She felt a flush of irritation, and then she blushed as she looked at him sprawled and her with her nightdress whipped around her calves.

"Wait here," Matthew said.

"As if I could go anywhere," Ruth said.

On hands and knees, Matthew made his way toward the door, tugging at Ruth who now couldn't keep from laughing.

"Thanks," she said when her bare feet were firm on the warm floor inside. "I couldn't have done that without you."

"We've sounded the alarm for breakfast, that's sure," he said.

Standing up safe, she nodded toward the tent. "Who do you suppose that is?"

"Wasn't there last night. Neither was that mount."

"Let him come to us," she said.

"Might take 'til noon, even if he started now," Matthew said.

It was probably just a traveler having to stop somewhere due to the storm. "Maybe the children will have their tradition now," Ruth said. "We'll pop some corn, play a game or two of jacks…not dead jacks," she said.

"Spend the day being a kid again. That sounds good."

"I wasn't going that far."

"Why not? You don't play enough, Ruth. Always so serious. Maybe Ned can teach you how to win at his string game. People grow different on you when you're playing with 'em," he said. Those piercing blue eyes seemed to stare right through her.

"I'm not walking there until the sun comes up and thaws some of this stuff out," she said, tucking the quilt up around a sleeping Jessie's neck.

"You think it'll thaw today, do you?"

"It will, won't it?"

Matthew looked out the window at the opaque sky, the mist drizzling ice. "Should," he said. "But I never was one to predict women or the weather."

Chita found Nehemiah at midday. He still sat where he'd read the letter, his hand gripped around the paper. "Oh, Señor Kossuth," she said. "I worry when I do not see fire from your chimney. You and Mrs. Kossuth are not well?" She gazed around the room. "Señora. She is not here?"

234

He handed her the letter. She pushed it back. "I do not read the English," she told him. "But I see her hand in it. You are like struck lightning," she said. "The news is good, yes?"

"That's right, I remember," he said. "Mrs. Kossuth thinks you should learn English, you know. I was the one who suggested she learn Spanish. Did she ever speak to you in Spanish? She's a very good student, you know. Very good."

"I fix you up something hot to drink. Build the fire. It is very cold out. You will feel better as soon as Chita fixes you something to eat. You can tell me of the news then. All of Crescent City should hear your news."

He frowned at her but let himself be led from the room and sat at the table while Chita worked, building the fire, patting flour and water into a round tortilla. He knew he wasn't thinking clearly. She was saying things, being cheerful, talking of Crescent City interests. What interest was it of anyone's that his wife had left him because he was a dolt, a man who bankrupted his life? An army couldn't have done a better job of destroying him.

A thick blanket draped his thoughts, wrapped him in a fog. The scent of Tipton lingered, from the lavender of her toilet water to the sachets she filled and scattered about the room. Everything his eye touched pierced him with her memory. Across the back of the couch draped his old flag with fifteen stripes. It had been changed to one with thirteen stripes with so many new states being added, but he could never rid himself of the old one. He knew as a veteran he was supposed to destroy the fifteen-stripe flag. And he'd been grateful when Tipton said it would make a lovely throw, something useful. The clock ticked. The clock she'd set on the lace-covered side table. Her hands had held that clock, had wound it tightly. It wasn't running now, he noticed. Time had stopped with her leaving.

"What did you say?" Chita asked, turning.

"Nothing. I didn't say anything," he said. He must have groaned out loud with the anguish of his loss.

"Señora Kossuth has gone to visit friends?"

He shook his head. He didn't want to say. It was none of anyone else's business what happened inside his household. No one need know what travesties occurred here, how he'd failed his wife.

"She will be back soon?"

"Soon. Very soon," he said and then stopped himself. He had gotten into this by not telling the truth. He looked at the woman who stood before him. She had kind eyes, had been good help. She didn't deserve his lies. "I…don't know, Chita. When she'll be back."

"She goes far away?" Chita turned back to her cooking. Her hands moved quickly as she turned the flat bread, then laid it in the hot spider. Grease spit back.

"The truth is, I don't know where she's gone or if she'll even come back."

"Oh, she will come back. The little one will bring her back."

"Little one? Little one what?"

Chita turned then, her face reddened against the natural cashew color of her skin. Her large brown eyes stared at him. "Does the letter not tell you? Is that not what you wanted me to see?"

"The letter says she's gone away. That's all. Nothing more." He picked it up, his hand shaking. He tried to hand it to her again, but she shook her head.

"It does not say about her baby? She does not tell you?"

"Baby? Tipton has a baby?"

"Not yet," Chita said. "But soon. She makes me say I will not tell you, but I think you know. You do not know?" Chita wailed, her floured hands squeezed on her cheeks. "She will be very unhappy with me when she finds this out."

He stood, almost knocking the lamp on the floor. He caught it and stared at Chita. "You're sure. You're sure she is…with child?"

"Sí. She does not know it herself until I tell her. Two months ago and then she fires me. I think she wants me to stay with a baby coming soon, but she says she wants to do things herself, for you. Take care of you and be ready for her baby. But she does not say she never tells you. Oh, *Madre, Madre.* She will never forgive me."

"She was afraid you'd say something. That's why she wanted to do everything here herself."

"And I do that, *sí?* Just what she doesn't want me to do." Chita looked nearly as bereft as he felt.

"She must have thought it her fault, that she'd done something wrong," he said. "That's why she wanted to go away. She signed the letter, 'Love, Tipton.' See here?" He pointed at the letter, then laid it down. "Never mind, Chita. Never mind." He straightened his shoulders, rubbed at his red beard. "I'll explain everything to her. Thank goodness, you told me. I have to find her, have to bring her back, let her know it's all right."

"You do not know where she goes?"

"Where would she go?" He wondered if he knew her well enough to know the answer to that question. He paced the room, feeling the heat from the stove, from the warmth inside him. Tipton carried his child! Where could she have gone? How far could she have gotten in the storm? She might have left a day, maybe even more, before. "Home," he decided. "I'll bet she's headed home."

"This is not her home, Señor Kossuth?"

"This is not her home, Chita. Shasta City is her home. And I tried to take her from it. She needed her mother, her family. That's what this is about. Shasta City. I'll go there as soon as the weather breaks, and I've got vittles in my stomach. Is that tortilla ready? This soon-to-be proud papa is starved."

From what Tipton could see, San Francisco was a bedlam of building and rebuilding. Blackened structures still smoked from the latest fire;

peddlers hawked pies at the street corners, and urchins not much shorter than Tipton spread their dirty palms out asking for handouts. Fast-walking men in dusty long coats and women with faces shadowed by bonnets brushed past her, made her feel dizzy with their pace. She felt spun around with the noise and the smells. Maybe this was a little more than she'd bargained for. Maybe she couldn't do this all by herself. She turned to look back up the gangplank. No, she couldn't get back on there. She would make this a better day. That was her new motto, she decided. *Make this a better day.*

Instead of being frightened, breathing fast to take her hands to tingling when something threatened to consume her, she'd remind herself that she had everything she needed to make this a better day.

Already she was grateful she'd arrived at dawn. It would give her time to trade in her sapphire-and-silver necklace for needed cash. She was sure she'd find a buyer, and with currency, she would find a room. Then work. Then a life. For her and her child.

Today she would pretend she walked behind a lantern at night, moving forward far enough to see in front of her if not exactly sure where she'd end up. Tomorrow she would set up her laundry business. She'd done it before. She could do it again.

"Step aside there, lass," a big burly man said. He motioned with a nightstick as one with port authority, giving directions. She stumbled against a man jostling behind her, pushing past. The burly man grabbed at her elbow, balanced her. "Wait for your family over there, lass. They'll be along. We've got to clear the gangplank. Move along. Move along."

"I have no family, sir," Tipton said. She blinked her eyelashes.

"Well, move anyway. There's no time for dawdling." He motioned behind her, and the gentleman pushed past. Cabs and shays came by and picked passengers up, let others off. The *Sea Gull* wasn't a big ship, but it would reload and head back, stopping in places like Crescent City, then heading north to Portland and eventually Seattle. Maybe Portland would be a better place for her, less congested, she thought.

No, she'd chosen San Francisco. She would make this work.

When the traffic slowed some, she tugged like a child on the burly man's sleeve.

"What, lass? You still waiting?"

"I have no family, as yet, kind sir." She stood sideways, so he could see the form of her. It was brazen, but she knew her baby would want to be of service.

The big man turned a shade of red Tipton had never seen before.

"Hush now, Miss. Missis. Sure and you're in need of help then. Have you no one to be meeting you, lass? 'Tis not a good place for a lady alone."

"I'm surprising them. What I need now is an address for the nearest…banking area. So I can safely deposit—"

"Shush now." He put his dirt-creased finger to his lips. "Not a good thing to be sharing." He lifted her carpet valise, handed it to her. "Carry it in front of you, Lass. Don't be talking about your valuables here in the open. There're nothing but rats and rogues waiting to take advantage. You take your valuables…and hire yourself a cab and go to Market Street."

"Why, thank you, sir," she said and curtsied.

Market Street. She'd been in San Francisco but an hour, and she already had a place to go. Tyrellie was right, the Lord did provide.

She used some of her precious cash to hire a cab, telling the driver to take her to the banking district. "What address, ma'am?"

"Oh, just any bank exchange," she said.

"You taking out or putting in?" the driver asked her.

Oddly, his question was the last thing she remembered until awakening that evening on the wharf, her face tender and sore, her traveling skirt torn and an empty valise jammed beneath her chin. Her underthings and other dress lay strewn across the dirty street. Her fists clutched her feathered hat. Frantic, she patted for the silver necklace. It and her remaining cash were gone.

She groaned, then quieted. *Lost it all!* How stupid she was. She noticed a dark form turn. Her heart pounded as she hugged the side of the building, wood slivers pushing against the cloth of her cape. Her hand brushed across her stomach. *Oh, Baby!* The dark form moved toward her, and she breathed a prayer. Maybe she couldn't make this a better day, alone.

As Ruth watched, the man stepped out of the canvas tent, slipping and sliding toward the cabin, his long arms touching the icy earth once or twice as he made an effort to keep his knees from hitting. He reached for the porch rail with one hand and sent his other out to Matthew, introducing himself as Burke Manes and saying that Burke was German for fortress and Manes—he pronounced it Man-ez—his father's last name too. "No aliases here either," Matthew said. He had a full head of sandy hair, and he smiled as he spoke. He stood taller than Matthew and leaned slightly at the shoulders as a man accustomed to carrying extra weight. He had a round face, short neck. He was not a handsome man. But he wore a cherub's smile.

"Not the way a man likes to greet folks," he said. "Coming at you in the early morning after having spent the night uninvited on your spread."

His eyes were hazel with white flecks in them; they were the most striking features of a wide tanned and lined face. He held his hat in his hand, reached out with the other to the boys who clustered behind Matthew, napkins stuck into the tops of their undershirts. He nodded his head to Ruth and said, "Ma'am."

"We've plenty for eating," Lura said. "Might as well sit a spell. Ain't going anywhere till the sun comes out."

"That, my good woman, is the truth for certain. Not to mention a fine reward for making it across the ice pond there." He bent to slip his boots off, his long coat falling open and Ruth thought then he was a man comfortable with himself, willing to be in his stocking feet within minutes of an introduction.

The others gave their names, and his eyes granted full attention to each, even the children. Ruth noticed that his shoulders bent lower when Sarah spoke. For her he almost went down on one knee to shake her little hand. Then his eyes cast to the cot near the fireplace and stopped, looked up in question. "My daughter. Jessie. She's…ill with the ague, they say. She's still asleep."

"Who says? Doc McCully?"

"Yes. And others, too."

"McCully's a good man. But it seems an odd time of the year for ague. Bread and milk helped her any?"

"Some," Lura interrupted. "Think a little whiskey might do her better."

"That is a common remedy for it," Burke said, removing his black wool coat. He looked around for a peg, found one and hung it there.

"That cure could be worse than the ailment, Ma," Matthew said.

"Relieves pain though," Lura said.

"Or gives a new one."

Ruth looked at Matt, detected something…singular in his voice. "She doesn't seem to be in much pain," Ruth said.

"That's a blessing," Burke said.

"Sometimes in the night she cries out. Could be dreams. She's had her share of troubles for someone so young. I don't know." Ruth turned away, embarrassed at the ease with which she spoke of such intimate things to this man.

"Johnnycakes are on," Lura said. "Who's eating?"

"I am!" both boys yelled in unison.

"I ain't deaf," she said.

"Yet," Matthew said and grinned as he directed Burke to the bench.

Lura laughed and threatened Matthew with the three-legged spider as she served, but he ducked, and she ruffled his hair instead.

"Join us, Mr. Manes?"

"Does your last name mean something special Mr. Man-ez?" Sarah asked. "You said your first name did."

"You pronounced it well, little lady," he said. "Some folks think it's like a horse's mane, but it isn't. And yes. Like I said, my first name means castle or fortress. Besides belonging to my father, the name Manes is an old Latin word that means 'revered spirit of someone who has died.' Someone you cared about, I might add."

"Speaking of things that've died that we might be revering, you didn't come across a dead red jack out there, did you?" Matthew asked.

"Can't say that I did. You lose one?"

"Revered?" Sarah asked.

"Holding them in high regard," Burke said, giving his attention back to Sarah.

She blinked. "The way I hold my mama and papa?" she said.

Burke looked over at Ruth. "She's my niece," Ruth said. "My brother and his wife died along the trail, on their way out here in '52."

He nodded. Then to Sarah he said. "I suspect just like that."

"Kind of nice carrying a name that says you hold people in high regard," Jason said.

"Even if they are dead ones," Ned added.

Burke laughed, a full belly laugh that made his eyes sparkle and the little lines like streams flow to the pool of them. He wasn't very old, Ruth thought. Maybe thirty at the most. "Nothing wrong with revering those we loved," he said. "As long as they don't hold us hostage to a memory that never was."

"What's that mean?" Mariah asked. "Pass the syrup, will you, Sarah?"

"Only that we don't remember things the way they really were. At least I don't think we do. We kind of form our own experience of it later. We think we remember it exact, but I'm convinced we don't. We get to have two experiences that way, for the price of one: what really happened, and what we remember. Most of us improve on the original, if it was one we didn't like. 'Course that means we've no excuse for carrying around bad memories because they can always be changed to better ones." He grinned, then broke into an elocutionary voice as though he stood on a stage and declaimed.

"What once we loved is memory now, tangled up with time.
Rooted deep.
Cradled through experience, it seeks to warm us;
Stay off erosion of the wounded heart."

They all sat staring, Matthew with his fork halfway to his mouth, the boys not chewing. "I'm still working on it," he said. Lura had turned from the fire, spatula in hand, squinting as though to hear it all. Even Mariah had dreamy eyes.

Burke brought his hand down, cleared his throat, then stuffed a piece of Lura's johnnycake in his mouth. "There's more to it," he said. "But I digress. So early of a morning." A crumb made its way onto the day-old growth of his stubbled beard.

"That's lovely," Ruth said.

"Who wrote it?" Jason asked.

"I take full blame, I do." He wiped at his face now with the back of his hand, and Mariah quickly handed him her napkin.

"It makes me think of…" Ruth hesitated then continued, "my friend, Mazy Bacon. She's always been fascinated with words and what they mean. And with putting them together in interesting ways. It sounds to me like her. What you just said."

"*Manes* means good then," Sarah said. "A good fortress."

"So it does," he said. "So it does. Like a solid home."

"That's fitting for Mazy, too," Mariah said. "Home means a lot to her."

"Where does she live then, this friend of yours?"

"In Shasta City," Ruth said. "But she came there from Wisconsin. With some reluctance. She's a widow." She'd have to ask Mr. Manes to write his poem down. It might be good to send it to Mazy, a way to open a gate a bad bull once closed.

They finished the meal, and Ned stepped out onto the porch to see if there was any change in the silver storm. If anything, the ice had grown thicker. Even the haystack had a sheen to it.

"Good thing we fed heavy yesterday," Jason said.

"Horses don't look too hungry right now," Mariah noted. The animals stood tails still, heads down, their backs a crystal mist and their noses white with ice. Ewald hadn't moved from where his head buried into the food bag. The paddock had been somewhat stomped down by the mares, but wherever they didn't stand, the ice had built up. The area between the cabin and the barn and lean-to shimmered in the foggy white. "It's getting colder," Mariah said. "See my breath?"

"Silver thaws usually don't last much more than a day or two in this country. But that's because it rarely stays cold. This one looks to hang on," Burke said.

"We can hold out for a week or more," Lura said. "Plenty of supplies."

"Feeding stock in this could be a trial," Ruth said.

"One we'll have to enter into tomorrow whether we like it or not," Matthew said.

"You'll have an extra hand at it, if you don't mind my staying a bit. Can't get far in this stuff."

"Where was it you were heading?" Lura asked. "Folks going to be expecting you?"

"Wherever the Lord leads," Burke said. "And folks rarely expect me. Actually, I'm your neighbor down a piece or two. Took a wrong turn." He smiled, whispered to Sarah, "I wasn't lost, mind you. Just powerful turned around for a day or two." To the rest he added, "I run some cattle. They're grazed out. And every traveling parson knows we're not really expected anywhere."

"You're a preacher?" Ned asked.

"I help lead the little Table Rock Baptists' meeting up in town. You're welcome to join us."

"We almost did," Matthew said. "Before Jessie got sick."

"Folks just seem to accept that a preacher will find his way to a hungering hearth."

"Wonder what God thinks you need to be feeding us here?" Ruth said, then turned when her daughter awoke and called out.

learning to receive

Seth hadn't thought that his presence in Suzanne's life would be anything but temporary. He'd looked for a dry place to stay on a wet night,
a friendly voice in a distant town. That was all. He should have located
a hotel or simple boardinghouse and just stayed there. But when he
arrived at Sister Esther's house where he and Mazy had visited earlier
that year, he'd surprised himself with the level of disappointment he felt
that Sister Esther wasn't there. Nor Miss Suzanne and her boys either.

He and Mazy and that bull had made their way with the directions
given. He hadn't remembered Suzanne being so lovely as she was when
Esther opened the door and Suzanne descended the stairs, inquiring
who was there. She was still "seeing with new eyes," and her enthusiasm
somehow framed her face with a deeper beauty than he'd seen before.
He shook his head. He hated thinking he'd done something to take that
serenity away, just by staying on, just by stealing that kiss. And with the
women doing good work like they were and him acting like a stream of
water dousing a going fire.

He took his writing set out, tried to put his thoughts into words.
Only dull and callow lines came out. He put the ink pen down, stared
into the lamplight. How had he gotten to this?

He'd dragged the bull south as a favor to Mazy, mostly, and hadn't
expected it would give him anything back. Life was funny that way.
Elizabeth Mueller had told him that once, that giving away was the yeast
in life. "It always raises more than it takes," she'd said. "You get a whole

loaf of bread from just a little tiny cake of yeast. That's what we're asked to do in life, Seth Forrester. Take what we've been given, give it away, and wait for more to come back. That's what you did in bringing us to safety. Now the good Lord will bless you by giving back. If you let him. You independent men don't much like receiving. Always on the giving end, wanting to fix things."

He'd scoffed at her, good-naturedly. Giving *was* easier than receiving. Any man knew that. It was a catalyst, she'd said, the way kindling built up a roaring fire or the way losing at poker for a few hands early could sweeten the final pot. No, not like that. He suspected Elizabeth would not approve of that analogy. That old woman with her baking heart had more wisdom wrapped up inside her pretzels than most padres in their catechisms. But she couldn't have known about his heart and how far away he stood from goodness, from being a worthy receiver.

See, here he was, bringing distress to Suzanne, all his "giving" meaning nothing. The man was just jealous, that was what Sterling Powder was. No need to be. Seth didn't intend anything. He was just a man helping a friend. And defending an unfair accusation of another. Still, what else could the man think but that he had intentions for Suzanne? Seth swallowed. Now where had that come from? A widow with two kids had no wish to intercept his wayward trail. Did they? And what about Powder?

Powder. Just a fluff of a name, but maybe the man himself had more substance. He had gotten Clayton to talk, after all. And the arrogance could camouflage a wounded soul.

Here it was well into January. He should have moved on. Maybe he was still reeling from Mazy's portrayal of their relationship. *More like a brother and sister.* That was what she'd said. If that was true, then what was this with Suzanne? There'd been something more in Suzanne's response to him than mere sisterhood. It was a passion. Had he drawn it from her? Or was she the yeast in what was yet to bake inside his own heart?

He stood up, paced the small guest room that held a bed with white flannel sheets and pillows with lace borders. A small writing desk sat beneath a window, and the light from the lamp flickered, a sign that the wick needed to be cut back. Seth's mother always told him that the quality of the light depended on the wick's being cut back. Why had he thought of that?

He heard Esther go out. She was a hard worker, that Esther. He could put some of his money into what they were trying to do. The investment would be a better use of it than sweetening a poker pot. And it would give him cause to connect with Suzanne more too. So what stumbled him, kept him from jumping in with both feet free?

Gambling. All life was that, so why ruminate like an old horse on a mouthful of stale grain? Winning at faro or poker or roulette left all men thirsting for more of something that could never fill them up. At least not at a poker table.

He heard the boys in the nursery next door, little Sason chattering, and the low, staccato jabs of words that must have been Clayton. Those scamps should be asleep. He thought about those boys, the sweet warm way they smelled, inviting as a bedroll on a cold morning. "Men holding babies are as catching as a cold," Elizabeth had said. A bell rang, and he heard the muffled voice of Sterling Powder. Probably telling the boys to quiet down. Two more days and that man would be gone. As far as Seth knew, Suzanne hadn't found any replacement. Maybe he should volunteer. He scoffed.

He pulled on his coat, brushed at the wide lapels, snapped his knuckles at the nap of his tall hat and pulled it onto his head. He needed some air, that was what it was. Fresh air.

A moon shown bright enough to make shadows as he walked. The light reflected on pools of water at the cobblestones, a thin layer of ice formed at the edges. The promise of cold that would disappear with the sun. He tripped on a tree root digging its way into the path, caught himself. He heard a pig grunt, a catfight begin and end in the distance. While he walked, he shook his head, turning his hands this way and that. He rehearsed what he would say to Suzanne in his head. *All I'm saying is that I'm sorry my being here has meant some disruption for you. Wouldn't want to hurt you. Don't know if going or staying does that.* Would that confuse her? Did it say more than he intended? *I am who I am, is all I'm saying. Not a perfect man. Not predictable.* What did a man say to a woman to move the caring forward when he didn't know for certain where his own heart was headed? A flash of lantern light flooded a circle of wet cobblestone before him. It illuminated his way for a moment, and then he walked right through. That was exactly how he felt: clarity for a second then stumbling on in darkness.

He tried to imagine what advice Elizabeth Mueller would give him about this. He had no mother to ask advice of, no father to show him the way, no brothers or sisters to cajole and correct him. He was an orphan just as sure as those Wintu Indian kids Mazy Bacon collected. Maybe that was what appealed to him about Mazy in the first place, that she took in strays. That was just what he was.

Well, he'd done his part in saving strays himself. He'd brought the women safely into Shasta City, and he'd placed a good chunk of his gambling winnings into Mazy's farm that now not only fed folks but was a place of business. Would Mazy think it was dirty money if she knew it came from gambling? He hoped not. She could take something unworthy and make it good. She had a soul for that. It was probably as close as he would get to sainthood. He snorted. He hadn't realized he hankered after sainthood. Now that was a losing gamble.

He looked up when he heard the music. Front Street. Bursts of laughter and the thump of feet tapping in time led him forward. Behind the tall doors of the brick building stood croupiers and dealers at blackjack and roulette tables. Smoke swirled like mist around them. Voices rattled the chandelier above the faro table, and heavy red drapes muffled the music of the five women dressed in pink playing cellos and fiddles onstage. There'd been a theater around here once, he'd been told, taken out by one of the floods.

A woman approached him. Dressed all in black except for a red satin flower attached to the side of her hip, a green stem trailing to the floor. She sidled up to him. "Looks like you know your way around." She fiddled with the diamond stickpin in his lapel, caressed his chest with the palm of her hand. He felt her heat against his leg. "Buy a girl a drink? Make you one happy man being kind to a needy girl."

He looked down at her. Was this his life then? Even without wishing to, this was what he drifted toward, wasn't it? He found his way here, when he sought direction, here to this den of drunken men and wasted women.

No, he hadn't sought it. He'd allowed himself to drift. That was what he did. Drift like a fishing line through a pool. These people before him represented the relationships he was capable of: shallow, temporary, depleting. He was a drifter. Well dressed, rich in worldly goods perhaps, but a drifter just the same.

She pressed against him. She smelled of whiskey and sweat. Face powder, mixed with lip rouge, caked at the corners of her mouth. A critter wiggled next to the fan spread open in her black hair.

"You're a man of good habits," she said. "I can tell that."

A man of good habits.

He stared at her. Was this what he was meant for then? To simply respond to the moment, to be led by his habits?

"What do you say?" she said. She had a crooked nose. She inhaled his scent, a long seductive breath, sniffed with her chin lifted.

"Looks like you might have had enough already," he said. "I know I have."

He pushed her aside and stepped backward, his eyes scanning the faces that swirled before him, the woman's included, her expression hurt, then angry. His heels hit the cobblestones none too soon. Then like a boy caught in the pumpkin patch by the farmer with his gun, he fled. He just didn't know where he was running.

❦

"Mrs. Kossuth? Tipton? Isn't that right? Tipton Kossuth. What on earth are you doing here? Here, let me help you up."

Tipton cowered back into the shadows, barely hearing her name over the pounding of her heart. She'd seen the form approaching, huge and bulky but now the person before her seemed almost tiny. Blurry but tiny. And she used her name. *Someone knew her name?* Tipton squinted, trying to make sense of where she was and how long she'd been here. Sea gulls cried out. She smelled murky seawater.

The form leaned into her. A woman. She let the woman take her elbow, help her sit up. She shivered, not sure if it was from fear or weakness. The woman brushed at her skirts. Tipton's head pounded like the thump of a water wheel against a river.

"You don't remember me, do you? I'm Esty Williams. Suzanne Cullver's friend. I helped her find her house in Shasta City. Remember?"

Tipton shook her head. That hurt even more. She held her head with both hands. She didn't remember who had found Suzanne's house, only that Suzanne moved into one before any of the others. She'd never seen this woman before. How could this Esty person possibly know her, let alone identify her from a dark shadow in a strange city?

"It doesn't matter. Are you hurt? Did you imbibe too much?"

"I'm fine," Tipton said, stiffening. "Just fine." She lowered her hands, straightened her short jacket at her hips. "How is it you know me?"

"I used to watch you, when you dragged those big baskets of laundry through the streets to the St. Charles Hotel. And Lura talked of you all, of course, what good friends you were. She mentioned you as the 'pretty one.' I knew your brother." She pushed a hatpin into her felt hat. "And I heard about your marriage after the fire."

"You did?"

"Where is Mr. Kossuth, by the way?" Esty looked around. "I can't imagine that he left you here unprotected like this. Did something happen to him?"

"Just what are you doing on this wharf so late?" Tipton challenged.

Esty tipped her head in a questioning way. "I'm waiting for the steamer to…you're bleeding. Your head is bleeding. Here." She reached into her reticule for a handkerchief, dabbed at the side of Tipton's head. "And it isn't late. It's morning. Early, yes, but the sun'll be up soon. How long have you been here?"

"I'll be all right," Tipton said, "I'll be all right." The dabbing at her wound stung, and her head pounded like unlatched shutters slamming in a windstorm. She swooned, falling against the woman. Maybe she could accept her help. She seemed kind enough. She was well-dressed, had a hat with feathers and flowers that swooped down to touch her narrow shoulders. A dragonfly hatpin held it at a cocky angle. She must have worked in the saloon if she knew Lura. Was she a banker? Or a woman of negotiable affections?

"Here," the woman said. "Come sit on my trunk." She led her to a flat-bottomed chest with the word "Millinery" stamped on the side. She picked up Tipton's flattened hat, pushed it out, and looked around for a pin. "There," she said and placed the hat on Tipton's head, pulling the dragonfly pin from her own to hold Tipton's on.

Tipton reached up to touch it. "It's heavy," she said. "Thank you, miss…"

"It's Esty," she repeated. "And the pin is brass."

"My head. It hurts terribly."

Esty hesitated, then said, "Take a smidgen of this." She pulled a small case from her reticule, turned it open to reveal a white powder.

"What's this?"

"Opium. The Chinese use it for pain. Just a little," she said. "My hip bothers me some, and this helps. Here." Esty took a pinch of the powder between her dark gloves and dropped it onto Tipton's tongue. "Sometimes it works faster underneath," she said. "But you've had quite a blow. Need to take it slowly."

The powder had a bitter taste at first, then her tongue felt numb, then nothing. Within minutes, the head-throbbing eased.

"Look," Esty said. "I don't know if you're awaiting a ship or have just arrived, but your bag has apparently been riffled through. And you're obviously hurt. Is your husband coming back? You can't stay here."

Tipton looked around. "I've…I've been…Nehemiah will be along. Thank you. I'm fine," she said. "This isn't where I arrived."

"You're on the dock for ships to Sacramento. That's where I'm headed. Suzanne lives there now. And Sister Esther. I'm sure they'd take you—"

"No! They can't know. No, we came to San Francisco."

"Where is Mr. Kossuth then?

"I'll stay right here. I'll…I'll wash clothes again, just like I did before. I'll—"

"Not do much until your head is stitched." Esty paused. She tapped her finger to her chin. "There'll be a doctor on board. You can stay with me for a time if you don't want Suzanne to know, though I can't imagine why not. Every one of you women who came across together share something special. You're so fortunate."

"I'm not resisting anything," Tipton said. "I'm just doing this on my own, is all. We have to do it alone."

"Suit yourself then," Esty said. "You can wash laundry in Sacramento if you've a bent to. I'd hire you myself. I barely have time for my own laundering with the millinery orders I have. Have you ever stitched hats?"

Tipton shook her head, stopped with the throbbing. She didn't *have* to settle on laundering, she guessed. If she took up millinery, she could work inside. It wouldn't be nearly the hard labor. But then Suzanne and Esther would know. And they'd tell Nehemiah, she was sure of it. No. She'd told herself laundry. If she didn't keep her own promises, how would she ever keep promises to her baby?

"I'd surely get that stitched, or it'll leave a disfiguring scar," Esty said.

Tipton's hand went up to the wet wound. She could feel a chunk of flesh just hanging, the soft tissue beneath it damp and exposed. It reminded her of her brother's ear all chopped off.

She was penniless, bruised, and alone in a strange city. What was she going to do? Her hand rubbed her abdomen. No, not alone. She could still choose. She wasn't breathing fast nor drifting away. She would make this a better day.

"If I could just take out a small loan. Until I get settled and find a place for the tubs and irons."

"That might be arranged," Esty said. "If you get that head looked at."

Tipton nodded. "All right. And should I have just a little more of the powder? Then I think I'll be strong enough to walk on board that ship to Sacramento."

They were into the tenth day of the silver storm. Matthew's early temper tantrum on the first day was a distant memory compared to the irritations each foiled on the other in the days since.

Ruth noticed this annoying habit Matthew had of cracking his knuckles and whistling without a tune. Lura hummed as she worked and smacked her lips when she kneaded the flour, loud as a pig. Mariah whined. She hadn't ever seen the girl do that before, though she had to admit, she'd rarely seen her playing jacks before either and losing to Sarah who got sassier than Ruth had ever seen her. She complained that Ned and Jason were hiding her pencils so she couldn't draw.

Ruth tried to stay out of their way, mediating, then working on her mecate. The boys had helped her spin the strands before the storm hit. She now had three, twenty-foot strands she was twisting into a rope. The singing and dancing led by Ned, followed by stories told by Matthew and Burke, too, had gotten them through most evenings. Sarah had cut and drawn an entire set of dominoes. Lura "uncovered" a deck of cards inside her spice box. But the diversions were wearing thin.

They were tired of venison stew. The flour would be gone that day, Lura announced. No more biscuits. Just meat and a few old vegetables to argue over. So much for the kindness of kinship, Ruth thought. This being under one roof day after day stretched any relationship. It was truly a miracle when two people stayed married, but divinely inspired if they lived through ten days of a silver storm and still spoke. Wasn't it Mei-Ling who had told her that the Chinese word for "trouble" was made up of two characters: one being the symbol for "under one roof" and the other being "two women"? They could certainly prove it here.

The first days had been...adventurous. They'd played games, learned some new songs led by the deep baritone of Burke Manes. Matthew had told stories of being along the Columbia River the year before. Ruth sensed he left some things out, but she found she liked what he remembered to share about landscape. They'd had things in common, and if it wasn't for her commitment to this land, this place, and her children, she might have allowed herself to speculate about what might someday have been with him.

Lura regaled them with mining camp tales, buttressed by Mariah and Ned's memories. Burke gave lively renditions of biblical stories, most Ruth had never even heard of, about widows and even women warriors, or at least women who strategized battle plans that the men carried out. No one had ever mentioned that before. She thought now that they'd all been holding their breath, assuming this storm wouldn't last long, couldn't last long. Each day they'd peer at the sky, hoping for the sun, and each night they sought the moon.

Then Mariah came in sobbing that one of the mares was down. She'd gotten so thin, Mariah worried that she'd miscarry. When they reached the barn, the mare struggled as though delivering early and then, huffing with exhaustion, died.

"They're not getting enough water," Ruth said patting Mariah's shoulder as the girl cried. They'd been chopping holes as best they could in the stream and hauling it from the spring that didn't freeze. But leading them up to the spring was treacherous, like walking across a frozen pond. The animals were stressed, not eating well and not drinking. And they'd had no salt now for almost a month.

Then one of Matthew's scrub mares, as she called them, fell on the ice and had to be put down. Ruth found herself hardly sleeping, just

standing and staring at the silver world. She could lose them all! All the
foals, all that was promised for that first payment in the spring just a few
months away.

At least Jessie was doing better. In an odd way, the girl seemed
strengthened by their togetherness, so Ruth would go out and help haul
water, chop at the haystack for an hour or two. And then the next day,
Jessie would be worse, not able to even bear weight on her legs. Ruth
wondered once if Lura gave her something to eat that weakened her, but
that made no sense at all.

Jessie's color seemed brighter since Burke's arrival, but perhaps it
was because she slept better. Burke had asked if he might pray with the
child that second day after he'd arrived. Ruth had hesitated, but
Matthew said, "What could it hurt, Ruth?" She'd consented, and that
night the child's breathing had been less labored.

"Color and breathing's better because of the little dab of whiskey I
put in her serving of soup," Lura confessed one day when Ruth mused
out loud about her daughter's strange healing.

"Don't do it again," Ruth said.

"And why not? Perfectly healthy. Even Doc McCully said so."

"I never heard that," Ruth said. "And I'm her mother. I'll decide
such things."

"Truth be known, you got a ways to go before you've had the years
of experience that I've had," Lura said.

"It's not the years, it's the miles," Ruth retorted.

"Not the tears, it's the smiles? Is that what you said?"

Everyone laughed, and for just a moment Ruth wondered if Lura
wasn't feigning deafness.

At least Burke hadn't been condemning of their efforts, or of Lura's
whiskey episode either. He wasn't at all what she expected a preacher to
be. He worked beside them, eased in at their table as though he
belonged, and never assumed he was wiser or more patient or better
than anyone else, though Ruth thought sure he was. The attention he
gave to the children proved that.

One night he'd stayed up at the fire while everyone else snored or tossed in their bedrolls around his feet. He just sat, whittling on a thin stick, "making toothpicks," he said. Ruth had lain awake, watching his gentle face in the firelight.

"Would you mind company?" she asked, wrapping herself in a blanket.

"Never do," he said.

She made her way quietly to sit across from him, her long braid falling over her shoulder, the plaid blanket pulled over under the opposite arm.

His features weren't really clear in the backlight of the fire so she wasn't sure how to read him. Finally she ventured, "We aren't, well, we're none of us married to each other," she said. "We're just staying together until spring comes, and then Lura and Matthew and Mariah, their family, will be getting a place of their own."

"Fortunate to have such friends who are willing to help out through a winter like this," he said.

She didn't know why she felt the need to explain to him. "They would have gone on already. Matthew has a place picked out north of Jacksonville, near the Table Rocks. He found it when he took my mares on ahead, after my brother and all the other men died. But when Jessie took sick…they stayed. To help get me settled. Us."

"Something looks like a tragedy turns out to be a good thing," he said. "I always find that interesting. Bible's full of those instances."

"Is it?"

"Take Joseph. Sold into slavery by his own kin, and it turns out he shows up being where he needs to be during a famine. Saves them all. What a celebration that must have been! Then after years in Egypt, his descendants end up living in exile, becomes a tragedy of its own as they're kept in slavery." He brushed wood slivers from his jeans. "But God cares about people we don't always think are worthy of his care. Little people, I like to call them. God cares that intimately about our lives, Ruth." She pulled the blanket tighter, suddenly chilled. "Then he led the Jewish people out through a wilderness, and they celebrated again. That triumph turns into forty years of being powerfully turned around. Not lost, mind you. Just seems to be the story of living, making our way through wilderness places, making mistakes, getting back on the trail. We find a new way and celebrate together, seeking the Promised Land."

"I suppose we do all long for Promised Land," Ruth said. "I thought this place would be that for me. But here we are. My daughter is, well, whatever she is. No longer the spitfire she used to be. And a bull destroyed my stallion and robbed me of my best friend. My whole herd, whole future for that matter, could be wiped out with ice. And a friendship is strained. I'm not sure I'm meant for connecting with people. Something always happens." She shook her head. "I must have done something terribly bad to have so much go wrong."

"Not part of God's will that we suffer," he said quietly. "Just part of his promise that he'll be there through it." Burke put his whittling knife up, folded his hands, and leaned forward, resting his forearms on his knees. "Do you have family other than your daughter and your nieces and nephews, Miss Martin?"

"Please. Call me Ruth. I had a child. Jessie's twin. He…died. My husband…he served time for it. In jail."

"I suspect you've served time too." Burke said. He said it so softly, with such compassion draped across his words that they arrived as a warming cape. She fought back tears, nodded.

"Hardest thing we have to live with sometimes is being the one still living. Next hardest is accepting forgiveness for whatever it is we've done. Big orders for our little hearts. Couldn't do it without the love of God to stretch us. I know I couldn't. Most important relationship of my life," he said. "Had the hardest time coming to accept that that's all God really wanted. The relationship. And for me to participate in it."

"You don't seem to have any troubles," Ruth said.

Burke smiled. She could feel it, even though she couldn't see it. "Ah, little lady, that's where our human eyes deceive." He leaned back. "The only difference between you and me is that I've found a way to accept what's been offered. I have to keep receiving day by day, but it's what makes living possible. Triumph is right over the hill from tragedy. Once you accept that, folks'll be saying things like that of you, too. Faith doesn't mean we have no problems. It only means we have someone who loves us just the way we are and will be there through the wilderness."

"As a friend of mine would say, I'll have to ponder on that."

By the twelfth day, they'd had to enter the cold silver world to tend to animals in earnest. The mares didn't like the iciness any more than Ruth did. Puff, the one Mariah had taken to, whinnied when anyone stood on the porch, but the rest of the herd was afraid to venture out even to the feed trough. So the boys skated in their manner, chipped ice from the haystack, then stacked flakes onto a makeshift sled Matthew rigged.

The animals ate little. Nervous, Ruth thought. And just when they needed to be bulking up to be ready for the spring deliveries, to fight off the bone-chilling cold. She hoped the one they lost earlier was already off her feed before this started. Now, looking at the others, she wasn't so sure.

Matthew had already put another mare down after she'd slipped and cracked her leg, the limb dangling like a broken branch. Ruth had stood in the cabin, heard the shot, then held Jessie who panted and screamed. Later, calmed, Jessie let Ruth slip her way outside to help cut the meat they'd be having for supper. Ruth broke off a two foot long icicle hanging at the roof when she walked by.

But by day fifteen, with the thermometer threatening to stay below freezing again, with the last of the haystack fed and gone, Ruth felt her brain would explode. The sameness of a sky as dark as a duck's bottom, the heaviness of watching tree limbs thicker than tree trunks finally crack with the load of ice, the agony of listening to her horses whinny and scream and lick at the corral poles, all pressed against her. And then the low moaning began through the night, of horses in pain, too weak to eat, with nothing to feed them now, nothing at all.

"If only we could find a way to get them to move into the grassy area. Couldn't they stomp it down, so they could eat, get some of the moisture from the blades of grass?" Ruth asked.

"Don't see how we could do that," Matthew said.

"They need rubber shoes," Jason said.

Matthew grunted. "Even if we had enough rubber to make up shoes, I doubt it would work. Might make it a short distance without a break, but…"

"Can't go on much longer," Burke said. "I've ridden these trails for a couple of years now, and it's never stayed on for more than a week. This is unusual."

"I…just…want us to think of a plan," Ruth said. She was sounding like Mazy with her talk of plans.

That night as she lay on the cot next to Jessie, she thought of what Burke had said, about tragedy being the other side of triumph. What could that mean for this ice storm, this struggle with watching horses starve or break bones or lose foals?

She thought she heard something outside, decided it wasn't likely. The silence of the storm proved eerie. No birds chirped during the day, no rabbits or rats or coyotes scurried, not even the squirrels. Wait! Maybe a thaw was starting, and the sound was ice dropping!

She stood up, made her way to the door, and opened it. Nothing had changed. Everything stood frozen stiff. Then the sound again—a distant braying? Could that be Carmine, still alive somewhere?

In the morning she got up just at dawn and while she made her way to the door for the wood, she heard the sound again. It came from the ridge. She couldn't see anything, just fog like old pewter. It did sound like a mule. Or perhaps an elk? Maybe, but it wasn't the same braying tone. There it was again! She was sure it must be Carmine.

"Matthew," she said, shaking his shoulder. "Matthew. Carmine's back."

"What? We can't bring him in now anyway," he mumbled. "Less the thaw's started." He sat up. "Has it?"

"No. But I have a feeling about something. I'm getting dressed, and I'm going to make my way up to that ridge."

"You're crazy, Woman."

"Coming with me or not?" she said. She turned her back to spill the heavy wool poncho over her head, and tucked her nightdress into her pants. Living here was like being in one huge family, Ruth thought. Modesty would just have to be put in its place.

Matthew groaned but he rolled out, pulled on his clothes, and grabbed at his coat. He slipped on his rubber boots as Ruth draped a square of canvas over her head to hold off the misting ice. "Guess we can try to bring some water in while we're out there," he said.

"Need help?" Burke asked sleepily.

"Just stay, pardner," Matthew said. "I've got a woman here with a wild idea. No sense having more than one man iced on this jack chase."

The rubber boots did help give a grip, and the ash bucket they took with them allowed them slight traction as they threw the gray powder onto the frozen mud before them. "I bet you didn't even see him," Matthew said. "Can't figure what he'd be doing. He can't get around any better than the mares can. Ewald sure hasn't ventured but a step or two."

"Just trust me in this," she said.

Her breathing came in short gasps. She was probably weaker than she realized from the sparse diet. She'd have to take a good look at the boys when she got back, make sure they weren't overdoing.

They ran out of ashes and set the tin beside the zigzag trail Ruth followed up into the timber. She was on hands and knees for some of it, able to stand upright when rocks broke through the ice if only for a foot or two. Her knees were bleeding and her gloves wet when she halted Matthew. "Listen," she said. "Hear it?"

"Yeah. But what is it? Doesn't sound like a mad jack to me."

"No, it doesn't. It sounds like water, Matthew. *Running* water. Not two-foot thick ice. Flowing stuff."

"You see the ice we're standing on, Woman? There's some trick being played on us," Matthew said. "Just can't be water."

But a few feet farther, and Ruth no longer crawled. She stood, then started to run.

"Hey!" Mathew said. "Careful!"

"Oh, Matthew, you have to see this, you have to!"

He pushed his way beside her and squinted.

"The sun is out up here. It's actually…warm," she said, pulling off the scarf that held her felt hat and had surrounded her throat. "It's warm. There's no ice. The water, it's a spring! Look over there. Carmine. He's been here all along, that stupid jack!" She was laughing now and crying at the same time.

"That stupid jack. He must have known something, tried to get the mares up here before the storm blew in." Matthew shook his head. "Not possible, it's just not."

"But it is. Look. Plenty of grass. Out of the wind. Water flowing. It's actually balmy. All we have to do is get them up here."

"They'll follow that stupid jack," Matthew said. "If we can get them across that ice field."

"Okay. Let's think on that. There's got to be a way. It's so close. So very close."

He turned around. "Look, Ruth."

Her eyes followed where he pointed. Below them lay a lake of fog, covering everything. Who could guess that beneath that fog stood mares and geldings and people with dreams and cabins and plowed fields, and wildflowers waiting, all frozen, not knowing that just yards beyond them, up higher, the sun shone. Water flowed.

"It's breathtaking," Ruth said.

"Yes, it is."

Matthew pulled Ruth to him then, and she startled, looked up into those azure eyes.

He kissed her.

It was as soft as a lamb's ear, as sweet as Mei-Ling's honey. Ruth Martin had never been kissed like that, not in all her twenty-five years. His lips lingered on hers at first, tentative, like a colt just learning to stand. His hands on either side of her face felt warm, his fingers soft dragonflies at her ears. She smelled leather, and then his tentativeness moved to something firmer, something safe and as strong as the log corrals that bound her horses. She drifted like a leaf caught in the backwater of a stream. A sound of surrender gathered at her throat, stopped the air that flowed. With the fingers of her free hand, she touched at the knot of hair caught beneath the brim of her wide hat. She felt rattled, uncertain. She pulled away, then rubbed at the back of her neck, swallowed, gathered her breath, her thoughts, her senses. "You're much too... This isn't..."

He put his finger to her lips, quieted her, and she looked at him again, for the first time. She saw goodness in that face, more experience than she'd believed. Wisdom. And strength.

"My Irish grandmother, on my ma's side, used to say, 'Better one good thing that is, than two good things that were, or three good things that might never come to pass.' This is a good thing, Ruth. Something rising from all the bad. We don't know what'll come of it or if it'll wipe out what's gone before." He kissed the back of her hand as he held it. "But we can accept this, just as it is."

She nodded and smiled up at him, feeling young and inexperienced, not the mother of one child, living, the auntie of three.

"Come on, let's go get us a drink," he said and pulled on her, a gentle bear, leading. "Nothing more refreshing than spring water."

Savor the moment, she told herself. *Hang on to what is.* It was a gift she could have. She just had to learn to receive.

one good thing that is

"I really wish you'd reconsider, Mr. Powder," Suzanne said. The handkerchief in her hand felt damp from her wringing it through her palm. Her heart was a broken melon, split open. He'd been so good for her boys. How could he leave them?

"I believe our parting of the ways is well advised. I'm sure your Mr. Forrester will amply fill my shoes."

"Oh, you've misunderstood. Mr. Forrester's being here has nothing to do with your excellent tutorage. It ought not cause you to—"

"I've done what I could. Under the circumstances, I'd hold no hope for change while things remain as they are. Indeed, I believe you like the…distractions. It's the very thing that rankles against my teaching."

Suzanne blushed. "I never meant to make your work with my sons difficult."

"Indeed. What we intend is often not the impact," he said.

She felt like a schoolgirl having disappointed her teacher.

"So then. It has been my privilege to serve you. I do hope you will grant me gracious letters of introduction for my next employer. I have been always honest, met your expectations, have I not?"

"More than I'd hoped in so short a time. I fear Clayton will lose his gain with you gone," Suzanne said.

"Something that should have come to you before you made the decision to disrupt methods already in place."

Esther brought the boys out to say good-bye. She heard the cats wail from their cages, listened while Sterling chastened the boys to pay attention to their mother, to follow Sister Esther's advice. What was that she heard in his words? Instruction, yes. A rightness. And compassion. But something more. Was his rigidity covering up a sense of failure? Was that why his words were as stiff as a disciplinary rod? She heard regret. He was going to miss them, too.

He clicked his heels. "Mrs. Cullver." She felt a wash of breeze as he must have bowed before her, reached for her hand and kissed it. The boys pulled at her skirt. "Good lady, I bid you adieu."

What was that Elizabeth sometimes said, about learning to do things differently if she wanted different results? She had to do something.

"Wait," she said. "I…you are absolutely correct, Mr. Powder. I did not take the needed conditions for your work as seriously as I might have. But we were learning…together, I thought. It's part of living, isn't it? Making choices, adjusting, correcting? We can set the clock again, can't we? Give ourselves more time?" She thought she might start crying. "I tried to adapt. We all did. The cats were welcomed. Even after Pig…I want so much to make this work, Mr. Powder. Especially now. You're a good person, a fine man. So very honest and…right." She knew he needed to have that acknowledged, understood. "Surely finding new strategies for continuing something important is as critical a lesson as teaching the value of routine?"

He'd stopped. She didn't hear his footsteps leaving.

"You've had many employers," she rushed on. "They wrote kindly of you, and yet they let you go. You left them. Perhaps your…honesty, bathed in judgment as it sometimes is, came out as…rude. Inconsiderate. I've been told as much myself. Different results—"

"It has been said, by previous employers," Sterling said quietly, "as you note, that I am often right." He sighed. "But that my way of letting others know of their imperfections needs some attention." Suzanne sniffed, squeezed the handkerchief wadded in her hand.

"Honesty is important," she said. "But perhaps it could be cloaked inside compassion and made easier then to hear. The way we say a thing can be as important as what is said," Suzanne said. "I learn that lesson daily."

"It is a sign of your graciousness that you would acknowledge your part in this, Mrs. Cullver." She heard his heels click together in salute. "And risk such…honest words to me."

"So you might reconsider?"

There was a long pause, and in it Suzanne sent a prayer. He wasn't the perfect tutor; she wasn't the perfect employer. But together, their efforts had helped her child make progress. She couldn't let that just drift away. What did it matter to her if she were right and ended up unhappy? She just hoped Esther would keep silent now, while she mediated this change.

"There must be no more moves. At least not without consultation. Can you assure me of that?" he said.

"Yes, oh, yes. But spontaneity must be permitted too. Children need to lead us, let us see the world through their eyes. That can't always be planned. And there may be other people…here at times. Their presence must be acceptable. It's part of a family life, people coming and going. Some may stay." She hoped Seth might. "But children learn from adjusting, not just from routine. The world won't make changes for them, Mr. Powder. You know that. It will service them well to learn how to live with others."

"It will," he said. "You're quite right."

"And I will do better at telling you when I believe you are right in principle, but your words make me want to disagree. If I feel judged unfairly or harshly—"

"I have never intended to be harsh," he defended.

"I suspected as much. Would my telling you when that occurs make your being here easier?"

"Indeed."

"We can both make alterations then," she said, "together." She put her hand out for him to take.

He accepted it. He would stay.

She would ask Seth to stay on too. Bravely risk telling him how she felt even if it meant he would back away. She would never know if he returned her feelings if she did not take the risk of asking. What mattered was that she could take care of herself and her boys…with help. There was nothing wrong with a little help. And nothing wrong with her. And for the first time in a very long time, Suzanne believed it.

Ruth and Matthew made their way back, zigzagging down the slippery trail and deciding to sit then slide on their bottoms for whatever distance they could. Ruth placed the canvas like a toboggan, the two sat and whooped until they spilled out and had to crawl again on hands and knees to the corrals, then gingerly make their way to the cabin.

Matthew pulled her up, holding her hand naturally.

Something had changed between them. Perhaps it was seeing the sun after sixteen days of frozen fog.

"It's sunny? Just up the hill?" Jason said, aghast. "It's just cold down here?"

"So we have to get them up there," Mariah said. "How far is it?"

"Quarter mile. Uphill and all ice," Matthew said. "This is where your thinking caps come in good."

Each joined in with possible solutions: Make a trail with dirt dumped on the ice. Burn more wood so more ashes could be spread. Cut branches and lay them down. Cut grass and lay it down. All had some merit. "None of them promises manna in our wilderness," Burke noted.

"We could cut up our slickers and make boots for the horses. Take a mare at a time and lead them up," Jason said.

Jessie awoke then, her lips white and pale. Ruth didn't think she'd ever get used to the fiery child lying spent as ash in her bed.

"We're thinking up ideas for how to get horses across ice," Ruth said. She ran the backs of her fingers across the child's forehead. It didn't feel hot. "Got any?"

"Give them skates," she said. Everyone laughed.

"That would do it, Sweet Pea, that surely would," Matthew said.

"Or claws like a cat's," Jessie added.

A clock ticked.

"I'm liking what Jessie said," Ruth said, an idea growing wings.

"About skates?"

"No, about a cat's claws. What would it take to put something on a horseshoe, something to keep an animal from slipping? To give them a grip, say at the toe?"

"A calk," Matthew said, striking the side of his head as though he were a dolt.

"A calk. We could calk all four shoes and lead them out, one by one, with rubber on our own feet so we won't slip as much," Ruth said. "Could you do it?"

"They put forged calks on stage horses. I've seen it done back in the States." Matthew ran his hands through his dark hair. "I don't know. These are young animals. Some ain't never been shod."

Ruth resisted correcting his grammar. "But they've been worked with, their feet trimmed and all."

"I don't have enough horseshoes," Matthew said. "We'd have to forge the calks, if we've got enough nails from the roof shakes left. Or pull some of the shakes for those shorter nails."

"I can help," Burke said.

"You've done horseshoeing?"

He grinned. "It's a pastor's job to keep things from slipping."

"We'd have to pull the shoes as soon as the animals got on top," Matthew said. "Only nail them on with two on each side instead of the usual four. We can reuse the shoes that way and it won't do so much damage to their hooves. We'll be making 'em up, putting 'em on, then taking 'em off."

"It's a lot of work, and it just might thaw tomorrow," Lura said.

"I'm tired of the waiting," Ruth said. "I'd rather do something, even if we later have to change our course."

"Agreed," Matthew said.

"I think I can pull the shoes off," Ruth said. "If you can forge the calks and Burke can shoe them, Mariah and I can lead them up and bring the shoes back down while you're making up others.

"You and Ned might try the plan of cutting grass and bringing it down," Matthew said to Jason. "It'll feed those left behind here and maybe give them the idea there's more where that came from. That's worth some effort."

"Sarah," Ruth said, "you'll stay with Jessie and Lura, keep them company and help Lura fix us vittles. We'll be starved before this day is through."

They had plans, the direction giving them excitement they hadn't felt for weeks. Matthew fired the forge before he sat down to eat breakfast. No one wanted to waste time eating while the call to action waited. But Lura insisted. Then with bellows pumping, Matthew began shaping the calk. The shorter house nails were bent over like cat's claws at the arc of the horseshoe, then heated to a fiery red. Matthew smacked them onto each shoe. Heat welded nail and shoe together. Four or five "claws" per shoe.

"A forged calk," Matthew said, holding up the finished product with the tong, then plunging it into the water to cool and set. Steam and the bitter smell of iron reached Ruth's nose. "You know, a real horse-shoer would have thought of that right off," he said.

"We needed a child to show us the way. It'll make for a better story, when you tell it by the fire next year," Ruth said.

"Whose fire? At your house or mine?"

Ruth swallowed, didn't answer. Instead, she watched Matthew pull the shoe out, turn it this way and that. The steam caused beads of sweat to form on his forehead.

"Ready," he said.

Burke took the set of calked shoes and lifted Koda's foot across the leather apron that reached almost to his boot tops. He pounded just two horseshoe nails on each side of each foot. "Hope they hold," he said while Matthew worked on a second set.

Koda would go first. Ruth figured he'd make a good leader for the mares, and if it worked for him, maybe they'd trust more that it would work for them.

Matthew had suggested they take Ewald first. If a jack went, they could count on the plan being considered safe by a "cautionary expert."

"Huh-uh," Ruth said. "If he doesn't like it, we'll never get the horses to even consider it. I'm counting on them wanting to please us; the jacks don't care so much. We'll will the horses to do this, scared as they'll be."

"You're the boss," he said, and she'd held those blue eyes of his, turning away before she blushed.

Burke finished pounding the last shoe on, and Ruth led Koda around the paddock a time or two to give him the feel of it in the crusty mud. He pressed through the day's ice, and then she took a deep breath. "This is it, Koda. You're my special one now." She rubbed in that place between his ears he liked. He nickered low.

"I think he knows how important this is," Mariah said.

"Let's go," Ruth said, nodding agreement. "Watch your step."

The horse followed gingerly, ears moving front to back as she led him out through the frozen wasteland. She could see his ribs, he'd lost so much weight.

Ruth wasn't aware she'd been holding her breath, but the sound of the iron shoe against ice clicked loud, and she exhaled. Koda dropped his nose, snorted, lifted his head and shook it once, twice, taking a tender step. If only it wasn't so steep, Ruth thought, this wouldn't be so dangerous. But it was. There was no point wishing that wasn't so. She did seem to have a habit of wanting things to be different instead of accepting what was. And it could have been so much worse, so much farther up the ridge and so much steeper…or no place where the sun shone at all.

Time dragged its feet before she heard, "Come on, Auntie." It was Ned, shouting from beyond the timber, calling from above the silver fog. "We can hear you."

"Get out of the way. Once he sees he can get a grip, he may come charging through," Ruth shouted. Koda stumbled and pawed, then pressed forward, back legs slipping then caught by the clawlike calk. "Come on, boy, you can do this. Just a little more."

"We're ready," Jason shouted back.

And so they were prepared when Koda did just as Ruth suspected. He sped up when he smelled the grass waving not with icy crystals but with a glint of sun shining against the brown. He leaped and lunged the last few feet, his neck arched, and he actually pranced when on solid ground. Still hanging to the lead rope, he dropped his head and snorted, twisting and jumping sideways. Ruth stepped out of his way as he found the top of the trail.

She whooped with him, tears of joy rising. "One down!" she shouted, not sure if they could hear her below.

"Fifteen-more-to-go," she heard Burke yell back.

"One-hoof-at-a-time," Ruth shouted, enunciating so they could hear her through the distant fog. One hoof step at a time. Just the way to walk through life.

Ruth had carried her whip with her, and as soon as she saw Carmine come trotting over to Koda, she handed off Koda's lead rope to Mariah, then snapped the whip around the jack's left foot.

"You're a great one," she said to the jack when he stopped, the thin cracker of the whip laced around his forelock. "But I can't have you chasing Koda out of here just now so you'll have to be hobbled." She slipped the leather pieces from her back pocket and tied the two front feet together. "You saved us, Carmine. You did. I wish we'd followed your lead before this storm hit, but we didn't. And I'll give you extra rations when they're all up here, I promise you, I will." He brayed, the long lashes over his eye blinking, his fuzzy ears alerted forward. She slapped him gently on his backside, and he hobbled off. She signaled Mariah to bring Koda over and hold him while she lifted his foot, pulled out her nippers and the little chisel to loosen the nails and straighten them. Then she yanked the shoes free. Sweat dripped from her forehead. It would be a long, long day. One shoe at a time.

Mazy buried her head in the belly of the cow. She liked the smell of the udder, the pungent odor of warm milk. A cat sauntered by, stopped, stood on its rear legs and batted at the spray of milk Mazy shot its way. She laughed. "A direct delivery," she said as the cat meowed for more. The cow stomped her feet, switched her tail in Mazy's face. Mazy turned back to the task at hand.

Beyond her, Oltipa worked, the woman's hands nearly as fast and firm as Mazy's. Oltipa tanned hides in the winter months, and Mazy suspected that was part of why her hands didn't cramp the way the hands of new milkmaids often did. Ben waddled up the alleyway that ran behind the two rows of cows. Mazy'd made a milking line so four could be worked at a time. Two being readied; two being milked while the first two were moved out and replaced. Organized into a routine. She loved it here, wondered again why she'd taken so much time to give herself the pleasure of Ruth's…no, her place.

Ben fast-walked after the calico cat, followed by Sula and a taller boy. Indian children watching after him, all passing through the end door into the hay shed. She heard them laugh and squeal and fully expected them all to burst back out in minutes, hay sticking out from their woolen hats, the cat no doubt still in the lead.

She took the full bucket of milk to the cart, poured it into the tin. With the milking finished, she skimmed the cream, poured it into the churn that Giles, the goat, turned into butter while he walked the treadmill. Giles. She'd found that name in one of the books she'd bought. It said it meant "goat shield," and she'd chuckled. She was looking for shields, all right, even a goat shield. Anything to put distance between herself and Charles Wilson.

She couldn't seem to avoid the man. He appeared to have nothing to do to occupy his time, and so he tried to occupy hers. Even with the Wintu women's help, she couldn't always escape him.

That she attracted men like Charles Wilson bothered her. Something must have been wrong with her. Jeremy had kept a shadow life from her; now a shady man pressed an interest that chilled her. Even Seth was a gambling man, though he'd at least accepted her no.

She finished her tasks and took the cart into town, letting old Ink lead the way. She endured Charles's leering, and after her deliveries she stopped at her mother's bakery, warming her chapped hands at the oven.

"Maybe you should let him think he's getting your interest," her mother advised when Mazy told her she'd been alternating her delivery times to avoid running into Charles Wilson. "Men like Charles often run the other way if they think the chase is won. Here. Try this sugar cookie. I put cinnamon in it. What do you think?"

"It's good," Mazy said, brushing the dark crumbs from her chin. She pulled the fingerless gloves off, laid them close to the fire to dry out. "With my luck, he'd find any interest stimulating and just come back for more. He's a loafer. I think he sees an easy way to have a steady income from my farm. Men like him miss the usual indicators—that a club beside the head means 'I'm busy.'"

"Not unless you marry him," Elizabeth said. "He can't have any steady income from you without that."

Mazy said, "I'm not the marrying kind."

"Seems I might be," Elizabeth said.

Mazy felt her face get hot. "You and Gus?"

Elizabeth directed her daughter to sit down at the small table. "He's asked me to be his wife, Mazy. Ponder that, at my age."

"What did you tell him?"

"What would you expect?"

Mazy swallowed, fidgeted with a ridge in her nail. "You're not that old, Mother. And your heart has always been young." She sounded stiff, even to her own ears. "It's your doing," Mazy said finally. She shrugged her shoulders.

"Mazy." Her mother reached over to her, lifted the girl's chin, and looked into her daughter's eyes. "I was worried how you'd take this. It don't mean I love you less; just that I've grown to love Gus, too. And it don't mean I didn't love your father. I did. I do yet, in my way. Once we love, I think we always do, even if what later happens shatters us like an old crock that never looks the same."

"Is that what death does? Shatters an old crock?"

"Shatters like a crock. But so can misunderstandings. Betrayals. Disappointments. People living under the same roof are bound to suffer those hurts no matter how much we love them. That's why we can't hope to do the mending by ourselves." Mazy nodded. She was one to want to do things alone and her way. "There's every likelihood you'll wed again, Mazy. And nothing that happened the first time means it's the way it'll be the next. Each loving is new, its own little traveling trunk waiting to be opened."

"I know," Mazy said. "It's just…I don't know what it is. I like Gus. He's a good man. I…"

"I don't need your approval, darling." She brushed a strand of hair behind Mazy's ear. The scent of yeast lingered. "I'd just like it. Same as I'd guess you'd like mine when that day comes again, if I'm fortunate enough to be around for it."

"Would you keep the bakery?"

"We'd own everything all together," she said.

"You could have an agreement about it. Beforehand."

"Gus isn't after my bakery," she said. "Beside, our agreement's in the Lord's hands. If he gives the nod of approval to the union, I suspect he's big enough to tend to each of us should something happen to the other."

"Gus is older than you. Quite a bit, isn't he?"

"He's nearly sixty."

"Don't you worry?... I mean, would you want to go through it again? His dying, leaving you a widow? The grieving and all that?"

"No guarantee I'd outlive him," Elizabeth said. "And besides, what's the choice?"

"Stay back. Don't step into it," Mazy said.

"And miss what love's been promised? Turn aside the filling up just because it might someday be emptied? Oh, Mazy," Elizabeth pulled her daughter into her arms. Her mother's shoulders felt thin, still firm. "That's what living is. Friendships, marriages, partnering, becoming a mama or a papa. Those kinships expand us like a yeast cake, and they drain as a dance. But it's where meaning lives." She took a bite of the cookie. "Too much spice," she said. "The only dance that don't deplete us is the one we choose with God. He don't ever step away."

"We do though," Mazy said.

"Think we all do at some point. That must grieve God great. But he never leaves. Always there when we step back. In this living we stumble and step on each other's toes, sometimes choose a poor partner. The partner walks outside, don't come back, and we have the choice: stay at the eggnog table or step back out onto the floor and try again." She gave Mazy a squeeze, held her hands around her daughter's waist. "I'm just pondering over you, my only child. Wanting the best for you."

"I've got the best," Mazy said. "A farm I can give myself to, children surrounding me, and my mother's love. What more could I need?" She kept her voice light.

"A little distance from Charles Wilson, from the sound of it," she laughed, patted Mazy's hand, and returned to her work. "Maybe you should fix him up with someone else so he'd leave you be."

"There's no one I dislike that much," Mazy said

Mazy wondered what held her back from fully embracing her mother's blissful state. She looked at her through new eyes. Elizabeth looked younger than she had in years. She'd bought new clothes. Had her old ones gotten large? Even her apron strings could go almost twice around her middle now. She wasn't ill, that was certain, not with that high color and her eyes full of sparkle. And she'd certainly chosen to dance again. That step onto the floor might be a little risky, but it brought a joyful spirit to her mother's life. Mazy envied her that. Maybe that was it, envy. Could she actually be jealous of her own mother? Was she wishing she had someone to tend to her as Gus tended? Was she missing companionship? How could she be? She had Ben and Oltipa and David Taylor close by. She could see her mother daily. It couldn't be jealousy.

Or could it? Perhaps she wasn't jealous of her mother's relationship with Gus but of her mother's willingness to risk, to keep her dancing slippers on the floor.

Ruth and Matthew and Burke and the crew finished half the horseshoeing and moving of mares on the first day. Tired and aching, they rose earlier for day two, figuring they'd be sore and slowed. And so they were.

Burke's gelding had gone up much as Koda had, pushing himself with the encouragement of Burke's voice. Once he hit the grassy slope, the animal had kicked his hindquarters, twisted and snorted and ran.

The last mare, a smallish bay, proved easiest of all, nearly running up the trail that was still iced over despite the tramping that had gone on by dozens of hooves before her. By the time they were finished and finally sat down at the top, horses stood contented, head to hindquarters of another, happy from their feasting. It was as though they'd always been there, sucking up the water pooled below the spring.

"Thank you, thank you, thank you," Ruth heard herself say.

"Who're you thanking?" Matthew asked.

"What? I don't know. Just grateful," she said. She dropped her eyes from his. He had a growth of beard. It aged him like fine leather. She looked out across the grazing stock. "Must be forty acres or so up here," Ruth said. "No wonder the Indians wintered it. I thought it was the bottomland they coveted, but this is where the real treasure lies. Maybe I should build near the spring, just let the hay barn stand where it is down there and use the cabin for foaling."

Matthew nodded. "Don't know as I'd build a house up here until the foaling's finished," he said. "Want to stay close by."

"I know that," she said, irritated.

He raised his hands in protest. "Not telling you how, just thinking out loud. Problem I seem to have with you."

She softened. "It's the spring that attracts. And not having the cold fog. Weather more like Ohio on this ridge," she said.

"Like New York, too," Matthew said. "It still amazes me to see that fog there, that grayness," Matthew said, "with this just above it." He shook his head. "This is some country."

"Challenges a soul, that's for sure," Burke said, approaching them, two pairs of horseshoes in his hands. He dropped them at their feet. "Looks like you people are up to it. Set your mind to a thing and do it."

"We're grateful for your help," Ruth said. "In every way."

Burke said, "In the Old Testament, there's a story of Abraham. He built an altar when he found his Promised Land. He was trying to find a place outside of Babylon where he could build a new nation, one without the idols his family had been exposed to. He named his place of belonging Bethel."

"No idols here," Ruth said.

"They come in all shapes and sizes," Burke said. "A lot of things hold us hostage, things we think we have to have so we'll pay a high price for them. Not just cash," he said. "But in bartering time."

"We still have work to do," Ruth said, moving away. She shouted to the boys to go back down, haul up some rope to make a corral for Carmine and Ewald, so they could take the hobbles off. She walked the perimeter, counting, gauging the distance and whether this might really be the best place for herself and the children. After a full circle, she found herself back where Matthew and Burke stood and talked.

"I'll be giving you folks back your privacy soon," Burke said. "Might need you to help me round my cattle out of the ravines and brambles come spring."

"We'll be glad to return the favor," Matthew said. "Anytime."

"I guess I'll slide my way back down and get my pack rolled up and my gear. Looks like I could ride out through there," he pointed to stands of pine and fir where a deer trail disappeared. "If I travel above the fog line, I can make it south to my place."

"You're welcome to stay on, though the meat's getting a bit familiar, I imagine, with no flour to disguise it. Surely by the end of the week this will be over, and we can make a run into Jacksonville for some salt at least," Ruth said.

"Looks like the whole valley's iced," Matthew said. "Wonder if any supplies have even gotten in."

"You may as well remain, Burke," Ruth said. "You may not find such luxurious accommodations as ours on the high road. All the population is in the valley, you know."

Burke laughed. "Is it now? Well, I'll keep that in mind. Valleys don't usually get good promotion. It's the mountaintops people seem to long for."

"Can be windy up on top," Ruth said. "Exposing."

"Ah, but the wind blows away the heaviness that threatens. And the view…" He spread his arms around. "I wonder if Abraham had such a view on his mountaintop."

"It's just fog," Ruth said.

"We all know what lies beneath that icy surface," Matthew said. He looked at Ruth. "Beauty unsurpassed."

Ruth grabbed at the whip on her hip, squeezed it and smiled. *She was happy.* She'd forgotten what that felt like. She wished she could say something snappy. She wanted to honor the occasion when friends helped friends outsmart fog. She hoped more than anything that this day marked the beginning of a willingness to celebrate life's little triumphs, when she'd allowed herself to feel the touch of one good man, the praise of another, and the satisfaction of accomplishing something hard, something that consumed them all, brought them all together in this place.

Burke tipped his hat and said he thought he'd catch up with his gelding, see what the boys were up to with those ropes they were trying to stretch between trees. He headed off.

"He's a nice man," Ruth said. She pulled at a string of loose sinew on the whip's handle.

"Knows when to exit," Matthew said.

"Does he?"

Matthew lifted her chin. "Maybe this is too soon. But I've been thinking. We could build *our* house here. Yours and mine. Together. Make this our Bethel."

She hesitated. Did she always hesitate when her heart felt full?

"We could. Maybe." She swallowed. "We've got foaling to get through. Breeding…I haven't heard from my lawyer yet. I'm still a married woman."

He straightened her felt hat, pushed it back on her forehead. "You've already made that decision. You're not going back on it?"

She shook her head. "I am still his wife. And until that's finished, I can't take another step toward matrimony. I can't. Won't."

"But you can take the next step toward us. Let the *we* that might be begin."

"And what would that look like?"

He smiled, then bent nearer to her face. "Like my grandma said, just admitting that this is 'one good thing that is.'" He put his hand at the small of her back, pulled her to him, and kissed her.

"One good thing that is," she said as he released her. "Yes. One good thing that is."

passages

Tipton located a Chinese doctor in Sacramento in no time at all. "They make excellent midwives," she told her baby. "Gentle hands. Isn't it funny how I once didn't want to have anything to do with Celestials and now, what would I do without them?" She patted her stomach. "I'll tell him about you, of course, but for now, his medicine really helps my headaches. It does, Baby, it does. And he thinks I'm just a chubby one. Do you hear how he says it? That I am a 'clubby lady.'" She laughed.

Except for the headaches and the occasional blurry vision, she was feeling so much better these days, not feeling alone, no longer wondering why she was here. She was taking charge of her life, doing for herself and her child just what she thought best. She weathered storms, all kinds of them, without the help of anyone, except her own wits.

Well, Esty had been a help. Tipton would pay the woman back, she would. Esty had gotten the steamer's doctor to sew up Tipton's head, and then she'd allowed Tipton to remain in her back room for a time. Tipton watched her twist the feathers, tie ribbon, and work the felt on her hats. She thought it a skill she could learn. A little like making a drawing, something she was once good at. But she wanted to be on her own. She'd accepted Esty's loan and now had found an abandoned shack near the Chinese district, though not in it. She would wash clothes. She'd done that before. And she didn't want Sister Esther or Suzanne to see her in this state.

The shack had four walls and a roof, a single window and door. She could tell that the whole window frame came out, which would be good when the days grew hot and she needed ventilation. A stove with a chimney would heat her irons and water in the two big pots she bought. She purchased two bars of Castile soap and a stick for stirring. One of her first customers, an actor named Flaubert, saw her need and brought her a table and two stools to go with her single bed. She felt richer than a queen.

Being near Chinatown meant she could divert miners and others making their way there from the Chinese launderers. They'd choose a pretty "chubby" American girl offering to clean boiled shirts and sheets, as well.

The room was all hers. It had a hook on the door, and she'd replaced the carpetbag for a buckwheat stuffed pillow for the cot. Her cape served as a blanket, not that she needed warmth once the tubs of water for washing heated up. She'd even grown accustomed to boiled dinners, which she supplemented with pressed fish imported from Canton. The actor had introduced her to that as well, and her Chinese doctor gave her incense that sweetened up the room.

And, oh yes, that opium. That white powder that took the edges off anything that felt rough.

Esty had promised to say nothing to Suzanne or Esther when she saw them; and she didn't hover once Tipton borrowed the money to secure the room. Tipton would pay it back with her first earnings. Well, part of it. The opium was a cost she had not expected, and she needed to save enough for it.

Ho Lin, the Chinese doctor, had given her herbs for her headaches, and she always tried to take them first. But the effects didn't last as long. Besides, in the hot room with steam rolling off the tubs and her back aching and her arms sore, she felt she deserved the gentle reprieve the powder gave. It took away the ache above her stomach that came when she lay still and tried to remember why it was she'd done this, gone away, what longing it was she truly sought to fill.

She finished the day's order and wrapped it in canvas, carried the heavy load to the back of the hotel where she collected her coins. She varied her path through the shanty-lined streets, not wanting anyone to notice her routine. They might realize she carried cash and take it from her, the way the cab driver had back in San Francisco. At least that was what she assumed happened. It was strange that she could not remember. Only details up to that time when he had asked for an address. After that, nothing. She'd asked Ho Lin about that. He said such memories were often lost close to the time of a blow to the head.

"Do they ever return?"

"If needed," he'd told her. "Mind protects and offers rescue, too." She'd frowned at him and wondered if he and Elizabeth Mueller might be kin.

Memory was strange. She could recall with great detail the last time she'd seen her fiancé, Tyrellie, but couldn't remember something that had happened just weeks before.

The scent of ginger oil marked her closeness to the board shacks. Pigs snorted in low pens nearby, their scent mixing with sweet smells of cooking. She had a sugar tooth and had thought herself fortunate that her arrival in Sacramento had happened before the Chinese New Year celebration. She'd collected sugared candies and watched a game of fan-tan. This year the Chinese had given all the women bracelets of smooth wood, and Tipton wore hers now as she approached the dirt-floor shanty of Ho Lin.

"Clubby Lady eary," Ho said.

It took Tipton a minute, then, "Yes, I'm early."

Ho turned back from a shelf he bent over, his thin queue still braided with the red and black silk ribbons worn to mark the New Year and to signal that all his debts were paid. The rest of his hair was shaved, but he wore a flat-top silk hat of red and gray when he saw patients.

He'd been standing before a glass cage filled with amber liquid and what looked like a piece of uncooked beef. Tipton stepped closer, squinting, then jumped back. "Is that a snake?" She squinted, leaned in again. A fat rattlesnake lay coiled inside, its head resting on a chunk of meat while malt whiskey swirled around.

"Is it…dead?" Tipton asked.

"Vely dead. You drink cup for aching bones," he said. "Make you move then vely fast, vely fast."

"I have no doubt," Tipton said. "You're not suggesting that for my headaches."

"No, no. For bones," he said and patted his own hip. "Vely good for bones. You got bad bones? I give."

The room felt hot and duskier today as Tipton sat on the small stool, declining his offer of the amber stew. A lily bulb perched in a jade pot on the floor beside the glass case, poking its green nose up through the dirt. The doctor examined the scar at the side of her head. He lifted her eyelid. His brows furrowed.

"What?" she said. "What is it?"

"You see? Eyes see good?"

"I'm fine," she lied. "Why. What do you see?"

"See Clubby Lady not say truth. Clubby Lady not clubby. Clubby Lady carry baby."

"You can tell that through my eyes?"

He scowled at her.

Tipton fidgeted. "I was going to tell you. I just didn't think it mattered. Yet."

"Baby come early."

"How would you know that? I've felt fine. Except for the headaches. Which the powder helps." He raised his gray eyebrow. "It does."

"Not good, Clubby Lady. No more. No more." He moved his hands before him as though wiping off a schoolgirl's slate.

"But you have to give me more. I have to work. The powder takes the ache away, so I can. Those herbs barely dull the throb. I need the powder. How will I work? How will I sleep?"

She felt her heart pound fast. How much powder did she have back at her room? Enough for one, maybe two days at the most, if she rationed it carefully, if she took her time.

What did he know? "The powder…it helps me." She stood up, knocked the stool over. "You've got to give it to me." She saw a pewter pipe. "I'll smoke it. It'll go slower, it won't hurt the baby that way. Please, don't do this now. Not when everything is going so well!"

He shook his head. "No good, Clubby Lady. No good. I fix for you. No powder. No more."

"I'll find it somewhere," she said. Hadn't she seen it sold in the Chinese apothecary? She took in deep breaths. She could weather this, too.

"I know what's best for me," Tipton said, and she pushed her way past him, kept her eyes out toward the street. Through the blurring and her head's throbbing, she failed to recognize the Chinese woman she bumped into carrying a frail baby in her arms.

What made Seth decide to head out to Mei-Ling's, he didn't know. Restlessness, he supposed. Avoiding talking with Suzanne because he didn't know what to say. She'd risked her thoughts and feelings with him, asked nothing in return, and he'd stood speechless. When he'd initiated a kiss, that had been fine. But when it was her leading a horse to water, the old mount just didn't know whether to drink or gallop away. He was procrastinating. It was already February, and he'd decided nothing. Except to ride out to see the little Celestial and her child.

"You do not come with Missy Suzanne or Missy Esther?" she said, her eyes looking past him.

"They had other plans," he said. He ran the reins through his hands, feeling the leather. "And I hadn't seen you for a spell. Got to stay in touch, or that baby of yours'll be walking and wearing pants before I even get to know him."

"Many moons before he walks," she said, lowering her lashes and blinking in that way she had. She'd invited him inside, served him tea as she knelt.

"You like Miss Suzanne?" Mei-Ling asked then.

"Well, sure." He fidgeted as he sat cross-legged on the rice mat covering the floor. "Doesn't everyone?"

"Ah. You do not tell yourself the truth yet, Seth Forrester."

"Yes I do."

"Truth. You look for reason not to find Missy Suzie special like a sugared nut. You afraid you not good enough for Missy Suzie."

"These are sure good," he said. "What'd you say it was?"

"Nut. Comes from China." She paused, poured a cup of tea. "Missy Suzie's baby is well?"

"Good as expected. That little Clayton's talking pretty good." He felt a twinge of…something. Powder was working hard as ever, and the man had been more than civil to him. He didn't think Suzanne held any special fondness for him, other than as a tutor. Of course she didn't. She'd told Seth as much when she shared her thoughts with him. And what had he done? Nodded his head. Shoot. To a blind woman, a nod was as good as a grimace and no help at all. She wasn't pushing at him. That was sure true. Maybe he just didn't know what to do with a woman who wasn't running from him.

"Seth Man is troubled," Mei-Ling said. She touched the back of his hand, light as a butterfly.

"When'd you become such wise counsel?"

"I see how you look at her last time you here. Missy Suzie see it too if her eyes work. But she sees it here," she said, patting her heart. "She does not tell you?"

He pulled at his collar. "Say, how're your bees doing? What are you and the mister up to?"

"We make plans. Leave soon," she told him as she served him dried abalone across the bamboo table. "From China too," she said, as he tasted it. "Very good, yes?"

"Different," Seth said. "So you're leaving? Where you going?"

"Oregon. Maybe."

"I hear Ruth has headed up that way, she and the Schmidtkes. You going to work mine tailings or what?"

"We plant gardens there, good ground. Here, Chinese not wanted. Even Indians not want us. Call us 'Chinee-Winto.' Chinese mine what others leave, pay big tax. They only collect from Chinese. No money to send home. No money to buy vegetables. No money to put into ground, plant trees."

"How're your bees doing?"

"Need many blossoms."

"Be a shame to leave what you've done here," Seth said.

"Home is where you warm," she said, touching her small fingers to her chest.

"You don't say." He chewed the abalone, evaluating the new tastes. "They say you'll need your umbrella in Oregon. Rains up that way."

"Here umbrella wards off rocks thrown when just walking with baby. Baby needs to grow where family honored."

"That doesn't happen much anywhere," Seth said.

"Wrong word chosen," she said and bowed, revealing more of the ivory sticks that held her hair in twists at the side of her head. "Need place where child sees parents live without lowering heads in shame."

"I hear you," Seth said. He picked up a little candy, unrolled the paper wrapper. "Every kid needs to see others looking up to their parents. Makes 'em feel valued."

"This is word I mean to choose. Valued." She nodded. "We are not valued here. Husband's work. Not valued. Our people. Not valued. In China, family greatest treasure. Here, gold greatest treasure."

"Ruth was heading to a place along Bear Creek, near a pair of flat-topped rocks. Table Rocks, they call them. Southern Oregon, north of Yreka."

Mei-Ling nodded. "Maybe we go there. See old friends again. Maybe."

"I'm sure you could stop over at Mazy's," he said. "She's got a whole passel of people staying there. Out where we camped that first night, you remember?" Mei-Ling nodded. "Calls it Poverty Flat, but it's rich bottom land. Hey, maybe you and your family could go there?" he said. "Grow all kinds of things on that river bottom."

Mei-Ling shook her head. "Must leave California. All rumor say soon all Chinese go, take nothing. We go now. Take bees."

"Guess you got a plan," he said. "But I'd wait 'til summer, is all I'm saying. Rivers be flooded this spring and traveling not good. If you can wait 'til May maybe. Sometime around there, it'd be better going."

He stood to leave, thought to offer to guide them north. But he wasn't sure where he'd be come May. "Guess I best say howdy and good-bye to your man there, Mei-Ling." They walked to where Mei-Ling's husband bent his narrow back at work along a short row of peach trees planted. Pleasantries exchanged, they started back. Mei-Ling pointed at this and that, sometimes cooing to the baby, sometimes stopping to let the child feel the tender branches; to show him something that he otherwise would have missed.

They had nearly reached Seth's tethered horse when he saw the woman running toward them, a bundle in her arms.

"What's that about?" he asked.

Mei-Ling stood on tiptoes, winced with the pain of that, then sheltered her eyes from the afternoon sun. The woman ran hard, looking back over her shoulder, reaching Seth's horse just as he and Mei-Ling did. "Whoa there, what's the matter?" Seth said to her. Did he know this woman?

She gasped for air, looked behind her. "He comes," she said. "Take baby. Go. Save baby." She thrust the child at Seth.

"Whoa, whoa, now," he said, raising his hands to object. "Baby needs its mother, isn't that right, Mei-Ling. Naomi? It's you, isn't it?"

"He kills me. He says he kills me," Naomi said. "You help me."

"Well, yes, but not by taking your baby."

The woman sobbed, her face streaked with tears and sweat and dirt, and then Seth noticed the blackness at her eyes and cheeks, the scars at her wrists as she held the baby up again, pushing it against his raised forearms. "Save baby, please!"

He thought he saw dust in the distance. He whistled to his big sorrel gelding, grabbed the reins at the post, tossed them up, and swung himself in. "Give me the child now," he said and he placed the bundle on the pommel before him, holding it with his legs. Then he lowered his hand to her.

Naomi turned to run off, but Mei-Ling blocked her way, and Seth leaned over and touched Naomi's shoulder. "You're coming too. I know a safe place for you both." At last, something he knew how to fix.

She was light as a feather, and he sat her up behind him. "You'll be all right?" he asked Mei-Ling.

She looked to the field. "I go there. Husband make safe for me. You go. Go!" she urged.

He kicked the big animal, and they sped off down the rows of trees, then through the cottonwoods that lined the creek bed. Seth looked back once to see Mei-Ling standing, her small husband running toward her just as a horse and rider broke through the dust and Seth descended over the side with his treasures.

Mazy was at Wilson's store when Nehemiah rode in. He brought a pack string of supplies with him though most he'd delivered at Weaverville. Then he'd come on over the Trinity Mountains to Shasta City.

She looked for Tipton and felt disappointed when Tipton didn't appear. Mazy knew it had been awhile since Tipton'd seen her mother. Adora seemed ready to mend the rip. Ruth came to mind.

Nehemiah looked cheerful, jovial almost, as he chatted with Adora. Charles's presence paused him some, but he didn't stand off nor stand to fight. Instead he acted as though he was a knight returning from battle almost.

"It's been a season," he told Charles. "Good trips and bad. Now this one, this one I was happy to be making, getting to see kin and all. Place has sure built up," he said. He looked around at the brick buildings, the heavy iron shutters on every window, to keep it from burning again. He craned his neck into the store. Was he looking for someone? "How was your winter?" he asked, turning back.

"Fine," Adora said. "Truth be known, our worst was '52, the year we got here. Nothing's been as bad since."

"Only been one winter since then, Mother," Charles corrected.

"And it was a mild one. Oregon folks didn't fare so well, I hear. Had a silver storm that lasted nearly a month. They had to send out an advance party to buy up the salt and set the price so it wouldn't be so inflated once they made Jacksonville. Heard that folks broke it open and ate it right there on the spot."

"I had trouble getting into Jacksonville myself," Nehemiah said. "So I'm glad for you that folks could make it over here, being milder and all." He craned his neck again toward the back of the store, turned back.

"How's Tipton?" Mazy asked then, and the look that crossed his face told her she'd asked the one question he hadn't wanted to answer.

He cleared his throat. "Fine. Just fine." He looked off to the side. "Oh, she hates having to wait alone while I'm gone, but in time, she'll be traveling with me on the campaign trail. Going to the state house for gatherings will tickle her fancy."

"I certainly hope you haven't forgotten about this store," Adora told him. "My Charles is just pushing himself to run it, and it could use a man accustomed to commerce, truth be known."

Mazy thought the vein in Charles's neck throbbed fast.

"That might be difficult with us living where we are, Mrs. Wilson," he said.

"Reason enough for you to move back over here."

"I'll consider it," he said. He cleared his throat again. "Might be good with the baby coming and all."

"A baby!" Adora clapped her hands to her face. "Charles! Did you hear? It's about time. Well, why didn't you say so? My goodness. I'll have to get some things together. Send it right on back with you. No wonder Tipton didn't join you. Goodness knows, travel for a woman in that condition wouldn't be wise. Not wise at all."

Mazy watched Nehemiah's face change like a man watching a mountain storm: moving from anticipation to dread, to an acquiescent calm.

"We wanted to…surprise you," he said. "You know Tipton."

"My little sister always did want to make an entrance," Charles said.

"Not unlike you," his mother chided. "You were the prissiest little boy, always wanting to dress meticulous and show off for us at the store. Must be some of the dramatic flair you both get from me," she said and pushed the hairpin into the bun at the base of her neck.

"I have to be getting back," Mazy said. "I hope you'll stay a day or so. Come out to the Flat." She had a second thought. "I'm going by Mother's first, if you'd care to join me."

"I would," Nehemiah said.

"Now you stop back by," Adora cooed. "I'll have a carpetbag of goodies for my little darling. A baby, Charles," she said again as she scurried back inside. Mazy shivered at the look on Charles's face before he saw that she was watching.

Nehemiah led the horse as they walked. Mazy ignored the hole she was sure Charles's stare was making in her back.

"She's gone, isn't she?" Mazy said. "You don't know where Tipton is."

He shook his head. "Left a month or more ago. Gave me a note saying she had to do things on her own. Didn't know anything about the baby until our housemaid told me." He took a deep breath. "I've been such an old fool."

"You're far from old, and Tipton never was one to do the predictable, except to be unpredictable," Mazy said.

"I thought she'd come here. To be with her mother."

"That does say something about what you don't know about that family. She might have made amends with her mother, but there's bad blood between her and Charles I doubt will ever be cleansed."

"Having to do with her first love," he said quietly.

"Even before that, I suspect. Charles didn't seem all too pleased to have Adora talk about your taking over the store." Mazy shivered.

"Tipton's so confused. Blames herself, I think. She's scared about this baby, she must be. Why else would she run away?"

"Paper is full of men seeking runaway wives," Mazy said. "Haven't you noticed? Most are ads from mean husbands or poor ones wanting their share of their wife's assets."

"Mean…" he said.

She stopped. "If you laid one hand on her—"

"I didn't. But I…we were distant. And I never talked of it. Never spoke of what she meant to me. She couldn't know. Something made her snap, and she left. She signed the letter she left with 'love.' Anything could happen to her."

"I doubt we'll be reading about her in the *National Police Gazette*," Mazy said.

"Those lurid crimes? You don't think—"

"No, no. I meant I think she's more resourceful than we know. Maybe than she knows. That could be what she's trying to discover— her way."

"If I just knew where she was, I'd leave her be if that was what she wanted. I just hope to tell her that I'm sorry. For not owning up to…some things."

"She should let you know she's all right."

"Don't condemn her, Mrs. Bacon. Please. You don't know all the details, all the things I did that sent her away." He lifted his hat, ran his hands through his reddish hair. His eyebrows lay like red caterpillars over troubled eyes. "How will I ever find her?"

"Allen Pinkerton finds people," Mazy offered.

"I was sure she'd be with kin."

They reached Elizabeth's bakery, looped Nehemiah's horse at the hitching posts, and stepped inside. Elizabeth greeted Nehemiah like a long-lost son. She embraced him, sat him down, gave him food and drink, and pulled a chair right beside him, giving him her undivided attention. It was another quality Mazy found she admired in her mother, always ready to embrace what was before her.

"So you're looking for Tipton," Elizabeth said after he'd filled her in, gave more details than he'd shared with Mazy. "Well, let me think."

"I just thought she'd go to family. To people she knew. Isn't that what people do, even when their family isn't always the most inviting?"

"Tipton marches to her own tune," Elizabeth said. "And if it wasn't for her carrying a wee one, I'd say let her be until she finds what tune she's hearing. But she might get addled with the changes a baby brings, her being high-strung and all."

"You're willing to meddle, Mother?" Mazy asked.

"To a point. Not always wise to stand by and just watch." Elizabeth drummed her fingers on the table. "I say we write to both Suzanne, south, and to Ruth, north. Both could be places she'd make her way to. If not now, as her time gets closer, I could see her seeking out a friendly face. She might even show up back at home. Which is where you best be, Nehemiah. There and doing what you intended doing. Wasn't you going to run for Congress? Ain't that what we heard?"

Nehemiah's face reddened. "County commissioner. That, too, might have pushed her off, my having to be gone a lot to campaign and more if I won."

"Why, I'd think she'd love the pomp and circumstance of all that folderol," Elizabeth said. "You give her a chance to go with you?"

He shook his head. Elizabeth patted his hand. "Never mind. We'll find her if she wants to be found. After all, didn't that Zane Randolph find his wife in the middle of the fastest growing state in the union?"

"But we were all together in one place then, Mother. Easy to find eleven widows traveling together, one wearing pants, and one blind, led by a black dog."

"Tipton'll stand out. You mark my word. We'll put our fishhooks out and see what we can catch."

Nehemiah said he'd finish up at Adora's store, then bring the string out to Mazy's, spend the night there at what Elizabeth said was fast becoming some kind of "stage stop" even without a stagecoach changing teams. "People just like coming to that place and camping out a night or two before heading on to the next phase of their journey. That bend in the river sure lured us to it."

Mazy drove the team with the empty milk wagon back down the Shasta road, puffing up reddish dust as she drove. Tipton on her own. Maybe the girl wasn't addled but just wanting to try living without a dozen people hovering, to see if she could make it. Sad she had to hurt Nehemiah to do it, but she had at least left him a note. Unlike what Jeremy had done to her. No note, no explanation, no nothing to help her understand why he'd lived a lie with her. *Mind mumbling.* She sighed. She'd loved him, and he had kept a secret he knew would hurt her. That was an act of love.

It wasn't so terrible to have loved him. She loved what she thought he was, and he tried to live up to that, in his way. Maybe he would have told her in time, and then she'd have had to contend with putting the lie away while he still lived. Testing her ability to forgive.

There had been many good things he'd done for her. He'd bought a farm for her—well, perhaps not *for her,* but for them. He'd insisted she stop her jam-making to walk through the woods, collecting morel mushrooms beneath blue columbines. He'd held her hands while they looked across the bluffs above the Mississippi, watching eagles weave through birches while grass waved in the wind. The sumac in the fall in Wisconsin turned red as her bloomers. Jeremy always made it a point too, on a dark night, to lift her needlework from her hands, and lead her out to the back stoop to stare up at the stars together.

"The Milky Way," he said. "North Star. Orion's Belt. See there?" She had actually found the stars that marked the constellation when he'd stood behind her, moved her head and held it with his hands so her eyes were guided perfectly to what he wanted her to see. She let herself be led, and he'd wrapped his arms around her and kissed the top of her head. Somehow that closeness had disappeared into the everyday routine of cooking and working and taking for granted. Oh, if she had it to do again, she would do it differently, she would.

She'd love a man who loved the stars…and her. He *had* loved her. That he loved another first did not mean he had loved her less. Who could explain or ever understand what made people do what they did? He had loved her, and she had loved him back. That was the truth of what was.

She turned down the lane to her farm. Between Ink's ears, she saw skiffs of snow marking the muddy track. A flock of geese had chosen to winter at the Flat, and they lifted now in the distance. People gathered near the barn, a few of the children squatted low as though clustered in trouble. *What now?* she thought.

She sighed. It was just what life was, she guessed, this deciding and sorting and responding and learning to love. She took a deep breath, asked herself what she wanted to experience with whatever challenge lay ahead: To be used up or invigorated? She guessed the choice was hers.

She pulled up around the far side of the barn, giving herself time to wrestle with the upcoming commotion.

Oltipa joined her, reaching up for the yoke at the mule's head. "You have visitor," she said.

Mazy took a wrap around the brake. "Another traveler?"

Oltipa grinned. Behind her, coming at Mazy as though out of a broken dream, trotted a dog. He was emaciated, dirty, covered with stickers and burrs, but she still recognized him as a gift her husband had given her for their first anniversary: a black dog she loved named Pig.

warder of the soul

In March, lilies sprouted along the walkways of Shasta City. Each year the Chinese gave the imported bulbs as gifts, and when they bloomed, Mazy found herself reminded of the generosity of others. She stood at the window of the bakery, the window box full of the stalks her mother had planted, the buds promising blooms. Pig pushed against her knees. "The lilies make me remember our first year here," Mazy told her mother.

Elizabeth said, "Bring him on in." She motioned toward Pig. "He can eat lots. He don't have to worry over ruining his figure. Now his memory," she tapped her temple with her finger, "that's right up there with the best."

"'The warder of the brain.' That's what Shakespeare called memory," Mazy said.

"Did he now. Ponder that. Memory may be the warder of the heart, too," her mother said. "Keeping good things from reaching us."

"I hadn't thought of that." Mazy stepped inside, looked back over her shoulder down the street, leaving the door open to the spring breeze.

"Charles Wilson sniffing around you this morning?" her mother teased.

"I think I've slipped into town early enough he isn't up yet. That's my new plan. It's working well. Deliver while Charles is still getting his beauty sleep and always have a pitchfork to hand him when he comes out. He is a strange one, Mother. And it bothers me how Adora puts up with him that way. Can't she see he uses her?"

"It might be good for Adora to push that rooster from the coop," Elizabeth nodded, "though I doubt she will."

Mazy shivered.

"You chilled?"

"Just by the likes of him."

"We need to remember, Daughter: Adora's getting something from tending him, or she wouldn't be doing it, I'll ponder. We all got needs. It's how much of ourselves we're willing to give up to get 'em met that matters. How far astray we'll go."

"I don't think I know what you mean," Mazy said. She sat down, Pig at her feet.

"Adora likes being needed."

"Tipton needed her mother, and Adora refused to go with her."

Elizabeth shrugged. "Adora saw her daughter was taken care of. Or maybe she didn't want to find out that she wasn't going to be the center of her daughter's life from then on. Takes a bit of getting used to, letting a child go."

"And Charles? What's he giving up to be taken care of?"

"Oh, he's worse off than most," Elizabeth said. "He gave up growing up."

"That won't cost him much as long as Adora's there to pluck worms for that rooster and keep his feathers fluffed."

"It'll cost him big, just the same. He may not realize it, but he's an empty man. He's keeping himself from sitting at the family table because he has to pass things around, learn to give and take. He'd rather be by himself, eating alone all the time with only his own company."

"Where do you come up with those ideas, Mother?"

"Eating's my passion, Child, don't you know that?" She patted her daughter's hand. "Pretty easy to spot someone undernourished when you've been feasting like I have all my life at the table of…risking and giving."

Mazy laid down the letter she carried, took Pig's big head in her hands and massaged his jowls, ran her thumbs on the bone between his eyes. He closed them as though asleep. "I didn't know how much I missed you," she said. "Isn't memory a gift? He had to remember how to get here, to swim rivers, avoid coyotes—"

"Oh, they wouldn't bother him none," Elizabeth said.

"He could have become someone's lunch," Mazy defended. "You just wanted to get home, didn't you, Pig? Eat at our table." He opened his eyes at his name, yawned wide, then slurped up at her face. She laughed. How she loved that dog! Someone to talk with, to walk with, to lie across her feet while she wrote at night. Someone to listen. "And Pig's big enough I don't trip over him like I do David's dog, Chance."

"You got people aplenty out there, I'll ponder."

Mazy nodded. The numbers of people she gathered around her tired her. She told herself that she wanted to respect David and Oltipa's privacy, suggesting a separate home not unlike the ones she'd built for the Indian workers. Oltipa had given her that squinted-eye look that Mazy had come to recognize as unspoken disagreement. Oltipa appeared to like the bustle of bodies around. Together, she and her Wintu friends wove grass for traditional mats and summer skirts and ground acorns into meal. They chattered in words Mazy didn't understand, laughing. Even when David took his day of rest, there were always others underfoot, not that David complained. So why should Mazy?

It was, after all, what she'd said she'd wanted. Being helpful to people. Using what she'd been given to make a safe place for others, speaking out because she could.

But she wanted distance, too. She was a boomerang tossed out to be with people, then swinging back to be alone. Maybe that was just the metaphor of her life.

"What did Suzanne have to say?" Elizabeth asked.

"About what?" Mazy asked, looking away from Pig.

"Where'd your mind go?" Elizabeth asked. She nodded toward the table. "That letter from her you said you got."

"Esther must have written it. Looks like she was tired when she did. Kind of a scraggly hand, almost like Seth's. Suzanne said she'd miss Pig terribly, but that a dog that made his way that far to find me deserved to be where he felt at home."

Her mother mumbled agreement, then brought chamomile tea for the two of them. "What else?"

"I didn't get it all read yet. Just drove on over here, hoping to avoid Charles." Mazy read to herself. "Well, Naomi is with her. She and her baby. A sickly thing, it sounds like. When she's better, they'll come north."

"Well, ponder that." Elizabeth leaned back in her chair.

"And if Ruth is willing, Suzanne thinks Naomi should go on north to her."

"Could be a chance for you to patch things up with Ruth," her mother said quietly.

"They weren't asking me to go. Besides, I wouldn't want to impose myself on Ruth. She's never written."

"Might take a little more effort with Ruth. She hasn't had much practice in chewing a thing until it swallows good. I expect she's choked more often than not when things go sour. Made her cautious."

Mazy nodded. "I should be bigger, I guess. A loving person would keep trying until the wound healed, wouldn't they?"

She patted her daughter's hand. Mazy turned back to her letter. Elizabeth stood, checked her oven.

"Oh, Mother. Listen. They've seen Tipton."

"They have? Where?"

"At a Chinese doctor's. Naomi even knows where she lives in Sacramento."

"So Nehemiah was right. She headed toward kin."

"I'm not sure…they haven't actually talked with her. But she's there."

"Ponder that. Our little Tipton in Sacramento."

Pig barked then, and Mazy looked around.

"You've saved me some travel," Charles Wilson said, his shoulder pressed against the open doorjamb in his lazy-lounge way.

"Charles! Eavesdropping. I might have guessed," Mazy said, folding the letter.

"Just helping my mother out. Being a good son. She's packed a few more things up for my lovely sister and the…child she'll have. The dear, dear grandchild, as Mother refers to it. Now I don't have to head to Crescent City to deliver them. I can go south."

"It doesn't say where she is," Mazy said.

"I'm sure my sister will make some dramatic entrance somewhere. Tipton can't thrive long without an audience. I'll find her in Sacramento, all right. Just take a little effort."

"Something that will tax you, I'm sure," Mazy said. For a fleeting moment she was almost glad he knew, that he had somewhere to go far away from her. But when she saw the menacing glint in his eyes, she took back that selfish thought. "You just leave her be, Charles Wilson. Tipton has a right to make her way. Haven't you done enough harm to her? She doesn't need any more of your meddling."

"Mrs. Bacon, Mrs. Bacon." He clucked his tongue. "That's more passion directed my way than I've ever seen from you." He ran his tongue along his upper lip, smiled. "You can give me a tongue-lashing anytime you choose."

She could hardly see straight for the fury his words brought; they burned her to the bone.

Zane Randolph lifted the iron rod above his head, his breathing deep and labored. Up, down, up, down, sweat beading on his upper lip. He counted in cadence, and each time he reached ten he started over. He glanced at the clock. Stupid Irishman. He was late again. Zane had things to do. He hated waiting. And O'Malley's constant cheeriness was as annoying as the laughter of children playing outside his window. Where was the man? How he hated needing him. Not long. Not for long now.

Zane's upper body had filled out, rippled with muscle. He noticed the tighter fit of his boiled shirts. After he bathed, he would pause to look at himself in the mirror, the triceps firm, his shoulders wide. Even the pulling and lifting he'd been doing getting in and out of the purple shay had strengthened him.

But he still needed the Irishman to harness the horse, bring the buggy about. He could get in alone now. Each time he dragged himself onto the seat, he cursed Ruth. Each time he lifted his leg to set it into the peg, he cursed the doctor. It was part of his litany, part of his…worship, as he'd come to think of it. Lifting the iron weight, then lifting their names. It was the ritual way he could live.

The Stub had healed enough to wear the contraption that went around his waist. "Fits tight as an oak peg, it does," his keeper had said. "Perfect fit."

There was nothing perfect about it.

He wore it a few hours a day, building up The Stub's endurance. He hadn't walked far on it yet. The crutch troubled him too. It was as plain as his wooden peg. He wanted a cane with a brass handle with a section of brass that could be opened out to act as a seat he could lean on. At the point end, he wanted a brass fitting as well, with room for a thin stiletto to slip under. He'd have a way to sit to rest wherever he was and a ready weapon for self-defense with just a bend toward the floor. It would distract people from The Stub, such an exquisite and unique cane. He'd have it before long. The undertaker who doubled as a wood-carver was making it up special. If the Irishman had done his duty by him, taken it there with his instructions and drawings.

He set the iron weight bar down. His eye caught the peg contraption laid across his bed. He hated the look of it, this reminder of what once was. He thought of himself as half now, just the upper half of a body. The lower half mutilated and riddled with pain, belonged to someone else, someone who stored the anguish and fury in The Stub. He would unleash it in time, when he "pulled himself together," as he thought of it, to take care of two people at once.

He lifted himself with his arms from the bench, stood and hopped toward the window to see if the Irishman approached. The throbbing of The Stub pierced him. Oh, how he hated the pain, almost as much as being told by his keeper that the pain shouldn't be so great now, should have passed on.

"Just give it a bit of push then, and you can go a little farther each day."

"I'm going far enough daily," Zane growled. "For all I know, there's more infection, into the thigh, and that's why it hurts. Foul doctor takes my foot, my leg, then leaves behind infection."

"The wound heals well," the Irishman said. " 'Tis the pain coming from your mind then. Something you can heal if you set your heart to it."

Zane growled at him. What did people like the Irishman know of pain anyway? He had two legs. He walked around without the aid of some tree limb rubbing his armpits raw, a chunk of oak as the headstone to his being half a man. What did any of them know?

He wanted to be agile enough to face Ruth in the spring, to look strong and sturdy, to have a well-cut suit fitted and to drive up in his purple shay, pull up to the hitching post in such a way that she might have forgotten—if that jehu even told her—that he missed a leg. He wouldn't give her the pleasure of knowing what she'd forced him to endure, how he had become half. He returned to his chair, picked up a heavier iron bar, lifted it above his head, then down, combining the weight with his worship.

He imagined the scene.

He would drive in with a spirited horse pulling the shay. He'd ask to speak with her from the wide-eyed nephew who would come out to greet him. She would step out. He would sweep his hat off to her, watching the startled look as she saw white hair and beard where there had been dark. He'd see the fear in her eyes with the recognition that his form was before her, powerful, stronger than he'd ever been, running his eyes over her body. *Delicious.*

She'd stare, be in shock from seeing him, right there in front of her, oblivious to the wisps of her hair dancing before her eyes.

He'd look around then at her ranch, her farm, whatever it was she would have. He knew she would have much. He'd seen the mares and yearlings in the corrals when he watched her from a distance, before she ever left Shasta. He'd been inside her house and touched what she surrounded herself with. Yes, she'd gotten their child back, but he knew what her real treasure was: independence. And the horses and land she would have acquired by now gave her that. Or so she thought.

He would have her, or no one else would.

He lowered the weight, his whitish chest hair wet with sweat. He reached for a huck towel, wiped himself. White chest hair. Something else to blame Ruth for.

Once while he rehearsed this scenario, lifting the iron bar, it occurred to Zane that she might just choose to forgo the divorce and act as though it did not matter if she had a paper confirming their separation. He had nearly dropped a weight onto his chest. He'd devised a plan for that as well. No matter what she chose to do, he had a plan to counter it. He was a very clever man.

He never prepared a delicious dessert without whipped cream to top it off.

Seth let Mei-Ling's words settle on his shoulders. He had now, for days. He guessed everyone could see it. He was the one with blinders on, not Suzanne. He sat in his room. His bedroll had been rolled up for a week, but he just couldn't seem to leave. He didn't have anywhere to go; but he didn't deserve to stay.

He could return and check on his investments with Mazy's farm. Maybe go on north into Oregon. Gold strikes there meant monte and roulette, too. Maybe head back East again. But somehow the excitement of riding to the edge of a ridge just for the joy of going over had lost its appeal. It was the thought of Suzanne that gave his heart a race now.

Fortunately she'd gotten Powder to remain. He wouldn't have wanted to live with the guilt of the tutor's leaving Suzanne in a lurch. She was a hardy soul. She'd make it. She didn't need Seth, and she wouldn't push him just to get her way. She'd been kind and gracious. The most intimate thing she'd spoken of had been wondering if he'd be willing to consider helping with the theater proposition she'd put to him. "I believe I can manage it," she said. "It might even work into a way to help with Esther's…service. At the very least, whenever you're in town, you'd have front row seats without a worry over the candle wax dripping on your hat." She'd smiled. She had the most fabulous smile, and she didn't even know it. She couldn't even see herself.

He swallowed. Was he afraid of being with someone who was… maimed? His stomach churned with the thought of it. Who *wasn't* maimed in some way? Hers was just out there for the world to see; his was deeper. And she'd seen through him, offered her love to him just as he was. And when he'd left her standing in the dark, she hadn't punished him nor made him feel like the worm he was. No, she'd talked to him of commerce, of making a life, of having some contact with him over time, whatever he'd allow. He didn't deserve such a woman. The candle flickered. He'd told himself he'd cut back that wick. The light would sure be better if he did.

The knock on his door was followed by Esther poking her head inside. "Naomi is well enough to travel," she told Seth. "It would be of great help if you would be willing to take her and the baby north to Mazy's. And then on to Ruth's."

"I sure want to help Naomi," he said. "But I don't know beyond that."

"It need be only for this one time."

"Just one step."

Esther nodded. "God gives direction for each step and a light unto our paths. We do not know what will happen with our efforts. But we have chosen to walk this road for now. A greater determination than that is not necessary."

"I'll leave first thing in the morning." He cleared his throat. "I need to find Suzanne."

He carried the flickering candle to her room, tapped on the door.

"Esther?" Suzanne said.

"No. It's me. Seth." He came into the darkness where she sat and placed the candle on the table. "I'm leaving in the morning. Taking Naomi."

"Oh, good. I know they'll be safe with you. Thank you. I'm sure Esther's grateful too." She smiled at him.

"I need to say something to you before I go. About what we talked about."

"The theater can wait, Seth. It may just be a dream I've swirled up on a day I've lost my focus." She chuckled low.

He put his hand over hers. "Suzanne...I...your hair," he said, pushing a strand back at the temples, "it's like spun gold." He ran his fingers down her jaw. "Your face, this man admires. And that smile, that smile invites an artist's brush." He touched her lips and felt her shiver. "And your heart fans this man's fire."

Her lips parted, she started to speak.

"I made a mistake, Suzanne. I wasn't thinking, haven't been thinking clearly for a long time."

"It's all right. We can—"

"My mistake was in not telling you that I love you. I love you, Suzanne."

Her mouth opened and closed slowly like a worn clasp of a treasured necklace.

"I have no right to seek your love, none at all. I can't promise you a predictable life, but I'll promise you a life where you are loved beyond measure. I'll be devoted to you and your boys. I want a wife, a family. I want you."

She tried again to speak. "My...vision...it's...won't...?"

"I'm blowing out the candle, Suzanne," Seth said. "So we'll begin at the same level of light."

Suzanne gasped, then reached, touching his chest. "I'm trying to focus on your face." He could feel her breath on his cheek. "Am I looking up high enough?

He took her hand in his and kissed the palm. "Perfectly," he said.

"Did you...did you just make that poem up?" she asked. "The one about an artist's brush?"

"I've been writing that poem my whole life long," he said as his finger removed her dark glasses. He bent to kiss her. "You just helped me say it out loud."

Tipton groaned on the bed, holding her belly. She'd been ironing when the ache overcame her like an ocean wave rising, then lapping the shore. She panted and turned onto her side. "Not now, Baby. Not yet." Was she supposed to rub her belly or not rub it when she felt this pain? She couldn't remember. The only birthing she'd been around had been Suzanne's delivering Sason back on the trail. What had they done then? Nothing, really. She and Mariah had just sat and talked while the women tended Suzanne, brought that baby into the world. Suzanne couldn't have done it alone. Tipton hadn't been all that interested except to remember the discussions she and Tyrell used to have about children, how many of their own they had wanted. Everything at that birth kept reminding her of Tyrell, his memory so fresh and fragile. She'd gone away in her mind when it became too painful. But she'd kept herself from the laudanum when Sason arrived. She wondered if she could deliver this baby alone.

The pain subsided and she waited to see if there would be another wave of it, but nothing happened. She had been straining with the twelve-pound iron. Men's pants needed that much ironed-weight for the pointed crease. Flaubert, the actor, insisted she use the heaviest irons. They tired her more than the washing. But he often stopped by and sometimes pushed the irons himself. He could make her laugh when he recited lines from the plays he was in. Once or twice, she helped him rehearse scenes. She thought he might be a little taken with her, and while she didn't encourage him, neither did she send him away.

She heard rustling next door. The walls were as thin as spring ice. She wasn't sure who that neighbor was. She rarely saw him. He slept during the days and was gone at night. A gambler perhaps. She had no idea what he must have thought she did on the other side of their shared wall.

A few shirts still dried. Sheets soaked in a heated tub, and she wondered if all the moisture was what made her head throb so much. She moaned. She had to finish the work. She tried to sit up and cried out, shouted almost, with the ache at her head.

"Hey! Quiet! Trying to sleep here." Her neighbor pounded against the canvas-covered boards, knocking her feathered hat from the peg. It fell on the bed, Esty's hatpin still attached. Hadn't her mother told her that a hat on the bed was bad luck? She should hang it back up. She rolled to do so, cried out again.

"Quiet!"

"Sorry." Tipton pounded back. Tears pressed against her eyes. She wouldn't be able to do this alone, not without help. Certainly not without the powder.

She'd been back to the Chinese doctor, and he'd agreed to help her with the baby when her time came, but she was not to use the opium. So she didn't. But her stomach had ached, and she'd been almost as sick as she'd been on the ship. She had taken just a pinch one day, hoping to slow the cramps. And he had looked at her suspiciously, gazed into her eyes as if he knew. She hadn't used it again, but it called to her, sitting there promising to ease her distress. She needed the doctor's help, she reminded herself. She didn't want to offend him.

Once, after leaving him, she nearly ran into a Chinese woman coming in to see him too. It might have been the woman who had been there that day her feet took her screaming away. She couldn't be sure through her blur. She thought the woman had lifted her hand as though to speak to Tipton, then lowered her eyes quickly.

She could see bruising on the girl's cheek and an odd disfigurement in her walk as she passed. Her baby made a cry like a kitten, pitiful. Had someone struck her? Tipton shivered. There was little worse than being attacked by someone a person thought would be safe. *Didn't she know that well?*

Tipton closed her eyes. She couldn't tell if the headaches she had now caused her eyes to blur or if the marred vision brought on the ache. It didn't matter. The powder would relieve it. She had to get up, finish the ironing so she could indulge. Not indulge, but take a treatment, that was what the opium was. She pushed herself up, waddled to the heating stove, and picked up the hot iron.

She still had a few coins, and when she finished this job, if she could finish it, Flaubert would pay her. She could buy more powder from the Chinese apothecary…or get something to eat. Flaubert would be by this evening to pick up his trousers and shirts. It was strange how she'd found herself a part of a family of misfits here. She'd even exchanged pleasantries with the fallen women who lived next door. Once she'd turned her nose up at "that kind of woman," and then the woman had brought a steaming stew to share, telling her food tasted better when "it were divvied up." She told Tipton of a closer place to get her water for washing too. And even the Chinese had proven themselves friendly as they shuffled by with laundry bags hung from shoulder yokes.

But Tipton liked the actors best. Most of them slept during the day and performed at night. They'd hired her to clean the costumes for the theater. This was a good place for her baby to be born.

Laundering was a good profession. Hadn't Nehemiah even read to her of a wardrobe manager whom King Josiah's priests sought advice from? What was her name? Oh yes, Huldah. A simple woman who led a nation back to God.

But she didn't need Nehemiah teaching her and treating her like a child. She didn't need Elizabeth to answer questions or her mother to remind her of whatever failings she had, how her *brother* was so much more perfect than she.

His memory made her shiver despite the steaming heat in the room. She needed nothing from Charles. She had a family right here. She was a woman complete unto herself. She set the iron down, wiped her brow with the back of her arm.

She'd been dependent on everyone once and afraid of everything, too: of Tyrell heading west without her, then of them not being able to marry, then of her parents and brother arriving. She'd worried about Tyrell—that he might get hurt or that she'd lose him to some western woman. She fretted about Charles, that his hatred for her grew and swept her mother's love from her. She even worried about being intimate with Nehemiah.

She'd been afraid of so much, and all that emotion had changed nothing. She'd gone with Tyrell, fluttered her way onto the wagon train, then lost Tyrell anyway. Nothing of her worrying had brought her gain. All alone she'd survived what she'd worried about most—the loss of a love.

Tipton put the iron down, tested the smaller one for heat. She pressed her hands against the low of her back, waited to see if the pain would strike again. A small pinch, little pain.

She'd survived a westward journey even though she didn't feel like living. She'd stood at a grave site now trodden over by a thousand oxen's feet. She'd dragged laundry through deep California snow to take care of her mother in a hard Shasta winter, then stepped forward in white, high-button shoes to marry Nehemiah. No one forced her. Not a soul. A picture of Nehemiah reading her note came to her mind, but she pushed it away.

Tyrell might not be happy with her, even though she had done this in his memory, for this baby, that it would be born to a strong woman who didn't need a teacher telling her how to do things.

She felt the baby kick. "Maybe panning for gold would be better, Baby," Tipton said. She stuck the stirring stick into a mass of sheets that swirled together like glue. She lifted the load out, shook one or two back to lighten it, then laid the shirts on the makeshift drying rack of layered sticks she'd built near the stove. She returned to the iron.

Sluicing the streams for gold. And what would she do with a baby then? "Put you on my back instead of in my belly and keep moving," she said to her child. That was what life required, that she keep moving.

She wiped the perspiration from her forehead with her apron, lifted the heavy irons from the fire to steam seams onto the pants when she heard the knock on the door.

"Come on in, Flaubert," she said. "I'm nearly finished."

"Yes, you are," she heard the voice say. She turned toward the door. Her heart pounded with recognition.

"How did you find me?"

"You're so easy," Charles Wilson said. "You leave tracks wherever those tiny slippers of yours take you, dear sister." He wiped his mouth with the back of his hand, gazed around. He sneered. "Mother would be distressed to see her darling Tipton so near the Celestials." He picked up the ceramic opium pipe, smashed it on the edge of the table. The scattered shards startled her, and she blinked as they fell to the floor. "All I did was ask for a pretty lady, a tiny little blond wisp of a woman, carrying a child in her belly and a laundry basket on her shoulder, and I got directed here. This is certainly beneath you, my darling Tipton," he said.

"Thin boards instead of the luxury of a hotel?" He clucked his tongue, took off his hat. With his fingers, he brushed his tightly curled hair behind his jagged ear. "Mother tells me you lived in the finest room at Kossuth's hotel. Before it burned, of course. Funny how that fire started so close to your rooms. Trouble does seem to follow my darling sister."

"How did you know that? And about my baby?"

"That the fire started near Kossuth's? Apparently it didn't spread quickly enough to the 'private rooms' of my darling sister and her mother."

"You set it," she whispered.

"Always the dramatic one," he said. "But, yes, now that you mention it. That's exactly what I did. And what did it get me? My mother, dragging out a trunk that would dress my darling sister in wedding white so she and her dear husband could take what should have been mine."

"But she loves you most. That's why she stayed behind. To be with you. She sold the mules for you." Her heart raced with the outrage of it, the startle of discovery, how lethal he truly was.

She wanted Flaubert to come. She wanted the neighbor who'd pounded on her wall to get angry and storm in. She wanted help. *Oh, please, God, please send help!*

"Ah, I see you understand," he said. "You always were a quick one. Vicious, too." He touched the jagged ear and started toward her.

Her thoughts raced. She backed up. She wanted to run. Her hand touched the heavy iron, her fingers gripping the warm but no longer hot handle.

He lunged for her, grabbed her wrist, splashing water onto the floor. "I'm no fool, Tipton," he said. He twisted her arm and she gasped, releasing the iron. He pulled her around the steaming washtub, knocked over the drying racks. He shoved her against the bed now, her head hitting the wall. Like a bull, he charged against her, pinning her to the bed. "Dear Mother can't say enough about her new grandbaby. Can't say enough about how wonderful it will be to see the next generation born Californian, how Mister Kossuth will come back someday to run my store. My store. But he will not run for office. Not after I let the world know his young wife lived in a brothel, an opium pipe in her bed, exposing her baby to disease and disgust and was most likely killed by a jealous lover."

"You're the disgusting one," she said. He struck her. She cowered on the bed, her eyes blurry, her head throbbing.

"Quiet over there! Can't a man get sleep?"

Tipton opened her mouth to scream, but Charles was too fast. He clamped his hand over her face. The smell of his cologne sickened her. She tried to bite, but his hands gouged her teeth against her lips. She tasted her own blood.

"Never fear, sir!" Charles shouted back. "My lady and I will strangle our enthusiasm for each other, in honor of your good sleep. Won't we, my dear," he whispered to her.

She tried to push him back. She tried to move him off her child. She tried to take in more air. His fingers mashed her nose. She groaned with the pain, and then it came back, the day she tore at his ear with her teeth to free herself from him. She clawed now at his hand, and with the other he wrenched her arm and shoved it back behind her, arching her chest and her baby toward him. Her hands felt tingly, as though they would soon go numb. Maybe she should just sink and drift away. Then the baby kicked.

My baby! I have to protect my baby!

"We must be quiet, quiet," he said to her. Spittle formed at the side of his mouth, his eyes glistened like a mad dog's. "So I will answer more questions in your curious eyes. That is curiosity, isn't it? Which we know killed the cat. So let me tell you about your dear Tyrellie. A godly man, he was going to marry a pretty lady. They were going to have a pretty child. The grandmother so wanted a child. The grandfather wanted a child too. And Tyrell, the good man, was going to oblige them when the pretty lady turned seventeen." He smiled. "Here's where the plot thickens, my dear. Listen carefully. It has a surprise ending. Tyrell was a weak man. A stupid man. And so he died." He chuckled, his eyes glazed. "It took almost nothing to kill him, Tipton. Nothing. All the hopes of the grandmother and grandfather dashed, the pretty lady almost dead of her dramatic grief. And later, we learn, almost dead of drink and laudanum. But she just couldn't do it, poor baby. Even with opium, she couldn't do it. Her poor pipe got broken. But the pretty lady still tried. She was just so slow in destroying herself. Now here comes the ending. She dramatically prolonged her grieving by getting married, by almost having that pretty baby. And then her big brother came to save her from her troubles. But alas, he was too late."

He pushed her arm back up behind her, pressed himself against her. She could feel the hotness of his breath, the smell of passion mixed with rage stronger than the scent of her fear.

Behind her, her fingers felt for the feather of her hat.

"Yours will be the more engaging death. Oh no, I won't quickly snuff out your life, dear Tipton. A kitten should be played with, teased. I'll simply snuff out your will to live. The world will know about Tipton Kossuth. And Nehemiah Kossuth will be laughed from his campaign. All your hopes shattered. Like puffs to the air."

When Charles said *puff* he released his hand from her arm just long enough to raise his fingers as though a dandelion fluff had been spun into the wind.

It was enough. Tipton bunched the felt hat until she gripped the hatpin. Her fingers clutched for the brass of the dragonfly rising at the end of the tempered steel shank.

In that moment Tipton knew: She could thrust the shank into his neck and take her brother's life. She could end the years of hoping that the future with him in it would be better. But in that moment she knew too: Charles had let a memory, a false memory, drive him down a lonely, rocky road. She was strong enough to live with what was; not be held hostage to what once she'd loved.

With a strength she'd never known she possessed, she wrenched her arm free, thrusting the shank's pointed end across the finely chiseled face of her only brother.

He bellowed like a mad bull, released her.

"Nehemiah won't care what you say about me. He loves me."

Charles clutched at his face, blood pouring over his fingers. "You hurt me," he said. The wound ripped from his ear lobe to his chin.

She squeezed out from beneath him.

He whimpered, "You hurt me. There's blood."

"If you do one thing to injure Nehemiah's reputation, to even suggest that I am less than his loving wife, I will tell them you confessed to starting the Shasta fire. And that you killed Tyrell. I'll have you sent where every day you'll work your lazy, lethal fingers to a bone."

"You hurt my face. There'll be a scar," he said.

Someone knocked on the door, and she yelled, "Come in! Come in!"

Flaubert's eyes scanned the room, the blood, her panting, the hatpin still a weapon in her hand. "Are you all right? Is this some play you are rehearsing without telling me?"

"My brother," she introduced, her breathing rapid as a hunted deer. "He's just done a scene where he confessed to arson and murder. But his plot to kill me has been permanently upstaged."

the same as praying

The sound of her own laughter enriched her. Ruth skimmed leaves from the water barrel and filled the bucket they used for drinking. She supposed it was the giddiness of their success that did it. All of them, working together, making it happen up there on spring ridge, as she called it, saving those mares and her future. Even Burke Manes had been provided just when they needed him. Who could have imagined that a man who lived not far away, who was never lost but "powerfully turned around a time or two" and who carried with him the mantle of a preacher unlike any Ruth had ever known, should show up on their night of misery? Suzanne was right: No eye could see the good God had in store for them.

Ruth smiled as she poured the water into the drinking bucket inside. She came out and nearly bumped her head on the supper triangle, the iron Lura clanged to bring them in from the field. So now she was attributing good things in her life to God. Wouldn't Mazy find that a surprise?

Mazy. Ruth ought to write, to tell Mazy of all this, but she didn't know how, couldn't even begin to put into words the emotional ride she'd been on.

Even the loss of another mare the first week after the thaw hadn't "pushed her to the outside," that place where she'd dismount and stand, just watching, as the Giant Stride turned around life's pole without her.

Matthew had noticed the mare with her head low, walking as though her legs were stuck in thick mud up on the spring ridge. He'd led her back to the barn, but they'd been able to do nothing for her, and the mare had died a heaving, wretched death.

"Why did it have to be Puff?" Mariah wailed when she heard.

Matthew held his little sister and just let her cry. She yelled about how unfair it was, how everything she loved got taken. He didn't try to argue. He didn't try to make it all right. Because he couldn't, Ruth decided. It was something about him she'd come to respect: that he didn't always try to fix what he couldn't, that he somehow had the presence of mind to know when to just listen and when to act. For someone so young, that was a marvel.

For someone so young. It was a phrase she wished didn't pop into her head quite so much. Still, when he leaned across her to reach for the shears to trim the boys' hair and his arm would brush her shoulder or when he asked her to give him the linseed oil to put on the bridle and his hand would linger over hers, she didn't think of his age. She thought about the racing of her heart, the strange sensations on her skin, the dryness of her mouth. And then that smile would come, breaking through a silver storm to warm her.

She hadn't ever felt this way with Zane. That courtship had been flattering more than unfolding. She'd felt swept away, not allowed to wade in at her own pace. But this...relationship made her feel like a flower being opened inside a protective hand. No wind to buffet, no pounding rain to strip the petals, no harsh sun to dry her up. She wasn't sure she could trust it or herself.

"Just let it be," Matthew told her once when she tried to explain her reservations about his age. "I'm what, five years younger."

"Six," she said.

They stood watching the horses graze. "What did you want in a partner?" he said.

"I wasn't looking for a partner," she told him.

"Well, if you had been. What would you want?"

She'd stepped away from him, to avoid the influence of those eyes. He had a full beard now, trimmed daily. "Someone who just took me as I am, I guess. Who didn't try to change me into what they thought I should be."

"And have I tried to change you?"

"No. It's just...too soon. You need to live your life. How can you know that I'm the one? Maybe...you're looking for someone to look after you and—"

He'd laughed, a big hearty, belly laugh. "Like my ma, you're thinking? Like I'm a kid needing his mama?"

She'd looked sheepish.

"Ain't nothing in the world about my ma I see inside you, Ruth Martin. Except maybe a good heart, even if it does come out sometimes twisted as a rope. And maybe a passel of power to get things to happen. I see that, too, in both of you. But I'm not looking for a keeper. Fact is, I wasn't looking at all. But I found. And I know a gem when I see it. No man with any sense will walk on by a treasure just because it came along the trail when he wasn't expecting."

"You think of me as a treasure?"

He nodded. "I only wish you thought that way about yourself."

She'd glowed then, she was sure of it. And she felt a softening that must have shown because later even Lura said she looked different. "Like your jaw came unclamped, and your mouth and ears decided to say howdy." Ruth had grinned. "See there?" Lura had looked at Matthew, then back to Ruth. "So that's how it is?" she'd said, raising an eyebrow. "Not so sure that's wise, you ask me."

"We didn't," Matthew said.

Even in late March, when she picked up the thick packet from her solicitor, Ruth's smile held. She would wait to open it until she was alone. She walked through the moist tall grass. Yellow starlike flowers with purple centerlines clustered on foot-high stems. She'd seen them before, near Shasta. Sarah had brought them to her in a fisted hand. Lura knew their names. She'd have to ask her again.

When she got home, Ruth sat ready to open the fat envelope. She'd written to the lawyer in Shasta, telling him where she thought Zane was and to press for the divorce if he had not yet heard from him. This letter would be the next step, she'd told Matthew. She wasn't just waiting for a thing to happen; she was making it happen. And for just a moment, she let herself believe that her life had turned around, that she could join in and not be bruised or battered, but gently sheltered while she played.

She opened the letter and read and reread it, feeling the smile on her face begin to fade.

Tipton stood serenely calm, a state that turned to frantic when Charles bolted from the door.

"Are you all right?" Flaubert asked again.

It pleased her more than she could say that the first words out of Flaubert's mouth questioned her safety. Almost a stranger to her, yet he was concerned about her protection.

She sank onto the bed, threw the hatpin down, and watched her hand shake. "He…he'll be back," she said. "He'll get his face sewn up, and he'll return. I've got to leave, get out." She stood up, turned, stepped on Flaubert's spilled shirts. "I'm sorry."

Her mind raced. What would she tell her mother? What would Charles say about what happened? He'd never said it was her who'd gouged his ear, not ever. But this. He could use this to hurt Nehemiah's election hopes anyway. And she'd made him mad now, madder than ever. Her finger felt numb. She held her breath.

"The clothes are of no matter." Flaubert swept off his cape, laying it on the bed. "You are."

Tipton bent then to pick up the broken pieces of the opium pipe, her hand shaking. She swirled around the room, tossing things inside her carpetbag. She grabbed her few coins, picked up the opium packet, looked at it, then threw it down as though it was hot enough to sear her fingers. What if she had been smoking it when Charles arrived? Both she and her baby would never have survived.

"It's all right, Baby," she said. "It's all right. Now. My other shoes. My hat. That's all we need. We'll tidy up here. Just tidy up."

"What will you do?" Flaubert said. Then, "Come home with me. I will take care of you."

"What? No, no. I…somewhere away from here." She thought of Esty. Suzanne. No, no. She couldn't go to Suzanne's. She'd been so stupid, so naive. She couldn't face their looks.

"Come with me to the theater," he said. "Rest in the wardrobe area until you decide."

She'd shivered. It was ironic, wasn't it? That someone who loved finery and fancy might take refuge amidst the clothes of actors.

"You have to find a place of rest," he'd said, his voice kind. "For your baby now."

Perhaps the theater was a good idea. She could stay unnoticed through the night at least. In the morning make her way to somewhere else. She needed to alert Nehemiah. Charles might pursue him.

On Third Street they stood in front of the Sacramento Theater. An outside ladder leading to the balcony broke up the otherwise smooth lines of the square building. "Inside there is a bar," the actor said. "We will walk past it as though we own it. Never mind who is there taking a drink. Go down the stairs to the right. That is where the actors dress. Once there, you must act as though you belong. The Rays will not be pleased to have a stowaway in their company. I must think of some way to explain…"

"They won't like it that the clothes you gave me for cleaning are ruined."

He tapped his finger on his long chin. "You will say you are a new wardrobe mistress I have hired to assist me," Flaubert said, his hand in the air as though onstage, making a pronouncement. "At least the red-striped pants I must wear for this evening's performance have a perfect crease," he said. "Flaubert announces it."

"Do you have another name?" she asked.

"Angus Flaubert."

She must have blinked. "You don't look like an 'Angus.'"

"It is a stage name," he said. "Taken to inspire me. You might wish to take one too. To become something other than you are."

"Will Ruth be expecting us?" Mazy asked. "We shouldn't intrude." She busied herself with the butter, patting the thick beige clump into the wooden mold, latching the top, then setting it into the cooler that Matthew Schmidtke left her so many months before. The work settled her thinking.

"She'll be expecting me and Naomi and her little tyke," Seth said. "Esther wrote to her. I'm sure she'd be pleased to see you, too. I'll fill her in on things in Sacramento." Seth rolled a cigarette, and Mazy watched him put a stick to the fire and light it, liking the scent of it, remembering. How pleasant were the scents of a good man's companionship, like fine tobacco, leather, and even wet wool.

Mazy said, "Speaking of Sacramento, did you ever see Tipton?"

"She disappeared like a jackrabbit in the shadow of a hawk. Even the Chinese doctor where Naomi saw her first said she hadn't been back. I found her room, following Naomi's directions. Somebody else had already moved in. They said all they found there was a hatpin with a dragonfly on the shank underneath the cot. No one's seen hide nor hair of her since."

"How odd. Maybe she'll seek out Sister Esther later, after the baby comes."

Seth nodded. "She'd be welcomed at Suzanne's."

"Are you going to become the boys' tutor?" Mazy teased.

Seth's face reddened. "In a way," he said. "But Powder's staying on."

The smallish girl child Naomi held in her arms fussed, and Mazy could hear her begin to cry. It would go to a high-pitched wail if they didn't somehow get her comforted. The baby rattled her more than it should. Seth and Naomi and the child had been at Poverty Flat a few days now, and the screaming of the infant, the wizened look of her, proved worrisome to Mazy.

So did the way Naomi looked. She'd been a round-faced woman with eyes like perfect ovals. Now one eye remained closed almost all the time, a wide, poorly mended jagged scar, diagonal across it as though a broken ale bottle had been jammed into her face. How people could do such vile things to each other was beyond Mazy's understanding.

Naomi stepped closer to her baby. "You're safe here," Mazy said. "You can disappear inside this crowd of people. There are almost as many folks here as on our wagon train when we started west."

"Too close," Naomi said.

"You're right about that. But there are places you can get by yourself. Across the meadow. Down by the creek."

"This place too close to Sacramento," Naomi clarified.

"Well, I suppose you know best," Mazy said. "It's just that your baby doesn't look well enough to make the journey. Just yet," she added quickly as she saw Naomi's face register fear.

"That's why we thought you coming along would be wise, Mazy," Seth said.

Mazy looked at him. Was the trip a way for him to get time with her again? she wondered. No. There was something different about him, something calming, as though he had found a fire inside to warm him that had nothing to do with her.

"There'll be others arriving," Mazy said. "Maybe I should stay here."

"Esther hoped you'd take Naomi north yourself. You and Ruth could help get her established."

The child's face twisted in distress, and Mazy wiggled her fingers toward Naomi who lifted the child up to Mazy's arms. "Hello, little Passion," Mazy sang out. "Pretty baby. Pretty Passion."

"I change name, maybe. New name for new place. To Chou-Jou."

"That'd be nice," Mazy said, lifting her voice above the squeal. "Always good to name kin after someone we cared for." Chou-Jou had made the journey west, been lost to hydrophobia before they ever reached the Black Rock Desert.

"Husband think girl child bad joss," Naomi said. "She keep him from sleep with her cries."

"She does wail," Mazy agreed. "Not badly," she said when she noticed Naomi's eyes begin to pool. She rocked from side to side, then turned and put the child on her shoulder. That made it worse, though Mazy patted and crooned. Pig barked as she talked to the child. "Jealous," she said as she walked to the door, opened it for him to go out. Chance, David Taylor's dog, yipped and followed. Mazy turned the infant away from her then, while she held one arm over the baby's chest, the other supported the baby's bottom. The little girl's legs draped over Mazy's arm as though sitting on a narrow branch, gazing outward as Mazy paced. The child felt floppy and soft as kneaded dough. Chou-Jou faced her mother but still screamed, and Mazy, without thinking of it, lifted her up and down in front of her while standing in one place. Chou-Jou quieted, appeared to look out then and see what was before her.

"She likes something you're doing," Seth said.

"Maybe so," Mazy said. As soon as the baby started to fuss again, Mazy lifted her up and down, feeling the child's little back move against Mazy's breast. The back of Chou-Jou's head was covered with thick, black hair against a slender neck. When she stopped the swinging motion, the child began fussing, but wasn't as frantic. Mazy lifted her again, three or four times more until her head nodded forward and Mazy felt drool on her arm. Mazy scooped the little feet, turned her around, then held her to her breast while she slept.

The ache of the infant's weight brought back a memory Mazy had never had, of the infant she'd never held. Tears sprang to her eyes.

It still startled her when someone asked her if she had children or not. She never knew quite how to answer, whether to say, "I lost an infant before it was born" or to say that she had none. It felt dishonoring to the infant who'd died to say nothing; a lie to say she'd had none. Would she, when and if she ever married again and had a baby, say that was her first child or only her "firstborn"? She handed the sleeping infant back to her mother.

"Safe in Oregon," Naomi said. "Safe there."

"You set a date for heading out?" David asked coming in through the door. With his foot he held Chance back, set Ben down. Oltipa followed behind. She had a basket full of white roots with stringy stems she plopped on her lap as she sat on a grass mat. She plucked at the roots, separating stems from tubers.

"Soon," Seth said. "If I can talk Mazy into joining us. Streams aren't so swollen as last year. I think we'll make the crossings without trouble."

"All will be well here," Oltipa said.

David nodded. "Oltipa and me, we got us some good news," David said. He grinned. "Ben here's going to have a little brother."

"That's wonderful," Mazy said. She dabbed at her eyes.

"Yup. And I'm thinking that if the offer is still open, Mazy, I'd consider farming more full-time. A fellow needs to be near his children, not be gone so much, if he wants to raise 'em right."

"I'm sure we can work that out," Mazy said. "I might be on the trail more myself." She cast a glance at Seth. "It'd be easier knowing this place is well tended."

"I hope to spend a bit more time closer to Suzanne's boys, too," Seth said. "Guess I can tell you all. Suzanne and I are getting married."

"You are!" Mazy said. "So that's why you look so…comfortable."

"Do I?" Seth grinned. "Figured it was time I said out loud what we've both been knowing but were too scared to say."

"Imagine, a man owning up to being scared," Mazy said.

"Matrimony is scary," Seth said. "That's why you got to be sure you have someone to hold you when it gets dark."

David laughed. "Never heard it expressed that way before, but it fits." He turned to Oltipa and grinned. "Like reins to a hand."

"And Suzanne will hold you in your darkness," Mazy said.

"And I'll hold her in hers," Seth said.

Mazy felt a flutter at her stomach. Had she somehow told herself that Seth would always be there? Someone for her to fall back on when she finally got desperate enough to admit she wanted companionship other than a dog? No, it wasn't loss nor envy neither. She was pleased for her friends. She just couldn't name what this hole inside her heart was.

"We'll be a good team," Seth said, his words coming faster with the rush of pleasure his disclosure carried. "Suzanne and I are talking about how both of us seem to need to keep water in the bucket swirling. We don't like to see dirt settle to the bottom. Just gets there, clear as a glass eye, and we stir it up again. Anyway, we thought we'd find a way to do that together. You tell your mother, Mazy, that I 'caught a cold' there in Sacramento. She'll know what I mean."

David clapped Seth's shoulder in congratulations. The man beamed.

Yearning, that's what this is, Mazy thought. She was yearning for something more. Walking through life alone was invigorating for a time. But she wasn't sure she wanted to do it for the rest of her days.

"Well, Naomi, are you ready for my company?" Mazy said. The Celestial nodded. "All right then, let's do it. We'll bundle Chou-Jou up against the April winds."

"We taking Pig to trot with us?" Seth said.

Mazy nodded. "A girl always needs a friend who accepts her as she is."

"You two will patch things up, that's what I'll ponder."

"I don't know. What happened was a terrible thing I could have prevented."

"That's not exactly so," her mother said. "We don't control much, except how we react to what we're given on this trail. Ruth's had a chance to find that out too. At least let yourself look forward to the journey," Elizabeth said. "Regardless of what happens when you arrive. Life's short. You got to celebrate often."

Mazy teased, "I won't miss a wedding, will I?"

"Ach," Elizabeth said and pushed her hand to the air. "Not to worry over that. You might just marry before me if you let yourself meet up with some nice man."

"I had a nice man." Her mother's eyebrows rose. "At least now I can remember nice things about him. And everything wasn't Jeremy's fault. I think I kept him…contained inside some boundary, Mother. I didn't tell him much, where the gates were. He didn't open doors for me to know him either. It was sad, really, that we missed knowing who each other was."

"That's good, Child. It is. To come to such a place of forgiveness. Letting go of being mad at him don't excuse what he did. You're a kind and loving woman. You can remember that young bride who married for love. And let her remind you that love can come again." Mazy blushed at the compliment. "I can pray for that, can't I? That your heart will be open to the man God chooses for you, as open as you are to helping others make their way?"

Mazy smiled. "What would you do if I said no?"

"Ponder it," she said. "It's the same as praying."

Zane Randolph smashed his fist against the wall of the livery in Yreka. Horses snorted and whinnied with the splintering of wood from his fist. "Hey now," said the hostler. "No need for that."

"I'll determine what there is need for," Zane said. He could not accept that the purple shay would have to stay. His well-laid plan was slipping from his grasp like an iron weight held by a sweaty hand.

"No buggy'll make it over the Siskiyous. That's just common sense, man," the hostler told him. "I'll buy this'n from you. You hire yourself a good freighter wagon to carry you and your leg there. Might be still early for them. They don't like the spring runoff, but I suspect you can convince 'em. Or you could ride yourself on a big horse. One peg leg like you're toting shouldn't throw you off too much."

"I need no advice from such as you," Zane seethed. He pulled himself into the shay, poked his cane at the hostler. "Bigger men than you have fallen by my hand," he said, then drove his shay out.

That had been several hours ago. Here he was now, at the mouth of Cottonwood Creek. At the foothills of the last mountains he would have to cross before he found his Ruth. He was closer to his destination than he'd been in months. But the horse resisted, wouldn't cross. It started forward as he whipped at its haunches, but pushed backward at the first step into water. She'd nearly killed him when she bolted back, turned the shay and set it up on one wheel.

Zane's heart had lurched into his throat while he waited what seemed hours for the wheel to set down on firm ground.

"You stupid beast!" he'd shouted, fury beading out on his forehead. *How dare this beast confound my plans! How dare it!* He whipped it again, and the horse's ears lay back flat as it pushed and pulled on the road.

"Might get farther if you give her a rest," a man with a New York accent shouted from a cabin beside the road.

Zane shook his fist, glad to have someone else to vent his outrage on.

"Suit yourself," the man said, shrugging his shoulders.

Zane breathed hard, could hear that rasping sound he made that he hated, a sound signaling defeat. Maybe he should see about a trade, his buggy for a riding horse. Or perhaps simply steal the man's mount and ride it across. That would serve him right for intruding.

He had to get across, and the idea of leaving behind the purple shay was just one more rock that Ruth threw in his road.

He yanked on the reins. "Whoa, now, you cursed beast! Whoa!" He'd need a decent gelding if he was to go on horseback, one he could test first—so stealing one would be useless. Impulsive. And he was not impulsive.

He hated it, how unbalanced everything was with a leg gone, wood where a limb should have been. He couldn't just choose a good-looking horse, couldn't just walk in and buy something, unnoticed. *Ruth. All Ruth's fault.*

He turned the shay around and headed back. It was growing dark, and before he reached Yreka he had to stop to light the side lanterns. It was an awkward affair to stand on one leg, use the peg for balance while he stood to light the flame. He disgusted even himself.

He left the shay at the livery, made his way across the dust-and-dung-covered streets, careful to place his brass-ended cane away from the piles. Inside, at the Yreka Hotel, he ignored the looks of gawkers slouched at the bar. They were nothing but gnats hovering at street manure. If they only knew what he had accomplished. If they only knew what he was about to do. He pounded the oak table with his cane, brushed off peanut shells with one sweep. "Bring me ale," he said. "Your best."

She would not get away with it. He would hire a freighter. Ride in a wagon up and over the mountains to his Ruth. Then rent a shay in Jacksonville. It might not be a purple carriage, but she would know royalty approached just the same.

"Use the cane Seth Forrester gave you," Esther directed Suzanne as they stepped out of the buggy. A night owl hooted, and Suzanne felt the cooler night breezes off the river.

"I usually do use it," Suzanne said.

"Yes, well, this theater is very dark, even in the daylight. And here we are at 3:00 A.M."

Suzanne laughed low. "Did you hear what you just said? About it being dark inside?"

"Oh."

Suzanne could imagine her blushing. "It's fine, Esther. It is. Perhaps I could lead you around, at least after the first time through. This will work perfectly," Suzanne said. "I just know it will."

"That remains to be seen."

Suzanne heard a heavy wooden door creak open. She stepped up. She could smell the linseed oil from the bar Esther said stood at the right, and noticed that the carpeted floor sloped slightly. She sniffed. A musty scent, of dampness from the river, she supposed, or perhaps mildew on the heavy curtains that would mark a distant stage. A cobweb drifted across her face.

"What time is she meeting us here?" Suzanne asked.

"Four o'clock, if all goes well. She's bringing in a child, she said. All battered and such. Soon as she arrives, we'll take her with us. But in the future, she may have to leave one or two here through the night. Then I'll bring them home after I come to clean."

"Material. We must get more clothing material. I wish I had that sewing machine Bryce insisted I bring."

"You might not have made it. Or ol' Cicero our ox might not have, if you had insisted it remain with you," Esther reminded her.

"I suppose. Are you lighting candles?" Suzanne asked.

"First thing I did."

Suzanne loved the smells here, of makeup paint, the heavy curtains, even the popcorn and peanuts ground into the thin carpet.

"Do you want to go downstairs?" Esther asked. "The costumes are there."

"I'll go on down."

"All right then. But if you hear something, come back up. We'll need to leave as soon as they arrive."

Suzanne tap-tapped her cane on the steps. She touched the wall at the turn in the stairwell and could smell the thick whitewash. The cool air of a large room greeted her, and she caught the scent of sweat clinging to costumes. Her eyes itched with the recognition of cloth newly dyed. She was aware of something else, too. She couldn't place it. She thought she heard something. She moved forward, tapping her cane and fluttering her fingers at her throat. Apprehension tickled her neck. Her boys were home safe. She hadn't risked them. She could feel a splendid sense of swirling, knowing here was something new.

riding the horse of intent

Ruth rode over to Burke Manes's farm, the packet from her lawyer in hand. It wasn't something she could share with Matthew. She wished Mazy were here to talk over this turn of events with, but she wasn't. And something in the eyes of Burke Manes told Ruth he might listen without judging.

Chickens pecked in the yard. Beyond, she saw Burke behind a single mule, a plow strap over his shoulder. He was readying a garden though there were still pumpkin vines covering the plot.

"I start on my circuit, and my land tending just gets neglected," he said. He sounded sheepish but not regretful. He invited her inside where she showed him the letter, reviewing in her own mind her options even while he read.

She could have her divorce all right, her solicitor told her. But Zane was suing for half of everything she had. *Half!* Half her horses. Half the ranch. And if she refused, he intended to sue her anyway, for half of what she had even if they stayed married! And he could keep on taking what she treasured, what she valued, and using it up as though it were whipped cream that could be replenished each time the cow gave milk.

"I'd heard of a case in California," Burke said, running his wide hands through his hair. "Where a wife sued her husband while they stayed married, to keep her half of their earnings from an eatery they ran. Seems he had a leaning to whiskey and she wanted a different kind of liquid asset to hang on to. She got it too."

"Everything is mortgaged," she said. "He…could take half, and the children and I would be left with nothing."

"Have you talked it over with Matthew?" Burke said.

She bristled. "It's really none of his affair."

And if Matthew knew, he'd kill Zane Randolph. She would never be free of the bad choice she'd made all those years before, marrying Zane. She could see that now. She'd been a fool to think otherwise, to think that she could have happiness without losing herself. To divorce him meant giving up the land. To stay married meant giving up the rest of her life.

Her solution she would share with no one. She could barely admit it to herself.

"A tough one," Burke Manes said then, handing her the letter back. He'd fixed a cup of coffee, which sat cooling before her. "Seems that, inside the challenges, that's the place where we learn those lessons we otherwise never would. It's when we find out how strong we really are. Who we really are," he said. "Think of what you learned during that ice storm."

"Too much ice break things," she said. "We lost more than one good mare to the stress of it. And Jessie. She hasn't gotten any better. So what I learned is that there will always be bad things happening to me. People around me will always have bad things happen to them. And it's foolish to think I deserve different."

"Unlike trees, we always have a way to buttress the load. We don't have to break the way those branches did."

"Relying on others," she snorted. "Who fail us too, in time. Or become broken themselves." She thought again of her brother and his wife, what they'd sacrificed for her.

"Here's how I see it," Burke said. "Life is like a trail headed to some sunny place. It's got holes to go around and rocks to step over, and sometimes how we deal with them teaches us more about what we're made of than anything else. The road's got nice scenery, too, most times, and we don't have to walk it alone."

"I don't think God wants me on that road. I just keep falling into those holes and stumbling over the rocks."

"It's just a part of what's there. When we get to the end of the road, then we'll get to understand."

"I want to understand now," Ruth said. "I want to know why we have to hurt so much now. I want answers. Why does a new black hole form itself just beyond one I crawl out of, ready to snare me as soon as I'm standing upright? What kind of a road is that?"

"A rocky one," Burke told her. "No one denying that."

"I can't do it anymore; I just can't," she said.

"Too many people would grieve your giving up," he said tenderly. "And who would be there for your Jessie, and Sarah and the boys?"

She wept then, hating that she couldn't seem to stop.

"Grief is the price we pay for loving," Burke said, his voice as soothing as a spring rain.

"It's too high a price. I can't barter or bargain. I have to do without. I don't want to take any more people onto the rocky road with me," she whispered. "It's not fair to them."

"Making the choice for them isn't fair either." He handed her his neckerchief. It smelled of sweat and earth. She blew her nose. "None of us can make it alone. It doesn't mean we're weak. Even the Lord had help, Ruth. Let the folks who care about you pull you out of the holes, point out the next ones, help you walk around, then celebrate your success."

"I want to go back to before all this started."

"It's what we all want to do when we're hit with something in the wilderness that we don't want to face. We don't get to go back, Ruth."

"No," she said. "We get pressure. To change."

The trip north to Jacksonville took them less than three weeks. Once she'd decided to go, Mazy did as her mother suggested: She enjoyed the journey, let it nurture her soul. The country was lovely. Red buds of oaks dotted hillsides, interspersed with the smoky green of digger pines. Pig sniffed and scouted and trotted back beneath oaks and red-barked madrones. He scrambled up over rocks and drank the cold water where boulders broke up rippling streams. Popcorn flowers with their yellow centers bloomed in the wet areas. Tiny yarrow clustered in thick patches. Colorful plants that looked like balsamroot, but for the leaves on their stems, bobbed in the breeze. "Mule's ears," Seth told her they were called. Pig frolicked through them all, the buttercups and Indian paintbrushes, chasing rabbits, barking at things that Mazy couldn't see.

"I'm glad you asked me along," she told Seth. "I like the idea of doing something good for Naomi, getting her out of a place she's not safe."

Seth nodded. "Just hope Ruth is willing to put her up for a time, 'til we can get her settled into Chinatown up there. Naomi's willing to work. She always liked the animals, she tells me. Helped Ruth back in Laramie looking after the stock."

"That's right, she did. And she was quite a cook, too, I remember. Lots of herbs and spices. Adora loved it. Lura, too. In fact, Lura always talked about cooking in an eatery someday. Maybe she and Naomi could partner up. They could—"

"*Owning* one is more like it, from what I remember about our Lura," Seth said. "Giving orders is more her way than negotiating together."

"You're right about that," Mazy laughed. "But then negotiating is important in any relationship. I hope we can use Poverty Flat to help Esther out," Mazy said.

"It's still in California," Seth said. "Esther seems to think Oregon's better. They need to be out of this state, if what I hear is true."

Mazy agreed. "Before they create a 'Chinese Protection Act' like they did for the Indians. And we can all see how the federal protection is keeping tribal people safe—genocidal neglect, I call it. Pretend they want to take care of the Indians, then let them die of disease and starvation." She pursed her lips in disgust. "Making widows and orphans nearly every day. I hear the tribes in Oregon are resisting being removed to reservations."

"Think the uprisings there are finally slowing down; they're more willing to talk."

"That's good. A sign that they still have hope."

"The resisting or the talking?" Seth asked.

"Both."

"Naomi's lagging behind some," Seth said. He reined up. "Don't think she's used to riding. Why don't you take the baby basket for a while? Give her a break."

They chose to ride rather than go by stage, stopping at hostelries for the night. At least their horses were well cared for there. More often than not, when people saw Naomi, they turned them away, told them they could grain the animals if they wished before moving on. They even saw a sign at one cabin beside the road: "Dogs and Indians stay out."

"I don't suppose they'd make an exception for Naomi or Pig then," Mazy fumed.

Outrage bubbled to the surface more than once, until Naomi touched Mazy's hand at a livery near Yreka and said, "It does no good for Chou-Jou to hear badness."

"I'm only defending you," Mazy said.

"You ride horse of good intent," Naomi said. "It does not arrive at destination."

Mazy knew her face burned red, but the woman was right. Her indignation didn't always get what she wanted, and it left Chou-Jou trembling, something none of them wanted. Who would have thought that such a little person could sense someone else's anger? Mazy vowed to keep her upset under her hat.

At Cottonwood Creek, in the foothills of the Siskiyou Mountains, they stopped to water their horses and met up with one of two Cole brothers, formerly of New York. Mazy played the "do you know?" game, asking about the Schmidtkes who had come from Putnam County, too.

"Can't say as I know them," Rufus Cole said. "Lots of folks changed their names, you know. Can't always say unless you meet them face up. Me and my brother only came out in '52."

"Why, that's when we came across," Mazy said.

"They farmers?"

Mazy nodded yes. "Had lots of Durhams. You might remember Lura Schmidtke. She's a little wiry woman who sharpened knives for a time, I guess. And she always wanted to open up a restaurant."

Rufus Cole smiled. "Thought of doing that myself. Right here." He gazed out over the low valley, prelude to the rapid rise of the Siskiyou Mountains. "Someday the stage'll come this far and farther. Go on into Jacksonville and up to Portland. They'll be needing swing and stage stations. Last year we had a local company bringing sporadic wagons in and over to Jacksonville from Yreka, but only when it's dry and only when the snow's out. You'll see. That trail's pretty rugged up and over, even for horse travel. Times like this, with the creek rising, wagon freighters make themselves scarce. Only pack animals make it. Big mules like you're riding there, ma'am." He nodded his chin to Mazy's mule, Ink. "We'll need the big boys to get into the act before we get a jehu to handle a Concord over these mountains." He looked to the road Mazy and Seth and Naomi would be taking.

"I know just the man who could drive it too," Seth said. "Used to drive for Baxter and Monroe."

Mazy said, "I think he's given up the rush of the road. For the sake of his family."

Mr. Cole tipped his hat at Naomi. "Might want to come into the house for a bit and let that little one have a taste of shade."

"Wish all our stops were like that one," Mazy said as they moved north after their respite.

Leaving Rufus Cole's shanty required a creek crossing of some challenge. Naomi's eyes grew large as she tried to kick her mount forward toward the rushing freshet. "Wait," Seth told her. "I'll go across, find the footing, then come back and lead you. You want to wait too, Mazy?"

"I'll follow you," she said. "I've got Chou-Jou with me."

Mazy watched Seth's big black gelding he'd picked up in Sacramento. The horse switched its tail once or twice, lowered its big head, snorted, then began his clop-clopping across the rocks and surging stream.

"He doesn't like it much," Seth shouted back over his shoulder. "But it's got a rock bottom. No quicksand. We'll be all right." Mazy followed. Ink didn't balk at all as they splashed quickly beside Seth.

"Why don't you lead Ink back and put Naomi on her," Mazy suggested. "Then go back and lead her horse."

"Good idea," Seth said as Mazy dismounted. As she waited for them, she looked around. She stood beneath a granary tree where woodpeckers congregated to store acorns for the winter. Upstream, broken tree roots and branches collected at rocks. Leaves and twigs from a season washed their way through the rushing water. There'd be more of these crossings, she suspected. If they were to truly transport Celestials safely out of California, they'd need sturdy, steady mounts, maybe find routes where people repaired bridges. And accomplices, people sympathetic to their cause.

Their cause. How quickly she'd taken it on. A wrong needing to be righted, that was what called her, that was what would fill her longing. Whether she found someone to share her life with as a partner or not. It was a good boundary. God knew her lot.

With Naomi safely across, they started up the twisting road, Pig's tail wagging in the distance. Yellow, jagged rocks with springs squeezing and dribbling black against them formed the inside ridge. Deep canyons pitched off to treetops below. Sometimes the ravines opened to the west, sometimes to the east. They could hear the roar of larger creeks rushing beneath them. More than once, huge sections of the road disappeared, the snowmelt pushing dirt and rocks and changing ridges in its wake.

"I hadn't thought about water being so strong," Mazy said. "It gouges and carves like a sculptor's knife."

"'The noblest of the elements,'" Seth said. "Pindar, I'm quoting now."

"You read Greek classics? Will wonders never cease?"

"My mother did," he said. "Water'll heal you, and it can kill you. Too little and you die, too much and you drown. But it's what we need for growing."

"Just the right balance of it," Mazy said. "So much of living is just the right balance."

Tipton had heard someone moving about upstairs the very first night she stayed, the night of Charles's assault. Stuffed into the bottom of the heavy oak wardrobe, she'd been crying, holding herself in sobs of self-pity. She was covered with crinolines and slippers and boots so that if anyone thought to look there, they would not see her cowering. She prayed, but they were words of questioning, filled with fear.

Then noise had startled her. She had crept up the stairs, surprised to see candles lit and someone, a woman, bent, picking things up off the floor. A broom leaned against the wall. A bucket of water sat inside the door. The cleaning person. Tipton backed out slowly and returned to her hiding place. She'd had to be extremely quiet. The night could be so exposing.

Then tonight she'd heard slippers on the stairs, whispering and shuffling sounds. Her heart pounded as she scrunched, hiding. Whispers. Silence. She creaked open the door, peeked out beneath her refuge of costumes. Bathed by a single candlelight, she stared into almond-shaped eyes.

The woman, well, girl almost, was smaller than Mei-Ling. She knelt, but Tipton imagined her feet were tiny like Mei-Ling's and her hands, if they hadn't been cupped inside wide silk sleeves, would surely have been small, too.

Tipton opened her mouth, but the girl quickly pulled her hand out of the silk and pressed her finger to her lips. Tipton nodded, lay back down, staring into the darkness. What had Nehemiah said once? That God often finds us in the morning darkness when we're less distracted. She was half asleep. Maybe it was a dream. But the girl's breathing could still be heard, raspy and wounded. Tipton winced, remembering the sores on her face too. And the Celestial was so thin, so alone. Tipton led a charmed life by comparison. She'd only been ill from her own poor choices, only been displaced by the imaginings of her distant mind. Even her brother would be no real threat if she would allow Nehemiah to truly be in her life, to love and protect her.

Shame flooded over her. She had been given so much, and still she put herself and her baby at risk, just because she thought she deserved more. What a mess she'd made. Nehemiah would be a fool to take someone like her back.

She crept out of the wardrobe. After making her way upstairs, she brought the water bucket and some rags back down. "Let me help," she told the Celestial, whose eyes widened in fear when Tipton kneeled beside her. Weak, the girl eased back, nodded yes. She wiped blood caked at the side of her face and tan flesh in the palms of her hands. Tipton began washing the girl's wounds.

Eventually Tipton returned to her wardrobe and slept. When she awoke, there was no sign of the Celestial, nothing at all to indicate she'd had a visitor in the theater. But somehow Tipton knew there would be more. Someone brought her, and someone else came to whisk her away. Many needed tending. She saw their presence as a gift.

She filled her days sewing buttons on costumes, repairing flounces on dresses, hemming men's pants. The thick wax makeup used to make the actors'—and sometimes actresses'—faces look larger so their audiences could see their expressions, also caked onto their collars and cuffs.

She scraped it off with a slender knife, even rubbed spots clean with sand. She'd planned to launder them, she would. But the thought of a steaming tub of water still made her ill.

Once or twice she'd watched a production, was captivated by the costumes and characters. "What did you think of our little play?" Flaubert asked her later.

"Lovely," she said.

"Maybe you will perform sometime?"

"My whole life's been a performance," she said. "I'm learning it's what goes on backstage that really counts."

She'd met Mrs. Henry Ray, the co-owner of the theater company and so far, the proprietress had found her work for Flaubert so satisfactory, she had hired her as "the official wardrobe keeper." It meant a wage. It meant meeting and talking and helping the actors. Her tending them kept other thoughts at bay.

The Rays would take the troop to San Francisco soon. Tipton had heard them discussing it when she watched them rehearse *The Wife* and *Charles II,* two plays that won them recognition when they'd performed them in San Francisco four years before. Tipton listened to the actors rehearse their lines, watched in fascination as the costumes and makeup and sets transformed not just the actors and actresses but the audience as well. Dozens of spectators hovered in the pit down front, hung over the balcony, or squeezed in with their glasses of ale on the wooden benches avoiding drips of candle wax on hats and capes as the night wore on. They listened, totally consumed by the extravaganza.

"Everyone needs to be transformed, to forget one's woes, if only for an evening," Henry Ray said. "That's what the theater does. And so they leave refreshed, the lowly and the royal, refitted to perform their tasks anew. It is the essence of art." His wife had nodded her agreement.

They spoke of things in front of her as she pinned a waistband or mended a tear. It was as if she wasn't there, as if she had gone away and yet she stayed. Listening, she learned. Mrs. Ray complained one day about the European actors. "They absolutely falter if the audience cheers or claps," she said. "'Tis the strangest thing."

Flaubert told the woman, "In France one only receives applause as a prelude to tomatoes."

"Ah," Mrs. Ray had said.

Tipton thought of that, how an action in one place could mean something quite the opposite somewhere else. No wonder people who came from different countries had trouble understanding each other. No wonder husbands and wives did too, she considered. They came from different families, different places. Only talking about their differences would lead to understanding. Only staying mattered, or coming back, giving, taking, simply holding.

She hoped the Rays would take her with them when they went to San Francisco. The trip was scheduled for late May. So was Baby's arrival.

She knew the Rays would not be pleased to know their "chubby wardrobe mistress" not only worked there by day and helped with the performances at night, but used the theater for her living quarters. She was always the "last to leave," Mrs. Ray commented, commending Tipton's dedication. Once Baby came, Mrs. Ray might have other words for it. She was rarely at a loss for words. Tipton wouldn't think about what word the arrival of Baby would prompt.

Every now and then, Tipton would awaken to yet another Celestial sitting like a lily pad quiet on the pool. The theater was a waiting room. For what, Tipton did not know, but she tended them, sometimes just sitting beside them until she heard sounds of those coming to move them to the next place, wherever that was.

It was her. Even in the darkness, Tipton knew. The tapping of a cane, the scent of lavender, even the swish of crinolines made her sure it was her. And then a woman had shouted down.

After the blind woman returned upstairs, Tipton followed. What business could Suzanne have here? Then she thought she recognized Esther's voice. On her hands and knees behind the bar, Tipton peeked out. She stumbled forward.

"Tipton!" Esther said.

She took it as her cue.

They took a room at the Crescent City Hotel, right next to the Table Rock Ten-Pin Bowling Saloon in Jacksonville. "I didn't expect to see a hotel named for a California city here in Oregon," Mazy said. She untied the overskirt, shook the dirt, then laid it across the saddle.

"And it's on the corner of California *and* Oregon Streets," Seth noted. "Hmmm. Smell that," he said.

"Smells like a French bakery," she said.

"There's another aroma coming from around that corner," he said. He walked the short distance to the corner of Third and Oregon, craned his neck, then came back. "It's a bakery and coffeehouse," he said.

"Mother would be in heaven."

They'd seen the steeple of a church when they'd rode in and, by all accounts, Mazy thought the town needed it. Shouts and curses blasted from the Palmetto Bowling Saloon where she heard ten pins roll and smelled malt whiskey, too. Other places announced faro and monte, tobacco and tunes. "It's a boom town, all right," Mazy said.

The proprietor squinted and frowned at Naomi as they entered the wood-framed hotel, but Mazy had already decided about what she'd say. And with Naomi's approval having been previously given she said, "This is my sister. The baby is my niece. We will be sharing a room, if you please."

"Might be more comfortable at the boardinghouse next door," the clerk said.

"If you have rooms, we'll be fine right here."

"Yes ma'am," the clerk said. The look he gave Seth pleased her: A look of pity for his having to travel with such a full-chisel woman.

In the morning they stopped at the desk to ask where Ruth Martin might be living and learned, surprisingly, that Lura and Matthew were south of town with them. "We must have ridden right by," Mazy said. "And never even knew it."

The agent followed them out of his office, and Mazy walked to free Pig from the stables. Seth saddled and led the mounts around to the front where they could see Naomi waiting with Chou-Jou. A man of Mazy's height leaned in toward the child.

"I should have stayed," Mazy said. "Someone's already harassing her. I hope bringing Chinese here will work, Seth."

"All in its own time, Mrs. Bacon," he said.

"Some things can't wait," she said. Mazy marched up and stood behind the man and cleared her throat. "This is my sister. May I help you?"

He turned, Chou-Jou in his arms.

He was not a handsome man. A large nose in a wide face. No beard or mustache. Hair curled at his coat collar. But Mazy was stunned by the color of his eyes. Hazel, with white flecks like snowflakes. They stared without reserve into her eyes. With one hand, he swept his hat from his head. "Ma'am," he said. "I meant no offense. I'm partial to babies, I'm afraid." He held the child with one brawny arm, without bouncing her. He turned to Chou-Jou then, gave her his full attention.

Mazy cautioned her tone. "She is a beauty, isn't she? Naomi? Are you all right?" She leaned in to touch the woman who nodded.

"Naomi? A biblical name," the man said, handing the baby back.

Seth came up, reins in hand. The horses behind him snorted. One stomped in readiness to leave. Ink bumped Mazy.

"Hey," she said. "Watch your manners."

"I've forgotten mine," the man said. "Name's Burke Manes." He shook Seth's hand, looked at her while Mazy introduced herself, Pig, Naomi again, and Chou-Jou. "And I took advantage of this baby's smile, I'm afraid. And her mother's kindness."

"Someone told me once that a man holding a baby was as catching as a cold," Seth said.

Burke laughed. "Could be true. Could be true." He spoke with the deepest baritone that vibrated against Mazy's heart. "You folks planning to stay in the area?" he asked.

"Just visiting," Seth said.

"And you, Naomi?" he asked. It was genuine interest and…compassion that Mazy heard.

"I stay with Ruth Martin."

"Ruth Martin!"

"Do you know her?" Mazy asked.

"I do," he said. "I live out that way. I'm heading back now. If you don't mind company, I can show you right where they are. I'm not always so good with directions, but I can lead you back to someplace I've been."

They mounted up, together splashing across Daisy Creek at the perimeter of town. Mazy found herself strangely quiet, just listening to the men. She'd missed that, hearing male voices speak of the price of things, the weather, the status of politics, and the signs of a worthy horse. She could talk of those things too, had opinions, but she came to them from a different place, and she'd missed hearing the views of those with deep tones. Too many women always around tended to insulate. As though they always stood in the necessary circle and never moved away.

"Miss Martin's had some tragedy," she heard Burke Manes say, and her ears perked. "Suppose you know?"

"No," Mazy said. "What happened?"

"Jessie," he said. "Little girl of Ruth's picked up something last fall. Left her legs weakened. She doesn't get out much. Miss Martin says she thought it came on earlier, having to do with a tragedy last summer. You folks may already know about her father."

"Oh, we do," Mazy said.

"I try to stop by and entertain the child, as much as my preaching and farming allows."

"You have a farm?" Mazy asked. *And he's a man of faith.*

"Oh, I try at it."

"Mrs. Bacon has a good-sized farm near Shasta City," Seth said.

"Do you now? Do you have pigs? I'm on a crusade against pigs," he added, though he grinned.

"What do you have against hogs?" Mazy asked.

"They destroy the camas bulbs," he said. "This country is full of them as I suspect your Shasta area is too. Camas feed the Indians. It's the Takelmas' staple food, and the pigs just wipe it out."

"I hadn't realized," Mazy said. "I was thinking of adding pigs for a while, but my skim milk went for a better cause."

"Camas-fed hogs aren't something we should profit from anyway. Changes the geography of a place forever."

"Rewriting the landscape," Mazy said.

"That's what the word *geography* means, all right," he said.

"I actually mean 'writing the land.' *Geo*—'land' and *graphy*—'write.'"

He looked at her, that white fleck in his eyes like candlelight in the dark. "I can see that the stories of words are important to you, Mrs. Bacon," he said.

"As they appear to be to you."

"We have something in common then," he answered, smiling full now, revealing a single dimple punched like a comma in the side of his cheek. Why had she just now noticed that?

Tipton resisted. "I can help here," she said. "Make it safer for the...ones you bring. I had no idea you came and got them. Some are so sick. I help tend them."

"Nehemiah is sick with worry," Esther said. "Go home to him, child. We can help you."

"I...want to be worthy before I go. He...I don't deserve—"

"We can't earn forgiveness," Esther said. "It's given."

"Yes, but…oh, now what?" Tipton looked disgusted at the stain deepening the color of her dress "I must have sat in some water."

"You're having your baby," Esther said.

They'd whisked Tipton away to Suzanne's. Esther went for the doctor while Tipton panted. "Oh-oh-oh-oh, here comes another one!"

"You are surprisingly strong," the doctor told her, "For one so tiny."

"All the ironing and washing I did," she panted between pains.

"Do you want laudanum?" he asked.

She shook her head. She wanted to be present for this, no more drifting away. God had answered her prayers. Many, many prayers. And she would never again seek refuge in potions or powders.

And then the child had arrived. Despite it all, her rash behavior, her willfulness and warped wishes, she'd been given a healthy child, eyes alert, staring, wanting to know Tipton as no other. "Let me see your face," she'd said to Baby. "Let me see your face."

Those first days, Tipton gazed in wonder at the sunrise-colored fuzz of hair, the tiny fingers gripping hers. She formed the *O* of the child's mouth, anticipated the smacking when she grazed the infant's cheek. She'd done what she needed to protect her child. But she'd also put the baby at risk. It had been a foolish thing, she realized. Baby needed her father, just as Tipton needed her husband. It would be good to have someone to walk beside her, especially when raising their child.

Clayton came in and signed something with his fingers. "What's he saying, Esther?" Tipton asked.

The older woman turned to look. "He'll tell you."

"Can you say it?" Tipton asked him.

He sighed. "Want hold baby," he said in his deep little voice. He grinned then.

"You sit. I'll put the baby in your arms, and we'll hold her together, all right?" He nodded, and she settled him on the chair, stood behind him to lay her baby in this older child's arms.

"I'm not certain that's wise," Esther said. "He might squeeze her too tightly."

"Oh, I think he'll be all right. I'm right here with her. I wish you could see his face, Suzanne. He's beaming."

"I think I can, in my way," Suzanne said. "There's something about joy that just seems to fire a hearth."

"You're thinking of your sweetheart," Esther said.

"I guess I am," Suzanne said, and she blushed.

"It's still a little strange to think of you and Mr. Forrester getting married," Tipton said. "Oh, oh, not too tight. Baby just wants you to be gentle."

"I can hardly believe I'm to have something so wonderful," Suzanne said.

Tipton lifted her daughter from Clayton's arms. "You did real well, Clayton," she said. "She's hungry now. You run along and let Mr. Powder know how you helped while I get her something to eat."

Clayton detoured to his mother, surprising her with his arms around her skirts in a calico-crushed hug. Tipton listened to the *click-click* of his shoes on the wood floor as she felt the tug of her child at her breast.

"Did you ever…" Suzanne began, clearing her throat. "Did you ever, with Tyrell, worry that something would happen to interfere with your joy? That something would stop you from…the fullness of it? From even marrying?"

"All the time," Tipton said. Her voice caught. Then, as though the infant knew of her discomfort, Baby shifted at her breast. Tipton smoothed her fingers over Baby's head. "And all my worry did me no good. Something did get in the way. I couldn't stop it. And instead of truly enjoying the time I had with him, I filled it with worry and wondering, and it turned out I couldn't stop a thing. Afterward I thought about it all the time. I felt…angry about what I didn't have for my future. Then I just…went away. I can't do that anymore."

"You've grown up, Tipton," Suzanne said.

Tipton wondered if she should tell Suzanne how one moment in a person's life changed everything. No, she suspected that was something Suzanne already knew.

"Some. I have amends to make. I've been asking myself what it is I really want for my life, for my daughter."

"You have an answer?"

"A beginning. I've written to Nehemiah, hoping he'll come to us."

Suzanne smiled. The ticking of the clock filled the silence. "I miss Seth," she said then. "I worry that something will happen to him before we're allowed to have the happiness of marriage. Isn't that…I don't know. I don't think I ever worried like that over Bryce. I feel as though I'm cheating on Bryce a bit." She adjusted her glasses.

"I felt that way about Tyrell too. Or did. I think that's why I…well, never mind that part. But now I know that giving your heart to someone or even something that matters is really all there is to do, even if it does mean some hurt will come when it changes. And it will change. People do…die. They go away. I don't understand it all. But loving them while they're here with us can be worth the pain of their leaving. The way I love Baby right now. Otherwise, we just go away. Or I do. Did."

"And never participate again," Suzanne said.

"Or even show up. I'd wager Bryce would want you happy. The second time for love doesn't mean you'll make it perfect, I don't think. Only that you get another chance to be filled up, maybe make it better."

Being filled up. Tipton supposed it was what she'd been seeking her whole life, expecting to always be satisfied. But even vineyards required dormant times. They didn't always have fruit to be plucked. Growing took time. What mattered was being grateful for the fruit when it arrived and not complaining that it wasn't always there for the picking. "I'm going back to Nehemiah," Tipton said. "If he'll have me."

"He won't be getting back the girl who left," Suzanne said.

"Well, ponder that," Tipton laughed.

within reach

Ruth pitched manure from the lean-to, sweat dripping from her fore-head. She lifted the felt hat, wiped her brow with the back of her hand, standing for a moment, her fingers gripped on the fork handle. So far, it had been a fair birthing season. Twelve standing foals. It was just enough to make the payment. Or she could have her divorce. If she asked him, she knew Matthew would tell her to take the divorce, that he still had his mares, his black jack, his option for free Oregon land. But she would forfeit everything. Zane would take half; Mr. Smith would take what was left. "We could start fresh together," Matthew would say, not under-standing that she couldn't—wouldn't—ever marry him with nothing but obligation brought to that union.

No, there was only one way out. She just wasn't sure how to make it happen.

She made herself think of something else.

The climate had proved to be as good as Matthew had claimed. Generally dry, not too hot, not too cold, rain when it was needed. She watched the clouds skip across the timbered ridge. Rain somewhere, she thought. She'd been refreshed by the feel of the seasons, with colors changing as they did back in Ohio and the sweet smells of spring drift-ing in the air. So far, there'd been none of the seeping, sweeping, sweating heat of back East. Of course, it was just early May. A perfect place, except for the occasional ice storm. But they knew how to weather them now.

Carmine pranced around his pen. One of the first mares to foal must have been in heat again, by the look of the jack. Ruth laid the fork up, signaled to Jason. "Bring up the bay mare," she said when he joined her at the barn. "We'll tease her and see if she's ready. Lead her over to the breeding ditch."

She expected good offspring. She'd already heard back from the adjutant at Fort Lane. It was just a stone toss away, and the army was seeking good mules. So her plan was already starting to work. The idea of breaking them to work cattle had come to her too. Matthew had snorted at that, but she had a good feeling that these animals might just be able to anticipate a cow's move and still be a size that didn't intimidate the way some horses did. She'd work on Matthew about that, help him see the possibilities. Even if she wasn't around to make it happen.

Freighters always had need of mules. And farmers. A whole new market grew from the tilling of soil in southeastern Oregon and northern California, using broke mules for running the mowers on the big ranches farther east. Harness-broke mules would bring a premium price to pull hay rakes and plows. They could even double as riding stock, which a good ox couldn't do. She'd had a good idea. It would be a good legacy to leave the children.

Matthew's fifteen head had all survived the winter, and it should have been a time of triumph. Yet heaviness weighed on her chest. Something Matthew said the night of the first foaling had almost deterred her. "Let me sort it out," he'd said while they waited together. She'd complained about not knowing anymore what mattered. It was as though she'd been falling her whole life into one of those holes in the road she told Burke of, and here was someone willing to help her avoid them or pull her out of them, no matter how difficult or how often. Letting him *help* her decide seemed the most natural thing in the world to do. Almost.

But now…well, he had his whole life ahead of him. He'd made her feel as though her age didn't matter. More, that no one else in the world mattered. She'd savor that, knowing someone saw her as central to his life in a way that nurtured instead of tearing apart. And if things had been different, she would have given herself to him now, truly believing she wouldn't be giving herself up.

Zane changed all that. Once again.

Think of other things, she told herself, tossing more manure. Jessie adored Matthew. She knew that. He'd taught her complicated hand shadows—animals, including a pig, a bird—and could even make hand shadows of emotions, like grumpy and fright. Her favorites were the stories of Mike and Mike's pig. He had even shown her a picture of Shakespeare once and could make a shadow that Ruth swore looked just like it.

When Matthew was around, Jessie didn't get that glazed look in her eye as much either. It was as though his presence made her feel…safe. Made all of them feel wrapped in a quilt of protection.

Ned and Jason, well, they'd accepted him as one of their own, twirling ropes in their spare moments with him and working with green-broke yearlings teaching them to lead. The children could stay on with the Schmidtkes, she was pretty sure of that. That might be the largest hurdle, deciding just how that mix of kin would cook together. Like one of Lura's stews, Ruth decided. Where the venison and potatoes and carrots and onions and all the rest could still be identified as unique but were brought together to make something better than what they'd been alone. Maybe not better, but different. She just wouldn't be around to make it happen.

She turned back to her work, then heard a dog bark. Matthew had been pushing for them to get one. The children and he were ganging up on her about it. Had he gone ahead without her? she wondered. She looked up. Lura had stepped out onto the porch, clanged on the triangle announcing lunch.

Ruth shaded her eyes with her hand. Squinted. It looked like Pig. If it was Pig, that would be Suzanne! And Seth? She recognized Burke

Manes, too. She'd been expecting Seth and Naomi. There the Celestial rode too. But had Seth also brought Suzanne? No. The woman waved to her then.

Mazy.

The closer they got to Ruth's, the more nervous Mazy got. She wasn't sure how to step into this wilderness relationship. She'd rehearsed what she'd say, how she'd say it. She wanted to give Ruth time to accept that she was here. She'd let Pig bring them together. Dogs did that, she found, made a subject for people to talk about when anything else was too risky, too dear. But when Mazy saw her standing there, her hands on her hips in that way that she had, her hat tipped to shadow her eyes, Mazy's heart swelled. Ruth was so dear to her. How could she not know that? *Please, God. Please, God. Please,* she'd said beneath her breath. *Let me do and say the right things, the things that will restore us, turn us around.* She kicked Ink and trotted ahead of the men and Naomi, pulled the mule to a dusty stop. Like a child headed for recess, she ran toward Ruth.

Ruth's eyes got large, and that almost stopped Mazy midstep. But it didn't. Maybe big eyes meant joy; maybe they meant hello; maybe just surprise. There was more than one way to see a thing. She'd not assume, but just hope that the horse of intent she rode in on would reach its destination.

She smiled, opened her arms. Ruth opened hers, too, and the two friends embraced.

"You are so precious to me," Mazy whispered into Ruth's ear. "Please, please forgive me." She was crying now, not able to help herself. The scent of hay and earth rose up. Mazy brushed a greenish flake from Ruth's brim. "I'm so sorry. So very, very sorry. I don't want anything to stand between us, not one thing, ever again."

Ruth said nothing, but held her, and Mazy could feel the warmth of her friend's hands on her back, the lean strength of Ruth's shoulders beneath her own. Mazy stepped away and wiped at her eyes with her fingers and looked down at her hands. For just a fleeting moment, she saw her mother's hands there. The same chapped knuckles, the same tapered nails. *We are all such extensions of our mothers.* She looked up. Ruth was thumbing her eyes too.

Ruth said, "I know it wasn't your fault. And yet when you wrote, I couldn't seem to find the words to tell you...anything. I should have written."

"It doesn't matter. It doesn't," Mazy said. "We're here now. Together. I was afraid you might ask me to leave."

"I'd never solve a problem that way."

Mazy laughed. "No, you'd just leave instead."

"Is that what you thought? That I'd left you?"

"You never wrote back. Didn't that mean you'd left me...at least in your heart?"

"I didn't know what to say," Ruth said. "Or how to say it."

Pig barked at her side now. "Hush," Mazy said to the dog, then to Ruth, "I haven't had much success in keeping friends." She scratched at Pig's neck. "Or making good ones like you are either. Single children seem to have that flaw. Or indulged children. We're not used to the give and take between equals, just pushing and pulling against grownups and always feeling like we've lost. But I don't want to lose you, not ever. You couldn't mean more to me if you were my own flesh and blood. You're the sister I never had, Ruth. The sister I'll claim if you don't mind being a part of our crazy kin."

"You've rehearsed," Ruth said, but she smiled.

"I'm rattling. I know. I'm just so pleased to see you, to have you welcome me after what Marvel did."

Ruth's eyes narrowed, then opened, a gesture as fleeting as a lamb's tail flickering.

"That's in the past," Ruth said. "Let's let it stay there."

She took Mazy's hand and walked back toward the men standing with Naomi and her child. Ruth greeted them, taking little Chou-Jou in her arms. By then, Matthew and Mariah arrived after taking long, matching strides across the meadow. The boys followed, accepting compliments from Seth with their heads down and the toes of their boots twisting in the dirt.

Lura stood at the porch and shouted, "You coming in to eat, or do I throw dinner to the dog?"

"I can see you folks have things to catch up on," Burke said. "Ma'am." He touched his gloved fingers to his hat while he looked at Ruth, then Mazy. "Course if I keep you talking, Lura might just throw dinner Pig's way, and I could wrestle him for it." He scratched at the dog's neck.

"My manners have gone to town," Ruth said, lifting her hands to her hat. "Stay, Burke. Stay for dinner. Stay for supper."

"Believe it or not," Mazy said. "I finally wheedled Mother's strudel recipe from her, and Seth and I picked up the ingredients in town. I'll fix it for supper, Ruth, if you'd like? If you don't mind waiting, Mr. Manes."

Burke grinned. "I like a woman with gastronomical intentions. And I'm always willing to wait for good things."

"Me, too," she said. "Some call it being stubborn; I call it being faithful." She noticed Seth smiling at her, felt her face flush with the warmth from his eyes.

The rain. Blasted rain. The creeks weren't swelled enough as it was. No, there had to be more rain. Zane had arrived on board a freighter, suffered the indignities of traveling with an illiterate laborer whose only virtue was hands strong enough to hold the horses and wagon on the treacherous trail. Zane had gotten over the Siskiyous, refreshed himself at a simple cabin owned by Major Barron and his bride. He hadn't told the man what he thought of the matrimonial state. Let him discover the betrayals on his own. He'd continued enduring the rough ride of the wagon until Jacksonville, the sores on his back reminders of all Ruth had caused him.

The journey had tired him, and he'd rested, forcing himself to wait to accomplish his task. He rented a beat-up old buggy at the Jacksonville Livery, reserved it and a horse for the morning, then spent the night at the rooming house next to the Robinson Hotel. The miners caroused all evening at the Robinson, and Zane positioned himself with the "businessmen" at the boardinghouse nearby. He could no longer disappear into the crowds as he had in Shasta City, a man with a peg leg. So he comported himself as the distinguished gentleman he was, the powerful person he'd become. After all, he'd soon be a very wealthy individual.

Making things happen as he wished was like consuming whiskey: The more he drank, the thirstier he became.

So he had slept well this past night, taken a good breakfast. He'd arrived first to the table and was already eating when the others appeared. He nodded. No need to rise. That was as he'd planned. He'd waited until the others left, then rose with his special cane and The Stub and made his way out the door.

The sky drizzled on him. The canvas of the buggy he'd hired was as thin as old flannel. He could almost see the gray up through it. It was all they had, and he was advised he should be "happy for it."

The horse at least hadn't shied away when he saw The Stub or his cane. He'd pulled himself into the carriage, trying not to seethe at having to leave the purple shay behind. At least the rain would give him reason to cover his legs to make his entrance as dramatic as he'd planned.

He knew where he headed. Jacob Orange, an attorney in town, had taken breakfast with him, and Zane had led him into a discussion of land and settlers. He'd had to listen to a litany of emigrants and showed no emotion whatsoever when the man had talked of the horsewoman southeast of Jacksonville. Judging by his description, he'd ridden right by Ruth's place on that stupid freighter.

The buggy wheel thumped through a hole in the road where someone had dug up a large rock but not bothered to fill it back in. The jar of it caused The Stub to jam against his thigh. How he hated this, the pain, the demand for adapting. He suffered both pitiful stares and frustration in achieving his goal. All because of Ruth.

As it happened, he didn't need to stop for directions. He came upon the horses grazing and just knew. He licked his lips, straightened himself, checked his pocket watch. Just after four. Plenty of time. Plenty of time to savor the impact of his visit.

The boys had put Carmine up; led Ewald to the pit. The mare had squealed and twisted her tail but shown no other signs of being ready, so they'd let her loose and took Ewald back to his pen. Mazy had stayed at the cabin, reading with Jessie. The window, frame and all, leaned against the wall, letting a breeze cool Lura's cookstove down.

Ruth and Matthew, Seth and Burke walked back from the garden area, talking to Naomi who held her baby at her shoulder, patting the child's back.

"I fear Naomi's right," Mazy said, stepping into the conversation as they came inside. "Expulsion of the Chinese isn't far away. The mining tax is supposed to be on all ore that's mined in California, but it's only enforced against them."

"Esther's people have been making escapes. Sometimes they send folks back to Asia when they're well, give them a small stake to help their families back in China. But we can move more through the north," Seth said. "If we can find more places for them. In orchards. As domestics. Cooks."

"Jacksonville isn't the most welcoming of towns, at times," Burke said. "Indians can tell you that."

"That African family, the Matthises, over on Butte Creek, have been accepted," Ruth said.

"One family that keeps to itself. Let's not kid ourselves. This won't be easy blending them in here."

"What we need," Mazy said, "is a way for them to get out and then disperse, like grass seed to the wind. Get them safe first. Then maybe we can help them land in places where the soil might be a little more inviting. Places like Portland or Seattle."

"I saw a few Celestials in The Dalles," Matthew said. "That place is growing."

"Poverty Flat will be an early stopover," Mazy said, aware of her planning voice. "But it being in California…well, a stopover may be all I can do. Maybe Nehemiah would work with us. We could get people to him on the coast, and he could put them on northbound ships."

"How are you financing all this?" Burke asked.

Seth cleared his throat. "I won quite big one night in Sacramento. Lost something, too, but sometimes losing is just the beginning of winning."

"Spoken like a true gambler," Mazy said. Seth winked at her.

"Anyway, I won enough that I miss the thrill of trying. That and my life's moved on to wanting more than just momentary pleasure. Suzanne and I are prepared to finance as much as we can. Maybe even form a theater company so we have a reason to be doing things in the night without others asking questions. Costumes and travel and people coming and going have been a good cover for Esther. But we'd rather not put other folks' diggings at risk either, like we are, using the Sacramento Theater."

"Everyone need own place," Naomi said.

"Right," Burke said. "Might not be a place tied to the land, though, but where your family is safe to live and love. Land matters, but not more than people."

Mazy looked at Burke as though seeing him for the first time. Had he been eavesdropping on her life? These were the very sentiments she'd struggled with since her husband said he'd sold their Wisconsin farm.

Ruth stood to offer Jessie a cup of water. The girl drank heartily, and Ruth smiled. "Hey, I think you're getting stronger."

They finished supper, and Ruth began the cleanup. "You go ahead out there," she said. "Matthew can show you the spring up the ridge." The boys jabbered about the silver storm, and Ruth watched out the open door as they all zigzagged up through the lush grass to Spring Ridge. Naomi and Lura trailed close behind.

"Too bad you're not feeling stronger, Jessie," Ruth said. "We could join them. You've never even seen that spring up there yet." She checked the black pot; the water wasn't boiling yet. "There's a rain slicker on the peg we could put on you if you want to try to stand and go on up."

"It's safer in here," she said.

"Safer," Ruth repeated. "There's nothing to be frightened of, Jessie. I just can't figure where that comes from." The girl had been surrounded by love and devotion, and it had simply not been enough. Ruth could see that. What Ruth could give would never be enough. Maybe what she planned to sacrifice would.

"They don't know yet, do they?" Lura said.

"Know what, Ma?" Matthew asked.

"Those two up there. Mazy and Burke Manes. That their lives are going to change." She nodded toward the couple that walked separated from the rest, Mazy's bonnet bouncing off her back, hands clasped behind her. She strode, stride for stride with Burke. They stopped. And Burke stood and pointed, then turned in another direction, shook his head, pointed again. Mazy had laughed, the sound ringing across the meadow.

"By Burke's getting involved in this underground?" Matthew said.

"You can be dense as a grinding stone," his mother said. "I don't know where you get that from."

Matthew laughed.

She elbowed her son. "They're falling in love," she said. "I can see it from here." He watched them, heads bent together, talking, not looking at colts, not noticing a darkening sky that threatened rain. Mariah stood with her hands on her hips well in front of them. She'd caught up a bay filly and waited for Mazy and Burke to notice. Matthew could almost see that next she'd be stomping her foot. Mazy and Burke didn't seem to notice anything but each other.

"Women are supposed to know that sort of thing," Matthew said.

"Well, Mazy don't yet, you ask me," Lura told him.

"No one has," he told her, but he smiled.

He wished he'd waited for Ruth, helped her with those dishes. Or insisted she join them up here. Maybe if they'd all come, Jessie would have been encouraged to try too. He hadn't had much luck convincing Ruth that when she stayed with Jessie, gave in to her demands like that, he thought that put a cap to that girl's thinking that she wasn't safe by herself. When he tried saying the words though, they came out self-serving almost, as if he was just envious of Ruth's attention. That wasn't it at all. The child wasn't doing it on purpose. More like she was reliving something bad that happened and not just remembering. And Ruth's being with her all the time or making sure someone always was, might have been as frightening to the child as discovering she could be left alone and not be harmed. She'd been powerless when Zane Randolph took her. She hadn't yet discovered how to get that power back.

He'd try again, telling Ruth. She'd been distant of late, holding herself from him the way a sick horse stood off to the side. All this worry over the land payment, he was sure, and Jessie, too. He heard the gentle cadence of Naomi cooing to her child, his mother's low reply, then Mazy's lilting laugh at something Burke said. He'd ask Mazy to talk to Ruth. Sometimes women listened better when words came to them carried in a sister's loving voice.

Jessie opened her eyes wide, looking past Ruth, through the door. "What is it?" Ruth said, turning. She heard the sound of a buggy. "It's just a visitor, Jessie. Goodness. Does everything have to be frightening? We'll be having more visitors. You'll have to get accustomed to that. Lura will sell her produce during harvesttime. There'll be Chinese coming here. Other travelers. And hopefully, people wanting to buy up a gelding or two and eventually, my dear, mules." She smiled, dropped her nose to her daughter's, and rubbed it. "Come on. Laugh a little, won't you?" She didn't have much time left to help Jessie. She'd be gone before long.

"Don't see nothing funny," Jessie scowled.

Ruth wiped her hands on the towel. Such a serious child. Ruth remembered her own mother had once used that phrase to describe her. She folded the linen, laid it on the table, then walked out. She lifted her rolled whip, held it at her side.

She didn't recognize him, a lone man. The horse pulled the buggy by, made a wide circle so it faced the way he had come in, stopping close to where Ruth stood. The horse snorted, breathed hard. It had a line of white froth at its chest, worked into lather on such a drizzle-threatened afternoon.

Ruth stepped off the stoop and watched as a white-haired man with a French-style beard lifted his hat from his head. Her stomach lurched a warning. She didn't know why.

"You don't recognize me, do you, dear Ruth?" she heard him say above the throbbing screams rising from inside her head.

She pitched back as though struck, gripping the whip.

Zane clucked his tongue.

"So you've come," she breathed. She reached for the door latch behind her, pulled it shut.

"Oh, don't shut off our dear daughter. I'm sure she's anxious to see her father after all this time."

"Leave her be. This is between you and me."

Her side ached, her heart pounded. She felt sweat dribble under her shirt, the whip handle slippery in her wet palms. If he took one step out, made one move toward Jessie, she would kill him.

"Where are all your friends, dear Ruth? Have they left you alone at last? Surely there's an unfortunate man somewhere, waiting for your...freedom?"

At least he had only her as an audience. There were no others to fuel this performance. If only they all stayed away, she could handle this. She had a plan. Everything felt spinning and hot. She had to get clear. Have courage.

"You knew I'd come," he said. "To claim my due. Half if you divorce me; half if you refuse. Not surprised? So. You know. But I neglected to have my solicitor tell you this: What you decide is of no matter. I'll have you Ruth Randolph. And I will have our child."

"Not Jessie," she seethed. "No court will give her to you. Not here. Not in California. Never."

"Oh, Ruthie, Ruthie. You always did put your hopes high in things like justice, law. It was your brother's doing, trusting that laws could bring you what you wished."

"They put you away where you belonged," she said.

He winced. "Where I belonged. For simply attempting to help my wife, my poor exhausted wife who couldn't take care of her son." He clucked his tongue. "For that I spent five years in prison."

"You killed him," Ruth hissed.

"You helped," he charged.

She couldn't let him control her. Could she rattle the horse so it took off with him? No. That would only prolong this. Could she step inside and get her pistol quickly enough? Could she kill him here while her daughter cowered inside? What was he saying? He looked frenzied, his eyes glazed almost.

"And she will be of good use. Every wounded father needs a loving daughter to assist him, especially when her mother is determined to divorce."

He'd force Jessie to…serve him?

Zane pulled the blanket covering his leg back then, revealing a wooden peg.

It startled her, the wooden limb. It was now. She had to act now. She lifted the whip and struck at him, the cracker splitting open the boiled shirt he wore. A dark stained formed at his chest. She'd drawn blood. She snapped the whip back and struck again, aiming for his throat. She would go to prison with his death. It was a price worth paying to protect her child.

This time, he grabbed the end of the whip with his gloved hands. He yanked it and her with it, his other hand pinching into her neck. He was strong as a mad jack. "The time has come, Ruth," he whispered into her ear as he seized her to him, his arm across her throat. "You first, and then my Jessie." She struggled, fury ripping at her arms. He laughed. He'd released the whip, but she was too close to him to gouge his eyes; he held her too tight. "Do you know how long I've imagined this? You, fighting and then speechless. All mine. Soon to be still." Then in an eye blink, he extended her at arm's length, raised a cane, and struck the side of her head. The blow, like an old tree felled, took her into darkness.

Tipton stood in the stateroom of the *Sea Gull*, a one-stack vessel sailing her home, her child cradled in her arms. "Oh, Baby, it's all right now. We're going back." She heard the steam whistle, felt the thud of the ship against the dock, the loud thump of the gangway let down. The smell of flotsam and fish mingled but didn't make her ill as it had before. Nothing would make her ill again, she decided. After what she'd been through, she'd discovered that about herself: She was as sturdy as a horse. She was also prone to impulse, self-indulgence, and vagaries. Nehemiah had been right about that, among other things.

She laid the baby down on the narrow bed, changed its napkin. She wished she'd taken the women's quilt with her when she'd left those months before, to wrap her child in; but she was taking nothing with her then, nothing from her past. And yet she'd taken everything with her, because memory insisted.

"Oh, Baby," she said. She still called her Baby. She just didn't want to name her by herself. "Baby, Baby. Your mama packed too many things for her journey. I should have remembered to throw things aside, just as we had to back on the trail." She remembered how pleased she'd been that her mother had saved her wedding dress and the heavy family trunk. The mules might have died trying to drag all those things across the desert, and yet Adora had risked that for a dress. Tipton had been proud of that—the very items her brother had been enraged to discover had endured both the journey and his arson. She shivered. She didn't know if he'd be silenced by her threats or if his wounds would only embolden him more. What would he tell their mother?

As a mother herself now, she vowed to do a better job, make better choices for what she saved from her past for her daughter, how she'd help her child thrive. "I only hope your father can forgive me," she said. Dealing with Charles would be bearable if she didn't have to do it alone; making good choices for Baby would be easier if she had help. If she accepted help. Like Suzanne, she was beginning to see that being a strong and independent woman didn't mean she had to do it alone. It meant allowing God to guide her life and being responsible to follow.

She could do it without Nehemiah though. If she had to. She wouldn't drift away again. For Baby's sake. For her sake, too.

After two days and a night's journey, the *Sea Gull* docked in Crescent City on a spring morning. It had only been two weeks since she had sent the letter to Nehemiah, telling him where she was, inviting him to come to Suzanne's. Each day since, she'd waited, hopeful. She didn't deserve his forgiveness—she knew that. But if she could only see him, convince him that she would be forever a worthy student, forever put her whims and notions aside, then she would spend her life a dutiful wife, one to make him proud. She'd make him forget whatever rumors Charles might spread.

Nehemiah's silence was her answer. She could have honored that, but she was hopeful, if nothing more. And she wanted Baby to at least see where she'd first begun. She'd show her Nehemiah's cabin, the beach that Tipton loved. And then they'd go away. Esther and Suzanne had given her enough money for the journey and to begin again. Maybe at Mazy's place, or maybe Elizabeth would open her arms and teach Tipton about making bread.

She walked down the gangplank, grateful that she had only the small carpetbag to carry. She could manage that and Baby, too.

Nehemiah was not here. Well, how could he be? He hadn't known she'd come back. She'd asked him to come to get them.

She bent to pick up her carpeted bag.

Perhaps, she thought, gazing around once more, hoping to see the familiar red beard of her husband. Perhaps she should go visit her mother. They would have something in common now, the raising of a child. No. Not with Charles there. And while she loved her mother, she truly did, she did not want to be a mother like her. Was that disloyal? No. She was required to make choices. Love did not mean agreement, only acceptance. She wondered if mothers everywhere vowed to be better mothers than they'd had? She couldn't imagine Mazy praying for that. Elizabeth was the best of mothers. Even someone as inexperienced as Tipton could see that. This baby wouldn't be enough to fix her family relationships, but it would change them. A baby always did that.

She looked around. "What is, just is, Baby," she said, sighing. "This is the beach I liked to walk on." Perhaps she could stay here in this coast city. It would be a good place to raise a child, the rocks of the coast a good view. Something about the ocean humbled a soul, reminded that people were small beings, and yet each was significant to God. It would give Nehemiah time to know his daughter. If they lived nearby. Tipton was certain that while he might not forgive her, he would fall profoundly in love with his child.

A man stood a distance down the wharf, talking to another. Her stomach tightened. It wasn't Nehemiah, as far as she could tell. She squinted. She needed glasses. A reminder always of her vagaries. Maybe with them, she could draw again. Fashion little picture stories for her child. She might just join the Crescentonian Club, a theater group. "Whimsical can be entertaining," she told Baby, "if we just don't let it get out of control."

She'd take a room for the night. Look for Chita in the morning, then make one more effort to meet her husband. Life would not end if she did not. She was strong as an ox, the doctor had said. It made her smile and think of ol' Cicero who had died on the trail, then come back to life.

"If you were a boy, I'd name you Cicero, Baby," she said to the roll of blankets in her arms. "But I'm holding out for Huldah, the wife of the wardrobe keeper. She was the wise one."

She kept her head high as she walked, glad for the feel of earth beneath her feet. The sky held horsetail clouds, wispy and wild with a hint of morning pink. A carriage rolled by, *clop-clopping*. She stepped out of the way.

She heard someone shout her name.

"Mrs. Kossuth," her husband said, jumping down from the carriage, a bag in his hand.

"Tipton, for you," she said, her heart in her throat. "Meet your daughter."

He dropped the bag, lifted the bundle from her arms. She tried not to wear the disappointment of his not reaching to hold her first. She had no right to expect it.

"I love her more than I ever thought possible," Tipton said.

"She looks just like you," he said, his voice husky.

"Does she?" She smiled. "You, too, I think. That fuzz of red hair—"

"She has your eyes. Blue as the sea."

"My mother used to say they were the color of Lake Michigan in October," Tipton said. "A somber, murky blue, I think she meant."

"I don't agree with your mother much," he said. He looked at her now, full in the face. "What did you name her?"

"I didn't. Not really. I call her Baby. Ever since I knew I'd keep her, maybe even before I admitted to myself that I was even…with child." She felt her ears grow hot. He turned back to his daughter, smiled and cooed into the infant's face. "You…you have a valise," Tipton said. "Were you leaving?"

"To find you," he said then, turning back. "I thought when you left it was to be alone. When Chita told me—"

"I knew she would! She—"

"I was sure you'd go to your mother's, to tell her. If Chita had kept silent, I don't know what I would have done, Tipton. Become a…a blue opal, cracked open." He held the baby in the crook of his elbow, reached for Tipton's hands. "It was my fault, my pressing you, not listening, believing I could teach you, guide you into someone who fit what I thought a wife should be. What I thought would be good for you to be. Not unlike your mother in that way, I guess. When I realized you were…carrying my child, I thought it was the change you were going through. I looked for you. I did. Then I knew you didn't want to be found."

"But I wrote to you. Charles…he's threatening terrible things that could hurt you and—"

"You were safe with Suzanne. I know you might have needed me, but I…I hoped instead you'd want me. An old man's thinking. You asked for help, and I wasn't there. Can you forgive me?"

"I'm the one needing forgiveness. I didn't need to come back, Nehemiah. I wanted to. Not just for our baby, but for myself. And to show you that I could be something I never thought I could be with you—within reach."

He wrapped his arms around her then and kissed her. It was not the chaste kiss of the man she'd married but the warm and passionate embrace of the man she'd grown to love. She'd just had to learn to love who she was too.

He released her. "We must always speak of whatever troubles us, Tipton. Risk whatever the answer might be, or the silence will destroy us."

"I know that now," she said.

"Let's go home." His eyes sought her luggage, his eyebrow raised in question.

"There's just the one bag," she said. "I've learned to travel lighter."

Mazy's definition of a virgin, of a woman being complete unto herself, was insufficient, Tipton thought as she stepped into the carriage surrounded by her family. A woman need never be alone if she accepted God's grace. And no one became complete until they could give themselves away.

the promise of a spring

Zane pushed an unconscious Ruth off of him and into the box of the buggy. He should leave now. Ruth would be his, she would disappear, and no one would know where she'd gone. It was the perfect crime! Her death, complete. He could return in a day or two, claim his child and the ranch.

But no, the child had seen him through the door. He was sure of that. He would have to silence her first, then leave with Ruth.

He hobbled from the buggy. The horse moved forward, then back. He should tie it; no time. He thump-walked to the porch, pushed open the door. His eyes adjusted to the dim room. He couldn't see her now. She'd been lying on a cot, had been able to stare out the door. Where had she gone? From the corner of his eye he saw a movement. He jerked aside, and the Dutch oven swung against the door instead of hitting his wooden leg.

"You brat," he seethed. With his cane, he struck at the girl who stood wobbly as a new colt. She went down. He should kill her, push a pillow over her face and be done with it. He heard the buggy shift outside. No time. Taking her with them would take too long, be too hard to manage with Ruth, too. When he returned, it would be a child's word against his, and no one would believe her. A court of law would listen to him. He was her father, after all.

He smiled and backed out, pulled the door shut and made his way to the buggy. It was perfect! Ruth his, at last, and he wouldn't even have to share the spoils!

Mazy hadn't laughed so much in…years, she decided. Burke Manes was a wonderful storyteller, especially telling tales of his own foibles. "Didn't you have a compass point to follow?" she said. "A reckoning device, something?"

"It would have done me little good. I knew which way was north. I just didn't know which direction I'd left my horse at."

Mazy scratched at Pig's head, watched him sniff after a covey of quail. "But you got the elk home. You found your pack animal? You didn't have to consume it out on the trail?"

"Eventually," he said. "Gave me time for pondering, wandering around in my own little southern Oregon wilderness."

"Deep thoughts, I'm sure." She liked that he used a word her mother was fond of too.

"In a way." He grinned at her, a single dimple in his check. "I decided I knew why the Israelites were lost for forty years in a stretch of desert only twenty miles wide."

"Why?" she said.

"Because the men refused to stop and ask for directions."

Mazy doubled over in laughter again. "Oh, Mister Manes," she said.

"Burke," he said. "It's Burke, and I do hope I have the privilege of calling on you again. Seldom does a man have such an attentive audience."

"I'm sure—"

"What's that?" Burke said, looking past her, holding his hand up for silence.

Mazy turned. She heard it now too, the clanging of the dinner triangle.

"Ruth must want us back there," Matthew said.

"I wonder what's got that terrapin in such a tizzy," Lura noted.

"Maybe something's happened to Jessie," Matthew said and started down the zigzag trail at a run.

At the house, Jessie was draped across the hitching rail with one hand, clanging as hard as she could against the iron with the other.

"Hey, hey," Matthew said, holding her up. "We're here. How'd you get out here? Where's your mama?" He looked beyond her.

"She ain't inside," Lura said, stepping past him to scan through the open door.

"He. Took. Her." Jessie gasped each word. "He. Took. Her."

"Who? Who took her?"

"Buggy tracks," Seth said. "Fresh ones."

"That man," Jessie said, and she wept. "Zane Randolph."

"Ma. You, Mariah, Mazy, you stay with Jessie here," Matthew ordered. "Boys, grab up our mounts."

"I'm going with you," Mazy said. "I'll take Ruth's Koda." They raced to the barn, bridled up. Mazy swung to ride astride, bareback. "Hold the gate," Mariah and Matthew shouted as one. When Mazy rode through, she spied a new horsehair rope. The one Ruth had been working on, she bet. She leaned, grabbed it, and kicked Koda to a gallop.

He hadn't even felt a need to rush. This was so delicious. He'd been calm. He had kept to his plan. It was sped up a bit; he'd had little time to let Ruth squirm, to let the realization of what he'd do to her fester within her. He'd squeeze from her every gold eagle she had earned. And then he'd take her life. He supposed he was fortunate no one else was there, though he would have loved to see the face of the man he'd bested once and for all. The child having seen him dampened things a bit. No matter. Even the drizzle couldn't drown his ecstasy, his triumph.

He'd keep her…no. He'd pull aside, finish what he started, then bury her in the timber.

The buggy slid on the road, and he realized the drizzle had turned the trail to muck. He didn't need this now. He certainly didn't want to get stuck in muddy ruts with Ruth beside him. He lifted the buggy whip, snapped it against the horse and shouted to keep the animal moving. He had that stream to cross, and then he could make it to the outskirts of Jacksonville, ride on through to One Horse Town. The Chinese and Kanaka would pay no attention to a woman left in their garbage heap. That would give him time to revive her, savor her terror before he finished his dessert.

Now that he'd decided, he couldn't make the horse move fast enough. He struck it again and mud flew up, pitting his hat. The horse slowed, and that was when he felt more than heard hooves thundering behind him.

Rain pelted their faces. "They're up ahead!" Matthew shouted, and he leaned forward on his horse. The Quarter-Pather seemed to tighten up, then explode in response to Matthew's knees. They could all see the buggy ahead. And beyond Mazy could see the creek Burke had said was called Daisy when they'd splashed through it early that morning. It was running full now. Even up onto the grassy bank. A tree had washed down, leaving the branches and roots tangled around a boulder and smaller rocks. It was right where the ford was. Too narrow for the buggy, she thought. He'd have to stop. They'd have him! And Ruth, too.

"What's he doing?" Seth shouted.

Mazy blinked. The rain came almost sideways now, the wind blowing with it. She felt blinded and lifted her skirt to wipe at her eyes. Could that be? He was trying to drive the buggy into the swollen stream, into the rush of the water.

"Hold back!" Matthew shouted. "Let them be! The man's crazy!"

They pulled up, the horses breathing hard.

Randolph pushed again, the poor buggy horse rearing, stepping backward while he whipped it forward. "Go! You blasted horse! Go, I say!"

The animal was frenzied now. Pig ran past Mazy, barking, which added to the sounds of rain, the splatter of mud, a screaming horse being driven beyond its limits.

"No, Pig!" Mazy called out. The dog stopped, but the buggy horse went on, entered the water. Zane drove it into the ford, into the branches and leaves being swept along, catching the wheels in the net of tree root and rock. "It's too narrow!" Mazy shouted.

Her words gave no halt to his effort. Water rose up to the horse's belly. It tried to rear, tried to move back, then lunge forward. They all watched as though in slow motion: The horse broke through the web of branches held firm there while the buggy pitched up on one wheel and came down jammed in the rocks. Zane jolted forward, and Ruth spread as limp as a whip across him and the box.

The horse pulled, attempted to rear, twisted by the harness and stiff side rods. It gave one last effort, the filly's throe shifting and tipping the buggy more. Zane appeared to be skewed deep into the wedge of the rock, his movement hampered by an unconscious Ruth.

"Ruth!" Mazy shouted. "Ruth! Can you hear us?"

Matthew had dismounted. He plunged, high-legged through the raging water, his knife drawn.

His leg! His leg was caught! And not The Stub. The good leg, his only leg. What was that? A bone! A bone exposed in his good leg! He felt numb like he had been in the river when the brat and that Indian woman had left him behind. Horses, always horses and women ruined him. Ruth moaned. He could hear his own raspy breathing. He had pushed too hard. He could have had it all legally. Why had he pushed the horse? Her fault. Ruth's fault. His cane with the stiletto knife drifted toward him, caught in Ruth's arm hanging limply across Zane's body. He looked up and saw a man in the water. A blade in his hand. He grabbed Ruth tighter.

What is that idiot doing? Trying to cut the reins? The harness free? What difference does it make? The animal will die! That must be Ruth's man! The horse can't live. Why is he bothering with it? Why isn't he helping me? It's a trick! He wants Ruth. He's moving to grab Ruth.

"Get my leg out! You fool! Idiot! Can't you see? Leave the horse be! Help me!"

He was coming closer. Yes, here he was.

"Pull up, under my arms. Do that!" Zane shouted to him. But the man was reaching for Ruth. "Don't bother with her." He grabbed at his cane, pushed the man back with it.

"Let her go, and I'll be able to help you!" Ruth's man shouted at him. He moved here and there, climbing above and around, yanking and pulling, trying to free Ruth from Zane's grasp. The pain seared into Zane's brain. "No! Get a rod, something! Anything. Free the leg. Free the leg!"

"It's wedged, I tell you. It's broken. Can't you see the bone? I can't get you out unless you give Ruth to me so I can cut you free!"

"What?"

Ruth's man came closer, almost over him now, holding a heavy knife. He was close enough to hear even over the noise of the horse screaming, the rage of the water, and a dog barking, barking. "You'll die unless I get your leg free. I can try to saw it off! Let Ruth go so I can reach it."

"My leg? You want to saw my leg?" *Cut my good leg?* "I'd sooner die," Zane shouted. *Ruth caused this, all of this. Dear Ruth.*

"You will," he was told.

371

Zane lunged for him then, felt searing pain from his leg to his back. "It's wedged, I tell you! Give me Ruth, and I'll cut you free."

The fool. Free? With two bad legs? Free? He could not carry out a plan with one bad leg; he could do nothing with two.

In that moment Zane knew what he would do.

He pushed at Ruth. The suddenness of it threw the man off balance, Zane grabbed for the heavy knife, used his own cane with one hand to hold Ruth in the swirling current, her white throat exposed.

"Ruth!" Zane heard the man yell as he struggled to stand against the current and slick rocks and roots. The man reached for Ruth, couldn't touch her.

Zane held the knife high, a warning. His knuckles on the blade were white as his broken bone. He controlled nothing now except this one thing—the thrust of a sharp knife. Then with his cane, he pushed Ruth into the stream, let his cane go. All that was left was this. With a singular force he plunged the blade deep into his chest.

Even from the bank Mazy could see Ruth's body twisting out of their reach in the water. She was faceup now, an arm tangled, then loosened. Matthew was so close, but the current pushed her out beyond his reach.

Help her, help her, help her. She spoke the prayer, squeezing her hands against the reins, then felt the rope.

"Matthew!" she screamed to him. "I'll toss the lariat!" She flung the coil, holding one end. It fell short. Ruth groaned, the water reviving her.

Burke rode up beside Mazy. "Let me toss it," he said as she pulled the line back in to make another throw.

But Pig had other plans. He grabbed the line being pulled back, ran partway down the shore then lumbered in, swimming with his nose high, in seconds at Ruth's side, the rope in his dark mouth.

"Ruth! Look at Pig!" Matthew shouted, and Mazy watched as her best friend's hand gripped the lariat still held by Pig.

Burke and Seth began pulling, and by then Matthew had come close enough to lift her from the waters of Daisy Creek.

❧

"He was a bad man," Jessie said.

"Yes, he was," Ruth told her, holding her close back at home. A blanket draped Ruth's shoulders. The rest of them stood near the stove, like stiff woolen socks drying out. "But even he couldn't stop you from getting help."

Jessie cried then. "I was just so scared," she said. "So scared. He hurt you. I had to make my legs work."

Matthew came to her then, and he wrapped his arms around them both, and Ruth thought she might have heard him stifle a sob. She pushed back.

"Are you all right, Matthew?" she said. He nodded, thumbed his eyes. She pushed the section of white hair that faded into the black away from his forehead. "Thank you. Mazy said you tried to save…him, too."

"I was trying to get to you. He…I wanted him to let you go. I couldn't get to you except through him."

"It was like a horrible dream," Ruth said.

"I didn't want you somehow blaming yourself for his dying in the river," Matthew said, his words clipped short.

"I wanted him dead," Ruth said quietly. "My being sent to jail for it would have been worth keeping Jessie…and you safe."

"Why didn't you tell me, Ruth? We could have come up with some other plan."

"Love means not telling all you know sometimes," she said.

"He'd have made you into something you never could be, Ruth. This place, your life, none of it's worth the price you were willing to pay for the likes of him."

"It wasn't for him. It was for my family. All of you."

Matthew held her closer, his other arm rubbing Jessie's shoulder. "It isn't ever going to be easy living with you. I've already resigned myself to that. But when I think of living any other way, I come up empty. You're all I ever wanted, Ruth. That, and family, these kids and maybe a handful of our own."

"I should have told you what he was planning, to take half if not all of everything. Then he said he'd use the law to get Jessie, too. But I could only see one way out, and I knew you would have stopped me."

Matthew said, "You don't have to stand up to people like that by yourself. There is always another way. We are never alone. I hope to prove that to you over the next fifty years. Even independent women have limits, Ruth. It takes a strong woman to accept that."

They sat at the fireside, consuming the cobbler Mazy had made. The sheriff had said he'd be out later to follow up on the suicide at the creek. Just the thought of it, of this day, caused Ruth to shiver. She stood to stoke the fire when Mariah burst in.

"There's a mare foaling. She's having trouble."

They headed for the barn, even Jessie, wobbly as a young colt. The mare was down, laboring hard.

"I massaged the mare's opening with some of ma's lard, but it didn't do anything," Mariah wailed. "I couldn't keep her walking."

"She can't go much longer," Ruth said, exhausted after this day.

"You should have called us sooner. Let's try to pull the foal," Matthew said. "Must be a big one."

Ruth reached inside, slipping her fingers and a rawhide strand around the unborn foal's feet that they could barely see. Matthew pulled then, the twine attached to a rope that strained against his broad back. Nothing.

"I don't want her to die," Mariah said.

"We're doing out best, Pipsqueak,"

But the mare raised her neck, snorted and moaned, lay back down.

Finally she just gave up. Mariah hovered at the horse's neck, talking and crooning, urging her to hold on, but she exhaled and was gone.

"Time to let go, Pipsqueak," Matthew told her.

"No!" Mariah said. "No!" Matthew leaned over the girl whose arms wrapped around the mare's neck like a child holding a feather pillow, wanting to sink in and disappear.

"Can we save the foal anyway?" Mazy said.

"The baby won't make it," Ruth said. "There's no sense."

Mariah wailed again.

"We'd have to cut it out and even then—"

"You had your horse cut up after he died, so what's the difference?" Mariah sobbed, her chest heaving against the side of the horse.

Her words pulled at Ruth's heartstrings.

"We might have a chance, Ruth," Burke said. "If we worked fast. The nose is nearly out, feet too. I actually think the thing is breathing. On its own."

"Keeping orphans alive—" Ruth began.

"We could try," Matthew said. "Ruth?"

"You don't do anything unless Ruth says," Mariah yelled at him.

"I do what I think is right, Mariah," he said. "That's what a brother does for a sister, what a man does for his family." To Ruth he said, "Some things are worth doing regardless of how they turn out."

Ruth hesitated then risked. "All right. I'll try to get some of the colostrums, from the mother's bag."

"That's my job," Mazy said.

"Jason, round up Lura's goat. Put her up on the lard barrel there, so she's the right height for this baby to suck the goat's milk when she or he stands. If it stands. We might have enough milk to keep the baby going. Burke, can you take the rope, let Matthew cut the baby out."

Ruth and Mazy worked swiftly, the reddish milk from the dead mare filling the bottom of a bucket Ruth held while Matthew sliced up through the belly of the horse.

The foal slipped out, slick and looking more like a newborn kitten than something that would stand taller than any of them if it lived.

"It's a stud colt," Matthew said.

Ruth cleaned its mouth with her fingers, let it suck against them. They wiped the clear sack from its coat, while she encouraged the colt to stand. Mazy poured the colostrum into a glove with a hole in it, to reward the baby as soon as it stood firm.

"He'll need to be fed every few hours, Mariah," Ruth said. "Put to that goat, or we'll milk it and glove feed it."

"He's alive," Mariah said.

And so are we, Ruth thought. One more rock climbed over. One more memory made.

The colt made a rocking motion as though it wanted to stand, and they helped it up, still rubbing its body with a rough towel, the way a mother might lick it with her tongue.

"I think he can do it alone," Burke said. "Mrs. Bacon, get your glove, then let's bring him over to that goat."

The colt sniffed and bunted. The goat bleated. And then with a little help, it jabbed against the udder of the goat that Jason held. The goat turned to look at the colt, went back to chewing the hay Ned and Sarah and Jessie had placed before it.

"You know," Ruth said, her eyes glistening. "He looks a lot like Jumper."

"So you'll be heading back with Seth then?" Burke Manes asked Mazy. The rain still drizzled onto the shake roof, but Mazy felt warmed by her shawl and Burke's presence as they sat beneath Ruth's porch.

"He's anxious to leave in the morning," she said. "Someone special waits for him in Sacramento. And I have people to arrange passage for, getting them north. Lura will be a big help here when the Celestials arrive. And those Ayrshires might just be missing me though Oltipa and little Sula and the others have taken to them too."

"Seth said you've risked much for people you don't know."

"Most of us don't even notice them, the Indians or the Chinese. I rail against that because each Yurok or Wintu or Hoopa or Cantonese bears something…distinct about them. To me. But others see them like similar stones they can dismiss."

"It should make it easier to move people in and out without notice that way," Burke said.

"I hadn't thought of that. But yes." She nodded. "'No eye has seen—'"

"'What God has prepared for those who love him.' First Corinthians two, nine," Burke finished. Mazy smiled, the comfort of being known flowering inside her like the first sprouts of spring. Pig's tail brushed Lura's basil plant, the scent punching the air. "I could use some advice on my gardening, Mrs. Bacon," Burke said. "Before you head back."

"Please. Call me Mazy. I like a good herb garden. And vegetables."

"I'm pretty good at preaching. Not all that good at gardening."

"That's not what I hear," Mazy said.

Burke had his hands folded over his stomach. A kerosene lamp flickered at their faces. "You got to watch who you talk to in these parts," he said. "Some of these Oregonians are horse-race-winning exaggerators."

"We used to tease Seth about that, about dividing by two and subtracting by four, whatever he told us." She leaned toward Burke so as not to let Seth, lying on his bedroll inside, hear them. Rainwater dribbled off the roof into a coopered barrel, soothing as a song. "He writes terrible poems, too. Did you know that? We all tell him that." She sat back.

"Uh-oh. I'm a bit of a bad poet myself."

"Are you?"

"Yes ma'am."

"Let me hear one." He looked bashful, his big round face with that comma dimple hidden in a childlike moment of being shy. "Come on," she urged. "I won't laugh. I won't."

"All right," he said. He cleared his throat. "It's called 'What Once We Loved.'

"What once we loved is memory now, rooted deep,
Tangled up with time.
Cradled through experience,
It threatens to erode our wounded hearts.
Time tends it.
Warms the earth around it.
Then brave, we journey forward,
Refuse to let the sharpened sides of memory be the fill.
Instead, we grieve and let loss change us,
Till and turn the soil,
And choose to love again."

"How do you know those things?" Mazy whispered. "How can you put it down like that, such feelings inside words?"

He shrugged. With his fingers, he combed the dip above his lip. "Been something I could do my whole life," he said.

"It's a gift," she said.

He nodded. "Just hope I use it well. I just want to encourage and teach and help people with the messes we sometimes make of our lives. To be God's hands and feet on the journey."

"I had this dream once," Mazy said. "I dream in color. Sometimes in a story, too. I was on a trip. I knew exactly where I was going, felt led almost. It was wonderful. An old friend said I was 'in service.' I ended up at a young couple's home helping slop their pigs, and I was as happy as if I'd found a cure for hydrophobia." She was quiet. "And isn't that what our lives are? Sometimes with formal lessons and sometimes what we're to learn is given through the everyday, where we'd least expect to find it. We just have to be willing to be on the trail, I guess. And accept the joy of knowing we're not alone."

378

They sat silent, the creak of the hickory rocker Burke sat in making crunching sounds on the mud-tracked porch.

"My mother says she'll remarry sometime this year," Mazy said. "That would be a lovely poem to read, if you wouldn't mind. To remind us all not to let the past be speaking too loudly into the present."

"Wouldn't want to intrude on a family affair," Burke said. "But it would be my pleasure to make the declamation at your mother's wedding. Might even offer to officiate, if she didn't mind a Baptist."

"Oh, Mother always said it wasn't the denomination that mattered but the relationship." He nodded. "You'd leave your farm?" she said then.

He turned to her, picked up her hand. She felt a tingling like a lightning storm crackling close. "I'm passionate about some things," he said, rubbing the back of her palm. "My farm is one. I wouldn't go on such a journey without a little planning. But you never know what a change of scenery will do for a soul."

"Oh, me, too," Mazy said, swallowing as she sank into his eyes. "I'd never choose to leave my home without a very, very good reason."

companions: breaking bread together

Upper Table Rock, 1859, five years later

"Come on, Grandmama! It's my birthday. Don't make us last!" Betha Manes, nearly four years old, could be as forceful as her mother. "Shall I carry your basket?" She offered then. Elizabeth nodded as little Betha rearranged the loaves of bread, adjusted the red-checkered cloth, and took her grandmother's hand. The child was as generous as her mother too, Elizabeth thought. Strong and kind. A good combination.

Together they wound their way up the deer trail to the top of Upper Table Rock, passing talus slopes, huge boulders and rocks that mimicked fence posts standing up together. They traveled to what Ruth said was almost the top of the world. "There's that cave Papa told us to stay away from," Betha said.

"That's right," Elizabeth told her. "You've a good memory."

Behind them on the footpath followed Mazy and Ruth and Tipton, the latter with a baby bouncing on her back. Tipton's Huldah, almost six already, stopped to pick a wildflower. She showed it to Suzanne whose fingers left Pig's harness to touch the leaves. She smiled at the child who stood before her.

This was a "Girl's Day Gathering," Mazy called it. The boys had elected to remain back at Spring Ridge, talking commerce and politics and mules and probably a little horse racing, if Elizabeth knew her Gus.

"Oh, look, Grandmama," Betha said and pointed. "Isn't it munificent?"

"It is indeed," Elizabeth said, inhaling.

Looking east out across the valley stood Mount McLoughlin, white as whipped cream atop a nine-thousand-foot cone. Elizabeth turned slowly to sight another butte, then Lower Table Rock, and then the Rogue River flowing through the agate desert below. Trees and fields bounded by split-rail fences dotted the land across the flat that spread for miles and miles toward the Siskiyou Mountains, then California. Western country never ceased to amaze her. No one would believe it looked this beautiful unless they journeyed here, dug their toes in God's footstool, this vast earth.

"Can you see your Aunt Ruth's mules grazing? Or your papa's farm he had before he moved to California to marry your mother?"

"People can't see that far," Betha told her, her grin unveiling a single dimple.

"Oh, just imagine it," Elizabeth said. "You'd be surprised how far you can see when you imagine a thing."

Betha pinched her eyes tight, then opened them wide. "Nope," she said, then set the basket down and headed for the rock's edge, stopping short and looking down. Grace, Jeremy's daughter, and Mariah approached, both of their white straw hats bobbing. They were home from school, both of them. Jessie strode close behind, hovering on every word.

"Truth be known, these baby baskets are a blessing to a hiker," Tipton said, fanning herself with her handkerchief. She lifted the frame, took the baby boy out. "Huldah, you be careful," she called out to the child standing next to Betha.

It was quite the gathering. The first when most of the wagon train women would try to meet in one place. Lura had said she wanted to be there, but cooking at Colestein's Stage Station kept her busy. And Naomi and Mei-Ling lived far away now, near the Columbia River; and

Adora had thought it best she stay in Shasta City and tend to her ailing son and their store.

Still a good showing. Elizabeth was pleased to be blessed by the companionship of so many women she treasured. Esty had been invited, too, their circle ever expanding. But with Esther's death last year, there'd been too much for her to do to take time away for playing. Elizabeth would miss Esther.

"Tell me what I see," Suzanne said as she caught her breath beside Elizabeth.

Elizabeth laughed. "Well, let's see. Kin," Elizabeth told her, "spread about like flowers dancing across a mat of grasses. A few trees and mountains in the distance. And the sky looks like smoke puffs out of Lura's old clay pipe. Feel like sitting?" Suzanne nodded. She was already showing, she and Seth expected a child to be born in the new decade.

The new decade. Six more months, and Elizabeth would be living in the sixties. Ponder that! Not an easy time for living with the expulsion of all Chinese from California talked about and strong words about cotton and slavery from the south. It didn't speak well of what the new decade would bring. But Oregon had become a state. It was no longer a "foreign land" as it had been, and she was glad to be alive to see all the Western Coast joined under the stars and stripes.

"Are there wildflowers?" Suzanne asked.

"Not many. Matthew says April and May are the months for that here. When the pools have water standing in them. I guess there are some strange little white flowers that bloom then. Only place in the world."

A bright red pileated woodpecker flitted by and landed on a branch of a granary tree before soaring off. "That's a treat," Ruth said as she approached. "I've heard those birds lots of times, just never noticed one up here."

"So much to see," Suzanne said.

"Mama, I need to…do a private thing," Betha said, pulling on Mazy's skirt.

"Can't you find no trees to squat behind?" Elizabeth teased her. Trees were a little scattered and distant up here. "Well, we'll just form up our necessary circle then," she said. "Mazy. Ruth. Mariah. Tipton. Come on over. We've got a reason to hold our skirts out and gossip."

They stood with their backs to the center where Betha hopped her skirts up out of the way. "Why, Ruth, your split skirt flares out right well, don't it? She's holding her wide leg pants out, Suzanne, and using almost as much material as your gown."

"It's serviceable," Ruth said. "And I don't get quite so many raised eyebrows."

"How's your vineyard doing, Ruth?" Tipton asked.

"Wistfully," Ruth said. "That photographer, Peter Britt, planted some vines in '52, and his're doing well. Ours just give me things to ponder about. Will the yellow jackets eat all the fruit this year? Will the birds get the sweetest grapes?" She grinned at Elizabeth. "It takes a lot of work. More than the orchards. And with the mules, well, there's hardly time in the day. And Nehemiah? Will he run again?"

"He plans to," Tipton said. "I hope to help more without being…with child like last time."

"Your brother Charles made some noises awhile back about maybe running for a house seat," Elizabeth said. "But then he got that terrible wound. It healed except for the spot at his mouth that gets irritated all the time. Just keeps weeping. I tried a salt pork poultice."

"I've heard bread and milk works good for cuts," Mazy said.

"Tried it. Got all sour. We tried pine pitch. It dries hard as nails. Just like tar and it don't wash off. Just has to wear off."

"I don't see how he can still eat so much. He rival's Pig," Mazy said.

"Guess he can't get filled up," Elizabeth said. "His gout and all."

Jessie asked something about the wagon trip across then, and people recalled sights and sounds and the things that gave them pause. No truths or lies rose up to fill the silence. Memories like mist drifted to each.

The circle finished, they made their way back to the baskets. Elizabeth handed out huck towels and spring water so they could wash their hands before sitting on the quilt which itself brought up new chatter, old stories mixed with new.

And then with the breeze lifting the lace collars of the women's dresses and the calls of blue jays, Elizabeth broke a single loaf of bread and passed it along. She followed it with clumps of butter on around. She felt…worshipful, almost, in this pleasant place. From a single loaf they'd become family. A single loaf bound them.

"What did you think of Wisconsin, Grace?" Suzanne asked the younger woman.

"Rolling hills, green, green grasses. Many fine farms and a button factory. Cassville's a pleasant place," she said. "To be from." She smiled at Mazy, took a bite of bread.

"And did you find the trip back an easy one, Mazy?" Tipton asked. "I don't think I'd want to see Papa's old store."

"I had good companions to share it with," Mazy said. "But it was… strange, to see the old place. The valley, or cooley, as we used to call it, was so much narrower than I remembered. Like a woman's shoe compared to a man's big boot of these Western slopes. And I remembered the bluffs being so much higher. And…the house needed lots of work. It's had several owners since we left, but they still kept the garden plot where I had it. And the bee tree is there. I took some lilac cuttings." She motioned for Betha to wipe some jam from her face. "And it was all smaller than I remembered. I cried a bit, and Betha said to me, 'It was the best choice, Mama.' How she knew what I was grieving, I'll never know."

"I'm glad Father left there," Grace said. "It was terribly hot and sticky, and little gnats bothered everywhere in an evening. You had to wave your hand before your face or they'd fly right into your mouth."

"That's why people from Wisconsin are always using their hands when they talk," Elizabeth said, and everyone laughed.

"So was it worth all the effort?" Suzanne asked. "Taking the ship and all?"

"It was for me," Mazy said. "It was nice to show Burke what I knew first. To introduce Grace to a place her father loved. And for Betha to see it. I doubt she'll remember much. But she may recall the cabin, the Mississippi River. And she saw an eagle there. She got all excited and talked about going home then. It made her homesick, I think, to see something that she sees here all the time. And she missed old Pig." The dog lifted his jowls from his paws, looked at her, then lowered his head and closed his eyes. Mazy sat quietly, still thinking.

"Truth be known," Tipton said, taking the bread from Elizabeth. "I've learned by studying Chita's Spanish that the word *companion* means 'with' and 'bread.' The word *bread* is 'pan.' Isn't that interesting?"

"And the beginning of words like *companion, compassion, and communion* one time meant 'the exchange of burdens,'" Mazy told her.

"I guess that's what friends do together, exchange burdens, so we can carry them together," Elizabeth said.

Elizabeth had pit-roasted camas bulbs in a clay jar, and she passed them now. Ruth bit into it and found the taste sweet. "These are good," she said.

"Oltipa told me how to fix them. And gave me some yellow jacket larvae. It's a delicacy, but I didn't think any of you would appreciate it."

"You can tell Ma about them," Mariah said. "She can serve them at the station and tell people they're tasty nuts."

"But I suppose the best thing about going back," Mazy said, "was that I finally understand the message in that old trail song. You remember, Suzanne. The one you accompanied with your harp that says:

> "'I'm not afraid of lightning or the wolf at my door
> I'm not afraid of dying, alone anymore.
> But when journeys are over, and there's fruit on the vine
> I'm afraid I'll be missing what we left behind.'"

The women had begun singing as Mazy recited and when they finished, Mazy said, "I don't miss what I left behind anymore. And the fruit that's on the vine of my life, right here, well it's sweeter than I ever could have imagined. So much is within my reach."

A silence settled over them. It would be broken later by firecrackers brought along to help celebrate Independence Day. But for now, as Elizabeth's eyes rested on the faces of those she loved here in this new place, she knew full well the truth of Mazy's favorite psalm, and felt blessed beyond measure. "Even in the wilderness times, the Lord does know our lot," she said. "And he always makes our boundaries fall on pleasant places."

Author's Notes and Acknowledgments

No writer writes alone. Though it is impossible to acknowledge all those whose words and research help a story grow, a few must be mentioned for *What Once We Loved.* My sister-in-law Barbara Rutschow provided information about dairying and horses, kinship and courage. My brother Craig continued to remind me of the meaning of family and pursuing one's passion. Clancy Rone, a fine writer in her own right, perused class notes, old library books, and oral stories of southern Oregon and Jacksonville in the early 1850s to help me create an authentic time and place. Then she read an unedited manuscript too. Dave Larson, a horseshoer extraordinaire, offered advice about calked shoes, mules, and strong women. My husband, Jerry, never failed to insist that I eat and take the dog for a walk; gave constructive feedback and provided unfailing encouragement. He is my earthly light, a constant gift of unconditional love.

The many capable women of my essential circle offered their presence, modeled kindness and a willingness to risk which served as inspiration for creation. Grateful thanks go to friends (you know who you are!) and family, the staff of the Confederated Tribes of the Warm Springs Indian Reservation's Early Childhood Center, and our church fellowship in Moro who tolerated my schedule and loved me anyway.

Special thanks go to you, the readers, who left messages on my Web page, came to signings and presentations, and told me what you hoped would happen for the *All Together* women. I cherished your suggestions, incorporated some into this story, and pondered them all and your willingness to take the time to share your thoughts with me. WaterBrook Press editors Lisa Bergren, Traci DePree, and Laura Wright inspired greater things than I thought I had to give. My thanks go to the entire WaterBrook/Random House team for commitment to quality and worthy stories. My agents, Joyce Hart of Hartline Marketing and Terry Porter of Agape Productions, all continue their belief in me for which I'm grateful.

Many details in *What Once We Loved* are true, as we know them. Californians and Oregonians have an early intertwining history that now spans three centuries including efforts as early as 1853 to form a new state from portions of both. The winter of 1852–53 was one of the worst in both northern California and southern Oregon record as noted in book two, *No Eye Can See.* However, the ice storm of that year that affected freighters from Crescent City arriving to save the town, actually occurred in January of 1853, not 1854 as I portrayed it. I hope readers will forgive my vagaries of weather. I've lived inside a silver storm like the one described, finding sunshine just a hundred feet above the pewter fog and crystal. Such storms, though rare, are real.

Dottie Smith's books on early Shasta County also provided details of Indian and Chinese life in northern California. Unfortunately the specific massacres mentioned did occur. The laws permitting annihilation of native people and the purging of Chinese are true. *The Dictionary of Early Shasta County History* and *The History of the Chinese in Shasta County* provided verification of the indentured status of Indian people in California by non-Indians and the discrimination of the Chinese, especially young women, along with efforts to assist them. In the Shasta area, there were local people who provided paid, protected work for Indian people as Mazy did. Ms. Smith also documented that, like Mazy and Elizabeth, at least one woman owned her own business in Shasta County as early as 1852. Women lived in mining towns; they had varied occupations. JoAnn Levy's works about women in the California gold rush offered information about the Rays and the Sacramento Theater as well as details of mining life. There is no evidence that the Chinese were protected and moved out of California via the theater; but the underground to protect them did exist in California and Oregon, and there is no reason to believe creative use of the arts would not have been employed as Esther, Suzanne, and Tipton envisioned.

In February 1859, the Chinese were expelled from California. The Act for the Government and Protection of the Indians known popularly as the Indenture Act was repealed in 1864 but continued to force natives into bondage well into the years after the Civil War.

The book *The Table Rocks of Jackson County: Islands in the Sky*, compiled and edited by Chris Reyes, provided detail not only of flora and fauna but also about the early Takelma and Rogue River people of southern Oregon. Stephen Dow Beckham's book *Requiem for a People* offered context for settlers seeking a new life in the land occupied by Indians on the California coast and in southern Oregon territory in 1853–54. The photography section of the Oregon History Center shared images of early Jackson County that inspired. There was a Baptist circuit rider that helped lead the Table Rock Baptist Church in 1853, but his name wasn't Burke Manes, a fictional name I just liked. Historic street and business information about Jacksonville came from *Jacksonville Oregon: The Making of a National Historic Landmark* by Bert and Margie Webber and from Barbara Hegne's book *Settling the Rogue Valley, the Tough Times—The Forgotten People,* which also provided records of women in the mining region and people of color in the Rogue Valley including the detail that the 1853–54 school term lasted only a month with the entrance of one lone African American girl. The Cole brothers had a cabin on Cottonwood Creek in the Siskiyou Mountains that later became Colestein's Stage Stop, which is in service today as a bed-and-breakfast. Photographer Peter Britt did come to Jacksonville in 1852 and planted a vineyard. Today the region is known for its lush orchards and vineyards nourished by a temperate climate and rich soils; and an international music festival is held yearly in Jacksonville, bearing Peter Britt's name. Visitors are welcome there as well as in historic Jacksonville. The entire town was added to the National Historic Registry in 1966. Shasta City, Crescent City, Sacramento, and Cassville, Wisconsin, are additional communities that offer rich opportunities to rediscover histories we didn't know we'd lost.

The Table Rocks of southern Oregon lure visitors still today. The views and vistas from their rim rocks confirm that wherever we allow, the Lord does know our lot and makes our boundaries fall on pleasant places.

Thank you again for following these women. It is my hope that you found nurture inside their stories and that their journeys have added to your lives.

Sincerely,
Jane Kirkpatrick

You may reach Jane at 99997 Starvation Lane, Moro, OR 97039 or by visiting her Web site at http://www.jkbooks.com.

If you would like to obtain a guide to help facilitate discussion of *What Once We Loved* with your book group, please visit http://www.waterbrookpress.com.